GUNSLINGERS

A Story of the Old West

JOHN LAYNE

NEWMAN SPRINGS PUBLISHING
320 Broad Street
Red Bank, NJ 07701

First originally published by Newman Springs Publishing 2019

ISBN 978-1-64531-079-2 (Paperback)
ISBN 978-1-64531-080-8 (Digital)

Printed in the United States of America

To Elizabeth

PREFACE

THE GREAT GUN BATTLES OF the Old West hadn't occurred yet. Deadwood, South Dakota; Dodge City, Kansas; Lincoln, New Mexico; and Tombstone, Arizona, where Wild Bill Hickock, Wyatt Earp, Doc Holiday, Billy the Kid, Pat Garrett, and others were immortalized.

The Indian territories and the Oklahoma Panhandle, known as No Man's Land, hosted many such battles. The difference was, they were fought by lesser-known men in a land that nobody cared about.

Consequently, none of those gunslingers rose to fame. Or did they?

This is the story of one of those battles and the men who fought it.

CHAPTER 1

THE SUN ASCENDED FROM ITS subhorizon slumber, sending purple and orange hues into a clear yawning sky. Creatures filled the prairie with the sound of dawn-breaking rituals. Jack Ryker paid no attention to nature's miracles as he roared across the untamed landscape. Years of sitting in prison dulled his senses to such marvels. On this day, Ryker's focus was dedicated to paying a valuable debt. The pounding hooves of nineteen charging horses roared like thunder from a broken sky. Ryker had assembled a gang of murderous and thieving men. He'd waited a long time for this day when he would descend upon his victim's ranch with the wrath of a rabid wolf. In less time that it would take Judge Parker to hang them, Ryker and his lawless bunch would cross the Oklahoma border from No Man's Land into Texas and prey on the man responsible for stealing ten years of Ryker's life. He would even the score and profit from it at the same time.

Moses Barber strolled out of the barn and was met by Elizabeth, who appeared to be in a heightened state of excitement.

"Where's Dad? I can't find him anywhere!" she shrieked in a voice sounding more like a rusted train wheel than a nineteen-year-old girl. Moses stopped and smiled. Had Elizabeth been home for more than a few days, she would know where her father, retired US Marshal Joel Thornton, was every morning about this time.

"Miss Elizabeth, you only been home for a couple days, and already you're fixin' to jump out of your skin!" exclaimed Moses.

"I know! I know!" she cried, short of breath.

Ole Moses was right. Elizabeth Thornton had just returned from Philadelphia, where she'd lived with her aunt and uncle for the past seven years. Her father sent her to live with them after her mother died. He had tried to explain to his then twelve-year-old daughter that she needed to experience the lifestyle of educated and sophisticated folks back East. His young daughter resisted, but Joel Thornton stood firm and insisted that the opportunity was one they couldn't refuse. Besides, he had decided to leave the Marshal's office soon and needed to concentrate on getting his cattle ranch up and running. Thornton knew if his daughter chose to return to this God-forsaken territory, he'd need a few years to prepare. On top of that, he knew his only child was on the verge of becoming a fine young lady, and she would require a woman's touch along the way.

Moses nodded his head to the right and motioned for Elizabeth to follow him around to the front of the barn. Dutifully, Elizabeth followed the man who had cared for her father since their days in the war together. Once in front of the barn, they could see a good portion of the five hundred acres her father named the Tilted T Ranch.

Moses stopped and, with a leathery right hand, pointed into the distance.

"There he is, up on that hill out yonder by the big mesquite tree. You can find him there just about every morning at this time."

Elizabeth shaded her eyes and peered out beyond the corral, pasture fences, and clumps of sagebrushes to see her father, tall in the saddle on King, his Steel Dust horse. King was erect standing motionless, but for the occasional flinch of his tail.

"What's he doing out there?" Elizabeth asked.

"Thinkin', just thinkin' about the old days, I guess. He rides up there and takes some time for himself before the day gets goin'. Been doin' that for quite a time now. He'll be down in a bit, take a bite of breakfast, then start the day. That reminds me, I best get a-cookin' before he gets back."

"I already finished the biscuits," Elizabeth announced over a wide smile.

"Yep. Smell mighty fine too." Moses chuckled.

As Moses headed to the house and his breakfast duties, Elizabeth turned and watched her father for a moment.

Thinking about the past? Elizabeth hoped he wasn't out there worrying about what he was going to do now that she had returned home. She was a big girl who could take care of herself, although her father wouldn't know that…yet.

Joel stepped through the front door pausing briefly to stomp the dust off his size 12 bull-hide boots, then made his way to the kitchen table where he was greeted with a basket of hot biscuits and black coffee. Moses was intently working the frying pan. According to the powerful aroma that had hit Joel in the face like a punch in the nose when he entered the house, Moses was cooking up eggs and bacon. Elizabeth, clad in a fine-print dress that brushed across her ankles, hurried from her room. Soaring across the kitchen, she wrapped her arms around her father's sunbaked neck before Moses set a full plate in front of him.

"Good morning, Dad!" she gushed.

Thornton smiled and returned the greeting.

"Sleep good, I presume?" he asked.

"Wonderful! I had forgotten how quiet it can be out here." Her eyes darted around the room. "The house looks fabulous. You and Moses must have been awfully busy."

"Well, we had seven years to work on it! Also had some fine help from Jake Rawlings. We added on here and there and put up the paneling after I sold last season's herd. It was a good cattle season and the market paid top dollar. Looking like this season may be as strong and we have twice the head to sell."

Elizabeth looked at her father with a scrunched nose.

"Jake Rawlings?"

Thornton smiled and leaned back in his chair as Moses filled his empty cup with black coffee.

"Yes, dear, that Jake Rawlings from the Double R. His father was kind enough to let me hire him to help out around here since Moses and I aren't getting any younger."

"Speak for yerself, old man!" Moses cracked, unable to hold back a loud laugh.

"Fine-looking young man that Jake Rawlings has turned out to be," Thornton added. "Darn near as tall as me, with shoulders I only wish I still had." Thornton looked up at Moses, who was leaning forward and looking hard out the front window. "What's wrong, Mose?" Thornton quickly asked, turning his head toward the front windows.

"Riders comin' fast," Moses answered quickly, heading for the den.

Thornton sprang to his feet and followed Moses to the den, where the guns were secured in fine oak cabinets mounted on the wall.

"Elizabeth, go to your room and lock the door until we find out what these riders are up to!" Thornton called back over his shoulder.

Elizabeth had already started for her room, but locking the door and hiding was the last thing on her mind. If trouble was coming, she would be ready. Thornton strapped on his gun and grabbed a Winchester from the cabinet. Moses did the same and took up a position next to Thornton at the den window.

"Looks like fifteen, twenty riders, boss," Moses stated under his breath.

"Yeah, and something tells me they're not coming for coffee," Thornton exhaled. "You stay here, crack the window and cover me, but stay out of sight until we figure out who they are and what they want." Thornton waved his right hand downward, letting Moses know he wanted him below the window.

Thornton stepped onto the front porch, leaving the door open behind him. His boot heels struck hard on the wood planks. Riders crossing the ranch wasn't uncommon, but these were coming fast, which Thornton found odd. Squinting to get a better look at the men, Thornton could see the front rider was a big man with long black hair and a full beard tumbling from under a black flat-brimmed hat.

"Mose, you recognize any of them yet?"

"No, boss, can't see 'em good enough."

"Okay, stay quiet, and don't fire unless you have to."

"Yes, sir, I'm ready."

The riders came to a stop, sending chunks of turf into the air. They kept their distance from where Thornton stood, his Winchester leveled and ready. Several of the horses stomped their hooves and snorted after their long fast ride. The lead rider walked his horse a few feet closer.

"Morning!" the bearded man shouted.

"Morning, what can I do for you fellas?"

"Well, we're on our way to town and decided to stop and see the town's namesake," said the big man with a hint of sarcasm.

"Believe y'all need to ride on then," Thornton stated in a forceful tone.

"Not so fast, not until you take a closer look at who you're talkin' to, Marshal," said the big man, showing rotted teeth behind a gaping smile.

Thornton froze at the word Marshal. No one had called him that in years.

"Now then," the big man continued, "I reckon it hasn't been that long that you can't recognize me and a couple of the boys here, Marshal."

Thornton narrowed his gaze and took a closer look at the big bearded man. He couldn't be certain, but—a bolt of lightning shot down his spine. Astride a horse in front of him appeared to be Jack Ryker, one of the most dangerous outlaws he ever brought back to Fort Smith.

"Ryker? That you? You look and sound different than I remember. The hair and beard hide you a bit."

Three of the other riders moved forward, taking positions next to Ryker. Thornton looked them over, recognizing Jake Morgan, Blackie Gillum, and Carlton Baines—all former fugitives of the law that had been hunted down back in the day by Thornton's fellow marshals.

"Morgan, Gillum, and Baines," Thornton acknowledged. "Well, Ryker, I see you're still picking your friends poorly," Thornton stated. "Y'all made your point, now get off of my land."

"Not until we take what we came for, Marshal Joel Thornton!" Ryker yelled out.

Thornton saw Ryker lean back in the saddle. Before Thornton could raise his Winchester and fire, he heard the crack of a rifle to his far left coming from a huge purple sage and felt the power of a bullet explode in his left side. The impact felt like a blacksmith's hammer and fire erupted inside his rib cage. As Thornton fell, he caught a glimpse of the outlaws scattering and heard Moses open fire from the den window. Thornton hit the wood planks with a thud and then rolled onto his back, getting off a wild shot with his rifle. Thornton's eyes darted up and fixed on Ryker, still on his horse, gun in hand, pointed directly at him.

"Greetings from Yuma Prison!" Thornton heard Ryker yell just before he saw the flash from the gun barrel and another hammer hit to his chest, ending the gunfight for retired Marshal Joel Thornton.

The outlaws were firing a fusillade of bullets toward Moses, who was doing his best to match the onslaught. Bullets pounded the window, sending shards of glass and splintered wood in every direction, including Moses's eyes and face, rendering him helpless. Kneeling on the floor, Moses dropped his Winchester and frantically attempted to clear the shrapnel from his eyes and face. Blood was streaming from his forehead down into his eyes, further complicating his efforts.

The gunfire stopped. An eerie silence took the place of cannonading gunfire. Moses heard the wisp of the afternoon breeze brush past the broken window. Several riders dismounted, their boots hitting the dry turf with a thud. Still unable to see much, Moses heard the boots of several men hit the porch, then enter the house. A single gunshot sounded and one of the outlaws hit the floor. Moses heard a second shot and subsequent scream from Elizabeth.

"Miss Elizabeth!" Moses yelled from his perch in the den.

Moses heard quick footsteps coming toward him and a man yelling, "The old man is still alive!"

Moses cleared leather with his Colt and fired at the faint image of the outlaw coming through the doorway. Moses's bullet hit Jake Morgan in the neck. He stumbled through the doorway and fired point-blank at Moses, hitting center mass. Moses Barber, former slave and civil war soldier, would not see his sixtieth birthday. Morgan then collapsed to the floor while the life oozed out of his severed artery, courtesy of Moses's final shot.

Blackie Gillum had been the second man through the doorway behind Donnie Smith when Elizabeth fired from the doorway of her room, striking Smith in the chest. Gillum had ducked behind a chair and fired at Elizabeth with a shot that creased the flesh of her right shoulder just enough to knock her off balance. She fell to the floor and dropped her Colt Peacemaker. Ryker walked into the Thornton house, paused, and surveyed the scene. Dead on the floor a few feet inside the doorway was Smith, whom Ryker barely knew. To his left lay Jake Morgan, apparently dead on the floor next to Thornton's cowhand, who also appeared to be done for. In the corner of the kitchen, crouching on the floor clutching a bleeding wound to her right shoulder was a young women Ryker had not planned for. Ryker walked toward Elizabeth and retrieved the Colt .45 Peacemaker from the floor.

"Yours?"

"Yes," she answered.

"And who are you?" Ryker demanded.

"I'm Elizabeth Thornton," she defiantly stated as blood streamed between her fingers, staining the sleeve of her dress a bright red.

"Elizabeth Thornton?" Ryker questioned.

"Yes, I'm Joel Thornton's daughter," Elizabeth said.

"I see," Ryker answered with a wide grin, putting his rotted teeth on display again. "I didn't know Marshal Thornton had a daughter. Had I known, I would have killed him anyway, but I would have enjoyed it more."

Elizabeth squeezed her eyes shut tight, fighting to hold back tears. She didn't want to give this murdering beast further satisfaction.

Ryker turned to Blackie Gillum and Carlton Baines, who had joined them in the house.

"Tell the rest to take the horses from the corral and herd the cattle we saw on the ride in. Forget about the others in the east pasture. Then we'll head back to the border," Ryker ordered. "I have some business here with Marshal Thornton's daughter before I leave."

Gillum turned to Baines, who nodded and left the room.

"Now, Miss Thornton, where did your father keep his safe?" Ryker asked as he reached down, squeezed Elizabeth's bloody shoulder, and pulled her up to her feet.

"I won't help you," Elizabeth managed through clenched teeth.

Ryker said nothing. He leaned over and pulled a large knife from inside his right boot. Ryker placed the business edge of the blade next to Elizabeth's throat and pressed enough to draw a line of blood. Elizabeth winced as the blade separated her skin.

"Don't think I won't stop there, Miss Thornton. Do as I say or I'll cut your throat, find the safe, and take what's inside anyway. Your decision…make it now," he demanded in a low voice, narrowing his black eyes.

Elizabeth gasped at the evil in his eyes and the stench of his breath. Her survival instincts took over. She wanted to stay alive, if for no other reason than to make this retch pay for what he had done.

"I believe the safe is inside a wooden cabinet in the den next to the gun rack."

Without hesitation, Blackie Gillum headed into the den, having to step over Morgan's body. He located the safe next to the open gun cabinet and checked the handle.

"It's locked! Need the combination!" Gillum hollered.

"Combination?" Ryker asked, edging his face closer to Elizabeth's. She closed her eyes and tried to pull herself free from the fiend's grasp. Ryker tightened his iron grip and grunted, spewing tobacco spittle onto her face. She gulped. Her lips trembled as she battled the need to vomit.

Ryker drew the knife away from her neck and loosened his grip. Elizabeth pulled herself away from Ryker's grasp. Thornton had given Elizabeth the combination to the safe shortly after she arrived in the event she needed any of its contents. She was now both saddened and relieved that she could open the safe even though she did not know the entirety of its contents. She retrieved a small piece of paper containing the three numbers from a cup inside the kitchen cabinet and walked to the den with Ryker close behind. After spinning the dial completely around to clear its mechanism with her bloodied hand, she began. Right 19, left 25, right 16. She pulled down on the lever, releasing the hardened steel catch. Ryker pushed her out of the way and opened the heavy door, exposing stacks of cash bills neatly wrapped in brown paper bands, several pieces of jewelry, a silver pocket watch, and what appeared to be a locket on a silver chain. Ryker grabbed the stacks of cash and the pocket watch. Elizabeth couldn't tell for certain, but there appeared to be several thousand dollars in crisp bills. Ryker told Gillum to get a saddlebag. Gillum hurried out and returned in a matter of seconds. Ryker filled the bag with the cash, placed the watch in his vest pocket, then scanned the remaining items. Ryker pulled the locket from the safe and opened it. As Elizabeth expected, the locket contained a picture of her mother.

"Your mother, I suspect?" Ryker asked without caring about the answer. Ryker threw the locket back into the safe and spun toward Gillum. "Get Smith and Morgan out of here and tie them over their horses. We'll take them with us."

"What about her?" Gillum snarled.

"Don't need the hassle of a woman along," proclaimed Ryker.

Elizabeth sat on the floor next to the safe and glanced into the gun cabinet. *I can't get them all, but maybe I can kill him*, she thought.

No! the voice of reason screamed inside her head. *Don't be a fool, Elizabeth! Just wait for them to leave. Your time will come.*

After the two dead men were taken out, Ryker came back into the room.

"Who are you anyway?" Elizabeth asked with tears now streaming down her face.

"Name's Ryker. I had the misfortune of being arrested by your father ten years ago. Went to prison for doing the same thing your famous father did, only I wasn't wearing a badge when I did it."

"My father is a great man!" Elizabeth shouted. "He was a federal marshal who tried to keep the likes of you away from decent people!" She sobbed, burying her face in her hands.

"Really?" replied Ryker. He leaned in toward Elizabeth. "Your father wasn't the lawman hero his reputation claims. How do you think he got the money to buy this ranch and get a town named after him? Marshal's pay? Your father wasn't any better than the outlaws he chased down and brought back to ole Parker in Fort Smith." Ryker laughed, licked his bearded lips, then stood up.

Elizabeth glared at Ryker with cold hard flinty eyes. Fury rose from her quivering body, reddening her once-insipid face. Her pulse raced.

"You'll pay for saying that," she promised.

"Maybe, maybe not, but he already has."

Ryker laughed, wheeled on his heel, and stomped out of the house. Elizabeth waited in the den until she heard Ryker mount his horse and ride away with the rest of the gang. She forced deep breaths in an effort to calm herself, then struggled to her feet and hurried to the doorway, hesitating, to see the outlaws riding through the pasture, pushing Tilted T horses and cattle north toward the border. Looking down she saw her father lying motionless on the porch.

Can it be? Is he really dead?

Elizabeth knelt next to her father, then leaned toward his face to see if he was still breathing. She felt his chest through his blood-stained shirt. The faint beat of his heart sent pulses of life to her hand. Excitedly she leaned closer to his face. A soft wisp of a breath touched her cheek.

He's alive!

CHAPTER 2

B LOOD RUSHED TO HER HEAD and caused her eyesight to dim
for a moment.

"Dad, Dad, can you hear me?" she asked in a muffled
tone. No response. Thornton was on his back atop bloodstained
planks. Elizabeth raced into the house and grabbed a pan of water
and a rag. She ran back to her father and with trembling hands began
dabbing his face with the wet rag. Realizing that he was still bleeding
from his wounds, she quickly retrieved towels and bandages from the
kitchen cabinet where just an hour ago she was preparing to clean
breakfast dishes. Swiftly she returned to her father's side and tore his
shirt away from the wounds. She then applied a thick bandage to
each wound.

How can I secure the bandages to his body?

Elizabeth scanned the area while she thought. Her gaze fell upon
her father's belt. Sure, she could use his belt to push the bandage on
his side toward his body to stop the bleeding. Elizabeth popped the
buckle and attempted to roll her father over onto his right side in
order to place the belt under his body and pull it around his waist. It
was then that Elizabeth felt the sharp pain in the right shoulder from
her own gunshot wound. The shock of witnessing her father and
Moses being gunned down and the fear of what Ryker would do to
her had eliminated the pain in her shoulder.

Elizabeth examined her wound and determined it wasn't too
bad. She balled up a rag and stuffed it inside her shirt sleeve over the
wound.

That will have to do, she thought. Elizabeth then leaned low on
the porch planks and pushed as hard as she could. Her father rolled
over onto his side. She slid the belt under his body as far as she could

and then rolled Thornton onto his back. She pulled the belt around and latched the buckle tight on his stomach, making sure the belt was over the top of the bandage on his left side. She examined the other wound. It was high up on the left side of his chest near his shoulder. Looking around the porch again, she saw a lariat neatly rolled up hanging on a post. She took the lariat and formed a makeshift sling around the belt, over the shoulder, and behind her father's back, tying it to the belt again. That would have to do for now. When she finished with the lariat, she looked at her father and realized he was looking at her.

Joel Thornton forced a slight smile and raised his left hand. Elizabeth clutched his hand and smiled back with tears falling from her flooded eyes.

"I'm here, Dad," Elizabeth softly assured him. Thornton swallowed hard, and then turned his gaze from his daughter's face to her bloodied shoulder.

"You're hurt," Thornton said in a weak voice.

"Just a scratch, no worries," was his daughter's reply.

"Mose?" Thornton asked.

She shook her head. "They shot him," Elizabeth reported.

Thornton closed his eyes, squeezing them hard in an attempt to fight his sorrow and anger.

"I need to get you into the house and onto your bed." Elizabeth's words brought Thornton back from his grief. "Can you help me move you? Do you think you can walk?"

"If you can get me up some, I think I can walk with your help," Thornton offered.

Thornton used his left arm as best he could while Elizabeth pulled up from behind her father's shoulders with all the strength she could muster. Thornton got to his knees, and with Elizabeth's bracing, he made it to his feet. Before he could take a step, he collapsed back onto the bloodstained planks. Pain like he had never imagined shot through his side and shoulder. Elizabeth let out a loud gasp.

"Are you okay?"

Anger flooded the big rancher's body and masked the pain.

"Get me back to my feet," Thornton called out in a wincing voice.

Elizabeth pulled up on her father's left shoulder again with all the strength she could, and watched in amazement as her father stood and slowly walked into the house. He made it to his bed and collapsed onto its blankets.

"Check on Moses again," Thornton told Elizabeth. "Just in case," he added.

Elizabeth nodded and went to the den where Moses lay facedown in a pool of blood—gun still clenched in his right hand. Elizabeth knelt and moved Moses's body slightly, but knew that it was no use. Another wave of sadness fell over her. She allowed herself to briefly reminisce. She remembered the first time she saw Moses. She was about seven. It was right after the war when her father returned. Her father explained to her mother that Moses had fought with him and had nowhere to go, so he brought him home as a ranch hand even though there was not much of a ranch to tend to.

A smile came to Elizabeth's lips as she recalled her mother questioning her father about hiring a ranch hand when there was no ranch work to do.

"Patience, Carol, patience. There will be a ranch to tend to soon enough," she recalled her father promising. Her father kept his promise. There was a ranch, but now her mother was gone and her father was clinging to life. Elizabeth ran her hand over Moses's face. She stood and looked again, then returned to her father.

Thornton looked over at this daughter as she entered the room. The look on Elizabeth's face told him all he needed to know. Elizabeth shook her head then pulled a chair next to the bed and sat down.

"I'm going to town and get Doc Langdon," Elizabeth told her father.

"Wait, tell me what happened first," Thornton insisted.

Elizabeth ran the sequence of events as she remembered them through her mind, then began, "I heard you talking to the men, then a shot was fired. Moses began shooting from the window, and the men started shooting at Moses and the front of the house. The shooting stopped, and two men came in through the front door. I shot the first one, but the second one shot at me and hit me in the arm. I dropped my gun and fell to the floor. Another—"

"You shot one of them?" Thornton couldn't believe his ears.

"Yes, Dad, I shot one. I know how to use a gun pretty well actually, but we don't have time to get into that."

Thornton forced another weak, but wide smile. Elizabeth continued.

"Moses called to me from the den, but the second one shot him before the one called Ryker came in. He forced me to open the safe. I'm sorry, but I'm certain he would have killed me if I hadn't. They stole the money, the horses and cattle."

Elizabeth's words hit Thornton like another bullet.

"Sky should be in the barn," Thornton said dejectedly. "Hook the buckboard to him and use that to go to town. I need some water."

Elizabeth quickly brought her father a cup of water, then went to the barn where she found their big draft horse, Sky, in his stall as if nothing had happened. Elizabeth hooked Sky up to the buckboard and returned to the house, where she found her father coughing violently.

"Are you okay?" Elizabeth cried. "What can I do?"

"Get Doc Langdon as quick as you can. I'll hang on until he gets here—I promise."

"I'll do my best," Elizabeth stated. She leaned down and kissed her father on the forehead.

Thornton squeezed her hand. "Find Ben Chance, Elizabeth. Find Chance and tell him what happened. He'll know what to do."

Elizabeth was confused. Ben Chance? She didn't know where to find him or what he even looked like. She hadn't seen Uncle Chance in ten years.

"Last I heard," Thornton continued, struggling to breathe, "he was down in Canyon Creek near Oneida. Take the stage. It will get you there." Thornton blurted before falling unconscious.

Elizabeth checked her father and confirmed he was still alive, and then she collected her Colt Peacemaker from the table, tucked it inside her satchel, and headed for the buckboard.

She had only been to the town named after her father once since returning home. The way was easily found following the well-worn road from the ranch to Thornton. Elizabeth recalled that it was about ten miles from the ranch. Having a big draft horse pulling the buckboard would mean at least an hour of travel time each way. Elizabeth slapped the reins and shouted at Sky, hoping for the best. The big horse moved along in a canter that was the best she was going to get. It was beginning to get hot as the noon sun set high overhead, sending beams of fire downward toward the Texas loam. Elizabeth slapped the reins again and hoped Sky wouldn't fade beneath the oppressive heat.

Elizabeth kept the pressure on Sky, snapping the reins and encouraging him along.

About halfway to town, Elizabeth thought while watching the road vanish under the buckboard. Suddenly, a lone rider up ahead came into view. Elizabeth fanned her hand over her eyes, shading the sun's brilliant light, and squinted for a better view. No doubt about it, it was a lone rider coming toward her. Since she didn't know anybody from Thornton, she could only hope it was friend and not foe. She noticed that the rider had sped up to a gallop, so she slowed Sky down to a slower gait. As the rider got closer, she noted it was a man dressed in brown chaps, vest, and a red shirt with a tan hat pulled down low to shield his eyes from the sun. Elizabeth also noticed a gun tied down to his right leg. She stopped the buckboard, and the rider approached, his horse now walking.

"Good afternoon, ma'am. I'm Jake Rawlings," he said in a pleasant voice.

"I'm Elizabeth Thornton, and I'm on my way to town to get the doctor. My father's been shot and he needs the doctor really bad."

"Mr. Thornton's been shot?" Rawlings shouted.

"Yes, he's in bad condition. Can you help me get to town faster?" Elizabeth asked.

Jake noticed the bloodstain on Elizabeth's sleeve.

"What about you! Are you okay?" Jake asked.

"Yes, I'm okay, but I need the doctor quickly!"

Jake Rawlings swung his bay around. "You head back to the ranch. I'll get Doc Langdon!"

Rawlings sped off without waiting for an answer. Elizabeth froze for a moment, not knowing if she should trust this stranger. Then his name hit her.

Jake Rawlings? Dad had said that he had helped him out at the ranch and was the same boy she played with at parties their parents had when they were kids.

Elizabeth turned the buckboard around and headed back to the ranch, praying her father would still be alive when she got there. She snapped the reins and yelled for Sky to move faster. Elizabeth needed every ounce of energy the horse could muster. A feeling of relief crept into her knowing help was on the way. She pushed Sky along the best she could. After about thirty minutes, she brought the buckboard to a stop in front of the house. Elizabeth ran into the house to check on her father. He was still alive, and it appeared to her novice eyes that the bleeding had stopped. She felt his forehead. It was on fire.

If the doctor could get here in time, she thought.

Elizabeth ran back out to the water trough where Sky was doing his best to drain it. She dipped a bucket and splashed water everywhere as she returned to the house. Plunging a towel into the bucket, she wiped down her father's face. He was breathing in short breaths and remained unconscious. All Elizabeth could do now was make her father as comfortable as possible and wait for the doctor.

CHAPTER 3

J AKE RAWLINGS CHARGED DOWN THE road, his bay's hooves pounding the dirt into dust beneath him. His horse was a good sprinter and was making his owner proud. Leaning forward with his head down, Jake yelled encouragement to his mount. Thoughts of Joel Thornton flew around in his head like a horde of sage hens flushed by a coyote. If Mr. Thornton died because of him, he would never forgive himself. It was Thornton who had first treated Jake like a man and cowhand. It was Thornton who taught him how to rope a calf, bring a stray back into the herd, and brand a hide. And then much to his mother's dismay, but with his father's permission, Thornton had taught him how to draw and shoot a gun. Jake's father had never been much of a cowboy and knew little about handling a six-shooter. They were farmers with a couple of oxen, a mule, and few horses. His father preferred a rifle and shotgun for hunting or a show of authority when it was needed, but a six-shooter? No, that was Mr. Thornton's expertise.

Jake saw the edge of town up ahead and knew a shortcut to Doc Langdon's place. He pulled on the reins to his left and cut through the rough terrain, doing his best to avoid the occasional rock or rut. Jake swung his horse in between McNally's general store and Mrs. Owens's boarding house, knocking over a barrel of grain perched next to the store in the process. He then cut across the street, nearly colliding with a wagon bringing goods to the store. The wagon's horses stopped and reared up, nearly causing the wagon and its driver to roll over. Jake swung off his horse with his boots hitting the ground before his horse came to a stop in front of Doc Langdon's office. Jake cleared the steps leading up to the door with a leap, not taking time to tie his horse to the hitching post. Jake's boot heels crashed onto the porch planks at the same time he hit the door with his shoulder, exploding into the front room, losing his balance and crashing to the floor like he'd been kicked by a mule. Jake looked up and saw Mrs. Owens sitting on a chair, eyes bulging from their sockets and mouth wide open.

"Jake Rawlings! What are you doing rushing in here like that?" she exclaimed.

"Mr. Thornton's been shot at his ranch. He's in bad shape!" Jake yelled out.

Doc Langdon opened the door of his treatment room and saw Jake getting up from the floor.

"Joel Thornton's been shot?" Langdon asked.

"Yes! I saw his daughter on the road and she told me. She also had blood on her dress! You're needed right away!" Jake advised.

Mrs. Owens's son followed Langdon out of the treatment room with a large bandage on his arm.

"Mrs. Owens, Billy will be fine. I cleaned the cut and applied an ointment that will help it heal. I'll check on him in a few days," Langdon hurriedly explained.

Byron Parker and Club Smith appeared at the doctor's door looking to see what all the excitement was about.

"Joel Thornton has been shot at his ranch. Can you two ride out there with Jake and I to see what has happened?" Langdon asked.

"Sure enough!" both men yelled in unison, then turned to get their horses.

"I'll get my bag and horse, then meet you in front," Langdon told Jake.

Jake paused, excused himself to Mrs. Owens, then rushed outside to his horse. As Jake mounted his bay, he heard Club Smith yelling in the street that Joel Thornton had been shot. Doc Langdon met Jake, and they rode over to the saloon where Club and Byron were mounting their horses. The four of them then headed for Tilted T.

Elizabeth finished wiping down her father's face and neck with a wet cloth, then went to the kitchen to boil some water in anticipation of the doctor requiring a sterile amount. After relighting the stove and filling a pot, Elizabeth hesitantly walked into the den where Moses lay in a pool of blood. The window he had been defending had been obliterated and would need to be boarded up. There were several bullet holes on the wall opposite the opening where the window had been. Elizabeth didn't know if there was wood for the jobs or not. She hoped that Jake Rawlings would come back with the doctor and help her take care of Moses and the repairs. She gazed down at Moses through tear-blurred eyes. She had known him a long time. He had been a member of the family. Again, she thought back to the day when her father returned from the war. She hadn't known what the war really was; all she knew was that it was scary and men died. Moses became much more than a farmhand. The memory was quite clear since Elizabeth had never seen a black man before. Her thoughts carried her away to moments of friendship, safety, and laughter with Moses. Now he was gone, killed because he was trying to keep her safe. She fought the urge to cry again. She decided her grief would have to wait. Anger was swiftly taking its place. Anger and the need to find Ryker and see him pay for what he had done.

I'll make him regret he didn't kill me when he had the chance, she thought.

Her father told her to find Ben Chance, that he would know what to do. Once her father was cared for, she would find her father's old partner. The man she used to call uncle even though he was no real relation to her. Elizabeth's arm was beginning to throb with pain.

I hope the doctor gets here soon.

Jake was frustrated. He wanted to move much faster than the doctor was able to ride.

"Come on, Doc!" he yelled again as he, Club, and Byron slowed their horses in order to let Langdon catch up.

"I'm doing the best I can, Jake. We're almost there if I remember correctly," Doc calmly replied.

Sure enough, Jake could see the ranch house in the distance.

"We'll ride on up," Jake called out before spurring his bay into a full gallop. Byron and Club did the same. Doc Langdon looked ahead as his escort hurried off. Langdon felt hollow inside. He was terribly concerned. He didn't know how long it had been since Thornton had been shot nor how severe the wounds were. All he knew was that with each passing minute, Thornton's chances of survival were diminishing. He wanted to ride faster, but he had never really mastered the art of being on horseback, and he was paying for it now. He only hoped that Joel Thornton would not pay for it with his life.

Jake, Club, and Byron rode up to the house with Club taking the reins of the three horses and heading for the corral. Jake and Byron hurried to the front door where they were met by Elizabeth, who waved for them to come in.

"Doc Langdon is right behind us," Jake assured Elizabeth.

"Howdy, ma'am. I'm Byron Parker." Byron introduced himself while extending his hand to Elizabeth, who accepted his hand with a faint smile.

"I'm Elizabeth Thornton, thank you for coming out with Jake."

Jake went to the door and waved Club Smith into the room.

"This is Club Smith," Jake announced. "Club, this is Mr. Thornton's daughter, Elizabeth."

Club removed his hat, pinned it to his side with his left arm, and cautiously approached Elizabeth with his head slightly bent down, offering his right hand.

"Pleased to meet you, ma'am."

Elizabeth accepted Club's hand and gently shook it, noticing that he did not have a left hand, but a stump starting just above the wrist.

"Thank you for coming, Mr. Smith," Elizabeth stated in a fluttered voice.

"Oh, just call me Club, ma'am, like everybody else. They call me Club since I don't have a left hand, and I sort of use my arm as a club when need be," he explained. "I don't rightfully know what my real last name was, so everybody just calls me Club Smith."

Elizabeth managed a soft laugh, then heard Doc Langdon ride up to the front of the house. Elizabeth met the doctor at the door and motioned him to her father's room without taking the time for introductions. Jake, Byron, and Club followed and stood behind Langdon, who put his bag down and removed his vest.

"What happened to you?" Langdon asked Elizabeth, noticing the blood stain on her sleeve.

"I was grazed by a bullet, but it just cut my skin. I'm okay for now."

"When did this happen?"

"Just after breakfast, around seven thirty. I found two gunshot wounds. One in his left side above his belt and another at the top of his chest on the right," she added.

Langdon was already at work cutting away the clothing surrounding the wounds.

"Do you know what type of guns fired the shots?" Langdon asked in a hopeful tone.

"No, not really, but I think the bullet in his side came from a rifle and the chest from a pistol," Elizabeth stated. "I boiled water in case you need it," she advised.

"Good, bring it in here with a clean towel. You fellas leave the room," he ordered. Jake followed Elizabeth to the kitchen.

"Anything we can do, Elizabeth?" Jake asked. Elizabeth turned and noticed Jake was very close. She looked up and met his blue eyes.

"Yes, could you take care of Moses. He's in the den. He's dead and I don't know what to do," Elizabeth responded.

"I'm sorry, I didn't know ole Mose was killed too. I forgot about him," Jake replied, his voice fading.

"We'll take care of Mose, you help Doc Langdon." Jake turned and met Byron and Club in the front room. Both men were looking at Moses's body on the floor in the den.

"Let's take Mose out of here and bury him," Jake stated.

Elizabeth quickly washed her hands, then carried the bowl of clean water to her father's room and set it on the bed table next to Langdon.

"Was he unconscious when you found him?" Landon asked.

"Yes, but he came to, and I spoke to him for several minutes before he went unconscious again. He hasn't been awake since."

"He's lost a lot of blood, but your bandaging helped a great deal. I need to try and remove the bullet from his chest first. You may want to wait in the other room," Langdon suggested.

"No, I'll stay here in case you need help."

With his patient already unconscious, Langdon chose not to inject morphine. There would be time to do that when Thornton awoke, if he awoke. Taking his bullet probe, he sunk the tip deep into the wound, moving the instrument in a slight circle as it traveled through the wounded flesh. Careful not to push the bullet further into the body, Langdon found the back side of the lead object. Slowly spreading the probe's tips apart, he caught the edges, squeezed, and slowly began the withdrawal. As the bullet left Thornton's body, the wound began to bleed again. Langdon applied a mixture of ergot to the wounded area and pressed a thick layer of gauze, holding pressure on the wound.

"What was that substance you put on the wound?" Elizabeth whispered as if not to wake her father.

"It's a mixture that includes ergot. It helps to slow bleeding by closing the blood vessels," Langdon explained. "Here, place your hand over the bandage and press down, keeping the pressure on," Langdon instructed. "I need to take a closer look at the wound in his side."

Elizabeth followed the instructions while Langdon examined the wound on Thornton's left side. The side wound was much worse. The skin was severely damaged with bruising around the entry point. Langdon felt the area and located a broken rib—no, two. The wound was still bleeding slightly. Langdon feared the bullet had penetrated the rib cage and damaged organs. He pressed firmly on the surface around the wound. It appeared that the bullet had missed the bottom of the lung and possibly entered below the stomach.

"Did you notice any blood in your father's mouth when he spoke to you?" Langdon asked.

"No."

"Good, the bullet may have missed his lung and stomach.

That leaves the kidney and the pancreas, Langdon thought. "I need to turn him onto his right side. Keep pressure on the chest," Langdon instructed Elizabeth as he pushed Thornton over onto his right side.

"I'm going to need to cut open the wound area to see if any organs have been damaged. Is that okay with you?" Langdon asked as a matter of courtesy, knowing what had to be done whether she granted permission or not. Elizabeth looked down and nodded in agreement. Scalpel already in hand, Langdon made an incision above and below the entry point to allow a larger open area to observe. Langdon instructed Elizabeth to leave the chest bandage and retrieve a candle for additional light. Elizabeth returned with the candle and held it as close as she could to the gaping wound, turning away from the ghastly scene. Langdon slowly probed the area until he located the bullet. Clamping onto the back end as he had done in Thornton's chest, he extracted the chunk of lead then inspected it to see if it had broken into fragments. Satisfied it had not, he dropped it into a small container with the other. Unable to determine the extent of the damage the bullet had done, he commenced to suturing the wound.

Club and Byron carried Moses from the house and brought his body to an elevated area behind the barn where Mrs. Thornton was buried. Jake went into the barn to see if there was wood to build a casket. Since there was no undertaker in town, Jake figured it best if he and the boys do the best they could. Jake located enough wood, a hammer, and nails and began to construct the casket. Moses wasn't a very big man, so the coffin would be on the small side. Club and Byron grabbed a shovel and pickax from the shed next to the barn and began to dig the grave. After about an hour of silent labor, Jake brought the makeshift casket out back where the grave-digging had been completed. Club and Byron placed Moses inside the box, and Jake nailed it shut.

"Wait here a moment," Jake told the boys, then headed for the house. Once inside, Jake saw that Doc and Elizabeth had finished with Thornton and were washing in the kitchen.

"How's Mr. Thornton?" Jake asked.

"He's breathing normal, but fever has already set in which isn't a good sign," Doc Langdon offered.

"We won't know much for a while," Elizabeth added.

"I built a casket for Moses, and the boys dug the grave out back of the barn. I hope that was okay, Elizabeth," Jake said.

"That's fine," Elizabeth answered.

"We can bury him now if you like," Jake asked, looking to Elizabeth for approval. Elizabeth looked at Doc Langdon.

"Would you join us, Doctor?"

"Certainly." Langdon smiled.

The three of them joined Club and Byron for an abbreviated funeral service, with Elizabeth managing a few words and a Bible verse before Club and Byron lowered the casket and filled the grave. The area was now the family graveyard instead of her mother's burial place.

Doc Langdon cleaned and bandaged Elizabeth's arm then instructed her to keep her father comfortable and warm. He promised he would return tomorrow before noon to check on his patient. Jake asked Club to stop by his parents' farm on the way back to town, tell them what had happened and where he was. Byron joined Club and Doc for the trip back to town. Jake returned to the barn and found wood planks that could be used to cover the shot-up window in the den and tackled the task without Elizabeth having to ask.

Elizabeth returned to the kitchen and began to clean the dishes that had been left on the table since this morning. The events of the day began to drift through her mind.

Who was this Ryker? What had he done to go to prison for ten years? Why was he so bent on revenge against her father? Why would he come to the ranch?

It wasn't just to shoot her father, kill Moses, and steal what he could. Was it? She knew her father had many enemies from his time as a marshal, but she never expected something like this to happen. And why did her father just walk out on the porch with his guard down? Didn't he recognize Ryker? Suspect trouble? He had sent her to her room anticipating trouble, and yet he left himself out in a position to be shot. That didn't make sense. Despite being gone for several years, she knew her father was a cautious man. Elizabeth wanted answers, and she didn't know if her father would ever recover to provide them. Her thoughts were shattered like breaking glass by Jake's voice.

"Elizabeth, you okay?"

Jake's words caused her to jump, sending the coffee mug in her hand to the floor, shattering in pieces.

"I'm sorry!" Jake said. He was standing in the front room near the table, still holding her father's hammer.

"No, that's all right. I was lost in what happened today and didn't hear you. Yes, I'll be all right. Just worried about Dad is all, and I'm trying not to think about Moses."

"I'll bring in some water and clean up in the den if you like," Jake offered.

"You don't have to do that, Jake. I'll take care of it shortly."

"Nope, you sit down and rest. I'll deal with the den," Jake insisted. "The window has been boarded up and I'll finish the den before I go." Elizabeth smiled and nodded, realizing she was too exhausted to argue. Jake hurried off to the job at hand. She took Jake's advice and sat down at the table. Immediately she found herself staring at the basket of biscuits she had made this morning that no one had time to eat. The morning seemed like forever ago. She reached over and picked up a cold biscuit and looked at it. A simple day. It was going to be a simple day started by a good breakfast and then maybe a trip into town to meet some people and shop at the general store. That's all she wanted today. Another day to find comfort in her new home and town. Then Ryker came and changed everything.

Who were all those men with him? Did they all have a grudge against Dad? Why so many of them? She couldn't see them all, but she knew there were many. Answers, she wanted answers. Elizabeth began to eat the biscuit by now, comprehending that she had not eaten all day and it was getting late. She would find her answers no matter how long it took or what she had to do.

CHAPTER 4

ELIZABETH WOKE TO THE SOUND of a crackling fire raging in the fireplace. Quickly looking around, she realized she had fallen asleep sitting in the kitchen chair, a half-eaten biscuit on her lap. Jake was seated in a big leather chair on the other side of the front room reading one of her father's books. Sensing she was awake, he closed the book and stood.

"I just checked in on Mr. Thornton. He's seems okay," Jake assured Elizabeth. "I didn't think that chair was very comfortable, but I didn't want to try and move you so I just left you alone."

Elizabeth sat up somewhat embarrassed by her actions. The table had been cleared and the kitchen cleaned.

"I can't believe I fell asleep!" she stated in an agitated manner, not quite knowing what to do.

"You had a pretty bad day, I'd say. You needed to sleep," Jake accurately observed.

"Yes, but not while I have a guest cleaning the house!"

"Well, first, I'm no guest, and second, I just picked up a few things in the kitchen. I wouldn't say I cleaned the house," Jake said, chuckling. "Now that you're up and around, I'll be heading out unless you need something."

"What time is it?" Elizabeth asked.

"About eight, I reckon," Jake guessed as there was no clock in sight.

"Would you like some coffee? I can warm some here quickly," Elizabeth asked, trying to mask her desire for him to stay.

"Sure, that'd be fine," Jake said, walking to the table and sitting down. Elizabeth heated the stove and put on the coffee.

"I don't have anything to eat," Elizabeth apologized.

"Sure, you do. I found a bowl of good lookin' biscuits on the table. I just covered them up and put them in that cupboard there," Jake explained, pointing to the cupboard next to the sink, smiling the whole time.

"Oh, those are from this morning, they're no good anymore," Elizabeth said.

"Nonsense, bust 'em out. If you made 'em, I bet they're great," Jake stated.

Elizabeth flashed a coy smile and retrieved the biscuits from the cupboard and placed them on the table along with two coffee cups. She then checked on the coffee.

After filling each cup, she sat down opposite Jake and looked closely at him.

"You don't look much like I remember," she declared.

Jake smiled. "No, I'm sure I don't. It's been a few years."

"Actually, it's been seven," Elizabeth offered.

"Yeah, I know. I been payin' attention," Jake admitted, looking down into his coffee.

"Really? Why is that?" she countered.

"Well, I been around this ranch with Mr. Thornton quite a lot helpin' out and learnin' some things."

"Learning some things?" Elizabeth inquired.

"Sure, Mr. Thornton taught me how to ride the right way, how to rope and heard cattle. He also taught me how to shoot. My pa didn't know much about those things, so he let Mr. Thornton—er, your father teach me."

"Are you a good shot?" Elizabeth asked.

Jake looked up at Elizabeth and saw a face with a frown and wrinkled forehead. "I reckon I'm better than some and not as good as others. Why?" Jake asked. Elizabeth let the question pass.

"You ever heard of an outlaw named Ryker?" she asked with a sense of urgency in her voice.

"Ryker? Nope, don't know that name," Jake answered.

"That's the name of the man who shot my father and stole our cattle. He forced me to open the safe so he could steal our money. He was with many other men. He is short two now though," Elizabeth stated as she stared into the distance. "Moses killed one, and I killed the other," she added.

"You killed the other!" Jake shouted, then realized how loud he had been. "Sorry, but you killed one of them?" Jake asked.

"Yes, I shot the first one that came into the house. The second one shot me in the arm, causing me to drop my gun and fall," Elizabeth stated without a scant sign of remorse or emotion. "Otherwise, I would have gotten him too," she added. Jake sat back in disbelief. Elizabeth looked at him and, seeing his reaction, smiled.

"Yes, Jake Rawlings, I know how to shoot pretty well."

Jake exhaled, shaking his head.

"Whoa! Where did you learn to shoot?" Jake asked, genuinely interested.

"In Philadelphia I met fella who had been in the war and was really good with guns. We got to know each other, and I asked him to teach me how to draw and shoot. I knew all along I was coming back here, and I didn't want to be one of those women who couldn't handle a gun or defend myself. I sure didn't think I would need to do that a few days after I got back though!" she exclaimed.

"Your aunt and uncle didn't care if you were shooting?" Jake asked.

"They didn't know about it. They thought I was with the other young ladies having tea and dreaming of being married or something."

Jake stood and announced he had to go. Elizabeth stood, shook Jake's hand, and thanked him for everything he had done.

"I'm not sure what I would have done without you today," she admitted.

"I'll bet you would have done just fine." Jake smiled and headed for the door. He stopped before leaving.

"If you like, I'll come back tomorrow and see how your father is and if you need anything?"

"Of course. I look forward to it," she replied.

Elizabeth extinguished the fire in the fireplace, checked on her father, who seemed to be breathing normally but still unconscious, then went to bed.

Jake swung up onto his horse and headed for home. The moon had punched a big white hole in the night sky, illuminating the path that lay in front of him.

Ryker, I need to find out who this killer is. Who would know? Jess McCoy! If anybody in town would know, it would be him. Saloon owners knew about everybody in the territory. He'd check with Mr. McCoy in the morning. Right now he needed to get home. He knew his ma and pa were waiting to hear all about what had happened to Mr. Thornton at the Tilted T.

Elizabeth lay on top of the bed staring at the ceiling, pondering her next move. She would need to find someone to look after her father while she was gone. She needed to find out where Canyon Creek was and how to get there. Her dad had said she could take the stage from town. She would consult with Dr. Langdon when he returned tomorrow. Chances were that he knew where Canyon Creek was and could direct her to the stage office. Hopefully he could suggest a lady in town she could hire to care for her father. She got up and checked her carpetbag. Ryker hadn't gotten all her money. She had one hundred dollars in currency and several coins. That would be plenty to hire a caretaker and stage fare to Canyon Creek, provided it wasn't too far away. Elizabeth felt better.

If only Dad would wake up, she thought before turning the oil light out and drifting to sleep.

CHAPTER 5

ENJAMIN FRANKLIN CHANCE HAD BECOME an unassuming man. He believed in doing the right thing, following the law, and earning a day's pay for a day's work. He had a sense of honor that was strong, even to him. He had been the son of a man who had headed West before it was the popular thing to do and a mother who had died giving him life. Due to his father's inability to settle down, Chance spent his formidable years moving from one settlement to another, then packing up and moving again. His father trusted no one and hammered that belief into his son at every opportunity. As a result, Chance found it difficult to form the bond of friendship with anyone. His distant relationship with his father mirrored that difficulty. He always felt his father blamed him for his mother's death. Because of that, he had consciously discarded his birthday, unwilling to remind himself of his mother's passing on that day. Subsequently, Chance was not completely certain of his age. Along the way, Chance learned to ride a horse and use a gun with the best of them. His first deadly gunfight occurred around the age of nineteen. These days, Chance was also skilled at his two favorite pastimes, drinking whiskey and playing poker. It was those two skills in action on this night. Maybe Chance was a simple man after all.

Chance lowered his head and glared beneath his hat across the table at the tall stranger who had been giving him fits all night. Although three other players sat at the table, the big visitor had been his only real challenge.

What'd he say his name was? Chance thought. He offered it up about four hours ago when this epic game began. Dakota Jones, the owner of the Creek Bed Saloon, came over to the table as Chance was about to shuffle the deck for another hand.

"Last hand! Gettin' late!" Jones barked in his usually abrupt manner. It wasn't that Jones was a rude man, but a fella over six feet and well past three hundred pounds couldn't help but be boisterous. Chance leaned over his shoulder and snapped at his host.

"Take it easy, big fella. We only need one final hand to settle the score tonight." Chance looked at the players and declared more than questioned. "Agreed?"

The four cowboys, including the tall stranger whose name Chance couldn't recall, agreed with a nod. One final hand, no limit with an ante of $20. After each player dropped his $20 in the middle of the table, Chance topped the pile with his own.

Chance finished shuffling. The cards looked like stamps in hands that accommodated his six-foot-four frame. He popped the deck on the table to his left, offering Clinton Smith the opportunity to cut the deck. Smith tapped the top of the deck with his right index finger, indicating he was satisfied with the shuffle. He followed with a wave of his left hand, motioning for Chance to deal. This wasn't the first time Chance and Smith had sat together at a card table in the Creek Bed. Smith couldn't remember how many times he had played poker with Chance in the year since Chance arrived in town. Like most folks, Smith liked Chance and trusted him at the card table. Smith couldn't say that about the tall stranger sitting across the table. Not that Smith had noticed any peculiar behavior or movements branded with cheating. He'd just never seen this fella before, and that alone was reason for caution.

With a quick left hand, Chance scooped the deck off the table and began his sharp method of dealing the cards by snapping a single card in front of each player. Five cards per player with each having the choice of discarding up to three and replacing each with a new card off the deck, thus the name of the game, five-card draw.

After finishing the deal, Chance set the remaining cards in front of him and gathered up his five. He took a quick peek at the top of each card. Not in any particular order, nor changing position of the cards. That was a sure sign of a greenhorn, to which he was far removed. Chance began his card-playing journey in a corral outside the stockyards in Fort Worth at the ripe age of fourteen or fifteen. He wasn't sure. All he knew was he'd been playing cards for near as long as he could remember and was pretty good at it.

Chance peered down at two kings, one three of hearts, one four of diamonds, and a jack of spades.

Hmm? Two kings are a good start, Chance thought.

After each player laid another $20 on the table, Chance turned to Smith. "Cards?" Chance asked.

Smith said nothing, just held up two fingers on his right hand. Chance peeled off two cards from the top of the deck, putting them directly in front of Smith facedown. Chance then looked next to Tom Davis, who was sitting to Smith's left. Davis also said nothing and held up three fingers on his left hand. Chance followed the same procedure he had completed with Smith, only this time sending three cards to the front of Davis. Chance gazed at the tall stranger across from him. The stranger let out a sigh.

"Two," was the mumbled response.

Chance rattled off two cards, putting both directly in front of the stranger. *Interesting*, thought Chance. The stranger had let out a breath and had spoken the word "two." There must be a purpose for those actions as Chance knew the stranger was no greenhorn himself. Before Chance could look to the next player sitting at his right, Albert Loman, the town's barber, pushed his five cards together and threw them into the center of the table.

"I'm through for tonight, gentlemen," Loman declared.

Chance revisited his cards and opted for three, keeping the two kings. He was rewarded for his decision as the king of diamonds joined his other two, a heart and a club. Unfortunately, the eight of hearts and the two of spades he dealt himself were no help at all. Three kings were a formidable hand, certainly reason to stay in the game until all remaining players showed their strength. Chance figured he was up about $100 or so anyway. Chance slid two $20 notes into the center of the table. Clinton Smith followed with two $20 of his own. Tom Davis paused, then tossed his cards down in front of himself.

"I'm out, boys, but I'll stay and watch the outcome of this one if nobody minds?"

The three remaining players nodded their heads with approval. The decision to stay or fold was now to the stranger whose name nobody could remember. The stranger took a long pause and looked carefully at the face of Chance then Smith. Without looking at his cards, the stranger placed $100 onto the pile of money in the center of the table.

"I'll stay and raise $60." The declaration was met with a grunt from Smith and a smile from Chance. Chance didn't know if the stranger was bluffing or not, but he did know it was going to take a damn good hand to beat his three kings.

"I'll match the $100 and raise another $50," Chance replied.

Tom Smith was already in the process of throwing his cards facedown on the table, mumbling something about the bet being too much for his blood.

The stranger leaned forward, resting his elbows on the table, looking at his cards with steel-gray eyes in a manner that Chance had seen many times before. Concern, doubt, indecision, the lines on the stranger's brow and the squint of his eyes told Chance he was all but guaranteed to be sweeping the money pile into his lap any moment. The stranger looked up from his cards, slowly reached down to the money that lay before him, and with fingers spread on his right hand, he moved $50 into the center of the table.

"Call," he whispered.

Without hesitation, Chance laid down his cards faceup toward the center of the table near the pile of cash.

"Three kings," stated Chance, neither confident nor contrite.

The stranger, holding his cards in his left hand while moving the other off the table down to his right side, laid down three aces and two queens.

"Full up," the stranger stated in a tone that mirrored Chance's prior decree. Chance leaned back in his chair, watching the stranger's actions.

"It's not necessary to cover your gun, stranger," Chance stated with a grin as he pushed back from the table and stood, keeping his own right hand ready. "But I believe your winning does mean you're buying the last round."

"I don't recall that being part of the wager," the stranger offered with his own grin. "But I like the idea, so let's order up with the big man behind the bar." The tall stranger collected his money from the center of the table. After folding it with his left hand, he tucked it inside his vest pocket next to his derringer.

The tall stranger whose name nobody could remember then strode across the near vacant saloon to the bar where Chance, Smith, Davis, and Loman were already being served whiskey in small clear glasses. The stranger leaned into a spot next to Chance and pushed his hat back.

"What'll you have, stranger?" Dakota Jones loudly asked.

"Whiskey," offered the stranger as he looked around the saloon using only his head turning from right to left then back again.

"You're an uneasy sort of fellow, aren't you?" Chance queried.

"Always, when I'm the new guy in town."

"Well, take it easy, kid. You're among honest men at the moment, I can guarantee that. What's your name? It's been buggin' me all night," Chance finally asked.

"Luxton Danner," replied the stranger, extending his right hand, which Chance gladly accepted.

"Luxton Danner? That name sounds familiar," Chance stated, looking down at the bar with a squint. "Have we met before?" he asked, his voice fading. Without waiting for an answer, he continued. "Ben Chance." He then reintroduced Clinton Smith, Tom Davis, and Albert Loman.

Danner nodded as each name was announced, then he downed his drink in one swallow.

A moment passed, then Danner nodded back at Chance.

"Ben Chance?" Danner clarified.

Chance finished his drink and nodded.

"Would that be US Deputy Marshal Benjamin Franklin Chance?" Danner asked.

Chance immediately angled his body and took a step back with his right foot moving his gun side away from Danner.

"Used to be," Chance slowly answered.

Danner watched every move Chance made, recognizing his defensive position. Danner shook his head.

"No reason to be cautious, Marshal." Danner extended his right hand a second time toward Chance. "I have reason to thank you, that's all." Chance relaxed and accepted Danner's second handshake.

"Now what did I do that would warrant a thank-you from a stranger?" Chance exhaled. Danner leaned on the bar and got comfortable.

"Well, awhile back, about three or four years ago, you went into the territories looking for a murderer by the name of Ellis Garner. I heard you found the no-good waste of human flesh hiding with a band of Indians. I understand you took him into custody and returned him to Fort Smith for trial. From what I've been told, you probably don't remember every outlaw you ever brought in, but I heard it was you that got ole Garner."

"I remember Ellis Garner all right. Not because he was anybody special, but because he stunk so bad and it took me two weeks to get him back to Fort Smith," Chance recalled with a frown. "It made Judge Parker happy though, me bringing Garner back alive. Parker got the satisfaction of hangin' him after he found him guilty of murder. What connection did Garner have to you?"

"No direct connection at all," replied Danner. "I never met the bastard. He killed a friend of mine back East. That was the murder warrant you served on him," Danner explained, staring into the mirror behind the bar.

It was the first real emotion Chance had detected in Danner all night.

"Glad to be of service," Chance stated, then turned and poured more whiskey into each empty glass on the bar.

"Goin' to be in town for a while?" Davis asked Danner.

"I don't know yet, haven't decided. Is the hotel down the street a good place to stay?" he asked to no one in particular.

"The Sundown, yep, good as any you'll find around here. Run by a fine-lookin' lady too," was Davis's response.

Chance quickly glanced at Davis with a scowl. Danner grinned.

"I believe I'll call it a night then." With that, Danner emptied his glass a second time, turned, and walked to the swinging doors of the Creek Bed Saloon. He pushed them open in one fluid motion and disappeared onto the dark street.

"Interesting fellow there, huh, Chance?" Loman stated.

"Young fella, packin' a pair of guns, but talks real good," Clinton Smith offered.

"Yep, seems like a smart one," Tom Davis chimed in. Chance wondered as he looked back at the Creek Bed doors still rocking back and forth from Danner's exit.

"Something about him seems familiar. Can't put my finger on it. Good night," Chance offered then hurried out of the saloon, his boot heels pounding the floor planks as he walked. Chance paused and took a good look up and down the street. Satisfied everything was okay, he crossed the street and walked over to the Sundown Hotel. Inside he found the owner, Rachel Christine Brennen, standing behind a large oak desk that served as the check-in point for guests. As Chance approached the desk, Rachel looked up and smiled. The glow of the oil lamp reflecting off the top of the polished desk illuminated Rachel's face in a soft radiance that exacerbated her long auburn hair. She was wrapped tight in a dark red robe that exposed a small helping of her pale white neck.

"Hello, Ben, or should I say good morning? It's a little later than usual tonight, isn't it?" she asked. Her voice radiated like a songbird's. His heart skipped a beat at the sound if it.

"It was a long game, and there was a stranger in town that insisted on buying the last round."

"Yes, I heard he won big and was told that meant he was buying." Rachel giggled as she spoke, causing a lock of hair to fall over her face. "He just came in, apologized for disturbing me so late, and then told me all about it."

"How many nights did he pay for?" Chance asked in a low, serious tone.

"Just one, but he said he might be in town for a while. Is there trouble?" Rachel didn't wait for an answer. "He seemed quite pleasant actually, not the usual kind I get in here."

"No, no trouble, just curious," Chance answered. "What room is he in?" Chance asked in a relaxed way, his face brightening up as he gazed at Rachel.

"I put him in five so he'd be several rooms away from yours," Rachel stated, standing straight. Chance grinned widely at Rachel.

"Always taking care of me, aren't you, Rach?" he said as he turned toward the massive oak staircase.

"Somebody has to!" she called back while she turned off the oil lamp that sat next to the register book. She locked the front doors and returned to her room.

CHAPTER 6

LIZABETH WOKE TO THE ALTERNATING sounds of singing of birds outside her window. She didn't know what kind of birds they were, but they were music to her hears. Suddenly, she leapt from her slumber and raced to her father's room. To her relief, he was still breathing normally and he looked a little better than yesterday, she thought. She checked his bandages and found a small amount of blood, and fluids had seeped through each one. Dr. Langdon had not instructed her to change the bandages although she was fighting the urge to do just that.

No, I'll wait for Dr. Langdon. He said he'd be back early today, she thought.

She washed and dressed quickly, wanting to be prepared if she had guests earlier than expected. After placing a fire in the stove, she prepared coffee and went out to the chicken coop to look for fresh eggs. Her father had not really wanted chickens on the ranch, but it was necessary in order to have fresh eggs on a regular basis. The coop was a small building about seventy-five paces from the east side of the house and held only a few hens. She looked over the twenty or so cows in the east pasture that Ryker had left behind. It appeared they were grazing fine with no hurry to add hay. A quick search of the nests brought four eggs into Elizabeth's basket. Returning to the house, she put the coffeepot on and prepared to fry the eggs. Shortly after finishing her breakfast and clearing the table, she heard a horse and carriage coming around the house.

Elizabeth met Dr. Langdon at the door. He offered an optimistic smile and removed his hat.

"Good morning, Miss Thornton. How's my patient this morning?" Langdon asked while entering the house.

"He looks a little better than yesterday, I thought, but he is still sleeping," Elizabeth advised. The smile on Langdon's face eroded into a frown.

"Let's have a look," Langdon stated, sounding neither optimistic nor discouraged. Langdon knew the longer Thornton was unconscious, the more likely malnutrition would set in, preventing the healing process and creating a second serious issue. Langdon removed his coat, washed his hands in the washbowl next to Thornton's bed, and removed the chest bandage first. After a thorough cleansing, he placed a fresh bandage over the wound. Repeating the same procedure for the wound on Thornton's left side, Langdon attempted to waken Thornton. Gently grasping the top of Thornton's shoulders, Langdon began to massage the shoulders and speak to his patient.

"Joel, can you hear me?" Langdon repeated several times. "It's Fred Langdon. "Can you hear me?" Langdon repeated as a hopeful Elizabeth looked on. After a few minutes with no response from his patient, Langdon ceased his efforts.

"What is it?" Elizabeth asked.

"I believe he is in what's called a coma. It's when the body shuts off after it has been damaged and needs time to recuperate. I admit I don't know much more than that. I read about it in a journal or two but have never experienced it with a patient before," Langdon explained. "Trouble is, in this condition, your father cannot eat, drink, or take any medication. I fear without food, at least a little, he will suffer from malnutrition," Langdon further explained.

"How long can he go being unconscious?" Elizabeth asked fearing the answer.

"I'm not certain. Your father is, or was a pretty healthy man before this, so I believe he could last longer." Langdon scratched his chin, looking down at Thornton. "The good news is that he is breathing normal and has a little more color in his face. The wounds don't look too bad, so we'll keep watch and hope he comes out of it soon." Langdon picked up his bag and followed Elizabeth to the kitchen, where she offered coffee. Langdon accepted and took a seat at the table.

"I'm sorry, but I didn't take the time to make biscuits this morning," Elizabeth stated.

"I wouldn't expect that or anything else after what you went through yesterday," Langdon said, smiling as he accepted his coffee cup. Elizabeth sat down opposite the doctor.

"I need to go to Canyon Creek as soon as possible," Elizabeth announced. "Would you know of a lady in town that I could hire to care for my father while I'm gone?" she asked. Langdon looked at her inquisitively.

"May I ask why you need to go to Canyon Creek right away?" Langdon asked. "Before my father passed out, he told me to go there and look for his old partner, Ben Chance. He said that Ben would know what to do regarding what had happened. He said the last he heard, Ben was the town marshal in Canyon Creek and could help me."

"Help you do what?" Langdon asked, no longer concerned about being meddlesome.

"The men that did this stole our horses, cattle, and money. I want to find these men and get back what they took from us," Elizabeth stated.

Dr. Langdon leaned forward and spoke in a stern, almost fatherly voice.

"I suggest you leave those things to the law, Miss Thornton."

Elizabeth looked down at her coffee cup.

The law? She hadn't even thought about that.

"Is there a marshal in town?" Elizabeth asked. "I've only been to Thornton once a few days ago, and I'm not familiar with anyone there except you," she added. Langdon picked up his cup.

"May I have more coffee?" he asked, realizing Elizabeth needed an overview of the town named after her father. He figured he was the currently the best one to provide it.

Elizabeth filled Langdon's cup, then returned the pot to the stove.

"Please sit down and I'll tell you as much about the town of Thornton as I know. But understand, I'm a newcomer of sorts. I've only been here two years."

Elizabeth smiled and leaned in, anxious to learn as much as the good doctor could tell her.

"As you probably know, the town started as a stop-off for the cattlemen moving their herds up from the south on their way to Kansas and beyond. Your father was instrumental in turning the camp area into a town with permanent residents, buildings, and such. From what I've been told, the town sort of sprang up overnight, as they say, which was no easy feat since there were no gold or silver strikes around here. As the cattle industry became stronger in the years after the war, there were more and more cattle and cowhands needing a place to rest, drink, and gamble. Those needs led to the hotel, boarding house, livery stable, blacksmith, saloon, store, and other establishments." Langdon chuckled. "We still only have one saloon. That tells you how small the town is." Langdon continued.

"A town hall and church were built. After a couple of problems with outlaws cropped up, the town elected a marshal and built what passes as a jail. Those two things just happened last year. Before that, the only law was the occasional visit by a ranger or US marshal. Just last year the county was founded and a sheriff was appointed, but he was over in Stratford several miles away. I've only seen him in Thornton three, maybe four times meeting with Marshal Thomas. John Thomas is the marshal in Thornton. He was handpicked by your father. A few of the businessmen in town sort of voted him in, myself included. The marshal's jurisdiction is the town and immediate surroundings. I don't believe it comes out this far, but I know John will help in any way he can. I know he can contact the sheriff and the rangers. He been over in Stratford the last couple of days. The sheriff there sent word for help. Seems like the fellas that came here may have gone there first and shot the town up—"

"I'll tell Marshal Thomas all about this, but I'm going to Canyon Creek to find Ben Chance," Elizabeth interrupted. "Dad told me to do that and I'm going to go," she added. "I need someone to care for Dad though."

"Well, I would suggest the store owner's wife, Mrs. McNally, or maybe Mrs. Rawlings. They both like your father and may be willing to come by for a few days," Langdon suggested.

"Very well, I'll try and get to town later today and see Mrs. McNally. I met her a few days ago when Dad took me to town. She was very pleasant toward me. I'll ask her first," Elizabeth stated as she collected Dr. Langdon's cup. Langdon stood and gathered his hat and bag.

"I'd gladly take you to town, but your father shouldn't be left alone," Langdon explained.

"Jake Rawlings said he was coming back today. When he gets here, I'll go into town then," Elizabeth advised. Doc Langdon said goodbye and headed for his carriage.

"I'll come back out tomorrow. If you need me sooner, send word," Langdon called over his shoulder. Elizabeth watched as the doctor's carriage headed for town.

Jake tied his bay to the hitching post outside the Tumbleweed Saloon and went inside. Even though he was twenty, he didn't visit the saloon very often, which was evident by the look on Jess McCoy's face when Jake walked through the swinging doors.

"Howdy, Jake! What brings you in today? How's ole Joel doin'?" McCoy added.

"Still alive as far as I know. He was last night when I left the ranch," Jake answered as he bellied up to the bar. The saloon was still empty except for a couple of regulars, Bob Sowell and Chili Daniels, who were already sipping beer at a corner table. Both Sowell and Daniels got up and joined McCoy and Jake at the bar, wanting to hear the scuttlebutt.

"Can I set you up, Jake?" Jess asked.

"Naw, thanks, Mr. McCoy. I was wonderin' if you had ever heard of a fella by the name of Ryker," Jake asked promptly.

Jess frowned and looked hard at Jake. "He the one who shot Joel?" Jess asked.

"Yep, that's what Mr. Thornton's daughter said."

McCoy nodded his head.

"Yeah, I heard of um," Jesse said slowly. "Been a lot of years though, back when I was in Abilene. Joel and Ben Chance used to stop by the saloon I worked in down there. I remember hearin' about this Ryker fella who was robbin' coaches. Heard Joel and Chance went into Injun territory and tracked him down. Joel and Ben rode together back then—"

"Elizabeth said that Mr. Thornton told her to find Ben Chance, that he'd know what to do," Jake interrupted.

"Oh, Chance will know what to do, all right." Jess smiled as he spoke. "Chance'll hunt him down and kill em for sure," Jess added.

"He'll hunt um down fer sure," Bob Sowell chimed in. Jake and Jess turned to Sowell.

"You know Ben Chance?" Jake asked as Jess leaned across the bar.

"Yep, I used to ride up in the territory years back. Everybody knew 'bout Chance and Thornton. Both were good, but Chance was lightnin' fast and didn't care if he had to pay for a funeral," Sowell stated.

"Pay for a funeral?" Jake asked.

"Yep, Chance and Thornton rode for Judge Parker over in Fort Smith. Deputy marshals they were. Parker wanted his deputies to bring back as many prisoners alive as possible. Didn't want his deputies out there killin' em all, so he made the deputies pay for the funerals for all they killed," Sowell explained. Jake stood in awe, his shoulders slumped, head up, and mouth open, leaning on the bar, not believing what he heard.

"How you know all this, Mr. Sowell?" Jake asked. Jess smiled and stayed quiet behind the bar.

"I knew my way around the Injun territory pretty good, so I would hire out as a guide to some of the marshals. I rode guide for Chance and Thornton a few times till they found their way and didn't need me anymore," Sowell answered. "Then I just heard the talk. You didn't want those two comin' after ya, that's fer damn sure." Sowell finished his beer and put the glass on the bar. Chili Daniels, who had stood still just listening to Sowell, did the same then left the saloon. "Pretty girl that daughter of Joel's," Sowell added, smiling at Jake before he headed for the swinging doors. Jake turned to McCoy.

"You know where Mr. Chance is?" he asked.

"I heard he was down in Canyon Creek, but that was a while ago. Don't know if he's still there." McCoy offered then cleared the empty beer glasses from the bar, wiping up the mess with a clean white towel he always carried over his shoulder.

"Elizabeth says she's goin' down to Canyon Creek to fetch Mr. Chance back here and go git Ryker and his gang."

McCoy shook his head. "Sounds bad for everyone to me."

"I think I'll go with her, make sure she's okay," Jake said out loud.

"I'd think long and hard 'bout that, son," McCoy answered. "We all love Joel, but sounds like yer lookin' ta git in a serious gunfight, kid. Better be sure you can handle it," he warned. "Yer ma and pa ain't gonna be happy with ya either."

"Thanks for your time, Mr. McCoy," Jake said, then turned and walked out into the street.

Club Smith was walking toward the Tumbleweed and saw Jake. "Howdy, Jake! Joel Thornton still alive?" he asked.

"I think so. I'm headin' out there now to find out."

"I'm thinkin' just 'bout everybody in town heard what happened to Joel," Club stated.

"Yeah, I'm sure you got around to everybody," Jake laughed as he swung up on his horse. "See ya later," Jake hollered then pulled his horse around and headed for the Tilted T leaving, a cloud of red dust behind.

Elizabeth felt lost. She hadn't been on a ranch since she was twelve years old. She wasn't sure what needed to be done. She made a pot of soup and left it on the stove in case her father woke up.

I better feed and water Sky, she thought then headed for the barn. She filled Sky's water bucket and feeder trough with grain then added some hay to his stall. She walked out of the barn and decided to take a look at her mother's and Moses's graves. Her mother's headstone was covered with a coating of green moss and dark mold. She brushed away some of the mess with her hand and read the stone.

Carol Haller Thornton
Born 1830
Died 1870
Beloved wife and mother

She paused and thought about her mother. Elizabeth smiled as she remembered how happy her mother always seemed to be despite working so hard on the farm every day while her father was away and the overflowing exhilaration when he returned home. She was a small woman with a big voice and heart to match. Long blond hair like her own and blue eyes. No wonder her father had been smitten by her and asked her grandfather for her hand.

That must have been daunting, Elizabeth thought. Her grandfather was a minister who had come to Texas from St. Louis to spread the Lord's word and make a new life for him and his daughter. Elizabeth couldn't remember much of her grandfather, only that he was a large man with a beard and was always speaking the Bible. Elizabeth knelt at the foot of her mother's grave. She closed her eyes and remembered the last time she saw her mother. What a sad time that had been. Elizabeth's thoughts were broken by the sound of her father coughing.

He's awake! Elizabeth ran to the house, rushed inside, and stopped at her father's door.

CHAPTER 7

THE NEXT MORNING DANNER WALKED down the stairs and into the dining room where he found Chance seated at the head for the table. Several other guests were gathered around having breakfast being served by a young girl. Chance made eye contact with Danner and with a swivel of his head motioned for him sit next to him. Danner looked around the room and noted that in addition to Chance and the girl serving, there were two men, one older and one younger, neither wearing guns, three women and two children, one boy and one girl. Chance had his gun on, which was no surprise to Danner as he figured that a former federal marshal, especially one with Chance's reputation, was always aware of possible trouble. Danner sat down on Chance's left and was immediately asked by the girl serving if he wanted coffee. After nodding yes, Danner looked at Chance.

"You a resident of this hotel, Mr. Chance?" he asked.

Chance finished chewing a forkful of eggs and looked at Danner.

"First, my name isn't Mr. Chance, it's Ben or Chance, and yes, I currently call the Sundown my home."

Rachel entered the dining room hurrying about with the purpose of making sure all her guests were being taken care of properly. Danner took a long look at Rachel and noted her long red hair, green eyes, and full red lips. She looked wonderful in her blue dress despite it being covered with a white albeit stained apron. Her apron was tied with neatly affixed bows behind her neck and at the middle of her back. Danner figured her to be about thirty-five, with an hourglass figure that would make any man take a second look. Her face was bright and lovely with a few lines here and there offering evidence that she had some life experiences behind her. Danner stood as she walked toward him holding a plate of steaming hot bacon and potatoes.

"Please sit down, Mr. Danner. You're my guest," Rachel politely stated. "Bacon, potatoes, eggs?" Rachel asked.

"Bacon and eggs would be just fine," Danner stated, smiling.

After Rachel had moved on to other guests, Chance leaned over to Danner and whispered.

"I know what you're thinking. What is a woman like that doing running a hotel by herself, right?" Keeping his eyes on Rachel, Danner nodded in agreement. Chance waited until Rachel left the dining room and returned to the kitchen for more food.

"She and her husband came here about four years ago from San Antonio. Her husband bought this hotel, and life was good until he was thrown from his horse one night riding back from Oneida. Hit his head pretty bad when he fell. He managed to get back here, but Doc Carson couldn't do anything for him. Doc said it was bleeding in the brain or something. He died leaving her with an eight-year-old daughter to deal with the hotel. The young girl you see serving in here is her daughter. Rachel's a strong woman, decided to run the hotel on her own. Nearly lost everything. She was robbed once, and a lot of the cowhands that stayed here didn't pay their share. A couple of whores tried to use the place as their setup, but she got some help from a few of the married men in town and took care of that. Things changed for her about a year ago, and she's doing pretty good now."

"Things changed? What changed a year ago?" Danner asked, wondering if she had found a new husband.

"I showed up," was Chance's reply. Danner leaned back in his chair and smiled. "Oh, so you and she—"

"Nope!" exclaimed Chance. "It's not like that at all. I just decided to stay here for a bit, and I made sure that everyone paid for the services rendered, if you know what I mean. So, Danner, what line of work are you in, or do I need to ask?" Chance inquired, taking a long look that made Danner a bit uneasy.

"Oh, the usual," Danner replied. "Cowhand mostly, although I've ridden guard on a few wagon trains."

"Riding guard?" Chance stated with a quainter tone in his voice. "Is that where you got the idea of wearing two guns?"

"Nope, just figured that two were better than one is all," Danner said.

"Only if you can handle both," Chance said as he stood, having finished his breakfast. "What do ya have there anyway?" Chance asked, narrowing his eyes, leaning forward, and peering at Danner's guns.

"'74 Russians in .45," Danner stated with a hint of pride in his voice.

"Thought so. Don't see many of those out here. I'm a Colt Army fella myself. Found I was faster with it than anything else I tried."

"I've been fast enough so far with these," Danner stated flatly, looking down at his plate of food. "Not that I walk around looking for another test," he continued.

"Nope, no sense looking for trouble. Wait around long enough and it finds you," Chance said as he turned and walked out of the dining room into the kitchen, no doubt to check on Rachel.

Danner stood, pivoted on his right boot heel, and walked out of the dining room through the bar area then out the front door of the hotel. Locating a wooden rocking chair with a comfortable-looking stuffed seat cushion on the front porch, he decided to sit a spell and let his meal settle.

The morning was bright and warm. The sun had pushed up on the east side of town. It burned an orange hole in the light blue sky. Danner took the opportunity to check out the lay of the land since he could see just about the whole town from his current vantage point. The Sundown was smack in the middle of Main Street, almost directly across from the Creek Bed Saloon.

Danner had immediately headed for the saloon last night after picketing his horse at the livery stable. The stable was down at the far east end of the town next to a couple of holding corrals. As custom for these Western towns, the blacksmith shop sat next to the livery stable and a couple of large warehouse buildings. There was a freight yard, and directly across from the blacksmith was what looked like a boarding house. Compared to the Sundown, it was small with what appeared to be four or five rooms for rent. Danner pictured a fine-looking woman, in the image of Rachel, running the boarding house, taking in an occasional female traveler or family that didn't want to be near the activity found at the saloon. West of the Sundown across the street was the general store and next to that a bank.

Danner found it interesting that a town this size had a bank, although Canyon Creek didn't qualify as a small town. It did have a stage line and a post office that looked like it was originally a pony express stop. He imagined the local cavalry troop commander might have commandeered it for temporary quarters from time to time. Danner leaned forward stretching his neck and looked to his right past the post office and identified the marshal's office and jail positioned on the same side of the street at the far west end of town.

Strange I didn't see the town marshal or a deputy yesterday, last night, or this morning, he thought. Especially since he was probably one of a few strangers in town. If trouble had started, there would have been a good chance it would have involved him. Danner laughed out loud just as Chance was walking out the front door of the Sundown.

"What's so funny?" Chance asked, looking around and seeing no one near the hotel porch.

"Nothing really," Danner replied. "I was just taking a look at the town and noticed the marshal's office and jail down on the west end. I realized I hadn't seen the marshal or a deputy since I've been here. That seemed odd to me as the Creek Bed was busy last night with a big stakes card game going. Then I figured I must have been the only threat of trouble in town since I seem to be the only stranger at the moment."

"Nope, don't consider yourself so special. Mrs. Tyler had a couple of cowhands come in last night at the boarding house."

"That's the boarding house down across from the blacksmith?" Danner asked.

"Yep, that's the one," Chance said as he looked east toward Mrs. Tyler's place. "And what makes you think you didn't see the marshal last night?" Chance questioned.

Danner's face contorted into a curvy mess as he looked at Chance. "Well, usually when a stranger comes to town and starts in on a poker game at the saloon, the law finds it necessary to make its presence known, that's all," Danner stated. "At least that's what I've encountered from personal experience."

Chance looked down at the seated Danner and pulled the left side of his vest away from his shirt exposing a bright silver star.

"You met the marshal last night, and he was highly interested in your activities."

Danner rocked back in his chair and laughed.

"I'll be damned!" he cried. "I can't believe you managed to get that past me. I'm usually far better at deducing clues around me."

"Well, my friend, I don't know what the hell 'deducing' means, but if it means knowing who you're playing cards and eating break-fast with, you've failed mightily." Chance stepped down from the porch and headed west toward the jail.

Danner stood up and watched Chance walk down to the jail and disappear into the office. Not sure what to do with himself, he went back into the Sundown and noticed the young girl cleaning up the dining room. Danner approached the girl.

"What's your name?"

"I'm Adeline," she stated in a clear voice. "I'm eleven and my mama owns this hotel. I work here and make my own money," she explained. Just then Rachel entered the room, having removed the food-stained apron, exposing her blue dress and beautiful figure.

"Well, Mr. Danner, I hope your stay last night and breakfast this morning was to your liking," she said. Her voice reminded Danner of a singing whip-poor-will. He quickly stood straight and removed his hat.

"Everything has been just fine, ma'am," he answered, the words stumbling from his lips. "Actually, if it's all right with you, I've decided to stay in town for a bit and would like to keep my room until further notice, if that's okay with you?" Danner repeated, sounding like a fool boy.

"It will be a pleasure to have such a well-spoken gentleman in the hotel. You sound like an educated man. Did you complete the grades?" Rachel asked.

"Yes, ma'am, actually I spent two years at Franklin & Marshall College in Lancaster, Pennsylvania, after the war."

Rachel looked up toward the ceiling with a faraway look in her green eyes.

"Is that near Philadelphia by chance?" she asked.

"Yes, ma'am, it's about eighty miles west of Philadelphia. Nice town, much smaller than Philadelphia," Danner explained.

"I've always wanted to see Philadelphia, Boston, and New York. They seem so far away from here, like another world," Rachel whispered.

"Mama!" Adeline shouted, abruptly extinguishing Rachel's daydream and bringing her back to the reality of Canyon Creek.

"Young lady, what have I told you about shouting like that?" Rachel scolded her daughter.

"Sorry, Mama, but shouldn't I get ready for school?"

"Yes, I assume so. Mrs. Tyler will be starting soon. Run upstairs and change into your gray dress, hurry now," Rachel said sharply. Adeline bolted for the stairs and was gone in a flash.

"I didn't realize there was a school here. I didn't see anything that looked like a school when I was looking around this morning," Danner said.

"It's easy to miss. It's a small building behind Mrs. Tyler's boarding house at the end of town. There has been talk of building a larger schoolhouse and hiring a teacher, but we haven't the number of families with children that we anticipated when the stage line came into town a few years ago. Many of the ranchers around here are pretty far away and don't send their children into town for schooling. We just started seeing some homesteaders come to town as a result of the lumber mill down on Cita Creek needing a few workers," Rachel explained.

"Which way is the mill?" Danner asked.

"Go west out of town about a mile or so, then turn north at the Coleman boulder," Rachel offered. "It's a large rock next to the trail. It marks the KC Coleman ranch boundary," Rachel further explained. "The mill is another mile or so at the creek."

"I wasn't aware there were enough trees around here to have a lumber mill." Danner laughed.

"There isn't really. There's some good-size timber further east from the mill, but mostly it's just a sawmill. Clayton Gibson owns the lumber supply store here in town. He and Sam Coleman had the sawmill built to cut the logs they bring over from the railroad station. The railroad is pretty far away, so they use big wagons to haul the logs from the rail station to the mill. I'm sorry, I'm just talking away." Rachel sighed.

"That's very interesting," Danner assured her. "This looks like a good town with a chance to grow," Danner added. Rachel looked out the front window onto the street.

"Yes, as long as the good people that come here stay, it will grow," she said.

"Good people like Ben Chance?" Danner asked.

"It's not like that, Mr. Danner. Ben has been very good to Adeline, me, and this town. He's been here a while, and I fear he's ready to move on," she said in a sad voice.

"Good people never stop coming," Danner said, trying to sound encouraging.

"True, so do bad," Rachel stated.

Danner wasn't sure what she meant by that. He chose not to inquire. Instead he excused himself and headed for the livery stable to claim his horse and head down to the lumber mill. If there were any new men in town looking for work, they'd probably be hanging around there. Danner hoped so, since he was looking for one in particular.

CHAPTER 8

J OEL THORNTON TURNED HIS HEAD slightly and gazed on his daughter through blurry eyes. Elizabeth moved to her father's side and sat next to his bed. She took his hand in hers and squeezed gently.

"How do you feel?" she plainly asked, not wanting to be emotional.

Thornton coughed again and grimaced.

"That hurts like hell," he said through gritted teeth. "Other than that, I'm starving," he added, forcing a faint smile.

"I made some soup!" Elizabeth shouted as she rose from her chair.

Thornton held on to her hand. "How long have I been out?"

"Since yesterday morning." Elizabeth attempted to minimize the agony of waiting that long.

"I'm sorry," he said, frowning, blinking several times in an attempt to see his daughter more clearly. "I'm sorry you were here and a part of this," he apologized again, wincing in pain.

"I'm not," she answered. "I'm glad I was here. You may have died if I wasn't. I'll get some soup for you. It should still be warm."

Elizabeth filled a bowl with the soup and returned to her father's bedside. She propped his head up with a pillow, then helped him eat. After several spoonfuls, he shook his head indicating that was enough. Elizabeth set the bowl on the bed table.

"As soon as you are stronger, I'm going to Canyon Creek to find Mr. Chance—"

"No! We don't have that much time!" her father stated. Elizabeth didn't understand.

"Not enough time?" she asked.

"No, Ryker will look to sell the horses to miners heading up to Colorado and Nevada and the cattle to the first cowhands moving a herd through the territory. It won't take more than a week for that to happen. It's a day and a half ride to Canyon Creek on the stage and another day and a half back. Then Chance will have to find Ryker, which won't be easy. He's no fool," Thornton said, closing his eyes and wincing with every word.

"I need to get Dr. Langdon back here with some medicine," Elizabeth told her father.

"No, too much time wasted for that!" Thornton said in as strong and loud a voice as he could stand.

"Nonsense!" Elizabeth shouted. "I'll send for Dr. Langdon, then go into town to catch the stage for Canyon Creek," Elizabeth insisted. Thornton looked at his daughter with tired eyes.

"You sound like your mother." He smiled.

"Well, someone has to talk some sense into you, and I'm just the one to do it," she said in a calmer voice and broad smile.

"Okay, okay, Miss Thornton," her father said. She removed the extra pillow from behind his head, and he closed his eyes, settling back into a deep sleep.

Elizabeth was energized. She felt much better now. She left the soup next to her father and went into her room to pack some clothes for the trip to Canyon Creek. Twenty minutes later she heard horses coming up the trail near the house. A quick look out the window confirmed it was Jake Rawlings leading a woman driving a single-horse carriage. Elizabeth quickly ran a brush through her hair, then walked out onto the porch and waited. Jake swung down off his horse then stopped the horse drawing the carriage and helped the woman down.

"This is my mother, Martha Rawlings," Jake said, allowing his mother to walk past him and greet Elizabeth.

"Oh my! What a beautiful woman you've become!" Martha said, leaning back so she could get a good look at Elizabeth. "I haven't seen you since you were a shy young thing!" Martha exclaimed, extending her arms out to each side just above her waist. "How's your father?" she whispered.

"Actually better, I think. He woke up and was able to eat some soup before falling back to sleep. I need to summon Dr. Langdon. I could tell he was in terrible pain," Elizabeth explained.

"That's why I'm here, dear," Martha Rawlings offered. "I will look after your father while you and Jake ride into town and fetch Doc Langdon back. You take my carriage," Martha insisted.

"Mrs. Rawlings, could I trouble you to look after my father for a few days while I go to Canyon Creek to attend to business? I know it's an awful lot to ask, but I can pay you for your time," Elizabeth advised. Martha frowned and looked back at her son, then again at Elizabeth.

"Jake has told me of your plans to find Mr. Chance. I don't mean to be impolite, but I don't believe it's a young woman's place to do such a thing," Martha said.

"I appreciate your advice, Mrs. Rawlings, but my father asked me to go and I can take care of myself quite well, I assure you," Elizabeth explained.

"Yes, Jake told me that also," Martha huffed, obviously appalled by what she had heard about Elizabeth killing a man.

"I wonder if there's anything Jake hasn't repeated from our conversation last night." Elizabeth looked at Jake with a frown on her lips and hands on her hips. Jake looked down at the ground and kicked at the dirt, saying nothing.

"Don't be angry with Jake. His pa and I were insistent on him telling us everything that happened. After all, we are neighbors and quite friendly with your father," Mrs. Rawlings explained. "He also told us you were hurt."

"I'm fine, really I am," Elizabeth interjected. "Please come inside. I can heat some water for tea," Elizabeth offered to Mrs. Rawlings. Elizabeth led Martha and Jake into the house, waving her hand toward the table for them to be seated.

"No, no," Martha Rawlings insisted. "You have Jake take you to town. I'll set about making tea and caring for your father. You know, your father has been a very important man to my Jake these past few years. His pa and I are very grateful for the attention your father has given him."

"I'm very glad to hear that, Mrs. Rawlings, and thank you so much for your assistance." Elizabeth looked at Jake. "I'm nearly finished packing. I'll be ready in a moment," she said, walking to her room.

Martha turned to her son. "You do everything you can to convince that girl not to go to Canyon Creek," she whispered. Jake nodded.

"I'll do what I can, but she's determined to follow Mr. Thornton's wishes."

"Joel Thornton must be out of his mind asking her to go find that gunfighter Ben Chance. Who knows if he's even in Canyon Creek?" Martha continued to whisper, shaking her hands then folding her arms across her blouse. Elizabeth walked into the room carrying her carpetbag and a small luggage carrier.

"I'm ready, Jake. Can we go?" she asked, heading for the door, not waiting for a reply. "I feel awful that I'm leaving after we just met, Mrs. Rawlings, but I feel I need to hurry as quickly as I can."

"My dear, I used to listen to your mother speak of you when you were a little girl. We haven't just met. Go fetch Dr. Langdon. It's all right."

Elizabeth hurried out to the carriage. Jake followed and saw Elizabeth already seated and waiting.

Here we go. This oughta be interestin', he thought as he climbed into the buggy.

"It was very kind of you to bring your mother over here," Elizabeth said, placing her hand on Jake's shoulder. Jake felt his pulse race from Elizabeth's touch.

"You're welcome, but it was her idea really. Pa told her it was okay if she was gone for a while," Jake explained. He then snapped the reins and started for town.

Both Jake and Elizabeth were quiet for a long time before Jake broke the silence.

"I could go to Canyon Creek and find Mr. Chance. That way you could stay here and take care of your father," Jake suggested.

Elizabeth stayed silent for several seconds before she responded. "I thought of asking someone else to go, but I've decided to go myself," she said. "I know you, your mother, and Dr. Langdon all feel that I'm making a mistake by going, but I've made up my mind. It's something I feel I have to do."

Jake said nothing just looked ahead down the road. Elizabeth wanted Jake to say it was okay, to affirm her decision. His silence hung over the carriage like a black thunder cloud ready to burst into a driving rain. Elizabeth couldn't wait any longer.

"Are you angry with me?" she asked.

"Nope, not my place to be angry. It's just that all of a sudden I'm afraid something bad will happen to ya, that's all. I can't rightly explain it."

Elizabeth smiled and hooked her arm under his.

"I like you too all of a sudden, Jake Rawlings," she said. Jake smiled, sat up straight, and snapped the reins again.

CHAPTER 9

J AKE PULLED THE CARRIAGE UP in front of the McNally general store. The stage office was next to it.

"Tell Mr. Wright you plan on takin' the stage to Canyon Creek, and here is the store in case you need somethin' before you go," Jake said, jumping down. Jake grabbed Elizabeth's luggage and carried it into the stage office, which was nothing more than an eight-by-eight-foot box with a roof, open window, and a bench in the front. A white sign with black letters announcing Randall County Stage Line hung above the open window. Bill Wright was seated on the bench scribbling something in a small ledger book. He had seen Jake's carriage arrive then went back to his task. He looked up when Elizabeth approached.

"Can I help you, ma'am?" Wright asked.

"Yes, please. I'm Elizabeth Thornton, and I would like stage fare to Canyon Creek," she said.

"I'm sorry to hear about your father, Miss Thornton. The stage isn't due in until noon or so provided there hasn't been any trouble." Wright looked at his silver pocket watch noting it was just past 10:00 a.m. "There's been some trouble 'tween here and Stratford. Rumor is that fella Ryker who shot your father is behind it all. Our stage usually doesn't carry a strong box, so it's been let alone so far," Wright continued. Wright was a tall slender man with a bald head and shaved face. He had a pleasant voice and a mild manner about him, Elizabeth thought.

"That's fine. I need to see Dr. Langdon, then I'd like to look around town before I leave," Elizabeth informed Wright. Wright smiled and nodded.

"Doc Langdon's office is just down the street next to Mrs. Owens's boarding house," Bill Wright said as he pointed to a white building past the general store on the other side of the street.

"After your business with Doc Langdon, the best place to start seeing the town is the store here or the hotel across the street," Wright offered. "No worry, I won't let the stage leave until you come back," he assured Elizabeth. She thanked Bill Wright and began to walk past the store when she abruptly stopped and turned back toward stage operator.

"Mr. Wright, what will the fare to Canyon Creek be?" she asked.

"That'll be three dollars, ma'am," Wright answered. Elizabeth smiled then continued past the store. Stopping momentarily to allow a couple of wagons to pass, she crossed the street and entered Doc Langdon's office. Her arrival was greeted with the sound of a bell hanging near the top of the windowed door. Doc Langdon entered the room and greeted Elizabeth with a smile.

"How are you, Elizabeth?" he asked in a low, comforting voice.

"I'm doing much better, thank you."

"And your father?" he asked.

"He seemed to be better. I was able to speak with him and he ate some soup before I left the ranch. Mrs. Rawlings agreed to stay with him while I go to Canyon Creek. He was in terrible pain though. Can you go out to the ranch and see him?"

"Of course. I will go out later this afternoon and see if I can help him with the pain. You leaving for Canyon Creek on today's stage?" Langdon asked.

"Yes, Mr. Wright said it should be here in a couple of hours. I thought I would look around town until then."

"Do I need to take a look at that shoulder of yours before you go?"

"I don't believe that'll be necessary. It's feeling much better."

"Very well then. I'll look for you when you return. Good luck."

Elizabeth walked out onto the street. The town was alive with activity. Wagons carrying various loads, carriages, and several cowboys crisscrossing the town reminded her of a busy street back in Philadelphia. After a deep breath, she crossed the street and headed for the general store. Once outside, she paused to look into the store windows at various items.

This looks like a very well stocked store for such a small town, she thought before entering through the green-painted front door.

This was the only place her father had brought her the day after she arrived.

Kate McNally was standing behind a neatly polished wooden counter which sat atop two shelves displaying various trinkets and dry goods. Jake was sitting on an old whiskey barrel next to her when Elizabeth entered.

"Elizabeth Thornton!" Kate McNally shouted when she saw Elizabeth. She then rushed to Elizabeth and completed her greeting with an immense bear hug. Kate McNally was tall for a woman and on the robust side. She wore a brown dress partially covered in a white apron tied around her waist. "Jake tells me your father is a little better—I'm so happy to hear that!" she continued in a loud voice. "Harold! Harold! Come down here! Elizabeth Thornton is here!" Mrs. McNally called up the stairs leading from behind the counter to the second floor. Elizabeth looked up and saw Mr. McNally coming down the stairs with a smile on his face.

Harold McNally was a small man, thin in the face with a short goatee and circle-rimmed eyeglasses perched low on his nose.

Mrs. McNally is much bigger than her husband, Elizabeth thought, covering her mouth to hide a chuckle. Harold McNally switched a ledger book to his left hand and extended his right to Elizabeth.

"Nice to see you again, Miss Thornton," he announced in a calm, clear voice.

"Isn't she the most beautiful girl you've ever seen!" gushed Mrs. McNally. "And that prairie skirt looks delightful," she added. Elizabeth looked down at her gray skirt and instinctively smoothed it out with her hands. The bottom had skimmed the dirt both at the ranch and in the street and was rimmed in red soil.

"It's a little dusty from the ride into town," Elizabeth acknowledged.

"Oh, I know!" Kate McNally declared. "This awful red Texas dust is mighty bad on ladies' clothes. Here, let me show you a new dress we just received from Fort Worth," she insisted. Putting her arm around Elizabeth, she guided her to the back of the store.

Harold McNally joined Jake near the counter.

"Mrs. McNally gets right excited at times," Jake said, watching the two women. McNally set his book on the counter, pulled a white handkerchief from his vest pocket, and began cleaning the lenses of his glasses.

"Yes, she's an excitable woman for sure, but more so with young ladies," he said. "We never had children, and she always wanted a daughter, so she gets this way from time to time." The door opened, and Ethan Michaelson walked in.

"Hello, Harold, Jake," Ethan said, then looked over at the commotion Mrs. McNally was creating by showing Elizabeth items for ladies.

"Must be Thornton's daughter," Ethan mumbled more to himself than to the men in front of him.

"Yep, her name's Elizabeth," Harold McNally informed Ethan.

"Pretty girl," Ethan offered—

"Oh?" Jake snapped, sliding down from the barrel. Ethan was a few years older than Jake and ran the livery stable in town. He had a reputation of sorts with the ladies.

"Take it easy, partner, just sayin' is all," Ethan said with a big grin. Jake said nothing and walked out of the store.

"What's with him?" Ethan asked McNally, shaking his head toward Jake and cracking another grin.

"He's been out at the Thornton ranch the last couple of days helpin' Elizabeth out. Heard he buried ole Moses Barber too. Been a lot for the boy, I guess," McNally said, placing his glasses back onto his face.

"I heard about ole Moses," Ethan sighed and nodded his head, keeping his eyes fixed on Elizabeth.

"What can I do for ya, Ethan?" McNally asked.

"I need some tobacco."

Harold walked behind the counter and reached into a large closed wooden box where he kept the tobacco. Harold selected a tin of Bull Durham that Michaelson favored and set it on the counter.

As Ethan dropped two coins down on the counter for the tobacco, Mrs. McNally and Elizabeth approached.

Mrs. McNally introduced Ethan. "Elizabeth Thornton, this is Ethan Michaelson. Ethan runs the livery stable."

Ethan removed his hat.

"Pleased to meet you, ma'am."

Elizabeth smiled and nodded her head. "Do you have any horses for sale?" Elizabeth asked, catching Ethan by surprise.

"Yes, ma'am, I have two at the moment. Burt Jamison's old mare and a younger Steel Dust I bought off a cowhand about a week ago. The Steel Dust looks to be a good horse," Ethan added.

"Steel Dust?" Elizabeth asked.

"Yes, ma'am, a quarter horse. Good all-around horse for whatever you need," Ethan explained.

"How much for that one?" Elizabeth asked. Ethan shifted his weight and looked down at the floor, uncomfortable with the question.

"Well, I'd like to get seventy-five dollars for it if I could—"

"Ethan Michaelson!" Mrs. McNally shouted. "How dare you ask such an amount from Elizabeth!"

"No! No!" Elizabeth stopped Mrs. McNally's rant. "I'm sure that's a fair price for a horse as fine as Mr. Michaelson has described." Elizabeth removed seventy-five dollars from her bag and handed it to Ethan. "Could you deliver the horse to our ranch in the next couple of days?" she asked.

"I sure can, ma'am," Ethan said, glancing at the frown on Mrs. McNally's rotund face. "Will you need a saddle?" Ethan inquired.

"No, we have a couple out at the ranch that should do," she answered.

"Very good. I'll bring the horse out tomorrow," Ethan stated, putting his hat back on.

"Thank you, Mr. Michaelson." Elizabeth smiled.

"It's just Ethan, ma'am," he replied.

"It's just Elizabeth," she responded.

Ethan smiled and walked out onto the street where Jake was leaning against his carriage. Ethan walked over to Jake.

"Elizabeth just bought that Steel Dust from me. Why she need a horse?" he asked Jake.

"That son-bitch Ryker stole all their horses, cattle, and money."

Ethan looked back at Elizabeth through the store window.

"I ain't heard that."

"Yep, now she's goin' down to Canyon Creek to find Ben Chance and see if he can get it all back."

"Ben Chance?" Ethan questioned.

"Yeah, Mr. Thornton told her he was down there."

"Yeah, he's there all right," Ethan confirmed. "I was just down there last month. Town marshal quite a few months ago and let out. Chance has been marshal ever since."

"New marshal? I'd better let Elizabeth know. Don't know how he can leave Canyon Creek if he's the marshal," Jake said. Jake started for the store when Ethan grabbed his arm.

"From what I hear of Ben Chance, he finds out Joel Thornton was shot, no marshal job gonna keep um from comin'," Ethan offered. "Let the girl alone. She's gonna do what she wants, and the likes of you ain't gonna stop her," Ethan said.

Jake thought a moment and knew Ethan was right. He'd already made his feelings known.

No sense makin' a fool of myself, Jake thought. Ethan separated twenty-five dollars from the money Elizabeth had given him for the horse.

"Here, take this $50 and give it back to Elizabeth," Ethan told Jake, handing him the money. "I didn't know about the stealin'," he said.

Jake rolled the cash and stuffed it into his shirt pocket.

Elizabeth and Mrs. McNally came out of the store.

"Now you two fellas move along!" Mrs. McNally shouted for no purpose. "I'm takin' Miss Elizabeth over to the hotel to meet Mrs. Henry!" The two women hurried across the street uselessly attempting to avoid the red Texas dust that kicked up from passing wagons and horses. Ethan meandered back to the stable, leaving Jake with his mother's carriage.

Jake walked over to Bill Wright, who had reclaimed his seat on the bench in front of the stage office.

"Mr. Wright, the stage been havin' any trouble out on the trail?" Jake asked.

"Plenty. Some Indian trouble, but trail riders mostly just stopping it to see if it's carryin' anything valuable," Wright added. "Shouldn't have no trouble goin' to Canyon Creek though if that's what's worryin' ya. Pretty girl, I'd say. I'd be worryin' too if I was yer age." Wright laughed. Jake turned and headed over to the hotel. If he wasn't needed anymore, he might as well head back home.

Elizabeth and Mrs. McNally were with Mrs. Henry in the parlor talking woman stuff when Jake entered.

"What is it now, Jake Rawlings!" cried Mrs. McNally.

"Just wantin' to know if Elizabeth needs anything else before I head back home is all, ma'am."

Elizabeth walked over to Jake, reached up, and kissed him on the cheek.

"Thank you for everything. I'll be back before you know it and we can visit. I'll be just fine," she assured her self-appointed guardian. Jake forced a smile and removed the money from his pocket, handing it to Elizabeth.

"Ethan wanted you to keep this, said he didn't know about your horses gettin' stolen. The horse probably wasn't worth the seventy-five he got from you anyway." He turned and left the hotel.

"It's a good thing that Ethan Michaelson came to his senses about that price!" Kate McNally exclaimed.

"Nice boy that Jake Rawlings," Mrs. Henry chimed in.

"Yes, he is," Elizabeth answered as she watched Jake cross the street, get into the carriage, and head out of town.

"Now, you'll wait for the stage here. I'll fix some tea," Mrs. Henry insisted before leaving the parlor to tend to a few duties before tea. Elizabeth sat down in an oversize red parlor chair with a floral print and fell into thought. Mrs. McNally was talking again, but Elizabeth had tuned her out. She didn't remember Ben Chance at all.

What was I, five, when I last saw him? What is he like now? Will he even come back with me? Help me get Dad's stock back? Only one way to find out, and she was determined to find him no matter what. She clutched the Colt Peacemaker concealed inside her bag. If it took killing more men, then so be it. Dropping that outlaw in the house wasn't her first go-around with a gun.

CHAPTER 10

MRS. HENRY RETURNED WITH A shiny silver tray holding three white cups, spoons, and a silver teapot. Placing the tray on the low marble table in the center of the parlor, she began pouring the steaming brown liquid into each cup. Elizabeth watched as each cup was filled and the pot returned to its place on the tray. She felt her heart beating inside her right shoulder. The pain was heightening where the outlaw's bullet had mangled her once-flawless skin. She could hear Mrs. Henry's voice but it resonated only as distant noise. Her focus was directed solely on her pain.

"Are you feeling okay, dear?" Mrs. Henry's inquiry snapped Elizabeth from her trance.

"Yes, ma'am. I'm sorry, I have been through a lot lately, and I guess I'm having difficulty concentrating."

"Well, it's no wonder you can even function, what with all you've been through!" exclaimed Mrs. McNally.

"All the more reason you should stay here in town and let us take care of you for a few days," Mrs. Henry offered while handing Elizabeth a cup of steaming tea.

"Yes, that is a perfect idea!" Mrs. McNally shouted in her normal high-pitched tone as she selected a warm cup from the tray.

"Maybe when I return from Canyon Creek, and if my father is doing well," Elizabeth stated with no intent of turning her statement into a reality.

"Nonsense!" Mrs. McNally replied, folding her arms across her buxom chest, spilling tea from the cup still clutched in her right hand.

"I just don't understand you, Miss Elizabeth Thornton," Mrs. McNally followed in a soft voice.

"Now, Kate, we women need to support each other. The times are changing. Young women are doing all kinds of things on their own." Kathryn Henry's statement was reminiscent of talk Elizabeth had heard in Philadelphia.

"Thank you for understanding, Mrs. Henry," Elizabeth said.

"I was back East about six months ago, and I saw what the ladies there were saying and doing. They might not be as tough as we ole girls here out West, but they know how to take care of themselves," Mrs. Henry declared. She smiled and picked her cup up from the tray.

Elizabeth took a sip of tea. Aside from its strength, she found its flavor satisfying.

"Tell us about your time in Philadelphia," Mrs. Henry asked, sipping from her own white China teacup. "How did you spend your time there?"

Elizabeth thought for a moment. Her mind drifted back to her aunt and uncle's majestic house, its tall white pillars framing the vast front porch. The double front doors painted a dark red around beautiful stained glass windows. Her expansive room complete with its Victorian four-post bed, matching hutch and full-length mirror. The images passing through her mind's eye were glorious. She smiled and took a deep breath.

"I don't know where to begin. I was there for seven years, but it seems like my whole life now. School is what I remember most, I guess. Shortly after I arrived, my aunt insisted that I attend the Girls Normal School. My aunt thought it was the best school for young ladies. Having grown up on a ranch in Texas, I wasn't very happy about it at first, but it became my sanctuary. Most of the teachers were young women, and the older I got, the more I admired them. My favorite subjects were mathematics and language. I found numbers fascinating, and the better a person could speak, the greater respect you gained. I really put forth a good effort and learned a great deal. When I completed the school, they wanted me to become a teacher, but they didn't pay very much and I wanted to return to Texas, so I refused the offer."

"What did your uncle do?" Mrs. McNally asked.

"He was a lawyer who helped people that arrived from foreign countries. He also helped land owners, but I'm not sure what he did for them. Because of school and my uncle's work, I had the opportunity to meet people from all over the world. There were so many people coming to Philadelphia from England, Germany, Poland, and Ireland that I had friends who spoke different languages and had so many different beliefs. It was amazing. I earned money tutoring women in English. I also helped my aunt make quilts and draperies. She is very good at stitching and needlepoint."

"You must have had young men wanting to court you," Mrs. McNally said, smiling and tilting her head downward, somewhat shy.

"Kate McNally!" Mrs. Henry shouted while giggling and leaning forward, wanting to hear Elizabeth's answer just as much as Kate McNally.

Elizabeth laughed loudly, causing her shoulder to announce its painful presence once more.

"There was one gentleman that came calling on occasion," Elizabeth admitted. "He was an officer in the Army Corps of Engineers stationed at Fort Mifflin. My aunt and uncle weren't very pleased because he was a bit older than me, but he was an officer and gentleman, so they allowed his visits." Elizabeth's face brightened at the thought of her former suitor.

"Did your father know about this young man?" Mrs. Henry asked.

"I mentioned him in a letter I sent Dad a couple of years ago, but he never spoke of him in his return letters. I'm not sure, but I don't believe he wanted to think of me as that grown up!" Elizabeth exclaimed.

The three women's laughs were cut short when Martin Henry entered the room.

"The stage is coming through the valley. Should be here in twenty minutes or so," Mr. Henry announced.

Elizabeth finished her tea and set the empty cup back onto the silver tray. "Thank you for your hospitality," she said.

Both Mrs. McNally and Mrs. Henry stood and looked at each other like mothers who were sending their daughter away for the winter. Mrs. McNally frowned and wiped her brow with a handkerchief she extracted from her dress pocket. Mrs. Henry smiled but with a hint of sadness around her eyes. Elizabeth hugged each lady then walked over to the front window to watch for the stagecoach that would take her to places unknown to see a man about revenge.

CHAPTER 11

D ANNER HEADED WEST FOR A bit when he noticed two riders heading east a short distance to his left. Danner kept an eye on them. As they passed, he noted that neither showed any interest in him.

That's odd, Danner thought. *Why not take a look over this way? Got something to hide?* Danner slowed his horse and looked back at the two disinterested cowboys for a long moment. Neither looked back at him, so he turned in the saddle and continued on.

Probably see them in town later, Danner supposed. A short time later he saw what had to be the Coleman rock described by Rachel. It was a towering bolder with jagged edges cut into its cragged surface. He reined his horse to the right and continued on following Rachel's directions.

Those two fellas must've been from the Coleman ranch, Danner told himself, still curious by their indifference.

Danner approached the creek and noticed a bustle of activity around the mill, which was larger than he had pictured in his mind. Men were running from area to area moving horses, logs, and lumber. The scene reminded Danner of an ant hill when it was kicked open, exposing the agitated occupants. An immense two-story wooden building large enough to hold a hundred horses was at the center of the commotion. Large white-wash letters on its side announced it was the Canyon Creek Sawmill. Long open areas where finished lumber was cut to various lengths was matched by an equal-size expanse holding uncut logs. The unloading area had a tall wooden and steel machine that threaded a thick rope through it over large iron pulley wheels. Men were unloading logs from large transport wagons onto smaller flat carts that were destined for the big cutting blades. He could hear the loud whine of the saw blade ripping through the fresh wood. The area smelled of fresh-cut and blade-burned wood. To the east of the mill were two large three-rail corrals filled with horses, both draft and quarter. Overall, Danner could see about twenty-five men working in the beating sun with more inside the building.

Danner rode up to one of the corrals barely noticed by the busy workers, and tied his horse to the second rail. A tall heavy fella wearing coveralls and a red shirt with sleeves rolled to the elbow was supervising the unloading of the big logs. He looked over at Danner and started his way in a slow walk.

"Help ya, stranger?" the man asked.

"Yes, sir, name's Luxton Danner. I'm looking for the owner or the foreman," he replied.

"Well, I'm Stoney Walsh, the mill foreman. Mr. Gibson is in his office upstairs. If yer lookin' for work, I don't think we're takin' anyone on at the moment though."

"Thanks. Not looking for a job. New in town and just curious about how lumber is made."

Walsh lowered his brow and cracked a half smile showing a wide gap where his two front teeth used to occupy.

"No offense, partner, but you don't look like a fella that cares about how lumber is made. You a lawman?"

Danner smiled. "No, sir," was all he offered.

"Well, okay, I'll show you around quick." The big man started with the log unloading area, explaining that most of the logs were transported via wagon from the railhead down closer to Oneida. The company ran three wagons at staged times in order to keep the timber coming regularly to the mill. The bark was rough cut off, and the timber was then cut into specified lengths and sizes of board before being loaded on the lumber transport wagons for town. As Danner walked around the mill grounds, he kept an alert eye out for the purpose of his visit. After catching a quick glance into the mill itself, Danner didn't see any recognizable faces.

Walsh walked Danner back toward the corral by his horse.

"Said yer name was Danner?" Walsh asked.

"That's right. Luxton Danner."

"Okay, Mr. Danner, now why did you really come out here?"

Danner smiled and nodded. "Okay, I'm looking for man named Albert Cullen. Goes by Bert. Small skinny fella with a thick purple scar on his chin and a real liking for whiskey," he admitted.

Stoney Walsh stopped and put his hands on his hips then laughed.

"Yep, Bert Cullen was here. He worked for us 'bout three weeks, I'd say. He was a wagon driver, but showed up drunk one too many times, so I fired him. Good man when he's sober, but getting paid put a stop to that."

"How long ago you fire him?"

Walsh scratched his unshaven chin with fingers the size of sausages and looked toward the sky. "'Bout three weeks ago, I'd say."

"By chance, he happen to say where he was heading?"

"Nope, he weren't too happy 'bout getting let go. He collected the pay he had coming and rode out. North toward the border was last I seen um. Probably headin' fer No Man's Land up in the territory be my guess."

Danner nodded in agreement.

"What he wanted fer?" Walsh asked.

Danner looked down and kicked at the red Texas dirt.

"Just a little misunderstanding is all," Danner said, scowling. "Thank you for your time, Mr. Walsh. Be seeing you around."

"You bet, Mr. Danner. Take care when you meet up with ole Bert. He carries a big ole knife in his left boot."

Danner untied his horse then swung up into his saddle.

"Thanks much. I'll remember that." Danner turned and headed back to town.

It was about two in the afternoon when Danner reached the western edge of Canyon Creek. As he was approaching town, he saw Chance mount his horse in front of the jail and head east toward the other side of town in a double-quick gallop. Danner spurred up his horse and quickened his pace. Riding up to the Sundown, he saw Rachel walk out onto the porch. She was nervously clutching her apron watching Chance rush down the street. Danner stopped in front of the Sundown.

"Something wrong?" Danner asked Rachel. Her concern showed in a wrinkled brow and frown.

"I don't know. I heard yelling on the street, then saw Ben ride by quickly and thought I'd take a look."

Danner stayed mounted and, with steady hands, instinctively checked his Russian .45s set loose in their holsters. Uncertain if he should intrude, he paused.

Davey Garcia was in a bad way. He couldn't breathe. His air was blocked by a thick forearm pressed against his throat. His boots were six inches above the ground, and sweat was rolling down into his burning eyes, blurring his vision. Blood was flowing from a gash on the side of his head. The cause of his agony had rushed into the livery stable and knocked him senseless with the crashing blow of a pistol to his head. He demanded money from the cash box, then pinned Davey against the wall with an arm the size of bedroll.

"Where's the cash box!" Pete Hanson demanded. "Tell me now or I'll break yer neck!" The thief eased off Davey's throat just enough to allow a feeble response.

"Under a plank shelf in the office behind me," Davey managed in broken English, gasping for air.

Pete Hanson was a no-good thief who had been sent from the KC ranch along with his equally worthless buddy Hank Evans. Their goal was to cause enough trouble to bring the marshal running to them. Picking up some extra money for the road was an added benefit. They decided robbing the livery stable would satisfy both needs.

"Hurry up, Pete! Rider comin' fast down the street," Hank Evans yelled. Hanson threw Frankie to the ground with a force that sent him rolling into a foul mixture of manure and hay. Hanson drew his gun, leveling it at Garcia.

"Don't get up!" Hanson darted into the small tack room Garcia used as an office and snatched the cash box. Pete heard the crack of his partner's pistol fire a double tap. Evans then ran past Pete, leaped over Garcia, and headed for the rear of the stable. Recognizing the situation was turning desperate, Hanson followed, finding Evans crouched behind a stack of baled hay.

"No way out?" Hanson barked.

"Nope," Evans gasped, sweating profusely, with his gun sited in a shaking hand. "And that damn Ben Chance is gonna come runnin' in here blastin' away any minute! I told Jenney this was a bad idea!" Evans hollered.

When Danner heard the shots, he decided it was time to intrude. He spurred his horse and headed for the livery stable. Recognizing a gunfight, people came out onto the boarded walkways to catch a view of the action. Those out on the street where running for cover. Danner was yelling to anyone that would listen to get off the street and inside.

Garcia crawled on his stomach out the front door. His head pounding with pain. He made it to the street then jumped to his feet and ran to meet Chance, who was swinging off his horse in full gallop, Winchester in hand.

"Chance! Chance! There's two of um." Frankie tried to think of the right words to say in English. "They hit me in the head and took the money box. They still in there!"

"You know who they are?" Chance asked, keeping an eye on the stable opening.

"I seen them before in town. I think they work at the KC," he offered, holding his bloody head with an unsteady hand.

"Get down to Doc Carson," Chance ordered. Then in a low crouch, he carefully stepped forward with the business end of his Winchester aimed at the open barn doors.

"You in the stable! Drop your guns and come out with your hands up!" Chance yelled, cocking his rifle with quick lever action. Chance's demand was met with silence. "No way out! Give it up!" Chance called again. The window on the left side of the doorway shattered, sending Chance's attention to his right.

Crack! Hanson's bullet smashed into Chance's left hip, knocking him sideways. As he was falling, he saw Pete Hanson in the window taking aim. Chance fired his Winchester and saw Hanson's face explode into a bloody mess. As Chance's right knee hit the dirt, his rifle hit the ground. The force knocked his rifle from his hands. Chance quickly tried to roll off his right side and draw his Colt Army pistol. Before he could clear leather, Hank Evans ran out of the stable doorway, his pistol leveled at Chance. *Boom!* A single shot put a Russian .45 bullet into Evans's chest, knocking him off his feet onto his back in a cloud of dust. Chance looked up to his left and saw Danner walking toward him, Russian .45 steady in his right hand.

"Any more?" Danner asked.

"Nope, not according to Davey," Chance replied, reaching down to check the wound on his hip. Danner holstered his Russian, then reached down to Chance.

"Need a hand, Marshal?" he asked with a smile.

"I need more than that," Chance said, doing his best to stand up. Danner wrapped Chance's left arm around his shoulders as a group of chattering folks ran up to the two gunfighters.

"Thanks, Danner, he had me cold," Chance said, looking over at Evans's body.

Danner said nothing. A fella called over the noise of the crowd that Doc Carson was on his way.

"Get me out of here," Chance told Danner.

A young boy had snuck through the crowd and picked up Chance's Winchester.

"He's your rifle, Mr. Chance," the boy said, handing the weapon to Chance.

"Joey! You get over here right now!" a woman yelled from the crowd, scolding the boy for handling the gun.

Chance thanked the boy and, with Danner's assistance, limped over to the bench in front of the livery stable's tack room. Chance leaned on his good hip on the bench. Chance pulled the blue bandana from his neck and stuffed a corner of it into his bleeding hip, wincing with closed eyes. When he opened them, Bart Steen, the town's undertaker, was standing in front of him.

"Heard the shooting, Marshal. Thought I'd come take a look."

"Got two for ya, Bart. There's one in the stable near the window in addition to the one in the street," Chance advised. "Bury um and send me the bill," Chance continued.

"Very good, Marshal. I will take care of everything." Steen motioned for two men to assist him, then carried on about his business.

"Know who they are?" Danner asked.

"No. I didn't see the one in the window very well."

"You won't recognize him now," Doc Carson said as he walked up to Chance with Rachel right behind.

"Took one in the hip, Doc." Chance removed his bandana from the wound. Doc Carson leaned down to take a closer look, moving the tattered cloth away, exposing a steady flow of dark red blood.

Carson frowned, then looked at Danner and Rachel.

"Get him over to my office at once."

"No, take him to the hotel. He'll be more comfortable there," Rachel insisted.

Carson nodded in agreement. Danner lifted up on Chance's left shoulder with Rachel taking the same position under his right. Chance insisted on walking despite barely able to limp. Chance gritted his teeth with each step. His muscles were rigid, causing the three to make their way slowly down the street toward the hotel. The trio entered the hotel, where they were met by Davey Garcia and his wife, Alita. Garcia's head was surrounded by a large white bandage holding a thick white pad to the left side. The pad had a hint of red caused by blood still oozing from his pistol-whipping. Alita stood and rapidly spoke in indiscernible Spanish, which prompted Garcia to stop her.

"She asks if Mr. Chance is okay," Frankie translated.

"I'll be fine as soon as Doc here gets to work," Chance answered, forcing a reassuring smile toward Alita.

"Let's get him up to his room," Rachel suggested.

Chance and his aides moved to the staircase where Chance attempted to navigate the first step. A piercing pain shot through him as if he'd been hit by lightning. Then nothing… Chance passed out.

CHAPTER 12

ANNER AND CARSON CARRIED CHANCE up the staircase to the hallway where they set him down for a moment to catch their breath. Doc Carson, breathing hard and pushing beads of sweat from his forehead, looked at Danner.

"I have a greater appreciation for those like you," Carson huffed at Danner.

"Like me, Doc?" Danner asked.

"Yep, big, strong, and young!"

Rachel followed the men up the stairway then moved around the trio in the hall.

"Room 8," she said, not stopping to look at her wounded friend sprawled on the floor. Danner reached under Chance's big shoulders and gripped hard with his immense hands, and Carson took an ankle into each of his. Together they moved the short distance to room 8, where Rachel had turned down the bed's quilt and sheets.

"You might want to remove those nice linens, Rachel," Carson suggested. "They're going to be blood soaked in a moment."

"Nonsense," she replied. "You just take care of him!" Rachel hurried out of the room into the hallway and retrieved Doc Carson's bag.

Danner and Carson lifted Chance onto the bed. Rachel returned with the medical bag and commenced to removing each of Chance's boots while Danner slipped off his gun belt.

"Trousers too," Doc Carson ordered. Removal of the trousers exposed a nasty wide open hole on Chance's left hip. The flesh was ragged around the perimeter with bloodied sinewy muscle visible. Carson rolled Chance onto his right side, elevating the wounded area.

"After all the gunshot wounds I've seen in my day, I never can get used to them," Carson sighed.

"It looks like he was hit with a pickax," Danner said.

Tears began to roll down Rachel's face. "What can I do, Doctor?" she asked.

"Boil some water and get me as many clean towels as you can."

Rachel ran from the room, closing the door behind her. Doc Carson removed a bottle of chloroform from his bag.

"Won't need that, Doc. He's out cold," Danner reminded the physician.

"He'll need it quick enough when I start digging around in there."

Carson set the chloroform on the table next to the bed. He grabbed his bullet probe and a handful of gauze pads from his black leather bag. "Hold him down, son," Doc ordered as he took a kneeing position on the bed next to Chance, then guided his probe into the gaping wound. Carson pushed the probe into the wound, slowly moving the tip in a small circular motion. The bullet had penetrated deep into the flesh and had hit bone. The beads of sweat that had formed earlier on his brow were now running down his face as if in competition of each other. The tip of the utensil stopped. It had found the final destination of the hunk of lead. Carson attempted to spread the probe's tips to latch onto the bullet. All at once Chance opened his eyes wide, jerked his body, and yelled loud enough for the town folk to hear.

"Chloroform!" Carson called out. Danner reached across Chance, grabbed the bottle and pad, then poured a spot of the potent liquid onto the dry pad. Danner then quickly put the sleeping solution in front of Chance's nostrils. Danner did his best to hold Chance still with his left arm while waiting for the chloroform to take effect. Three quick seconds and Chance was out.

"Whew!" exclaimed Danner. "I've heard of pain bad enough to put a man down, but never to wake a man up," he said, looking at Carson.

"The bullet is lodged in the hip bone just below the joint. I'll make another try to loosen and remove it, but if it won't move,

I'll have to stop." Carson began to move the tips of the probe and attempted to squeeze the tips onto the back end of the bullet. The stubborn lead wouldn't budge. Carson carefully removed the probe. A knock sounded on the door. "Come in," Carson stated. Rachel entered with a bowl of steaming water and large rags draped over her left forearm.

"How is it going?" she inquired with a sullen look on her face. Carson said nothing, just dropped his probe into the bowl of hot water. He wiped blood away from the wound then took a rag and soaked it in the water. He looked at Rachel.

"I'm not able to remove the bullet. It's lodged in the bone. The top of the femur is cracked. If I keep digging around in there, he may never walk again." Carson covered the wound with the steaming rag and applied pressure. Rachel looked at Danner, doing her best to hold back further tears.

"What now, Doc?" Danner asked, breaking the silence like shattering glass.

"I'll get the bleeding under control, close the wound up best I can, and hope for the best."

"Hope for the best?" Rachel questioned Carson's comment.

Carson said nothing, just went about his business. Danner took the remaining rags from Rachel, then pointed to the door.

"Take care of your hotel. We'll let you know when he wakes up."

Rachel forced a brief smile, turned, and left the room.

"Appears she has feelings for Chance, huh, Doc?"

Carson was in the process of closing the gaping wound with stitches he didn't care to count.

"More than appears, young fella. Everybody knows she carries a torch for ole man here…except maybe him." Carson laughed, needing to stop stitching for a moment.

"How could he not know?" Danner asked.

"Not really not knowing, it's that he doesn't want to know, I reckon. Chance was just passing through about a year back. Had no intention of sticking around, but saw that Rachel was struggling. So, for some reason, he decided to take it upon himself to help her out. Word was that he didn't ask for, nor wanted, anything in return.

That made him sort of a hero with the folks in this town. Usually, a stranger comes around, stays for a spell, then leaves. If he does something to help out the town or its people, he usually wants or expects payment in some way. Not Chance. He just wanted Rachel to succeed, I guess."

Carson finished bandaging Chance's hip then pulled the linen and quilt over him. "Now we wait."

Carson cleaned his equipment and loaded it back into his bag.

"Can you stay and watch him for a bit?" Carson asked Danner.

"Sure thing, Doc. I got nowhere else to be right away."

"Good. Rachel will need some assistance. I can stay for a while, then I need to get back to my office."

Carson sat in a wooden rocking chair in the corner of the room. Danner took his gun belt off and hung it on the back of the four-post chair opposite Carson. Danner sat down and extended his tree-trunk legs out straight in front of him.

"Six-five?" Carson asked.

"Six-six, 245, I was told. Some time ago a fella bet me he could guess my weight. He gambled on everything. They put me on a scale used for weighing government beef at Fort Sill. The fella bet me $50 and guessed 250 pounds. After they called out 245, he started yelling that the scale was fixed since it weighed government beef for the Indians. He carried on so much I told him to keep his $50."

Doc Carson laughed. "That was it?"

"Yep. The next night, he was caught cheating in a poker game and was shot. That was the end of that. What's your story, Doc? How'd you come to be here in Canyon Creek?"

"I studied medicine in Boston before the war. When the war broke out, I joined the Union Army as a medic and worked with a surgeon. Learned more doing that than anything I did in a classroom. Anyway, after that nonsense ended, I went back to Boston, but got restless. Decided to head West. See the country I read and heard about from a bunch of soldiers from Texas." Carson paused and shook his head. "I was surprised how many Texas men were fighting on the Union side. I made my way to Fort Worth, stayed for a while, then boarded a stagecoach and ended up here. The town was growing and there was no doctor. The people were good folks. I helped Sam Coleman recover from the fever, and he convinced me to stay. That was about three years ago."

"Who is this Sam Coleman? I know he runs a big ranch outside of town."

"I heard he came back here before the war. He was a colonel in the Confederate Army. His family has owned the ranch for years. Five thousand acres, I believe. Raises cattle and horses. He employs most of the men that don't run a business in town or work at the mill. Good man from what I've seen and heard. Highly respected. Dakota Jones over at the Creekbed was in his regiment. At least that's what Jones claims. I've never spoke to Coleman about him."

"Those two fellas over at the stable, I believe I saw them ridin' toward town earlier today. It looked like they were coming from Coleman's ranch. Chance might want to head out there and check when he's up and around again."

Doc Carson looked over at Chance with a frown. "Chance isn't going to be up and around for some time, I'm afraid. That bullet is in a bad place. I believe we'll need a new marshal or at least a deputy to help him out." Carson looked back at Danner with a smile. "Any chance you'd be looking for a job, Mr. Danner?"

"Me? I'm just a stranger passin' through, Doc. Nobody knows anything about me—"

"They all saw what you did for Chance out there today. Saved his life, I figure. That'll be enough for these folks to support you."

"I don't know, Doc. I hadn't planned on staying very long."

Danner stood up and walked over to look at Chance. A knock on the door was followed by Rachel entering.

"Anything new, Doctor?" Rachel asked. She held a tray with two cups of steaming coffee. Placing the tray on the table between the chairs Carson and Danner had occupied, she joined Danner at Chance's bedside.

"Let's wake him up, see how he feels," Carson stated, reaching into his bag to pluck a small vial. Carson opened the vial and moved it back and forth under Chance's nose. Chance shook his head slowly and opened his eyes. After mumbling a few incoherent words, he lifted his head and looked at his audience.

"What happened?" Chance asked. He attempted to move, then winced and stopped.

"Don't move too much," Doc Carson suggested.

Chance looked at Carson, then pulled the linen away from his hip, displaying the large white bandage.

"Get the bullet out, Doc?"

"Nope, it's still in there," Carson replied.

"Well, let's get after it then. What are you waiting for?"

"I can't do it, Chance. The bullet is lodged in the bone just below the joint. If I was to dig around too much, I might cripple you for good. You need a good surgeon in a hospital to get it done right."

"What now then?" Chance asked.

"I believe you'll heal all right. Main concern is to keep infection out. You need to take it easy, not walk much and keep the wound clean. When you can, have it taken care of."

"Not walk! How's that gonna work, Doc! I'm the only marshal in town. That damn sheriff over in Oneida ain't gonna send any deputies over here."

"Don't you worry about that, Ben Chance!" Rachel hollered at him. "You're going to do just what the doctor says or I'll kill you myself!"

Danner laughed. "Well, Marshal, looks like you've been overruled."

"Look, Danner, just because you saved my ass out there doesn't mean *you* can start telling me what to do!"

"I'll leave this problem to you folks. I need to get back to my office," Carson stated as he picked up his bag and cup of coffee. "Good luck you two," he added, looking at Danner and Rachel. Heading for the door, he stopped, turned, and looked at Chance with a glare of seriousness.

"Don't push it, Ben. If you do, you may never walk again." With that, Carson shook his head and headed down the hall.

CHAPTER 13

THE SILENCE HUNG IN THE room like a black cloud of despair. After a long delay, Danner spoke up.

"Chance, if you'd like, I'll watch over the jail for a couple of days until you get back on your feet." Danner strapped on his gun belt then retrieved the cup of coffee from the table.

Chance took a long look at Danner with raised eyebrows and tilted head.

"Before any of that happens, tell me the real reason you're in this town. I know you're here for a purpose and I need to know what it is before I go deputizing you."

Danner returned the look with a squinted gaze. "Let's just say I'm looking for someone and they're not here. How about I check with you before I get into any trouble. That good enough?"

Chance paused and looked at Rachel. She smiled and nodded her head in approval.

"Fine. Go over to the office. You'll find a deputy badge in the top right drawer of the desk. Bring it back here and I'll deputize you so it'll be official." Chance looked at Rachel. "Get a few business owners together and let them know what is happening. Tell them Danner is the new temporary deputy. Tell them if any of 'em has a problem with that to let me know. Now, is there any chance of getting a drink around here?" Danner held out his cup of coffee. "Put a shot of whiskey in it and I'll think about it."

"I'll be right back with coffee…and some food," Rachel said with a sound of relief in her voice. She left the room, closing the door behind her. Danner picked his hat up off the bedpost and started for the door.

"Danner, who the hell were those two at the stable? Any ideas?"

"I think they came from the Coleman ranch. I passed two riders out near the Coleman rock. They were headin' for town this morning from the direction where I figure the ranch is. I thought they were a bit suspicious, both kept their heads and hats down over their eyes. Neither one looked my way despite us passing pretty close. I went on to the mill. I should have paid closer attention."

"Nope, not your concern. The fella you're looking for. He been out at the mill?"

Danner smiled. "I'll go check on the jail and get that badge." Danner picked up Chance's gun belt from the floor and put it on the bed within his reach. "You never know," he said before walking out, closing the door behind him.

Chance tried to move his left leg. Pain shot through his hip, making his eyes water.

What the hell he shot me with? A damn cannon? he thought. He stared up at the ceiling.

Now what? He had planned on leaving in a month or two. Planned on getting the townspeople together to vote in a new marshal, freeing him up to head out. Where, he wasn't sure, but head out was in the plan. Now, he didn't know if he could walk, let alone ride a horse.

And just who the hell is this Luxton Danner anyway? And why is he here? Danner gnawed at him like a beaver on a woodpile. He seemed familiar. He saved his life. That Chance was grateful for. *You think too much.* Chance closed his eyes and fought the pain.

Danner made his way down the street toward the jail. Several folks came up to him with thanks for helping Chance. One short old man with long gray hair had retrieved his horse, and a fine-looking woman with short black hair in a brown dress handed him a basket of fresh bread rolls. Danner smiled and nodded his head in appreciation.

This hero thing isn't too bad, he thought. He reached the jail and stepped into the office. He located the deputy badge in the desk drawer. He took a long hard look at the badge.

I hope this isn't a mistake, he thought. Before leaving the office, he stopped and looked over the Wanted posters on the desk, thumbing through each one. He stopped on the seventh poster. He recognized the one that he had killed. Hank Evans. No doubt about it. Horse thief wanted in the Oklahoma territory. Five-hundred-dollar reward, dead or alive. Danner folded the poster up and put it in his pocket. He'd need to get a couple of witnesses who could read and write to sign the poster in order to collect the ransom. Danner thought for a moment.

Hadn't somebody told him that Coleman always had his cowhands checked by the marshal before he hired them? Danner finished looking though the posters then picked up the key ring. He looked out the window and saw about ten men on horseback ride up to the front of the jail and stop. None dismounted, obviously waiting for him to come out. He slowly opened the door and looked out, taking cover behind the door as much as possible. A man about fifty-five or so, well-dressed in black trousers, gray shirt, and a black leather vest, walked his horse forward a few steps.

"I'm Sam Coleman. I own the KC ranch. One of my men rode out and told me two fellas I fired were killed here this afternoon. They tell me one of um shot Ben Chance. You know anything about that, mister?"

Danner stepped out from behind the door, then closed and locked it.

"Yes, sir, Mr. Coleman. Marshal Chance took a slug in the hip. Both fellas were killed. One by Chance, the other by me. One of um was Hank Evans. I don't know who the other one was."

"Who might you be, stranger?" Coleman asked.

"Name's Luxton Danner. Just got into town yesterday."

"How is it that a fella gets into town yesterday and today finds himself in a gunfight with the town marshal?"

Danner didn't like answering questions from a man who had nothing to do with his business.

"I reckon that's not your concern, Mr. Coleman."

Coleman wasn't used to men talking back to him. He took a deep breath. "Understand, fella, I'm grateful you stepped in and helped out Ben Chance. I consider Ben a friend of mine. I make it my business when two men that I hired come into town, cause trouble, and shoot my friend."

"Your two former cowhands are down at the undertaker's place. You can identify Evans. The other is missing a face. Chance is at the hotel with a bullet in his hip, and I'm the new deputy for the moment. Now if you'll excuse me, I've got work to do." Danner walked out and swung up onto his horse next to Coleman. The two men's eyes met.

"Good day, Mr. Danner," Coleman sneered as he tipped his hat toward the new deputy. Coleman reined his horse right and led his group of riders into town.

Danner waited until Coleman and his men were down the street. Then he spurred his horse and rode down to the hotel.

Danner stopped in front of the Sundown and sat atop his horse for a moment, watching Coleman and his men. Coleman pointed over to the undertaker's place, then a lone rider headed that way.

It makes sense Coleman would send a man over there, Danner thought. *Probably wants to make sure it was his men.* Danner dismounted and tethered his horse to the hitching post next to the Sundown entrance. He stepped up onto the porch and continued to watch Coleman and his men. They all rode over to the Creek Bed, tied their horses, and went inside.

Danner strolled into the Sundown lobby and noticed Rachel behind the big front desk tending to a new customer, a short man wearing a brown suit and carrying a large bag. No guns were visible, and Danner decided he didn't look the seditious type. Rachel looked over and smiled as he headed up the staircase. Once at the top of the stairs, Danner took a quick look around the corner down the hall and in the dining room. All clear. He then went up to Chance's room and knocked.

"Who is it?" Chance's voice was a tad weaker than he was used to.

Danner announced himself, then entered the room, staring down the barrel of Chance's .45.

"What took you so long?" Chance asked, obviously annoyed.

"Took a look through the Wanted posters and was held up by Mr. Coleman and his boys."

"What did he want?"

"Information, I guess. Was more interested in me than anything else. He heard about the shootout and already knew I was part of it. I wasn't in the mood to answer many questions, so he and his boys rode on down to the Creek Bed. Except for one of 'em. Coleman sent him over to the undertaker's."

"Don't worry about Coleman. He's all right. Most of his hired hands are solid cowboys. Can't answer for 'em all. There's always a few that slip through when you hire out as many as he does."

Danner pulled the deputy badge from his pocket and showed it to Chance.

"Raise your right hand. Do you solemnly swear to uphold the law and protect the people of Canyon Creek in the County of Randal in the State of Texas?"

"I do."

"You're now my deputy, like it or not." Chance managed a smile.

Danner pinned the badge onto his vest, then removed the Wanted poster from his pocket and opened it. He leaned over and held the poster in front of Chance's face.

"This is for the fella I killed out there—Evans. Five-hundred-dollar reward, dead or alive. I'da killed him anyway, but I'll take the money," Danner declared, tipping his head back, looking over the poster at Chance's face.

"Very well, I'll see to it when I get back over to the jail. I'll sign it, then you can collect over in Oneida."

"What now, Marshal?" Danner picked up his big boot, set it on the bed's foot rail, and leaned forward.

"The usual, take a look around town a couple of times this evening, especially in the saloon. Make sure the card games are straight and none of the men are harassing the ladies too much. Keep a light burning in front of the jail until midnight or so…then check back here. They'll be two stages arriving tomorrow. One from Oneida and the other from up north near the border. The Oneida stage should get here around ten in the morning and the one from Thornton about two, three in the afternoon. Any questions?"

Danner stepped down from the bed rail and pushed his hat back on his head. "Ladies at the saloon?"

"Yes, Danner, ladies at the saloon, you know, dance hall girls, whores. We have them here in Canyon Creek too."

"Well, I wasn't aware we had those opportunities here in town."

"You haven't been in town long enough to know much of anything. Just make sure nobody gets killed while I'm up here getting bossed around by the hotel owner!"

Danner wheeled around on his heels and stopped. Without looking over his shoulder at Chance, he laughed. "I'm not so sure you don't like being bossed around by the owner."

Chance grabbed his hat from the bedpost and slung it at Danner as he reached the door. The hat hit its bull's-eye square in Danner's back. Danner looked down at the hat.

"Good luck pickin' that up." Danner left and closed the door behind him. He paused outside the door.

I didn't see any girls at the saloon last night.

With any luck, it would be a quiet night in Canyon Creek.

CHAPTER 14

ELIZABETH STOOD AT THE FRONT window of the hotel. The sound of horses crashing down the street seized her attention. She looked out and saw six horses rumble past with the crimson-and-gold Randall stage in tow. Red dust billowed up from the street, veiling the buildings on the other side. She watched the stage until it came to a roaring halt in front of Mr. Wright's overland office. Men ran up to the horses and began to unhitch the team. The driver and another man leapt to the ground from the high front seat. The side door opened, and a man wearing a long black coat and matching sou'wester stepped out. There appeared to be other passengers inside the coach, but between the dust and the commotion around the stage, she couldn't tell for certain.

"I must be going," Elizabeth said, turning toward her hostesses.

"My dear, are you sure about this?" Mrs. McNally said. "I should think a young lady like yourself would be much better off staying here and letting someone go on to Canyon Creek on your behalf."

"I completely agree with Mrs. McNally," Mrs. Henry chimed in. "I'm sure you could get any number of young men here in Thornton to carry your message to Mr. Chance."

"Thank you both for your concern, but I promised my father that I'd go and find Mr. Chance. I hope you both understand my position. Thank you for the tea, Mrs. Henry. I'm sure I'll be back in a couple of days." Elizabeth hurried out the parlor and quickly crossed the street, pulling her skirt up to minimize the dirt soiling it. As she stepped up onto the walkway in front of the store, Mr. McNally stepped out and handed her a bag bulging with unknown surprises.

"I've prepared some food and drink for your trip," he explained with a smile.

Elizabeth stopped and accepted the bag of supplies.

She gasped. "How much do I owe you, Mr. McNally?"

"Nothing. Just come back as quickly as you can."

Elizabeth thanked him and walked over to the stage office, where Bill Wright was busily scribbling in his ledger.

"Hello again, Miss Thornton." Wright offered a smile with his greeting. "We'll be loading the coach in about fifteen minutes with passengers to follow right ahead. Your driver will be Cletus Bradley, and Dave Jennings will ride with him on this trip. You may wait inside if you like. Less dust in there!"

"Thank you kindly, Mr. Wright. I believe I will step inside." Elizabeth stepped into the small room and took one of the two chairs at the back. It was quiet inside the stage office and much cleaner than the walkway next to the street. She paused and let her mind wander for a moment.

I hope I'm doing the right thing. Maybe I should have stayed with Dad and sought a messenger? No, Dad will be in good hands with Mrs. Rawlings. I must go.

Elizabeth pulled the carpetbag from her lap and attempted to set it down on the floor next to her. A sharp pain pierced her right shoulder, causing the bag to slam against the floor. Before she could control her reaction, a loud scream exited her lips. Her eyes immediately filled with tears, blurring her vision. The door swung open, and before she knew it, Bill Wright was standing over her.

"What's wrong, Miss Thornton?"

"Oh, I'm sorry, Mr. Wight. I just dropped my bag is all."

Wright leaned down and took a close look at Elizabeth's grimacing face, noting the tears.

"I'm usually not one to pry, miss, but you look to be in some kind discomfort."

"Well, my arm is a little sore is all. Really I'm fine. Will we be boarding the coach soon?"

"Just a few more minutes." Wright spun on his heel and went back out to the stagecoach to speak to Cletus.

Elizabeth rolled up the sleeve of her blouse, exposing a bloody bandage covering the wound compliments of Blackie Gillum. She peeled back the gauze, then gasped for breath at the sight. The flesh had separated and was bleeding. The area surrounding the opening was swollen and bright red. She quickly withdrew a fresh bandage from her bag and replaced the soiled one.

I'll deal with this later, she thought. Wright walked in as she rolled her sleeve back into place.

"We're about ready, Miss Thornton."

Elizabeth retrieved her bag from the floor, stood, and made her way outside to the waiting stagecoach. As she approached the carriage, Cletus opened the door and offered a hand to assist her in stepping up into the compartment. Elizabeth accepted the assistance and entered the carriage. She looked up and was startled by the bright green eyes of a man peering at her. Gasping and losing her balance, she fell backward onto the unoccupied front seat. Her bag fell to the floor, sending her Colt Peacemaker out with a thud. With catlike quickness, the stranger scooped her bag off the floor and held it in front of her. She accepted the bag with her left hand and placed it next to her. Keeping his eyes fixed on hers, he reached down and retrieved the gun. The stranger moved his gaze from Elizabeth to the firearm and slowly examined it. Without a word, he twirled the Colt around to expose the grip toward Elizabeth.

"Yours, ma'am?"

Elizabeth wrapped her hand around the handle of the Colt and waited for the stranger to release his tight grip. The stranger's hand slowly opened, allowing her to carefully return it to her bag.

"Yes, thank you," she replied.

"My apologies, ma'am. I didn't know I was traveling with a lady. If so I would have delayed my entrance into the coach." The stranger removed his black hat. "Allow me to introduce myself. I'm Vin Packard, from Kansas City, at your service, ma'am." Packard smiled and bowed his head.

Elizabeth felt her face burn with a sense of embarrassment. She forced a smile. "I'm Elizabeth Thornton, and no apology is necessary, Mr. Packard. I was just surprised to see you."

Bill Wright stuck his bald head into the coach.

"Your bag is strapped down up top, Miss Thornton. Should ride just fine to Walker Wells."

"Walker Wells?" Elizabeth asked.

"Yes, that's where the stage will stay tonight before heading out to Canyon Creek in the morning. Jacob and Martha Walker have a farm down there, and they have accommodations for the stage and its passengers. You'll like Mrs. Walker. She's a real fine lady." Wright swung the door shut and twisted the handle until the crossbar locked into position.

"Have you traveled by stagecoach much, Miss Thornton?" Packard asked.

"When I was a child. I took the train just recently when I returned from back East."

"Back East?"

"Yes, I lived in Philadelphia for several years. I just returned home to Thornton about two weeks ago." Elizabeth wasn't sure if she should be offering this stranger so much of her personal happenings. Still, he had a way about him that put her at ease.

"What takes you on a trip so soon after returning home?"

"I'm going to Canyon Creek to locate a friend of my father's." Elizabeth knew better than to say too much about her mission. Both passengers were then treated to Mr. Wright announcing the coach's departure.

"Last call for the Randall stage! Stratford! Cactus! Walker Wells! Westwind and Canyon Creek!"

"Looks like just the two of us, Miss Thornton," Packard said with a faint straight-line grin beneath his wide-brimmed hat.

Elizabeth smiled and nodded. The crack of a whip followed a "Giddyup" from Cletus. The six fresh horses swiftly responded, setting the coach on its way to Stratford. The carriage rocked from side to side, forcing Elizabeth to steady herself with her hands. Her right shoulder bit with pain on each impact. She slid sideways on the seat to give her right arm a rest. She examined her travel partner from the corner of her eye. He was looking directly at her, arms folded across his chest. Dressed completely in black, all she could see were his green eyes glowing above a sharp nose and trimmed goatee under the brim of his hat. No longer at ease, she began to feel uncomfortable in his presence. She redirected her attention to the open window on her right and watched the town of Thornton fade into the bright brown hues of the landscape.

CHAPTER 15

THE RANDALL STAGE COMPANY HAD taken great care in the craftsmanship of their overland stagecoaches, adding extra padding to the benches and newly designed metal springs to the axles. These added luxuries were not found in many of their competitors' coaches. With the expansion of the railroad, the use of stagecoaches was in decline. Still, there were vast areas of country that required travel by horse. Canyon Creek, Texas, was one of those destinations.

Cletus Bradley had been driving stagecoaches as long as he could remember. This Randall coach was better than some and not as good as others, but today it was cutting nicely through the sun-splashed valley. Despite the endless drought, the sage was in bloom, painting the rolling land with colors of faint green and vibrant purple. The cactus was lagging behind with occasional yellow blooms trapped in between long needles, awaiting their next victim. Cletus snapped his whip and called out to his six-horse team with yelps of praise. Only the oppressive heat beaming down from the sun could hinder this journey. That was as long as there were no outlaws along the path looking for easy prey. Cletus had left Thornton without the safety of a shotgun rider with him. He would feel better when they reached Stratford and picked up Dave Jennings, who would ride guard the rest of the way to Canyon Creek.

Elizabeth was doing her best to avoid engaging her fellow passenger, who seemed perfectly content to ride in silence, casting a constant gaze toward her. Her slender body swayed with the movement of the coach, and if not for the intense heat and her aching arm, she felt alive with the excitement of her mission. She wondered how her meeting with Ben Chance would go and if he would agree to accompany her back to Thornton and her father's side. She thought of her father and his condition, pushing out any thoughts of him not recovering from his wounds.

He's in good care with Mrs. Rawlings, she reminder herself. *He should be checked on by Dr. Langdon again. That would improve his chances of recovery.*

"You appear to be in deep thought," Vin Packard stated. His comment startled Elizabeth, causing her to flinch and let out a short shriek.

"I apologize for disturbing you, ma'am. That wasn't my intention."

"Everything all right in there!" Cletus called down into the coach while slowing the horses a bit.

"Yes, sir, Mr. Bradley!" Elizabeth shouted back. "We're fine!"

Without responding, Cletus cracked his whip and returned the team to its traveling speed.

"We've been riding in silence for quite some time and I thought I would make an attempt at conversation. I failed miserably, I'm afraid," Packard added.

"Not at all, Mr. Packard. I guess I just drifted away."

"Please call me Vin. Mr. Packard sounds far too official, and some would not consider me a gentleman after all."

Elizabeth was curious at Packard's statement.

"Why would you not be considered a gentleman, if I may ask?"

"I suppose I enjoy my cards and liquor a bit too much for some folk."

"Are you good at cards?"

"I'm able to avoid other forms of employment, if that is what you mean."

"I've only watched men play a few times. I admit I don't understand the game very well."

"Well then, you've met the right man to teach you the some-times-honorable game of poker." Packard removed a deck of cards from his vest pocket and began to shuffle. "There are many games of poker, so we'll start with one of the simpler games."

Elizabeth sat up straight and moved slightly forward on the bench in order to see the cards that Packard was dealing into two piles on his bench seat.

"How many cards do I receive for this game?" she asked.

"For this one, each player gets five cards to begin," Packard explained.

Suddenly the coach began to slow and calls of "whoa" were called out by Cletus. Elizabeth fell toward the front of the coach while Packard lunged forward, attempting to catch the cards that were now flying onto the floorboard. The coach came to a stop.

"What the hell's the trouble, driver!" Packard yelled, then immediately apologized to Elizabeth for his language.

"Stay quiet," Cletus said in a low voice. "Mr. Packard, are you armed?"

Vin Packard's eyes narrowed, and his mouth turned into a quick frown.

"Yes, sir," was the only response needed. Packard looked out the window but saw nothing that would be viewed as dangerous. "What is it?" he asked.

Cletus tied off the reins on the long brake handle next to him. He slowly got down from his high seat and walked to the coach window keeping his eyes forward down the trail.

"Looks like a pack of Indians on horseback a-ways down the trail. Eight or ten of em, just sittin' on their horses."

Packard leaned out the window and looked down the trail.

"I heard some Comanches left the reservation a few months ago and were attacking buffalo hunters," Packard said.

Cletus pushed his hat back on his head, leaned forward, and squinted in order to get a better look.

"Yeah, I heard same thing. Been a few small raids too. I ain't seen none on this trail in a long time though."

"What you aim to do?" Packard asked.

"Well, with no shotgun rider and just the two of us—"

"Three," Elizabeth corrected, drawing the Peacemaker from her handbag.

Cletus looked down at the pistol and smiled.

"Even with three, ma'am, I reckon we'll wait here a bit and see if they move on. We're already too far from Thornton to go back."

"Heard of Indians attacking a stagecoach lately?" Packard asked.

"Yep, further south near Fort Concho a while back after word got out that Crazy Horse was killed," Cletus answered. "If I recall, shotgun rider and a passenger were killed in that fracas."

"How far are we from Stratford?" Packard asked.

"Not far t'all. 'Bout five miles, maybe less," Cletus answered, keeping his eyes fixed on his adversaries. "Well, shouldn't sit here any longer, we're sittin' ducks out here in the open. I'll ride slow toward 'em. We'll see what they do. They may just watch us ride by."

"I hope you're right," Elizabeth said.

"So do I," Cletus responded with a smile. "Stay down on the floor and don't come up shootin' unless I start," Cletus ordered.

Both Packard and Elizabeth nodded and took positions on each side of the floorboard.

Cletus stepped up onto the foot rail and peered ahead.

"There's flat ground along the west side of the trail near the hills. I'll head that way and give 'em a wide berth. The ride'll be a lot rougher, but it beats takin' a bullet or arrow," he called to his reluctant but prepared Indian fighters. Cletus snapped his whip and started the team forward at a slow pace.

Pulling on the reins to his right, the team eased off the trail and onto the rugged surface of the landscape. Sage and cactus succumbed to the coach's metal-wrapped wood-spoked wheels sounding like the blade of a plow busting cropland in the spring. The carriage rocked in six different directions, knocking Packard and Elizabeth against the seats, doors, and each other.

Packard clutched Elizabeth's left shoulder in a dual effort to minimize her movement and speak to her.

"If the shooting starts, stay down unless I get hit," he said in a stern, loud voice.

"This is no time for chivalry, Mr. Packard," she answered, matching his demanding tone.

Packard looked her in the eyes and saw less fear than he had anticipated.

This is no daunted woman. She'll be all right, he thought.

"Here we go! They're headin' this way!" Cletus's voice broke Packard from his thoughts.

Cletus snapped his whip and brought the team to a full run. He could barely keep his seat as the coach bound and banged against the uneven floor of the valley. He could see the raiding party clearer now as they came closer with each passing second. The leader was in full headdress yelling out to his band of face-painted warriors. Worse, Cletus saw several braves armed with repeating rifles, the first of which lowered his weapon and fired. Cletus saw the puff of smoke from the barrel a split second before he heard the crack of the bullet. He pulled hard to the right, turning the team away from the charging Indians toward the summit of the hills. What he would give for his crack-shot partner Dave Jennings sprawled across the top of the coach firing his Winchester at this moment. The coach was rocking so violently now that Cletus couldn't draw his Colt and return fire. Both hands were needed on the reins as he did his best to keep the Randall rig from catapulting into the brush.

Packard took hold of the door window frame and steadied himself as best he could. Looking out, he saw their pursuers were close off the left rear of the coach. Packard fired his Colt Peacemaker in the direction of the charging Indians, hoping for the best. There was no chance of aiming at a specific target in these conditions. Elizabeth, having pushed herself up onto the front seat, fired out the window in a useless attempt at defending the trio.

"Hold your fire!" Packard shouted. "Save your ammunition! We'll need it when they catch us!" Packard continued. Packard looked at his young womanly partner.

I can't let them get her alive, he told himself, wincing at the thought of killing this beautiful girl he wanted to learn more about. It was absolutely necessary. Allowing her to be captured alive would be the greatest sin in a long list of sins he had amassed in his unfulfilled life. A bullet was a far better fate than the rape and torture she would certainly suffer if captured alive. He could not allow it. If nothing else, he thought of himself as a gentleman when it came to ladies like Elizabeth Thornton. Packard returned to the task at hand and swung himself out the door, hanging on the frame with his left hand. He fired the five shots he had left in his gun, seeing two Indians fall from their mounts as a result. Elizabeth grabbed his coat and pulled him back into the coach.

"Thank you!" Packard reloaded quickly. He moved back to the window and fired again, sending another brave to the ground. Bullets hit the side of the coach, splintering the once-polished crimson wood. An arrow flew through the window, just missing Elizabeth and ripping the back padding of her seat. Packard leaned out the window and fired wildly. The coach was bouncing so violently, he couldn't hit his target. The crack from an Indian rifle ended with a piercing thud into Packard's neck shattering his collarbone and thrusting him backward into the coach's interior. The door was swinging back and forth, banging against the coach's crimson-colored surface, sending fragments of wood into Elizabeth's face. The Indians were right next to the coach now. She covered her face and fired another shot out the window.

CHAPTER 16

WES PAYNE HAD HAD ENOUGH of the oppressive heat beating down on him and his stallion, Ringo. Delaying his journey to who knew where, he decided to seek refuge inside the yawning hollow of a rock some might call a cave. The cooler air was a welcome pleasure for him and Ringo as they took a respite from the day's long ride. Ringo was nudging the worn bullhide boots that capped the long legs of his partner, who had laid back to enjoy the peace of the valley when the first ping of a rifle shot was heard. Ringo, who had been underneath Captain Wes Payne for the entire four years of battle against the Union Army, snapped to attention. Payne threw his hat back off his face and listened intently. Ringo snorted and bobbed his head, announcing danger was present.

"Easy, buddy, easy," Payne told his companion of fifteen years. Payne stood, brushed the dust off his chaps, and moved to a position outside his relaxed domicile and looked toward the rifle sound. The response from a pistol answered the rifle shot. Leaning against a ragged old mesquite tree whose branches hung down like a grizzly's grasp, Payne witnessed the source of the trouble. He quickly counted nine mounted Indians in pursuit of a stagecoach that looked ready to run clean off its wheels. Payne spun in one fluid motion, set his stirrup, and swung onto Ringo, who had dutifully followed his partner to the old mesquite. Payne snapped Ringo forward, and in lightning-bolt fashion, the duo shot down through a gap of terrain and headed toward the fleeing stage in full sprint.

Cletus was pushing his team as hard as he could, but the six fleeing horses were beginning to tire. Standing on the coach board, he yelled and pleaded with his source of escape, but the team began to slow. A quick glance over his shoulder confirmed his fear. The hostiles were about to overtake his coach. A bullet struck the coach, blowing up the wooden frame that held the once-leather-covered seat. A large splinter punctured the flesh of Cletus's left leg, knocking him to one knee on the driver's platform. He held on and managed to keep control of the reins, then continued to yell out to the horses.

Elizabeth was hanging on inside the coach, which now felt like the confines of a coffin. An Indian jumped from his mount onto the open doorway, then flung himself inside the coach's box, falling on top of the unconscious gambler who had been a mysterious stranger but was now her insentient protector. Elizabeth screamed and fired her Peacemaker point-blank at her assailant, splitting his skull in half. Blood, bone, and brain splashed across the back wall of the compartment, sending Elizabeth into a spinning vortex of darkness. The sound of another rifle shot was the last thing she heard before fainting into oblivion.

Cletus saw the lone rider approaching fast from his left. The cowboy's fists were full of pistol with his rein looped behind his neck. Both guns were firing in unison as the cowboy sped past the coach and charged headlong into the band of warriors who were now falling from their ponies. Cletus pulled back on the reins with every ounce of strength he had left, bringing the Randall stagecoach to a crawl. Looking back, Cletus saw the cowboy savior shoot two more hostiles off their ponies. That sent the last few marauders twirling around and fleeing into the distance. Cletus stopped the coach. His leg was burning with the wooden implement lodged deep into his limb. Grasping the protrusion with his left hand, he closed his eyes and yanked as quick as he could. Pain shot up his leg, as though he had been kicked by an ornary mule. Leaning over, he found the box of bandages that served as a medical kit on the Randall stages. After he hastily covered the wound and securing it with his bandana, he jumped down and looked inside the carriage, hoping his travelers had survived the onslaught. A quick scan of the scene put Cletus into action. He grasped the dead Indian and pulled him through the gaping doorway then threw him to the ground. Packard was still unconscious and bleeding badly from a grotesque wound to his right neck and shoulder. Elizabeth lay listless on the front seat covered in splattered blood, still clutching the Colt Peacemaker in her right hand. Cletus reached over Packard and peeled Elizabeth's fingers from the gun's grip, taking it and setting it on the seat. He could see blood was still flowing though the swollen vein on Elizabeth's neck. Cletus heard the cowboy ride up behind him and dismount. Stepping away from the coach, Cletus extended his hand to the stranger who had saved his and his passengers' lives.

"I can't thank you enough, stranger. You saved us from an awful fate," Cletus offered.

"Don't mention it, name's Wes Payne," was the reply along with a powerful handshake.

"Everybody okay?" Payne asked as he brushed past Cletus to peer inside the coach. Payne reached down and felt the undamaged side of Packard's neck. Payne felt a faint push of blood, confirming life remained in the black-clad gambler. Payne directed his attention to Elizabeth.

"She's alive, all right," Cletus assured the hulking cowboy. "I reckon that's Injun blood all over her," he added.

Payne swiftly looked over her and noted blood oozing from her right shoulder.

"Looks like she took one in the arm. She's bleeding from inside her shirt," Payne stated. He moved Packard to the rear of the coach's floor, placing him on his back, then reached in and grasped Elizabeth with his massive hands. He lifted her from the seat and out of the coach as though she was a doll. Slipping his arms under her legs and back, he turned and placed her on the ground shaded from the sun next to the coach. Payne removed his vest, folded it, and placed it under Elizabeth's head, ordering Cletus to fetch some water. The old stage driver limped to the front of the coach and retrieved a canteen from the compartment under the rider's seat then returned to Payne's side. Payne took off his red bandana, soaked it with water, and began to wipe the bloody mess from Elizabeth's face and neck with the soggy neckerchief. His efforts revealed a beautiful narrow face with flawless skin and lips. Elizabeth moaned and opened her eyes, jerking sideways from the abrupt sight of her caregiver.

"It's okay, you're all right now. You fainted," Payne advised her in the best soothing voice he could muster. "You've had quite an experience, ma'am," he added, offering her a drink of water.

Elizabeth attempted to sit up, but fell back under the pain from her right arm. She yelped and closed her eyes tightly, fighting back the pain.

Cletus knelt and cut the bloody cloth away from Elizabeth's right arm. The wound had torn open during the jostling in the coach and was bleeding. Of more concern was the yellow fluid seeping from the wound.

"Looks like infection has set in, ma'am," Payne stated. "How long you had this?" he asked.

"A couple of days," Elizabeth answered. "I was shot during a robbery at my father's ranch in Thornton."

Payne's eyes widened.

"The Tilted T Ranch?" Payne inquired, helping Elizabeth up into a sitting position.

"Yes, it's my father Joel Thornton's ranch," Elizabeth explained before swallowing another gulp of water.

Cletus stood and returned to the coach and Vin Packard. Packard remained unconscious. Cletus returned to the front seat compartment and retrieved a box of bandages then quickly attended to the wounded gambler. The thick pile of gauze was all Cletus had available. It would have to do for now.

Payne lifted Elizabeth to her feet and began to introduce himself. She looked past him and asked Cletus if Packard was okay.

"He's hurt real bad, miss, but still alive. He might make it if we can get to Stratford quick enough."

Payne checked on the horses then returned to Cletus, who was about finished with his patient.

"Horses are about let out, but I think they can make it to Stratford," Payne advised. "You check on the harnesses and wheels, and I'll bandage this young lady's arm," Payne instructed. Cletus hurried to check on the team.

"I'm sorry, I'm Elizabeth Thornton. My manners have left me with all this happening."

"No apologies, ma'am. Wes Payne, nice to meet you. I'm glad I came along when I did. I fear what may have happened to you if Ringo and I hadn't decided to stop and rest a spell in the hills."

"What did happen? And who's Ringo?"

Payne laughed and whistled for his companion. Ringo walked up to Payne and nickered. "This is Ringo. Ringo, meet Miss Elizabeth Thornton." Ringo bobbed his head.

"Oh, I see," Elizabeth said with a smile.

"Well, ma'am—"

"Call me Elizabeth, please, Mr. Payne," she insisted.

"And I'm Wes," he asserted. "I heard the shots from the hills, and when I saw you were being chased by that raiding party, I decided to ride down and see if I could help out. Fortunately, I was able to convince your hostile friends to turn back after a little argument."

"A little argument?" Elizabeth asked as she looked back to see several dead men strewn about the sage and cactus.

"Yes, ma'am," Payne confirmed, looking back toward the fallen warriors.

"Horses look good enough. The hames and traces are tight and ready. The wheels have seen better days, but I think they'll make it," Cletus reported.

"Good," answered Payne. "I'll follow you into Stratford." Payne grabbed the door, which was hanging loosely from a single hinge. He pulled the door from its lone crux and set it inside the coach. After helping Elizabeth back to her front seat, he swung up on Ringo and motioned to Cletus to get back on the trail and head south to Stratford. Cletus snapped his reins and pulled to the left, bringing the team back onto its course. Payne dropped back a few feet from the coach's rear and kept pace.

Elizabeth looked down on Packard, whose body appeared lifeless. She felt ashamed that she had felt uncomfortable with this man. He had defended her and the coach gallantly in her mind. Now, he might die in her presence.

How many men have I seen die since I returned from Philadelphia? Was it seven, eight? She couldn't recall. She had killed two herself. She closed her eyes.

Too many, she thought.

CHAPTER 17

ESPITE ITS FLEDGLING EXISTENCE, STRATFORD had most of the big-town amenities. Like most towns on the Texas cattle trail, it sprouted from a tent city along Cita Creek. Stratford grew with each cattle drive that passed through. The main street was lined with a hotel, two saloons, a blacksmith shop, general store, feed and tack supply, and sporadic shacks that served as housing for some of the town's residents. Newer to Stratford was the stagecoach and telegraph offices at the end of town. A livery stable, school, and brand-new church filled its boundaries.

Jerry Crowley was a small nervous fellow who had made his way west as part of a large wagon train that stalled in the general vicinity of Stratford a few years back. When the train finally decided to continue on to California, he elected to remain in Stratford and help it grow. An educated and aspiring businessman, he lobbied the Randall Stage Company to stop in Stratford, assuring he would operate an acceptable office. Once satisfied, the Randall Company agreed, and now he was the town's official transportation director. As such, he was worried because the Thornton stage was overdue, which was unusual. Crowley stood on the step of his office and looked to the north, straining his eyes in the hope of catching a glimpse of dust kicked up by its carriage. Finally, after an hour of anxiety, the coach came into view amidst a cloud of valley trail dust. Relieved, he removed his round spectacles and wiped them clean with his handkerchief, then stepped back into his office.

Taking his bright silver pocket watch from its perch inside his neatly tailored brown vest, he recorded the time in his ledger book, adding a note that the stage was an hour late. Lucky Louis Ogalsby, the town's happy-go-lucky drunk, walked by the office.

"Stage's comin'!" he announced, then kept his stagger toward the Cita Saloon, which was the only one in town that would allow him in.

Crowley walked out onto the office steps and greeted the oncoming Cletus with a friendly wave. Crowley saw the coach's door was missing on the left side and the team looked weary. Running across the street to the blacksmith shop, he yelled for young Jimmy Prescott to fetch the doctor. John Prescott, the town's gargantuan blacksmith, took a break from hammering fire-blazed horseshoes and came out from the back. At six foot eight inches tall and three hundred pounds, John Prescott had become known simply as Big John.

"What's the trouble?" Big John asked, still holding a large black hammer in his left hand.

"Stage is coming in an hour late and one of its doors is missing," answered Crowley.

The big blacksmith set his hammer down and pulled off the thick leather apron he wore for protection against the soaring bits of scorching iron he sent into the atmosphere with every strike of his hammer.

Crowley and Big John hurried back to the stage office as Cletus pulled the reins and settled the horses down at its steps.

"Big trouble, Jerry!" Cletus announced. "Indian raiding party hit us. I got a fella in the back bad hurt, a young lady with a bad arm, and I took some lumber in the leg!"

Wes stopped Ringo at the back of the coach and dismounted. Cletus made his way down from the splintered board that had been a fine bench seat when it left Thornton.

"If it weren't for this feller here, we'd all have less hair right now!" Cletus stated, pointing back at Payne. "He rode right into all of 'em hostiles firin' both guns!"

"Thanks, stranger." Crowley nodded to Payne. Payne said nothing, just waved his hand.

Big John helped Elizabeth from the coach and saw Packard on the floor. The big blacksmith leaned in and shook his head. "This one's dead, Jerry. Doc can't help him."

Payne looked into the coach and a glance at Packard's gray face confirmed the big man's diagnosis. By now, several people had begun to gather around the rattled stagecoach. Herbert Kent, led by Jimmy Prescott, approached Crowley.

"This young lady needs your help, Doc, and Cletus's leg needs attending. There's a fella in the back that's dead," Crowley informed Stratford's physician.

"Don't mind me, Doc. This leg's nothing a drink won't cure," Cletus announced.

Doc Kent guided Elizabeth into the stage office and commenced attending to her arm. Big John lifted Packard's body out of the stage and ordered his son to get the flat wagon from his shop. He carried Packard to his shop and placed him on the wagon Jimmy had pushed up front. The big blacksmith then gathered up some tools.

"Jimmy, take this man over to the undertaker's," John ordered his son.

Crowley told Cletus to sit down on the waiting bench and tell what happened. A crowd gathered around to listen.

"Hold on!" came a voice from the back of the crowd. Everybody turned and saw Marshal Lon Barry making his way through the human obstacle course.

"Heard we had trouble on the trail, Jerry," the marshal said.

"Yes, sir, Indian attack. Cletus here was about to tell us all about it," Crowley answered.

"That's right, Marshal. We were comin' down the valley near the foothills about four, five miles out when I see this band of injuns on horseback waitin' on the trail up ahead. I stopped the stage and talked to that feller and young lady about what we should do. We all decided to try and go around 'em off the trail, but they come a-yel-lin' and shootin'. I tried to outrun 'em, but they caught up, and if it weren't for this gunslinger here, we'd all be like that Mr. Packard."

Barry looked toward Payne.

"Who are you?" he asked.

"Name's Wes Payne, Marshal. I was up in the hills when I heard shootin' down in the valley. Saw what was happening, so I rode in to help."

"He charged down from the hills with two guns blastin', Marshal! Killed half of 'em Injuns his-self." Cletus exclaimed.

"Much obliged, Mr. Payne," Marshal Barry said, shaking Payne's hand.

"Sorry I was late. If I'd heard sooner, that fella might still be alive," Wes stated. He tipped his hat, then swung up onto Ringo. "Marshal, if you need me, I'll be down at the saloon."

Crowley recruited several men to change out the team, and asked Big John to look over the coach's wheels and springs to see if it was trail ready. He then retrieved a bucket from the step and headed over to a nearby trough to collect water for cleaning the mess inside the coach. Elizabeth was sitting in the stage office staring into space. Doc Kent worked on her arm with some urgency.

"When did this happen, young lady?" he asked.

Elizabeth shook her head, slowly keeping her gaze straight into nothing. All she heard was muffled noise. No voice, no words.

Doc Kent continued working on her arm, doing his best to drain the poison. Herbert Kent was an educated man with enough medical knowledge to recognize an infection when he saw it. The only question now was how far the toxin had spread. Certainly, into the shoulder, which contained a bright red blotch inside a dark bluish-purple border that faded into the skin. Kent placed his hand on the shoulder and squeezed firmly. Elizabeth let out a scream that brought Jerry Crowley running into the office.

"What happened!" Crowley yelled.

Elizabeth jerked her body away from Kent, clutching her arm, folding herself at the waist to ease the pain.

"I'm sorry, miss, but I needed to know how bad the infection has gotten," the doctor explained. "When did this happen?" he asked a second time.

"A couple of days ago," Elizabeth managed the words through gritted teeth.

"I need you to come to my office. I want to open the shoulder and see if I can remove most of the toxin."

Elizabeth was exhausted, sick, and in terrible pain.

"Okay," was all she said.

Kent lifted his patient up from the chair and slowly walked her to the door.

"We'll be over at my office."

"Very well," Crowley answered, then resumed his cleaning duties in the coach.

Big John returned to the stagecoach with the tools to repair the door. Crowley finished his duties, thanked his handy blacksmith, then headed for his desk to write the day's events into his ledger.

Wes was standing at the bar in the Cita Saloon trying to finish a mug of beer in between answering questions about his actions from the afternoon. The bartender set another full mug in front of Payne followed by an "On the house!" when Marshal Barry approached Payne.

"Speak with you a bit, Mr. Payne?" Barry pointed over to a table in the corner of the saloon. Payne nodded and followed the lawman to the table, taking a chair in the corner where he could see the rest of the room.

"You happen to see what kind of Indians attacked the stage?"

"Comanche," was the singular response.

"You sure?"

"Yep."

"That's what I figured. Since word of Cochise being killed got out, I heard a bunch of Comanche left the reservations and formed small raiding parties. Been hittin' the buffalo hunters and rustling cattle, but this is the first I heard of them attacking a stage."

"I was further east about a month ago. A party of Comanche and Apache riding together attacked a ranch, killin' the rancher and his wife. Right after, a couple of buffalo hunters were killed and their skins stolen."

"Apache?"

"Yep. I didn't see any Apache in this bunch though. About ten, er, twelve total, most with Winchesters. Might want to let your folks know to stay close to town for a while."

"I could use a deputy for a bit till things calm down. Interested?"

"Nope, on my way north. Might hook on with a cattle drive headin' to Kansas City."

"Thanks for your time, Mr. Payne. Good luck." Barry stood, shook Payne's hand, turned, and hurried out of the tavern, which had become a loud raucous throng with what looked like the whole town's population crowding through the swinging door.

Payne leaned back and removed his hat. One of the local girls scurried over and sat down.

"You're a downright hero, stranger," she exclaimed with a big smile and turn of her head. "Interested in a reward?"

"No, ma'am, I wish I had the time, but I got to get on."

Payne's self-appointed reward frowned, stood, then wrestled her way through the thick crowd back to where she came from. Payne hadn't been completely truthful to his bar beauty. He was headin' north, but he wanted to know more about Miss Elizabeth Thornton. He finished his beer, then forced his way through the crowd, receiving numerous pats on the back along the way to the street. Payne was on his way back to the stagecoach office when he met Cletus coming the other way.

"Howdy, Mr. Payne?"

"Cletus. You takin' the stage onward this afternoon?"

"Yep. That fuss-budget Crowley says the stage will be good to go in about a half hour. Trouble is, I was supposed to pick up my guard Dave Jennings here, but now I hear he's down in Cactus. So it'll be me and that pretty lady if she can make it."

"If she can make it?"

"Yep, Doc Kent has her over to his office. Says that arm's pretty bad."

"You know where his office is?"

"Yep, right there across the street. It's the one with the white shutters. I'm gonna get me a drink 'fore we go. If I don't see ya, thanks again, gunslinger."

Payne nodded and walked across the street with the stride of a puma. Reaching the doctor's door, he barged through with the force of an angry bear. Doc Kent appeared from behind a curtain.

"Anything wrong, sir?"

"No, sorry for the uproar. Stage driver told me you had that young lady from the stage in here."

Elizabeth pulled the curtain back.

"Yes, Mr. Payne, I'm here."

Payne looked over the cause of his angst. Her once fine white shirt was now torn and tattered with bloody red accents scattered all over. A large white bandage donned her right shoulder.

"How you feelin'?" Payne asked.

"Better now that Dr. Kent has fixed me up."

"I've suggested that she remain here in Stratford for a few days so I can monitor that arm, but she insists she has important business in Canyon Creek that can't wait."

"I don't mean to get in your business, ma'am, but—"

"Don't concern yourself, Mr. Payne. I'll be fine. I have a friend in Canyon Creek." Elizabeth's face was pale, and beads of sweat were dotting her forehead. Her eyes were dark as though she had been struck in each.

"Is the stage continuing on?" Kent asked.

"Yes, I just talked to the driver. About a half hour, he said."

"Then I must be going," Elizabeth informed Kent. "Thank you for everything. I feel much better, and I'm sure there's a doctor in Canyon Creek."

Kent handed Elizabeth a sack of clean bandages.

"Have Mrs. Walker change the dressing when you reach her farm tonight."

"I will, I promise."

Payne stepped aside and opened the door for Elizabeth, who walked out to the street in a robust manner, attempting to convince Kent and Payne she was sturdy enough to make the trip. Payne rambled to her side.

"The coach's guard was not here like the driver thought. He's down in Cactus."

Elizabeth stopped on the walkway in front of the stage office and looked at Payne. She was unable to mask her frown, and lines of concern streaked across her face.

"I'm riding guard," Payne announced, then ambled over to the hitching post where Ringo was neighing. Payne swung up on Ringo and waited next to the coach's team. Elizabeth entered the office where Crowley was scratching away in his ledger.

"The stage will be leaving momentarily, ma'am. Was Doc able to fix your arm up?"

"Yes, it feels much better. Do you know when we might arrive at the Walker farm?"

Crowley's bright face darkened into a frown.

"Should be about eight o'clock or so, ma'am. I'm sorry. We haven't had any Indian trouble around here for some time, and I guess we got lazy. Cletus shouldn't have taken the stage out without ole Dave or someone else riding shotgun. Best get aboard." Crowley turned and escorted Elizabeth out to the stage.

Cletus made his way out of the saloon and headed back to where Crowley and Elizabeth were waiting. He'd been through an Indian raid or two in his day, so this was business as usual. He had to admit though that he worried a bit about his lone passenger.

This is no place for an unescorted lady. Sure, would be good if that gunslinger would ride along for a spell, he thought. "Ready to go, Cletus?" Crowley asked as he approached. "Looks like you have a guard after all," Crowley continued, looking up at Payne and smiling.

"Well, righty good!" Cletus shouted. "Always good to have a gunslinger along for the ride!"

"All aboard! Cactus! Walker Wells! Canyon Creek!" Crowley announced.

Cletus crawled up onto the splintered driver bench, cussing under his breath about his bandaged leg.

Crowley eyed Wes Payne mounted straight and looking like a force to be reckoned with.

"I'll ride down to Cactus where your shotgun rider is supposed to be. I'll move on from there," Payne answered Crowley's unasked question.

"Wait just a minute, Cletus!" Crowley ran back into the office and quickly drew ten dollars from the cash box he had hidden under his desk. Spinning on his heels, he ran back out to Payne and reached up as far as he could to offer the cash to his auxiliary guard.

"No need, Mr. Crowley, my decision."

"No, sir, the stage line already owes you a great debt. Please take it. I've approval for such situations."

Elizabeth had seated herself in the coach and was watching Payne carefully. Payne snuck a side glace over to Elizabeth, who smiled and nodded her head in approval. Payne tipped his hat and collected the money with a left hand that bore a hideous scar in the middle of its back. Crowley noticed the mark and gasped. Elizabeth also found herself catching a short breath as though she had just blown out an obstinate candle. Payne jerked his hand back, reined Ringo to the right, and rode out in front of the team.

"I'll ride ahead for a bit," he growled, obviously irritated that his desecration had been discovered.

"See ya on the way back, Jerry!" Cletus hollered then snapped the reins, which started his six-horse team into action.

"Git on up! Let's go!" The stage rocked forward and kicked up a cloud of red dust that spun dust devils spinning on each side of the carriage. Big John and Jimmy Prescott stepped out from their black iron furnace and waved, eliciting a mirrored response from Elizabeth as the coach rumbled away. As she waved, her shoulder bit like a rabid coyote, causing her to bite hard with closed eyes. She was alone in the coach now, Mr. Packard's memory and bloodstained seat her only companions.

For the first time since her father told her to find Ben Chance, she doubted her decision.

Had everyone been right? Should she have hired someone to find Chance? How was her father? Was he still alive? Would she make it to Canyon Creek and back?

The stage roared down the vale that led to Cactus, leaving a long trail of dust that resembled a diamondback slithering through the valley.

A short distance ahead, high atop a knoll stood a shrouded band of Comanches in full war paint watching the snake crawl onward.

CHAPTER 18

Tenahpu Tama had not been anointed a chief in the Comanche nation. He had been deprived of that honor by the white man who had all but hemmed his people into neat little pens called reservations. The great Comanche raids were a distant memory, but warriors like Tenahpu Tama were poised to make a stand for pride and honor. With the great nations' chiefs held in captivity across the land, restless warriors like Red Young Man and Tenahpu Tama, meaning "man thunder," had broken from the reservations and were leading raids of livestock thefts and stagecoach and buffalo hunter attacks. This lone stagecoach would be another small victory feather in Tenahpu Tama's private war bonnet.

The would-be Comanche chief raised his spear, then in a silent swift motion dipped the point toward the stage. Nine braves banged their heels into their ponies haunches and lurched forward following their leader. In single file the proud Comanche warriors sped to intercept their prey like an eagle's talons honing in on its quarry.

The beating hooves of the stage's team were rhythmic music to Cletus's ears. With each ending stomp of the horses' efforts, Cletus snapped his whip and let out a yell. Elizabeth had fallen into a rhythm of her own, rocking with the movement of the coach. Her arm felt good and her spirits were high as she studied Wes, effortlessly gliding on Ringo outside the coach. The scorching air had become tolerable as it whisked past her face in the open window. They would be in Cactus soon, then onto the Walker farm for the night. She looked forward to an uneventful journey.

Suddenly she noticed Wes pull Ringo around, then an unintelligible shout to Cletus. The coach sped up and turned sharply to the right, vacating the worn trail path for the rugged terrain surface.

Not needing an appraisal of the situation, she reached for her Colt Peacemaker and slid over to the left side of the coach. In the distance, she saw the cause for the change of direction. Indians were charging hard toward them. Veiled in single file, she wasn't able to tell their number, but she knew Wes and Cletus would need all the help she could provide.

Wes stopped Ringo near a large rock, dismounted, and forced Ringo down onto his side. Drawing his Winchester, he laid it across his saddle and took careful aim at the lead Indian. *Wait… Wait…* The lead Indian broke to the left, exposing the rest of the band. Wes carefully squeezed the trigger. *Crack!* The rifle responded smoothly, and the shot was true. The would-be Comanche chief Tenahpu Tama flipped backward off his pony, crashing to the ground. A quick and unceremonious ending for a proud warrior. In one easy motion, Wes cocked his Winchester, took aim on the next in line, and fired a second round. Another charging brave was sent backward, abandoning his pony. A third shot and another rider-less pony halted the charge. The remaining braves turned and sped off, not wanting to challenge Wes's aim again. He stood pulling on his saddle, letting Ringo know it was safe to rise. He considered riding out to identify the dead attackers, but decided against it.

The others may decide on a second charge, he thought. And he was beginning to think his luck was running thin.

Cletus glanced over his shoulder at the sound of the first rifle shot and saw Wes's plan. As such, he brought the stagecoach back onto the path to get more speed. No sense hanging around. If Wes couldn't hold 'em, he figured the more distance he got, the better. A second glance after the shooting stopped let Cletus know he could ease off on the team.

With all this action, we need a doggone army escort, he thought. Cletus worked the team back into a rhythm and called down to Elizabeth that everything looked okay.

Elizabeth had watched in awe as Wes had single-handedly saved her and Cletus again.

Who is this man? Where is he from? Why is he here? She decided she wanted answers to these questions and more. She hoped to convince him to ride along all the way to Canyon Creek.

Wes rode up past the coach next to Cletus.

"Thanks again, big fella!" Cletus called down from his perch. "Any idea what they were?" he asked.

"Not sure! Comanche, I'm guessin' though! Didn't want to wait around and see! About thirty minutes to Cactus, I reckon," Wes called out.

"Yep! Should be there in a jiffy!"

Cletus cracked his whip, and the Randall stage followed the snake-shaped trail twisting and turning its way into the small town of Cactus.

Like many West Texas towns in 1877, Cactus was still in the process of being settled. The livery stable doubled as the stage office, and most of the town's business was handled in the store or the saloon. Since a cattle drive would occasionally stop for a day or two, there was a boarding house and blacksmith available for those cowhands who had money left after a visit with the ladies in the bawdy house at the far end of town. The rest of the town consisted of a few wooden structures and several tents. Just enough to appear on a map.

Cletus brought the stage to a rest in front of the livery stable, pulled on the brake handle, and gingerly stepped down from his driver's platform. His leg was still barking, thanks to the slice of wood that found its way into his flesh during the first Indian raid on what seemed like a never-ending run.

Hank Rigglesby, the operator of the Rigglesby Livery Stable & Stage Office, made his way out from the bowels of the barn bringing clumps of manure and hay flying off his muck boots.

"Hey there, Cletus!" Rigglesby hollered, spitting tobacco juice through a toothless smile. "Heard ole Dave Jennings let out on ya."

"Let out on me? I ain't heard nothin', ain't seen hide nor hair of Dave," Cletus answered. "He was supposed to meet up with me down the road. Been ridin' without a shotgunner the whole way. Thanks to this here fella, we're still in one piece!" Cletus poked his thumb toward Wes as he walked around the coach and opened the door for Elizabeth.

"Had two Injun attacks today alone," Cletus continued. "Lost one of my passengers in the first one. Would have lost both, but this young lady knows how to handle a pistol. That's for sure!" Cletus stopped abruptly and removed his hat as Elizabeth stepped down from the coach. Hank Rigglesby did the same.

"This here is Elizabeth Thornton, Joel Thornton's daughter," Cletus announced. "This here is Hank Rigglesby. He runs this place."

"Pleased to meet you, ma'am," Rigglesby stated, wiping brown juice from his stained whiskers with an equally stained shirt sleeve.

"Nice to meet you, Mr. Rigglesby. Is there any place I can clean up?" Elizabeth asked.

"Yes, ma'am, over to the store. Ronnie keeps some clean water in a pitcher," Rigglesby announced with pride in his voice and a nod across the street.

"I'll take you over while they water the team," Wes stated, looping his arm under Elizabeth's, then guiding her across the street.

"So that's Joel's daughter, huh," Rigglesby asked out loud. "I heard she come back from out East."

"Yep, about a week ago," Cletus spoke, for the record. "Then Joel got shot—"

"What! Joel Thornton shot! He alive?" Rigglesby blurted out.

"Last we heard this morning he was still alive, but don't know for sure now. Guess it was real bad. Bunch of outlaws rode up to the ranch, shot Joel, killed his man Moses Barber, and winged the girl there before stealing his cattle and horses. She's headin; down to Canyon Creek to fetch Ben Chance."

Rigglesby had put his hat back on and was listening intently with squinted eyes and clenched teeth. After a moment, he began to nod his head and smile.

"Oh yeah, Chance and Thornton rode together in their marshal days. Wouldn't want to be the fella to cross Ben Chance," Rigglesby stated.

"Nope, nor me," Cletus agreed. "Help me get the horses watered. I need to get to damn Walker Wells before too late!"

Wes opened the Cactus Mercantile door, sounding a small bell that announced their arrival. Elizabeth smiled as she passed through the threshold onto the clean wooden floor. Storekeeper Ronnie Bolton entered the area from a room in the back.

"Good afternoon, folks. What can I do for you?" Bolton asked in a high-pitched voice as if he hadn't had a customer in weeks.

"I was told I may wash up here," Elizabeth stated, putting her best manners on display.

"Yes, ma'am, right this way. There's a washroom right back here with clean water, soap, and towels." Bolton motioned with both hands toward a narrow door behind the sales desk. As Elizabeth closed the door behind her, Bolton turned his attention to Wes.

"Anything for you, sir?"

"Got any ammunition? I need bullets for my Colt and Winchester."

Bolton frowned and shook his head.

"No, I'm sorry. Any ammunition I get in sells pretty fast, especially if a cattle drive comes by. I only get a supply shipment every six to eight weeks, and ammunition less than that."

Wes looked around and spotted some canned food on a shelf.

"I'll take a can of peaches and corn," he said, removing a can of each from the shelf.

Wes paid for the food as Elizabeth appeared from the washroom. Wes held up the cans.

"It's not Delmonico's, but it may hold you over until we get to the Walker place," Wes offered.

Elizabeth smiled.

"It looks wonderful," she said. "Thank you for the use of your washroom. Do I owe you any money?" she asked.

"No, ma'am, the stage line gives me a couple of dollars a month to make it available to the passengers," Bolton explained.

Wes and Elizabeth began to leave when Bolton called out, "Wait!"

Bolton retrieved a fork from a drawer and handed it to Elizabeth.

"Can't eat without that." He laughed, holding up his right hand in a stop motion. "No charge. Have a safe trip down to Walker's."

"Thank you again," Elizabeth said, placing the utensil inside her carpetbag.

Wes and Elizabeth took a short stroll down the street then crossed over and made their way back to the stage where Cletus was about finished tending to the team.

"Ready to go when y'all are," Cletus advised.

Wes opened the coach door, and Elizabeth climbed back in for what she hoped would be the last time of the day. Wes pulled a knife from inside his vest and opened the can of peaches, cutting a three-edged box in the top then bending the square lid back.

"Nothin' fancy," he said, handing the can to Elizabeth.

Elizabeth smiled and accepted the container.

"Too bad I lost the bag of food Mr. McNally gave me before we left Stratford. I guess it fell out of the coach when Mr. Packard was shot. I didn't get to see what it contained. This looks perfect," she said, holding up her gift utensil.

Wes closed and cranked the handle, locking the bar. Elizabeth glanced down and caught a glimpse of the mangled skin on Wes's hand before he could pull it away. Their eyes met.

"Ready?" Wes asked without a smile.

Elizabeth nodded and looked away.

Cletus had taken his place high up on the platform and was watching the exchange between his passenger and guard.

"Hold on, I'm going to ride shotgun and give Ringo's back a break," Wes informed Cletus.

"Sounds good! Like the company!"

Wes untied Ringo from the water trough then hitched his rein to the rear of the coach. He drew his Winchester from its scabbard and retrieved the few rounds he had left from his saddlebag.

Taking his place next to Cletus, he opened his hand and showed the old driver eight rifle cartridges.

"Don't get us in more trouble than this," he said with a tight-lipped grin.

Cletus let out a cackle then cracked his whip and started for Walker Wells.

Elizabeth watched the town of Cactus pass by like flipping pages of a book.

It's a long way from Philadelphia, she thought. She looked down at her dirty skirt and blood-specked blouse. She didn't know if she should feel sorry for herself or just angry at what transpired in such a short period of time. It'll be better when she found Ben Chance. It had to be.

CHAPTER 19

C LETUS GUIDED THE STAGE AT an easy pace, knowing Ringo was keeping up behind the coach. Wes hadn't said a word for quite a time, so Cletus broke the silence.

"Pretty gal that Elizabeth Thornton," he said, looking to spur a response. Wes said nothing.

"Good-lookin' woman who can work her way around a pistol. Don't see that much out here," he added.

Wes stared ahead, keeping his lips pressed tight.

"Aw, come on now, partner. I know yer thinkin' about her. I can see it in yer face."

Wes looked down at the footboard and grimaced as though he was in pain.

"Look, old-timer, the last thing I need to do right now is get caught up with a woman. I've probably lost out on that cattle drive I was headin' to when you saw fit to get yourself attacked by them Indians. Besides, gal like her ain't gonna be interested in a drifter like me."

"Never can tell what's goin' on in a female's mind," Cletus cackled.

"You just get us down to the next stop without any shootin'," Wes demanded.

"Can do! Young fella, can do! Just about there now. Won't be another hour!"

The Randall stage rolled along gliding over the worn trail like a West Texas sidewinder. As Cletus promised, the Walker farm came into sight in less time than he had figured.

John Walker had claimed these three hundred acres of bottom land in between a couple of tall hills ten years earlier. After a month or so of digging, he found water, dug a well, and began building around it. First the house, then the barn, tack building, corral, pens, and another barn. His wife, Martha, joined him after the well was dug and the house was built. Two large stock ponds made available to the local Indian tribes kept him and Martha on sociable terms and his ranch free from flaming arrows. The Randall stage line came calling about three years ago, making John and Martha Walker an offer they couldn't refuse. Steady income from the stage line helped expand his heard and paid for the two rooms added onto the house for overnight guests. The place had become well known and was a common stop for travelers making their way south to run cattle or west to the promise of silver and gold in Colorado and Nevada.

"Stage is comin'!" John called to Martha, who had been doing her best to keep dinner warm for over an hour.

"It's about time!" was Martha's frustrated response.

Jacob Walker came running up to the front porch where his father was examining every movement of the stagecoach and what he could see of Cletus.

"Any trouble, Pa?" twelve-year-old Jacob asked with a hint of excitement.

"No, can't tell really 'cept that it's two hours late," his father replied. "Let's get over to the barn and give Cletus a hand with the team," John instructed his enthusiastic son.

The sun was setting behind Walker hill, pushing bright orange and purple rings into the clear blue sky.

"There's a friendly site, my friend!" Cletus called to Wes. "Been lookin' forward to Mrs. Walker's biscuits for a couple hours now," he added.

John and Jacob had taken positions in front of the big barn that was used to house the Randall stage teams for the night. The barn was equipped with water and grain troughs, eight hay-filled stalls, and a tack and shoe area if needed.

Cletus brought the stage to a stop in front of the barn, cranked back on the long brake handle, then tied the reins around it for good measure.

"Hello, John, good to finally get here this evening," Cletus said as he climbed down from his bullet-damaged seat.

Wes slid down the passenger side and poked his face into the open coach window. Elizabeth was doing her best to smooth out her worn prairie skirt and tattered blouse. Wes smiled and opened the door.

John shook hands with Cletus and noticed Jacob watching Wes intently.

"Looks like you had a bit of trouble this time," John said, noticing the bullet-riddled coach and driver bench.

"I'll say we did! If it weren't for this big fella here, we'd never made it."

Wes helped Elizabeth down from the coach, then turned to John and Jacob.

"Good evening, sir, name's Wes Payne," he stated as he extended his right hand to John.

"John Walker, and this is my son, Jacob."

Wes leaned down and shook Jacob's hand.

"Howdy, Jacob? I'm Wes."

Young Jacob Walker said nothing. His eyes were wide open and his mouth gaped in a huge grin.

"Are you a gunfighter?" Jacob rapidly asked.

Wes smiled and let the question die on the young boy's lips.

"This is Elizabeth Thornton, she's the lone passenger on this trip," Wes introduced her to the Walker men.

"How do you do? I'm sorry I'm not more presentable, but it was an eventful journey, I'm afraid." Elizabeth's words were hard evidence of her fatigue.

"Pleased to have you as our guest here at Walker Wells, ma'am," John responded. "Jacob, you help Cletus unhitch the team and get them ready for the night. Miss Thornton and Mr. Payne, if you'll follow me to the house, I'll show you to the washroom. My wife has dinner waiting if you're hungry."

"Wes, would you please get my bag down from the top of the coach. I need to get out of this terrible blouse," Elizabeth asked.

Wes jumped up onto the stage, quickly untied the bag, and jumped back down.

"Go on ahead, partner. Jacob and I will take care of Ringo," Cletus advised.

The three then headed for the house.

"Give me a hand with these harnesses, Jacob," Cletus directed his young assistant.

Jacob obliged and grabbed hold of the two lead horses' bridles while Cletus took to disconnecting the team from the coach.

"That fella a real gunfighter, Mr. Cletus?"

"I'll say he is! We were bein' attacked by some Injuns, and he come ridin' down from the hill guns in both hands and his rein behind his neck firin' away! Took care of them Injuns single-handed, he did! Saved our hides! That's for sure!"

"Golly," Jacob gushed. "Is that his horse?"

"Yes, sir, that's Ringo. Why don't you untie him and put him in the barn for Mr. Payne," Cletus suggested, knowing the boy would relish the opportunity to take care of a real gunfighter's horse.

Jacob ran to the back and untied Ringo, then led him into the barn for water and grain.

John Walker opened the front door and waved Elizabeth and Wes inside. Martha hurried from the kitchen to the front room to greet her guests.

"Martha, this is Elizabeth Thornton and Wes Payne. They're the only two passengers tonight. Cletus is alone. Dave Jennings isn't with him."

Martha introduced herself then directed Elizabeth to the washroom to clean up and change. The two women disappeared into another room.

"Mr. Payne, I hope my boy didn't make you uncomfortable out there. He's not used to seein' anybody other than ole Dave Jennings with Cletus. He sees a big man carrying a couple of guns and, well, he gets a little excited."

Wes offered a brief smile and looked out the window toward the barn. "No problem, sir. I remember how I was when I was his age."

"What kind of trouble did y'all run into out there?"

"Comanches hit the stage twice. First outside Stratford, then again near Cactus. I happened to be near by the first time, then decided to ride along to your place here."

"I've heard about the buffalo hunters havin' some Indian trouble, and a few of the ranchers have blamed some recent rustling on them, but hitting the stage is another thing. Better send word to the fort and let the army know," John stated.

"Yep, heard about the hunters and the rustling, but attacking the stage was new to me. Look, Mr. Walker, I'm not really one of the stage passengers, if it's okay with you, I'll bed down out in the barn for the night."

"No, sir, I won't hear of that. You're welcome here like all stage passengers and employees. I'll make sure my boy doesn't bother you too much."

"Don't worry about that. I'm not much of a storyteller. He'll get bored, I'm sure."

Martha Walker entered the room.

"Looks like that young lady has had a bad time of it," she announced to both men. "Her blouse is ruined, and I don't know about that skirt either." She sighed.

"Mr. Payne—"

"Please, it's Wes," he stated.

"Wes was telling me that the stage was attacked twice by Indians during the trip from Thornton," John informed his wife.

Martha's shoulders slumped, and a frown appeared on her lips.

"That's certainly bad news," she replied. "I'm surprised we haven't been visited by the soldiers yet," she continued.

"Possible they don't know about all this activity," John suggested.

"There hasn't been Indian trouble for a while. Why now?" Martha asked, looking toward Wes.

"Well, ma'am, some of the younger Comanche and Apache have gotten angry over the way the reservations have been handled, and word got out Cochise was killed by soldiers. I reckon they figure they have a right to fight back," Wes said.

"Sounds like you might agree with their behavior, Mr. Payne," Martha stated, making John shift his weight in discomfort at his wife's words and tone.

"Well, ma'am, if my people were being treated the way that they are, yes, I figure I'd fight back too," Wes defended his position.

"I can't say I disagree," John offered. "But I'd hoped we were past all that," he added.

Elizabeth emerged from the washroom with fresh clothes and a bright smile.

"I sure feel better. Thank you, Mrs. Walker. I really needed that!" she exclaimed.

Wes looked hard at Elizabeth. She was radiant. More beautiful than he had thought. It was the first time he had seen her without bloodstains and trail dust.

Martha Walker looked at Wes and saw the admiration in his face.

"Mr. Payne, the washroom is available if you like," she said.

Wes said nothing, just quickly made his way out of the room.

"You look beautiful, my dear," Martha ensured her lady guest. "And it wasn't lost on Mr. Payne either!" she stated with a smile.

Just then the front door flew open, and Jacob came running into the house followed by Cletus.

"Jacob Walker! You slow down, young man!" His mother's voice caused Cletus to quickly remove his hat and stand still.

"Come in, Cletus. Mr. Payne should be finished in a moment and then you can wash your hands before dinner," she informed the old stage driver.

"Um, yes, ma'am," Cletus replied.

John Walker laughed and retrieved a bottle of whiskey from a nearby cabinet.

"I believe a quick drink before dinner is in order. It's been a rough ride today," John pronounced, showing the bottle to Cletus.

John poured whiskey into the three glasses he had placed on a small table in the front room anticipating Wes joining him and Cletus. Wes entered the room as John was returning the bottle to the cabinet.

"Join us in a quick drink before dinner, Wes?" John asked, holding up a glass toward Wes.

"Don't mind if I do," Wes answered, accepting the libation.

The three men raised their glasses in salute to each other and then downed their pick-me-up in unison.

Jacob was silent watching every move Wes made with wide eyes and an open mouth that appeared like it wanted to speak but was incapable.

Martha and Elizabeth were in the kitchen, where Martha was placing her delayed meal on the table. Elizabeth had taken a seat at the table after being told her assistance was not needed by a stern Martha Walker.

"You men come on and eat this food I've been trying to keep warm all evening," Martha demanded.

The four men promptly responded and sat down at the big oak table that John had built himself about five years prior.

"Cletus Bradley! I didn't see you wash them hands! God knowns what they've been into this day!" Martha bellowed at her regular guest.

Cletus leaped to his feet and hustled toward the washroom to take care of his business.

"Jumpin' grasshoppers! Fightin' Indians all day and now this!" he exclaimed as he headed for the door.

Everyone laughed and dug into their meal.

After dinner, the men settled into the front room for a post-meal drink and cigars that John had saved for a special occasion. Martha, Elizabeth, and Jacob, after a brief dispute, cleaned the table and kitchen in preparation for breakfast the next morning. Martha then showed Elizabeth to her room and announced to the men that it was time to turn in. John showed Wes to his quarters while Cletus headed to his usual cubby near the washroom, and Jacob his place in the loft. Martha extinguished the oil lamp and headed to bed, satisfied her guests were comfortable.

CHAPTER 20

MARTHA RAWLINGS FINISHED CLEANING UP the kitchen, then checked in on Joel, who had been noisily sleeping for several hours. His breathing was irregular, intermittently disrupted by a nasty-sounding cough. Martha looked down on her patient with a frown and wrinkled brow. She was not as optimistic about her patient's condition as his daughter had been when she left. Martha was a hardened woman of the West and had seen plenty of wounded and ill people pass before their time. Joel Thornton had the look of a man that was nearing his end. Martha hoped she was mistaken this time.

Doc Langdon brought his carriage to a halt in front of the Thornton house and tied his horse to the hitching post in front of the porch. Grabbing his bag, he turned and saw the front door opening with a somber-looking Martha Rawlings in the entryway.

"Mrs. Rawlings, good of you to care for my patient," Langdon offered in a high voice meant to be uplifting.

"I just wish I could do something for the man," Martha answered, shaking her head.

Doc Langdon made his way up the steps and into the house, removing his hat and placing it on a hook next to the door.

"Has he taken a bad turn?" Langdon asked, now quiet and concerned.

"Well, I didn't see him initially, but he's having difficulty breathing and is coughing regularly. The color has drained from his face. He doesn't look like the man I saw last week," Martha answered.

"Let's have a look," Langdon said as he walked to Thornton's room. He reached down and felt Thornton's forehead. His touch revealed a fiery surface with beads of sweat doting the once-vibrant man's face.

Keeping his eyes on his patient, Langdon asked Martha to fetch some cool clean water and a towel. Langdon commenced to removing the bandages from Thornton's chest and side. Both were soaked with blood and fluid that emitted a pungent odor associated with infection. Langdon cleaned the wounds and attached fresh clean bandages over the ghastly injuries.

Martha returned with a pan of water and a clean towel. Langdon wiped his patients face and chest, attempting to cool the heated skin. Thornton coughed and woke, jerking his body and head, startled by Langdon staring down at him.

"Hey, Doc, you startled me," Thornton said, eyes wide open now, seeing Martha Rawlings standing behind his physician. "Well, looks like I have an audience. Hello, Martha, what are you doing here?" Thornton asked his neighbor.

"I told that daughter of yours that I would watch over you while she ran off to find that gunfighter Ben Chance!" Martha couldn't hold back her angst over Thornton's decision to send his daughter off on a dangerous journey.

Thornton forced a smile and looked at Doc Langdon.

"Seems my request of Elizabeth was not favorable to my neighbor," he stated.

Doc Langdon met Thornton's smile with one of his own.

"Well, sometimes women don't quite understand the decisions we men make."

"Oh!" Martha Rawlings huffed, spun, and left the room in a pout.

Thornton and Langdon both let out with laughter, which was cut short by Thornton violently coughing and wincing. Langdon opened his bag and withdrew a syringe of morphine.

"That really necessary, Doc?" Thornton asked.

"I don't have much of this, so I only use it when it's really necessary. Joel, I'll be honest with you. Your chest will heal fine, but this one in your side…"

"I know, Fred," Thornton cut in. "I'm thinkin' I'm not gonna make it this time. That's why I need Chance to find the heard and any money that's left. Elizabeth is going to need that money when I'm gone. I had hoped to send Mose, but those bastards got him. Didn't have the cash to hire out a messenger, so I did what I thought was right."

"Doesn't matter now, she's on her way. I just hope she gets back here in time."

"Don't worry, Fred. I'm not ready to go just yet. Something about that Ryker I need to talk to Chance about. Something was wrong, just can't put my finger on it yet."

Langdon sent the morphine into Thornton's arm.

"I'll be back out tomorrow to change the bandages. Sleep as much as you can."

Langdon stood and closed his eyes. Thornton hadn't called him Fred since his arrival three years ago. He feared his patient and friend had decided this was it. Hard to treat a patient who was giving up the fight. He turned and closed the door behind him. Martha was rocking in a chair in the den knitting some kind of garment.

"I'm sorry, Doctor, but him sending that girl off just wasn't necessary," she reasoned.

"I know it appears that way, Martha, but he had his reasons. I believe she'll be all right and a better, if not stronger woman when she returns. Do you need anything before I go? I'll be back tomorrow afternoon to change the bandages and see how he's doing."

"No, sir. The house is stocked quite nicely. Moses Barber was a good hand. Took good care of Joel Thornton and this house. I miss his colorful conversation," Martha admitted, wiping a tear from her eye with the corner of whatever she was knitting.

"Very well then. I'll be on my way. I need to stop over to the Henderson place and check on Mrs. Henderson. She's about to have that baby any day now."

"I saw Jack Henderson in town last week. He said she was tired of carrying that child without using her arms!" Martha laughed.

"I'm not surprised!" Langdon lifted his hat from its hook. "I'll let myself out, Martha," he called out then shut the heavy door behind him. Langdon stopped on the front porch and lit the lantern. The light brought the blood-stained planks into view.

Fred Langdon wasn't a violent man, but he had been out West long enough to understand the fact that violence was a way of life for many men. Why it had come to his friend's ranch at this time, he didn't know, but he admitted to himself that he was looking forward to Ben Chance's arrival. If Chance was half the man he had heard about, this Ryker fella was in for all he could handle.

Something about that Ryker I need to talk to Chance about. Something's wrong, just can't put my finger on it yet. Thornton's words went through Langdon's mind.

What did he mean by that?

Langdon untied his horse and stepped up into his carriage.

Yep, sure will be interesting when Chance gets here, he thought before snapping the reins and heading for the Henderson place.

CHAPTER 21

THE MOONLIGHT ALLOWED RYKER TO see his riders herding what appeared to be a few hundred cattle and another fifty horses. Ryker let out a yelp and spurred his horse on to catch up to his fellow bandits. Along with the cash in his saddlebag, he had scored bigger than he ever thought possible. Get the herd back into No Man's Land, then look to sell the horses to anyone heading west to Colorado, Nevada, or beyond. They'd fetch a better price from the miners than any of the cowhands heading north to the rail lines.

Blackie Gillum was calling out orders to the thieves-turned-cowhands when Ryker rode up to him.

"Any idea on the head count yet?" Ryker asked.

"Not yet, but I'm guessin' close to five hundred cows and another fifty or so horses."

"Better take than I thought," Ryker added.

"Yep, good of Thornton to have his main herd in the north pasture for us." Blackie laughed. "Made it too easy to take 'em. I reckon they'll send out a party after us, huh?"

"Yeah, I figure it'll take way too long to do any good though. By the time Thomas gets back from Stratford and finds out what happened, we'll be movin' the herd into the territory and sold most of the horses."

"Figure on sellin' 'em to the miners?"

"Yep, get better price than from the cowhands. We'll keep a dozen or so for the next drive that passes. We'll move over the border then head 'em into the gulch over by Carrizo Canyon. Plenty of water and grass there," Ryker stated. "We'll take a head count and camp for the night."

"Why you keepin' a dozen horses?" Blackie asked, concerned over lost money.

"Been told to hang on to that many, that's why!" Ryker howled.

"Been told by who?"

"Never mind. I have it all taken care of. You and the boys just get the herd over to the Carrizo and wait. I gotta go meet the boss. I'll be back tomorrow."

Ryker and his sixteen crude cowhands pushed their prize across the bone-dry prairie, kicking up a powder cloud reminiscent of an Oklahoma dust storm. After moving the herd into the canyon, Ryker met with Gillum.

"Stay here tonight, then head out in the morning. Don't wait for me. I'll catch up later in the day," Ryker advised then headed back south.

Gillum watched until Ryker faded into the night. He knew who they were working for but didn't like Ryker keeping secrets from him. If there was another plan, he wanted to know about it. Gillum had an uneasy feeling about this job, and his feeling was rarely wrong.

This ain't gonna play out like planned, he thought.

Grateful for the view of the land, compliments of the moon's efforts, Ryker kept a quick pace. He looked forward to counting the money. That was not part of the bargain he had agreed to. Nor were the horses. That meant more money than he had thought. Along with everyone looking for Jack Ryker, and not him, this venture was working out really well.

Now I just have to get rid of the herd, he thought.

This meeting should go a long way to accomplishing that. Then all he had to worry about was a posse from Thornton.

How much can a few men do? Ryker laughed to himself. It won't be enough—that much he was certain. He cut to the west and slowed his horse. The meeting place wasn't that far now. No reason to rush. He took the opportunity to think about taking care of any posse that might come after them. He figured they wouldn't just rush him and his boys.

Too many of us for that, he reasoned. *We'll ambush 'em. I'll find a good spot along the way and leave a couple of boys to take care of him and his men before they catch us. Yep, ambush.* He couldn't believe he hadn't thought of it earlier. He noticed a large group of trees up ahead. *Good place to stop for the night and count money,* he thought.

After securing his horse, he built a small fire then opened the saddlebag. There were fifteen stacks of greenbacks, each wrapped in a nice brown paper band. He saw that each stack contained $10 banknotes. The first stack held fifty banknotes. He wasn't sure, but he guessed the stack was $500 worth of greenbacks. If each stack was the same, that would be fifteen stacks of $500. He counted a second, then third stack. Each was the same, $10 banknotes and fifty greenbacks. He wasn't sure how much he had, but he knew it was thousands.

He thought for a moment. *Who saw me take these out of the safe? Blackie for sure. Baines? No, he left the house. Only Blackie knew of the money for sure. Good.* He'd only need to give Blackie a couple of stacks and keep the rest for himself. He returned the money to the saddlebag and tucked it under his saddle near the fire. After checking his pistol and rifle, he leaned back against the saddle and closed his eyes.

Ambush the posse, if one was even coming, and get rid of the herd as quick as possible. He'd report that to the boss tomorrow. He reached into his mouth and hooked a finger behind his chaw of tobacco and pulled it out. He threw it into the fire and watched it burn for a minute. A cloud passed in front of the moon, extinguishing its light. The last flicker of the fire disappeared, sending a cloak of darkness over the camp. Ryker closed his eyes and smiled before drifting off to sleep.

CHAPTER 22

THE SUN HAD DIPPED BEHIND the western peaks of the Guadalupe Mountains and was replaced by a bright, near full moon. The mountaintops looked like a black iron wedge against the night sky. Canyon Creek had settled down. A few riders were moving up and down Main Street with most of the wagons finding their night's destination. Danner could hear piano music coming from the saloon with a splash of laughter now and again. He swiped a match against his gun belt and lit the oil lamp mounted to the left of the door of the marshal's office. The flickering flame illuminated the entire narrow porch in a low glow of yellow light.

So far, so good, Danner thought of his first night as a Canyon Creek lawman. He leaned up against the door frame and scanned the town. To his left, he noticed a woman carrying a basket making her way across the street from near the general store. Danner wasn't sure, but she appeared to be the same girl that handed him the basket of bread after he had left the Sundown earlier in the day. Like it or not, he was about to have a visitor. As she came closer into view, Danner stepped forward toward the railing that rimmed the office porch.

"Good evening, Mr. Danner," the young lady announced.

"Good evening, ma'am," Danner replied, removing his hat. Danner confirmed it was the same girl that had offered up baked goods earlier. She was beautiful with dark features and hair to match. Her lips were painted bright red, and she wore a silver roped necklace around her slender neck.

"I'm at a disadvantage, ma'am. You know my name, but I'm yet to attain yours."

"I'm sorry, I'm Delores Loman. My parents own the general store here in town," she replied, nodding her head toward the store.

"I asked Miss Rachel about you this afternoon. I hope you don't mind. I thought you might be hungry, so my mother and I made up a basket for dinner." She held up the basket as Danner stepped to the stair where Delores Loman was standing.

"I'm very grateful to you and your mother," Danner answered, accepting the dinner basket. I hadn't given much thought to eating with everything that has happened today," he explained.

Delores Loman said nothing, just smiled.

"Actually, I'll trade this basket for the one you gave me this afternoon." Danner turned and began to step into the office when he stopped and looked back at his visitor. "Would you like to step inside?" he asked.

"I'll just wait here on the porch, if that's okay?" she replied, brushing her raven-black hair back and stepping up onto the entryway.

Danner smiled and quickly stepped inside. A hasty glance around the room led to his target sitting unassuming on a small table in the corner behind the hot stove. Danner snatched up the empty basket and swiftly returned to his guest on the porch.

"Here you go, Miss Loman," Danner stated as he handed the basket to her. The exchange caused their hands to touch.

"Oh!" Delores shouted, causing Danner to pull his hand back with lightning speed. Delores looked down, her shoulders twitching.

"Have a good evening, Mr. Danner," she called as she turned and ran across the street toward the store. Danner watched the girl run all the way until he heard the front door slam shut.

Interesting, he thought. Danner's preoccupation with his evening visitor was abruptly shattered by the sound of several horses galloping down the street. The moon wasn't quite full but provided enough light for him to see five riders slowing their mounts as they entered the town to his right. Danner stepped back into the doorway out of the oil lamp's illumination and watched the five men ride past. Three older bearded men were in the lead with a couple of younger cowhands following two horse lengths behind. All appeared armed. None appeared to be the outlaw type. Nevertheless, Danner decided to follow his new visitors and confirm his observations.

Choosing to leave his horse at the office, Danner walked down the street close to the businesses on the same side of the street as the marshal's office. As expected, all five riders stopped at the saloon, tied their horses in front, then brushed through the swinging doors. The first thing Danner noted was that the piano music did not stop when the cowboys walked in. A good sign. Next, a couple of locals came out of the same swinging doors under their own power. Another good sign.

"Mr. Danner!"

Danner looked over his shoulder to see Doc Carson approaching from the middle of the street.

"Hello, Doc. How are things?" replied Danner.

"Well, I was hoping you could tell me," Carson said with a chuckle.

"So far, so good as far as I can tell, sir," was Danner's jovial response.

"Glad to hear it. I'm on my over to the Sundown to check on our boy Chance. Care to join me?"

"I'll be along in a few minutes. Just want to check the Creek Bed and make sure Dakota doesn't need me," Danner advised.

"Very well, I'll see you later," Carson stated, not stopping to say anything further.

Danner approached the Creek Bed, stopping briefly to look in through the window before entering. The place was hopping with a combination of range riders, cowhands, and those who appeared to be locals by the way they were dressed. Several girls in bright-colored dresses were making their way from table to table looking for a drink or a client. Danner hadn't seen them the night before and wondered briefly why. After a deep breath, a glance down to the badge on his vest, and hand checks on each of his Russians, newly minted deputy marshal Luxton Danner swung open the Creek Bed doors and walked inside.

At that moment, Doc Carson was entering the Sundown Hotel where Rachel was wiping the top of the big oak desk that served as the welcoming station for her guests. A bright smile welcomed the clinician, who mirrored her warm greeting.

"Good evening, Doctor. How are you?" Rachel asked.

"Just fine, Rachel. How is our favorite patient doing?"

Rachel exchanged her smile with a frown.

"I don't know what to do with that man!" she exhaled. "He has been alternating between kind and callous for the last several hours, and I finally told him that if he knew what was really good for him, he would settle down or he would find himself sleeping over at the jail!"

Doc Carson laughed and headed for the staircase. "I take that as a very good sign," he proclaimed.

Carson ascended the stairs, made a sharp right turn at the top of the staircase, and headed for Chance's room. A door opened at the end of the hall, and a short man dressed in a brown suit and bowler hat stepped out, then closed and locked the door.

"Good evening, sir," the round-faced man said as he approached Carson.

"Good evening," Carson replied and stepped aside, allowing the man to pass.

The man stopped and removed his hat. "Excuse me, sir, but could you tell me if there will be a good game at the saloon tonight? I'm new in town and quite enjoy a good game of poker when I can find one."

"I should think so. There seems to be a large crowd over at the Creek Bed tonight. I would guess there'd be at least one, maybe two," Carson answered.

"Very good. Thank you," the squeaky-voiced man answered then went about his way.

Carson knocked on the door.

"Who is it?" was the crotchety answer to Carson's knuckle rap.

"Doc Carson," was the simple response before Carson opened the door and let himself in to find Chance sitting up in bed with a gun in his hand.

"You oughta know better than to knock on a man's door!" Chance hollered.

"I didn't know there was another way," Carson said bluntly, setting his bag on the chair next to the bed.

"Aw, I'm sorry, Doc. I'm just not used to being bedridden, I guess."

"How you feeling?"

"Considering I have a hole in my hip the size of a shot glass, okay."

"Let's take a look at that shot glass."

Doc Carson helped Chance over onto his side and removed the thick bandage that was no longer lily white, but various colors of red. Carson plucked a bottle of alcohol from his bag and opened it.

"This is gonna sting," Carson understated as he poured the antiseptic onto a gauze pad. Carson pressed the soaked pad against the stitched wound, eliciting a grumble from his patient. "Looks pretty good, all things considered. How's the pain?"

"I'll deal with it—when can I get up and move around?"

Doc Carson leaned back. Carson's face was stoic. No squint, smile, frown, or glare.

"I'll just say this. You should stay in bed as long as you can stand it and off your feet as much as possible after that. I wouldn't be too anxious to ride a horse either. The longer you give that hip an opportunity to heal, the better off you'll be. The town seems to be in good hands with this young fella Danner."

"I've been lucky. Been winged a time or two, thrown by a couple of horses I was breakin' in, but I never been laid up like this. I must be losing my touch."

"Nonsense, you were bushwhacked by those fellas. Who in their right mind is gonna beat up Davey Garcia and steal his money in the middle of the day? It was like they wanted to get into it with you. That's what everybody's saying. It was like an ambush."

Chance sat up straight and peered ahead, lowering his brow in the process.

"I didn't think of that, Doc. It doesn't make sense, does it? Why would they want to tangle with the marshal?"

Carson shrugged his shoulders and finished tying on the fresh bandage. "Maybe it wasn't the marshal, but you. Try and get some sleep. I don't think there'll be any trouble in town tonight." Doc Carson retrieved his bag and headed for the door.

"Doc," Chance called after him.

Carson stopped with his hand on the doorknob and looked over his shoulder.

"You really think Danner is okay? Damn guy has only been in town a couple of days."

"Yep, no doubt in my mind. Take it easy, Ben." Carson closed the door behind him and headed down the hall.

CHAPTER 23

E LIZABETH WOKE TO THE CROWING of a rooster outside her window announcing the break of dawn. The sun's warm rays were penetrating the room via clear panes of glass above her head. For a glorious moment, the weight of her journey lifted from her shoulders, allowing her to soak in the sounds and smells of a new day. Her senses alerted her to the aroma and echoes of biscuits, bacon, and eggs cooking up in the kitchen. A feeling of guilt quickly passed through her as she felt she should be helping in the kitchen. She heard Cletus announce that the team was hitched and ready to go as soon as breakfast was finished. That announcement brought the motivation to get up and prepare for the day.

Wes followed Cletus into the house with Jacob fresh on his heels.

"Dad!" Jacob eagerly gulped. "Wes says he's been to Mexico and the mountains in Colorado!"

"Take it easy, son, and leave Mr. Payne alone," his father reminded the boy.

"That's all right, it's been quite a while since anybody has been interested in anywhere I've been," Wes assured his host.

"Look! Wes gave me this pouch he got from a real Indian!" Jacob gushed, showing his prize to his father. John Walker looked at Wes, who immediately qualified his gift to his young admirer. "Only if your mother and father approve, Jacob," Wes explained.

John Walker glanced at his wife, who nodded in approval.

"Okay, son, make sure you thank Mr. Payne," John reminded his impressionable boy.

"Oh, he has many times already," Wes assured.

"Come and sit down at the table," Martha announced to her guests, which included a freshly prepared Elizabeth entering the kitchen from her room.

"Good morning everyone, I'm sorry to be the last one to the table," Elizabeth offered, mildly embarrassed.

"Nonsense, I told the men to be quiet and let you sleep a little extra this morning," Martha advised.

"How long will it take to get to Canyon Creek today?" Elizabeth asked anyone who might know.

"We should be there about noon or so," Cletus spoke up. "That's if we leave pretty quick, that is," he added.

Breakfast went quick as did the hugs and farewell speeches. Before the sun had cleared the distant hilltops, Cletus was snapping his team into action, and the stagecoach roared out of Walker Wells on its way to Canyon Creek under the watchful eye of Wes, who had decided he would stay with the stage until it arrived safely in Canyon Creek. Wes kept a good distance in front of the coach, scouting the trail ahead.

After about an hour, Cletus slowed the team to rest, allowing Wes to ride back to the coach with his scouting report.

"Nothing I can see for miles, Cletus," was music to the old reinsman's ears.

"We could use a humdrum trip after yesterday!" Cletus hollered above the clangs and slaps of the team's hames and lines.

"Bring her to a stop and I'll ride along for a bit," Wes stated. Cletus pulled gently on the reins and brought the coach to a rest while Wes tied Ringo to the rear boot.

"All okay, Elizabeth?" Wes asked, poking his head into the window.

"Just fine, Mr. Payne," she replied, gliding her hands down her skirt in an attempt to smooth the wrinkles.

Wes jumped up into the shotgun seat, sliding his Winchester into the scabbard mounted on the box. Cletus snapped the team back into action and headed south.

Another hour passed with the only conversation being that of Cletus with himself, occasionally mumbling under his bushy mustache. Wes had leaned back with arms crossed, having tipped his hat down over his eyes for protection from the beating sun. Cletus slowed the coach down, then stopped altogether.

Wes looked up and scanned the area.

"Anything wrong, Mr. Bradley?" Elizabeth asked, popping her head out the right window.

"No, ma'am, just restin' the horses for a spell. You can get out and stretch yer legs if you like."

"Thank you, I believe I will." Elizabeth opened the door and stepped down onto the dusty rut that passed for a road.

"Don't stray off the path too far, ma'am. Them rattlers can get up on ya perty quick," Cletus warned. Elizabeth quickly looked around her feet then walked to the back of the stage, where Wes was untying Ringo and getting some water for him and his mount.

"Drink?" Wes asked, extending the ladle of water to Elizabeth.

"Yes, please. How long until we reach Canyon Creek?" she asked.

"Less than an hour, I'd say," Wes answered, looking down the trail as if he could see their destination.

"What will you do when we arrive?" Elizabeth asked with a wisp of hesitation in her voice.

"I'll check and see if there's an outfit I can join heading north to the railhead. If not, I'll decide what else to do then. I'm guessin' you'll be in good hands with Ben Chance," Wes flatly stated.

"Yes, I'm sure I will."

"Okay, you two, let's get under way!" Cletus yelled out.

Wes opened the door and helped Elizabeth back into the coach, then swung up onto Ringo.

"I'll ride up ahead the rest of the way, Cletus," he barked as he galloped down the trail.

"Well, what's got into him?" Cletus mumbled. "Aaah," he then let out a cackle and cracked his whip.

Comin' to the end of the line with the young lady, he thought.

A short time later Cletus saw the edge of town sprouting up like bluebonnets in a field.

"Canyon Creek dead ahead!" Cletus hollered loud enough for Elizabeth to hear. Glancing out the window through the endless cloud of dust, she could see the town her father had ordered her to. A sudden sick feeling came over her. Her heart began to race and her stomach fluttered as though it was filled with butterflies that were trying to escape.

What if Ben Chance wasn't there? What if her father had been wrong and he was unable or unwilling to return to Thornton with her? What if? She stopped her thoughts right there. If her father said Ben Chance was in Canyon Creek and he would help them, then he would be there and help decide what to do. She peered down the road and saw Wes riding tall in the saddle, leading the way. *Besides, if Ben Chance isn't available, I'll hire Wes to return to Thornton with me,* she thought. *He wouldn't say no, would he?*

The stagecoach rumbled on, gliding over the improved road leading into Canyon Creek's overland station.

CHAPTER 24

THE RANDALL STAGE, SCARRED FROM its journey, roared to a halt in front of the Canyon Creek stage office, bringing with it a cloud of red dust the size of a buffalo stampede. Cletus tied off his line on the tall wooden brake lever and jumped down off the box like a man twenty years younger. The hostlers rushed to the team and began their work. Elmer "Bart" Barton, the station keeper, stepped out of the office, journal in hand, writing as he approached Cletus and company.

"'Bout time, ya old whip!" Barton called out at Cletus, extending a right hand for a friendly shake. "Twelve thirty-five, not bad at all," Barton followed up, not waiting for a response.

"Boy, if you knew what we'd been through on this one, you'd be thankful we's here at all!" Cletus's answered his old friend.

"Had some trouble, I see," Barton said in a low, more serious tone as he inspected his peppered carriage.

"A couple of Injun attacks, Bart. Killed one of my passenger's short time outta Thornton," Cletus explained. He opened the door to allow Elizabeth's exit. "Weren't fer this young lady's talents with a six-shooter and that fella there, I'd a lost both 'em," he added, nodding toward Wes. "By the way, speakin' of this fella, he's owed shotgun pay since Dave Jennings never showed up," Cletus informed his boss.

"No," Wes announced, holding up both hands, scarred palms forward in a stop sign. "I told Cletus that wasn't necessary as I was already headin' this way."

"That's mighty nice of ya, stranger, but I'll put you down for guard duty pay and square up with ya right quick. Don't leave," Barton demanded. He then turned his attention to Elizabeth and stood straight with his journal clutched to his chest in his left hand. "Elmer Barton, ma'am. I'm the station keeper here. Welcome to Canyon Creek. I'll make arrangements for your luggage. Shall I have it taken over to the hotel?"

"Pleased to meet you, Mr. Barton." Elizabeth was again pressing her right hand against her skirt attempting to smooth the creases while holding her carpetbag with the left. "Yes, I would appreciate it if you could have my large case brought to the hotel. It's the only one in the compartment in the back," she added.

"Very well, it will be taken care of immediately," Barton advised. He then snapped his fingers toward one of the hostlers and pointed to the back of the coach. "Take, Miss…" Barton paused a moment and looked at Elizabeth.

"Oh, I'm sorry! My manners have left me on this trip! I'm Elizabeth Thornton, from Thornton, Texas," she exclaimed.

Barton smiled. "Take Miss Thornton's bag over to the Sundown and leave it with Mrs. Brennen at the front desk." The young hostler circled around the coach, removed the brown leather case from the boot, and scurried across the street to the Sundown Hotel, where Adeline was watching the excitement from the open front door.

"Mr. Barton, can you direct me to the marshal's office? I would like to speak to Marshal Ben Chance as soon as possible," Elizabeth asked.

"Yes, ma'am, the marshal's office is down toward the end of town, but you'll find Ben Chance over at the hotel. If you need the marshal, we got a young deputy watchin' the town these days," Barton explained.

"No, no, I just need to see Mr. Chance, thank you."

"Very well, if you'll excuse me," Barton stated, then turned his attention to Cletus and Wes.

"Bart, this here is Wes Payne," Cletus announced while Wes and Barton shook hands.

"Glad to know you, Mr. Payne. Please come inside so I can issue you payment." Barton then led Cletus into the office as Wes stepped toward Elizabeth.

"I'll be around for bit if you need me." Wes tipped his hat, then walked into the office without another word.

Elizabeth paused, fighting the urge to follow Wes into the office. Thinking better of it, she turned and walked over to the Sundown Hotel for her long-anticipated meeting with Ben Chance.

Adeline greeted Elizabeth as she stepped up onto the Sundown's front porch.

"Hello, welcome to the Sundown Hotel," Adeline recited what her mother had instructed her to say.

"Good afternoon, I'm Elizabeth. What's your name?"

"Adeline. My mommy owns the hotel. I can take you to her."

"That would be very nice."

Elizabeth followed her escort into the hotel lobby, where Rachel was working behind the desk.

"Mommy, this is Elizabeth. She just came on the stagecoach."

Rachel stepped around the desk and brushed a lock of red hair away from her face.

"Good afternoon, I'm Rachel Brennen, the owner of the hotel."

"Good afternoon, I'm Elizabeth Thornton. I've traveled from Thornton to see Mr. Ben Chance. It's terribly important."

Rachel's smile disappeared. She peered at Elizabeth.

"I don't mean to intrude, but Ben is up in his room resting. I'm a close friend. May I ask the purpose of your visit?" Rachel asked, a bit embarrassed and uneasy.

Elizabeth paused and sensed something was wrong.

"Well, my father requested that I travel here to ask Mr. Chance for help. You see, my father is an old friend of Mr. Chance, and he is in need of his assistance right away," Elizabeth explained without going into detail.

"I'll be happy to show you upstairs to Ben's room, but I don't believe he will be of much assistance right now. Ben was shot yesterday and he cannot walk."

Elizabeth gasped, placing her hand over her mouth, then collapsed into a nearby chair, moving both hands over her eyes in an attempt to keep from crying. Rachel knelt before Elizabeth and placed her hand on Elizabeth's arm in an attempt to comfort her newly arrived guest.

"What is it, dear? What has happened? You can tell me," she pleaded, feeling responsible for breaking bad news.

Elizabeth gained her composure, sat up, and took a deep breath. She looked into Rachel's eyes and believed she could trust her with her story.

"Two days ago, my father, Joel Thornton, was shot by outlaws who stole our cattle, horses, and money. My father was wounded badly and insisted I come to Canyon Creek and tell Mr. Chance. My father was a United States marshal with Mr. Chance many years ago. With Mr. Chance's assistance, I hoped to find the men responsible and recover as much of our property as possible. We couldn't have known about Mr. Chance being shot. Now, I'm uncertain what to do."

Rachel stood up and thought for a moment. Danner was upstairs now with Ben. They would know what to do.

"Okay, I'll go up with you and see Ben. He'll know what to do," Rachel assured her visitor.

Elizabeth reached the top of the staircase with Rachel close behind. She turned and saw Danner standing outside an open doorway.

"Oh my," she quipped.

Danner, hearing Elizabeth's comment, spun his head and locked eyes with the young woman who would become his damsel in distress. Elizabeth stopped and smiled, transforming her already striking appearance from lovely to glamorous.

Danner turned, his right spur catching the back of his left boot as he attempted to remove his hat. Stumbling forward, the gray Stetson glanced off his fingertips and landed on the floor.

Elizabeth let out a girlish giggle, the kind a child makes when they're amazed by a shiny object. Danner quickly retrieved his hat, stood straight, and returned his visitor's smile. Elizabeth mimicked Danner's snap to attention and proceeded to walk calculatingly toward the tall rock-jawed cowboy with shoulders as wide as the hallway. Stopping a stride away from Danner, she formally announced herself.

"Good afternoon, sir. I'm Elizabeth Thornton, and I was told that I could find Mr. Ben Chance up here."

"Luxton Danner, at your service, ma'am," Danner declared, bowing slightly at the waist. "I'm currently the marshal of Canyon Creek," he added.

Elizabeth's bright expression quickly faded to a dark frown and wrinkled brow.

"I'm sorry, I was informed that Ben Chance was the marshal here," she stated in a low, defeated voice.

"Yes, ma'am, but…"

"What the hell's going on out there, Danner?" Chance yelled from his medicinal prison.

Danner peered into Chance's room. "There's a young lady here to see you, Chance," Danner explained.

"Well then, send her in already," was the gruff command.

Danner stepped aside and waved Elizabeth toward the open door. Elizabeth took a deep breath and stepped forward into the doorway and gazed upon her anticipated savior. Instead of seeing the mountain of a man she had envisioned during her journey, see witnessed a bedridden patient who appeared ill and weak. Optimism rushed out of her like a wild mustang fleeing a corral. Her shoulders slumped and her gaze dropped to the floor. She looked back at Rachel, tears welling up in her blue eyes.

Chance sat up in bed, straightened his shoulders, and made himself look as strong as possible, noting his visitor's obvious disappointment in his appearance.

"What can I do for you, miss?" Chance asked in a loud forceful tone.

Elizabeth reclaimed her composure and looked straight into Chance's eyes. "I'm Elizabeth Thornton, and my father, Joel Thornton, sent me to find you and request your assistance."

Chance met the introduction with a grin as big as Texas. "Elizabeth Thornton, well, I'll be… I haven't seen you since you were a little girl heading for Philadelphia. How's that ole crusty father of yours anyway?"

"Clinging to life the last I saw him. Men came to the ranch, shot Dad, and took the cattle, horses, and money." Elizabeth sighed, holding back tears.

Chance's expression turned dark, his eyes narrowing and grin quickly turning to a frown as he gritted his teeth. "How bad is he?" Chance managed to ask through a clenched jaw.

"Very serious, I'm afraid. He was shot in the side and chest. Dr. Langdon is very concerned. He looked a little better when I left two days ago."

"Who did it?" Chance demanded, leaning forward, burning a hole through his visitor's gaze.

"The man called himself Ryker. Said Dad was an outlaw just like him. Said the only difference was Dad hid behind a badge. That's not true, is it, Mr. Chance!"

Chance looked down at himself, lying in a bed while his friend was clinging to life. Chance knew it was bad if Joel had to send his daughter for help. He grabbed a fistful of bedsheets in each hand. His head spun with flashing thoughts and images of him and Joel Thornton over the years. They had been trail partners, deputy marshals, and most importantly, friends for longer than Chance could remember.

"No, it's not—Danner!" Chance called for his deputy marshal.

Danner stepped into the room from his position at the doorway with Rachel right behind. Chance stopped and looked at Rachel, forcing a thin smile.

"No argument," he directed toward his caregiver. "Take Elizabeth downstairs and get her whatever she needs. Get Doc Carson over here right away!" Chance looked at Elizabeth. "Give me an hour or so, and we'll start back to your father's ranch. Don't worry, your father's the toughest man I ever met. He'll still be kickin' when we get there," Chance assured his anxious messenger. Rachel grabbed Danner's arm.

"I'll take care of Miss Thornton, you get Doc Carson," she ordered.

"Danner!" Chance yelled. "After you see Doc Carson, go over to the livery stable and tell Davey I'll need a buckboard and an extra horse. A small buckboard, not one of the big ones they use for logging. I won't need the extra horse saddled. Rachel, I'll also need a couple days' rations for two."

Danner turned to Rachel and held up three fingers where Chance couldn't see. Rachel let out a sigh of relief and nodded to Danner. She and Elizabeth then left the room. Danner closed the door and turned to see Chance sliding sideways and sitting up on the edge of the bed. Chance winced in pain and took a deep breath.

"I have no inclination to try and stop you, but you really think you can make it with that hip?" Danner asked, knowing the answer.

"You just get Carson over here to bandage this thing up and worry about yourself."

"I'm going with you," Danner announced.

"What! Why! What stake do you have in this?" Chance shouted, forcing himself to stand and gauge his stability.

"I don't have an answer at the moment," Danner replied, then quickly exited the room before Chance could say anything else. Danner was met at the bottom of the staircase by Rachel, whose pressed lips and look of anguish told Danner all he needed to know.

"I know. It'll be all right. The look on Chance's face when she told him her father had been shot was all I needed to see. That hip isn't going to stop him. At least not until he's finished with this Ryker fellow," Danner stated.

"That's what worries me. It's not the hip stopping him, but this Ryker," Rachel replied. "You ever heard of him?" Rachel asked.

"No. Don't know that name. You?"

Rachel shook her head. "Chance hasn't told me much about his past. What I've learned about him has come from others in town or passing through. His reputation has traveled far, I guess."

"You'd have to have been living under a rock to not have heard of Ben Chance and his exploits," Danner acknowledged. "I'll go get Doc Carson," Danner stated and began to hurry past Rachel, who clutched his arm again.

"I'm grateful you're going with him." She smiled then hurried into the kitchen to gather the provisions Chance had requested.

Danner pushed through the front door of the Sundown, wondering what he was getting himself into.

CHAPTER 25

*N*ONSENSE, YOU KNEW WHAT YOU *were getting into when you set out looking for Ben Chance,* Danner corrected himself. *I'm grateful I'm actually needed.* Danner hurried across the street to Doc Carson's place and let himself inside. A bell on the door sounded his arrival. Doc Carson emerged from behind a white curtain hung from the ceiling to the floor.

"Hello, Marshal. What brings you in here this afternoon?" Carson asked in a pleasant tone.

"Doc, I need you to head over to the Sundown and bandage Chance up so he can take a ride," Danner asked.

"A ride? Ben Chance shouldn't be thinking about walking, let alone riding anywhere," Carson blurted.

"I know, but this girl came in on the stage and told Chance about an old buddy that had been shot and all his livestock stolen, and that's all it took for Chance to heal immediately," Danner explained.

Doc Carson frowned and began to hurriedly place items from a shelf into his bag.

"What girl? What old buddy?" Carson demanded as he reached for his spectacles that were resting on his desk.

"Girl's name is Elizabeth Thornton. Her father is Joel Thornton," Danner answered quickly.

Doc Carson stopped and turned to Danner. His face turning pale and emotionless.

"Joel Thornton dead?" Carson asked.

"The girl said he is still alive when she left him a couple days ago. I guess no one knows if he's still alive or not."

Energized by the thought that Thornton might still be alive, Carson snatched up his coat and bag and walked past Danner.

"Let's go, son. If I know Ben Chance, he won't wait long for me."

Danner spun and was right on Doc Carson's heels as they broke through the door onto the street.

"Doc, I gotta go over to the livery stable and get the horses ready, I'll see you in a bit," Danner called to the focused physician, who didn't seem to pay attention. Danner then headed to see Garcia.

Carson came through the front doors of the Sundown like a bull leading a stampede, taking no time for pleasantries from a startled Elizabeth and Rachel. Carson headed up the big staircase then down the hall to his patient's open door.

"Don't give me any back talk, Doc. I need you to wrap this thing up tight. I got business to tend to," Chance hollered at his doctor.

"Settle down, Ben, settle down. I know better than to try and talk sense into ya right now," was Carson's abrupt response. "Get back down on that bed so I can take a look and see what we're dealin' with!" Carson ordered his patient in a don't-mess-with-me tone.

Chance paused then followed orders and leaned back on the bed, exposing his left hip to Carson.

"Sorry, Doc, but I just heard—"

"I know!" Carson interrupted. "Danner told me what happened and to whom."

"Then you know I got no choice. Joel and I go way back. He'd do the same for me."

"I know he would," Carson's mumbled. Carson cut the crimson bandage off Chance's hip and stared into the gaping wound being held together with strained sutures pulling at the surrounding purple flesh. Carson thought for a moment.

No, there's nothing more I can do, he thought. Carson dropped his chin to his chest and rubbed his forehead with a steady hand. *Pressure, direct pressure on the center of the wound would be the best tactic. Pressure would cause pain though. Pain would hinder thought, reflexes, movement. I have no choice. If the wound tears open, he'll bleed to death or succumb to infection. No, no choice.* Carson removed gauze from his bag and molded it into a large white ball. Chance said nothing, just watched Carson's hands.

"Okay, Ben, here's what you need to do. You need to have pressure on this. As much as you can stand. There will be pain, but we can't avoid that. I'm going to place this ball over the wound and then wrap it tight. That will put direct pressure on the opening. Change this bandage every day if you can. Don't let it get too dirty or infection will set in and kill you before you do any good for Thornton."

"I just need a few days, maybe a week, Doc," Chance stated, looking Carson in the eye. "It won't matter after that."

Carson didn't bother to hide his concern. Chance saw the grim look on his friend's face. Carson nodded in agreement and began wrapping his patient's nemesis. No gunslinger would present more of a distraction or hindrance than this mess that was once Ben Chance's left hip.

"There you go, Ben. That's the best I can do," Carson declared.

"Good enough, Doc. Feels better already." Chance chuckled.

"Liar."

Doc Carson gathered his things in silence then stopped at the door.

"I'll expect to see you back here in a couple of weeks. I'll get you healed up then." Carson smiled and left the room.

Danner found Davey Garcia in the livery office.

"How's the head?" Danner asked the diminutive barn owner.

"*Sufrimiento cabeza,*" Garcia replied, rubbing the bandage on his head.

"Maybe some tequila later will help," Danner said, cracking a smile.

"*Si*, yes, maybe later."

"Can you get Chance's horse saddled and ready to go? We'll also need a small buckboard and an extra horse, no saddle," Danner asked.

"Yes, sir. Maybe fifteen minutes or so, *señor.*"

"Good, we'll stop by in about a half hour."

Davy Garcia nodded and disappeared into the back of the stable.

Danner headed back to the Sundown and met Doc Carson on the street in front of the hotel.

"Well, Doc?" Danner asked.

"Keep an eye on him. If he starts with a fever, get him to a doctor as quickly as possible. He should be okay for a few days. I left plenty of antiseptic and clean bandages with Rachel. If the antiseptic runs out, pour whisky on the wound. I'm sure you'll have some of that along. Also, put this in your saddlebag. It's laudanum. It'll help with the pain if you can get him to take some."

Danner accepted the bottle.

"Thanks, Doc. Hope to see you in a couple of weeks," Danner added, then bounded up the steps into the hotel.

Danner was met by Elizabeth, who had washed and changed into a pair of black riding pants and a fresh long-sleeved gray blouse. Her long blond hair was pulled back into a ponytail, exposing a small, solemn, yet bright face highlighted with red lips. Danner stopped and looked closely at Elizabeth for what seemed several minutes.

"Mr. Danner?" Elizabeth asked.

Startled by her words, Danner snapped out of his momentary trance and removed his hat.

"I'm sorry, ma'am, I was, I mean I couldn't help but—"

"Are there no pretty girls in Charleston, Mr. Danner?" Rachel asked with a laugh as she entered the room.

"Yes, ma'am, of course, I just haven't seen—"

"Never mind. Go up and see if that friend of ours can make it down the stairs on his own legs," Rachel instructed.

"I'll make it down just fine, madam!" Chance called out from the top of the staircase.

"Don't you 'madam' me, Ben Chance!" was the rebuttal.

Chance made his way down carrying a bag, which Danner grabbed at the base of the stairway with no objection from Chance. Chance stepped into the room with an obvious limp but no expression of pain on his face.

"Elizabeth, can you drive a buckboard?" Chance asked.

"Yes, sir, no problem. I can also handle a gun, if need be," she added.

"Oh?" Chance tipped his head back in disbelief.

"Yes, I learned to shoot quite well back in Philadelphia and have unfortunately had to prove my skills twice since my return to Texas."

Chance, Danner, and Rachel all leaned in toward Elizabeth.

"What happened?" Chance asked in a curt voice.

Elizabeth looked down to the floor. "I killed one of the men at the ranch and another on the stagecoach when we were being attacked." Rachel stepped in and put her arm around Elizabeth and squeezed lightly, causing Elizabeth to wince in pain.

"What's wrong, my dear?" a startled Rachel queried.

"I was wounded in my right shoulder at the ranch. A bullet cut my arm."

Chance and Danner looked at each other, neither having to verbalize their disbelief.

"Let me take a look at that arm before you go," Rachel demanded and quickly hurried Elizabeth into the washroom near the kitchen.

"Shootin' at a woman, huh," Chance muttered, squeezing the handle of his holstered Colt. "Looks like we're in for a fight, my friend. Sure you still wanna go?"

"Now more than ever."

"That's what I hoped you'd say."

"I'll bring the buckboard up and load the supplies," Danner advised.

"Bring my horse along too. The less I have to walk right now, the better," Chance said, grinning at his fellow gunslinger.

CHAPTER 26

D ANNER MADE HIS WAY DOWN the street where Davey was waiting in front of the livery stable. He had the buckboard hitched up to a fine-looking chestnut plow horse, Chance's tall bay stallion, and a paint tied to the back. The buckboard had three sacks of grain stacked behind the bench with a small wooden keg tied off on the sideboard.

"Everything look good, *señor*?" Davey asked.

"Looks great, Davey."

"I have three sacks of grain and a keg of water."

"Perfect. We'll square up with you when we get back."

"No worries, Mr. Chance has a bill," Davey informed his new customer.

Danner hopped up on the buckboard and snapped the reins, sending the wagon toward the Sundown.

Rachel and Elizabeth returned to the lobby, where Chance was walking back and forth testing his hip.

"Everything okay?" Chance asked.

"I put a fresh bandage on it. It's not too bad," Rachel answered. "How about you?" she asked.

"I'll get along."

The trio heard the buckboard's arrival out front. Danner came in and took up Chance's and Elizabeth's bags, turned, and headed back out without a word.

Elizabeth thanked Rachel and gathered her carpetbag and the two satchels of food that Rachel had prepared. Elizabeth walked to the front door where she was met by Danner, who took the satchels and held the door open for her. The door swung closed, leaving

Rachel and Chance alone in the lobby. Rachel held back tears as she stepped into Chance's arms, burying her face in his chest.

"You come back here, Ben Chance," she said. "I don't know what I'll do if you don't."

Chance uneasily returned the hug, carefully resting his chin on top of Rachel's flowing red hair.

"I'll be back before you know it," Chance said in a firm, confident voice. Rachel took a half step back and looked up at the only man she had ever had feelings for after her husband died. Chance leaned down and kissed her like he had never done before. "I'll see ya, Rach," he added, then turned and limped out the door.

"It's not like that, huh, Chance?" Danner asked, grinning from ear to ear.

"If you know what's good for ya, you'll mind yer own business, kid. Now help me up on my horse."

Elizabeth and Danner shared a laugh as Danner boosted Chance up on his horse.

"I need to pick up my horse and a few things from the jail on the way out," Danner informed his two saddle partners.

Chance looked down the street and saw several mounted riders waiting in front of the jail.

"You expecting company?" Chance asked, pointing down toward the jail.

Danner followed Chance's gaze and noted five mounted riders in front of the marshal's office.

"Nope, no idea what they want," Danner offered.

"Well, let's go see what they're up to," Chance announced then spurred his horse onward. Danner snapped the reins and turned the buckboard around in the street and followed Chance down to the jail.

As Chance approached the five men, he recognized Sam Coleman and one of his foreman with three other cowhands.

"Good afternoon, Sam," Chance greeted the town's cattle baron.

"Good to see you up and about, Ben," Coleman jovially replied. "I didn't know if I'd get to speak with you," he added.

"What can I do for you, Sam?" Ben asked, bringing his horse to a halt in front of Coleman's. Coleman looked past Chance and noted Danner driving the buckboard with a female passenger.

"I heard you might be leaving for bit, so I figured on seeing you off is all."

Chance nodded his head.

"And talk about a new marshal, no doubt."

"Well, Ben, I've got a lot invested in this town, and I need to keep it in order. You understand that, I'm sure."

"I understand you're a rich man and pay a lot of people to make sure you stay that way," Chance replied, catching Coleman off guard.

"Ben! You know I'm an honest man running an honest business. I help keep this town going every way I can!"

"I know, Sam. I guess I'm a little edgy right now. Got a few problems of my own I need to take care of. Do me a favor, get with Doc Carson, Dakota, Loman, and Gibson and have them agree to who the new marshal will be."

"No problem, Ben. I wouldn't have it any other way. You figuring on coming back?"

"Don't know just yet. Maybe, maybe not. Depends on how good me and Danner here are, I reckon."

Chance nodded toward Danner, who had stepped down from the wagon and taken a position on Chance's left flank. Since Chance was right-handed, Danner knew the optimum position was to his non-gun side. Coleman's men also seemed to recognize this and moved accordingly behind their boss.

Coleman looked down at Danner, smiled, and touched the brim of his hat then looked back at Chance.

"Gun trouble, huh?" he asked, tilting his head to the side. "Seems like bad timing with that hip and all. I'll send a couple of my men with you if you like. Might even the odds a bit," Coleman said.

Danner began to speak, but Chance held out his hand and stopped him.

"Thanks, Sam, but that won't be necessary. We'll manage just fine. Don't you have a drive fixin' to get started?"

"Yep, a day or two and I'll be ready to send a herd up north."

"I'm sure you'll need all the men you can get for that. So long, Sam," Chance abruptly stated, signaling Coleman the conversation was over.

"Take care, Ben," Coleman called out as he spurred his horse on, heading into town, his four riders jumping into action without needing to be told.

Chance turned his horse and watched Coleman carefully ride down the street. Danner glanced back then looked up at Chance. Chance's wrinkled brow and narrow eyes indicated that he was in deep thought. Danner waited a moment then spoke up.

"I thought you said Coleman was all right," Danner asked, somewhat uncomfortable with the question.

"I did," Chance said, keeping his eye on Coleman and company. "But that was before these last couple of days."

"What do you mean?" Danner asked.

Chance looked down at Danner. "Get your things out of the office and let's go. We're burning daylight."

Danner ran up the jail steps and disappeared into the office.

Chance turned his attention to his friend's daughter.

"Miss Thornton, I'm going to need you to handle that buckboard off the main road. I know a trail that'll get us to your father's ranch a good half day quicker. It's a little rough, but that wagon should make it. You game for the challenge?"

"Yes, sir, Mr. Chance, I'll do my best," Elizabeth answered.

"Very well, we should be at the campsite I have in mind by tonight. Danner! Let's move!" Chance yelled toward the front door.

On cue, Danner emerged with his rifle, bedroll, and saddlebags, which he quickly tied down on his horse.

"Ready to go, boss!" he hollered as he swung up onto his horse.

"'Bout damn time!" Chance grinned. "Let's go." Chance nudged his bay stallion, and the troop headed north out of Canyon Creek, Chance glancing over his shoulder, wondering if he'd ever see it again.

CHAPTER 27

THE AIR WAS WARM AND the sky crystal clear, signaling another hot and dry day ahead. The drought had lasted what seemed like an eternity with the lack of rain, causing crops and cattle herds to suffer like never before. Chance's trail was as rough as advertised, but passable. The ground was hard and cracked. The clumps of talus and bunchgrass along the way begged for water. Since the trail was not heavily used, there was little dust kicking up from the hooves and wheels, which pleased both Chance and Danner as neither wanted their presence detected. Both knew they were prime targets for outlaws or the small bands of Indians raiding the area.

Chance led the way, keeping his horse at an easy gait, allowing Elizabeth to keep up with the wagon. Danner rode behind the wagon, keeping close watch to the rear. After about ninety minutes, Chance stopped under the shade of a large cottonwood tree and dismounted. His hip was weak, and he buckled under the immense pain, catching himself by his saddle horn. Elizabeth drew back on the reins and stopped under the relief of the shade.

"Are you okay, Mr. Chance?" she asked, seeing for herself that he was not.

"Just a little stiff," Chance replied in a low voice. "Another thing, don't call me 'mister.' Just Ben or Chance will do," he said, forcing a smile. "I feel old enough without being a mister."

"Very well then. It'll be Ben from now on," Elizabeth assured. Ben nodded in approval then sat down on a large rock looking down the trail, watching Danner's arrival.

"Anyone following?" Chance asked.

"Yep, near as I can tell, it's a single rider keeping a good distance back," Danner replied.

"You sure it's a single rider?" Ben asked, removing his hat and wiping beads of sweat from his face with a dark blue bandana.

"Hard to tell with this rock-hard ground, but I think so. I heard a whinny not long after we started, but haven't seen any dust to confirm.

"Not much dust when yer ridin' on rock," Chance declared, swinging his hat across the trail edge. "We'll rest here a few minutes then ride on," Chance advised.

Danner swung down from his horse and tied him off on a sagebush. Elizabeth pulled hard on the brake lever then stood to get down from the wagon. Danner quickly moved around the rear of the wagon to assist Elizabeth, who accepted his outstretched arms. Finding a clear spot on the side of the trail, she stood and leaned against a branch from the cottonwood. The branch reached out toward the trail like the inviting arm of a friend. Danner removed his bandana and soaked it with water from his canteen. He offered it to Elizabeth, who slowly wiped her face and neck. The heat had caused her to sweat like she had never experienced before. Patches of soaked material dotted her blouse, causing her embarrassment.

"I'm sure I look just awful," she flatly stated. Chance said nothing as he moved his hip in an attempt to quell the pain.

"Not at all," Danner offered with a smile. "Now that fella over there, he looks awful," Danner said, trying not to laugh too hard as he nodded toward Chance. Elizabeth giggled.

"You should look this good when you're my age and a bullet in yer hip!" Chance called back in defense of himself. "All right, enough of this, grab a drink and let's get going," Chance ordered. He carefully stepped into the stirrup, grabbing his saddle horn with one hand and the cantle with the other, then heaved himself up onto the saddle, crying out in pain. Neither Danner nor Elizabeth spoke a word. Danner helped Elizabeth onto the wagon then swung up onto his horse.

Chance started down the trail, first walking his horse then picking up to a canter. Elizabeth reined her horse on, keeping the wagon on pace. Danner stayed further back than he had, constantly checking over his shoulder, wondering who might be following them. He was surprised a bit that Chance had not had more to say about being followed. It was as if he expected it and was not terribly worried. Danner admitted to himself that he would not be as concerned if Elizabeth was not along for the ride. He couldn't wait to get to the Thornton ranch and leave her safely behind.

The sun had crossed its pinnacle and was beginning its descent to the western horizon when Chance pulled up and stopped abruptly. The trail had led upward on the edge of a small canyon which Chance was now scanning intently. Elizabeth stopped the wagon about twenty yards behind Chance and waited. Danner spurred his horse and rode past Elizabeth to join Chance.

"What is it?" Danner asked, coming to a stop next to the big man.

"Down on the canyon floor a little north of that dry creek bed," Chance answered, pointing. Danner looked down and saw what had stopped Chance. A small group of riders on horseback were mulling around a cluster of purple sage near the creek bed. A closer look confirmed their suspicion. It was a band of Indians. Ten or twelve mounted on bareback ponies. Danner dismounted, removed his hat, and dropped to his hands and knees, crawling toward the edge of the canyon wall. They were only thirty feet or so up from the summit of the canyon floor. After a brief examination, he returned to Chance, who had backed his horse away from the area to provide concealment.

"Ten or twelve Indians. Can't see if they're armed, but they must be out here this far from any reservation I know of," Danner reported. Chance nodded then motioned to move back toward Elizabeth and the wagon. Elizabeth, sensing danger, had stepped down from the wagon and was keeping her horse quiet by rubbing his mane and head under the bridle. Her father had taught her how to keep her horse quiet when she was a child for times like these.

"There's a small band of Indians down on the canyon floor," Danner whispered to Elizabeth. Chance rode up behind Danner.

"We'll wait here for them to move on before we continue. They may have seen us moving along the trail since it's in the open and we're not very high up. Leave the wagon here."

Danner and Chance dismounted and moved their horses to the opposite side to the trail where they could be hidden in brush and trees. Danner then returned to the edge of the canyon and kept an eye on their uninvited guests. Twenty minutes later the would-be raiding party began heading east toward the opposite side of the expansive gulch. Danner stepped over to where Chance and Elizabeth had taken refuge among sagebrush and snowberry junipers.

"They're headin' east toward the other side of the canyon. I think we're okay now," Danner reported.

"Good, if we pick up the pace a little, we can still make the campsite around sunset," Chance advised.

Moving steadily onward through the snakelike trail, the oppressive heat grew less intense as day turned to evening. Elizabeth was beginning to tire as the wagon seemed to find every bump and rut on the path's surface. At least the sun was beginning to crouch below the spiked peaks to the west and the trail was now mostly covered by a canopy of trees and vines. Chance had ridden further up the trail to scout the area, and Danner was still riding far behind, consumed with whoever was following them. Elizabeth's mind wandered back to the ranch, wondering if her father was alive or dead. She had tried to prepare herself for the worst, knowing that her father's wounds were serious and that he might not recover. The thought of her father's condition filled her memory with images of the day that began so wonderful and ended so horrible. Finding Ben and meeting Danner had soothed her thoughts, but now, feeling alone in the middle of nowhere, her mind rushed back to reality and the purpose of her travels. For a moment, she wished she had never left Philadelphia.

It was getting dark, so Elizabeth had to strain her eyes in order to see Chance stop in the middle of the trail, waiting. Elizabeth brought the wagon to a stop.

"Everything okay, Ben?" she asked.

"Everything is fine. We'll camp just around the bend of the trail. There's a clearing with an underground spring pushing water up to green grass for the horses. We'll wait for Danner here."

After a few minutes, Chance and Elizabeth heard Danner's horse hooves tapping the path's fire-dried surface. Danner rode up next to the wagon without a word.

"We'll camp around the bend for the night," Chance whispered. Danner nodded and waited for Chance to lead the way. A few minutes later an opening appeared on the west side of the trail. Despite the darkness, Elizabeth and Danner could sense the green grass and smell fresh water. The air was clear and filled with lively fireflies that dotted the black landscape with tiny points of light. The cool air embraced Elizabeth, sending a chill down her spine. The horses snorted in agreement with Chance's campsite selection. The crescent moon had sliced a wedge in the dark sky and provided a glimmer of light as Elizabeth brought the wagon to its night's resting place. Chance and Danner dismounted and picketed the horses along the edge of the tree line. Elizabeth stood and stretched before jumping down from the wagon's perch.

"We'll put the campfire between the wagon and the tree line. That'll give us some protection from the trail if we get a visit during the night," Chance advised. After disconnecting the plough horse from the wagon, Danner retrieved some grain and took it to the horses. Chance walked back and forth trying to lessen the pain in his hip. He had not taken any of the laudanum that Doc Carson had given Danner. He was determined to keep away from that poison unless he had no choice.

Danner returned with an armful of wood to start a small fire. Elizabeth gathered the satchels of food Rachel had provided. It wasn't long before Danner had the fire in full flame and Elizabeth a coffeepot brewing. The fire illuminated the three of them, and Elizabeth noticed that Chance looked weak. His face was pale despite the hot sun, and lines cut deep into his cheeks from his sideburns down to his chin. Elizabeth had offered to cook, but Chance had suggested only dried beef and bread for dinner. Elizabeth poured coffee for each of them and returned the pot to the rim of the fire.

"Do you think we'll make it to the ranch tomorrow?" Elizabeth asked Chance. He finished a big gulp of coffee and complimented Elizabeth on her brewing skills.

"Yes, we should make it just before sundown. We'll avoid the towns and cut right across the valley," Chance advised. Danner perked up and looked at Chance.

"Cutting across the valley will expose us to whatever is out there. You think that's the best plan?" Danner asked.

"Nope, it's not the best plan, but we're running out of time. Every day we lose lets those sons o' bitches get rid of Joel's stock. We can't let that happen," Chance explained. Danner nodded in agreement, then got about setting up his bedroll and saddle.

"Elizabeth, you'll sleep in the wagon. Danner and I will take turns on watch tonight from down here. Should be a quiet night," Chance offered in his best comforting tone. Elizabeth smiled and finished her coffee.

"I'm heading to bed right now. Shall I leave the coffeepot on the fire?" she asked.

"Please do," Danner answered before Chance could speak.

"Goodnight then, and thank you both. I wouldn't have known what to do if it weren't for the two of you." Without waiting for a response, she turned and disappeared into the bed of the wagon.

CHAPTER 28

ANNER LEANED UP AGAINST HIS saddle and stretched his long legs out toward the fire. Chance was doing the same on the other side, staring into the flames with a look that suggested his thoughts were far from the campsite. After a half hour of silence, Danner felt the time was right for the conversation he had been carrying around with him for twelve years.

"Chance, you mind if I ask you a personal question?" Danner asked in a serious tone.

"Why not? If I don't care to answer, I won't," was Chance's matter-of-fact response.

"Were you in the war?" Danner asked with a slight sound of hesitation in his voice.

"Yep," was the singular reply. When Chance offered no further information, Danner continued.

"Would it be improper to ask what side you were on?" Danner inquired.

"Nope, not really, I guess. I was a captain in the army of the Confederate States of America," Chance stated with pride and no apologies. "Why?" he demanded.

"I was just curious, is all," answered Danner.

"Nope, there's more to it than that, now what is it?"

Danner looked hard at Chance. He thought he was prepared for this discussion, but now he found himself searching for the right words. Chance's question hung in the air like an anvil, waiting to crash down on Danner and his fool question. But it wasn't a fool question. He wanted—no, needed to know for sure. Just then, Elizabeth approached the fire and broke the tension.

"Is there any coffee left?" she asked.

"Yep," Chance answered and leaned toward the fire where the coffeepot was keeping warm.

"Here you go, kid," Chance offered as he poured coffee into Elizabeth's tin cup.

"Did I interrupt something?" Elizabeth asked, knowing she had crossed the threshold of small talk.

"No, not at all," Danner quickly blurted out, hoping Chance would let the issue lie until a later time.

"Actually, you did arrive just in time to bail out our young friend here," Chance said through a wide smile. "Mr. Danner was just asking me about my participation in the late war. I haven't quite figured out his interest just yet."

"I'm sorry," Elizabeth offered, embarrassed that she interfered.

"Nonsense, kid! I have no secrets about my contribution to that chaos," Chance stated. He then asked Elizabeth to join them and looked over at Danner. "Now, Mr. Danner, shall we continue?"

The additional time Elizabeth had bought him wasn't enough.

"Like I said, I was just curious, that's all. I had heard of your exploits as a federal marshal and wondered if you had taken part in the war," Danner unconvincingly stated. "I'd heard that some of the Texas boys decided to not get involved," Danner added.

"That's a damn lie!" Chance grunted. "Some Texas boys went north, some south, but they were involved!" Chance bellowed. "You appear to be a little young to have taken up sides in the war—"

"No, I was old enough," Danner said in a low voice.

"Well, partner, what side did you join up with? Or do I need to ask?" Chance queried.

"I was a Union soldier," was Danner's surprising answer. Chance's narrowed eyes and wrinkled brow presented a puzzled look. Elizabeth said nothing, just watched the two men engage each other.

"You may have been a blue belly, but you're no Yank," Chance stated with confidence, leaning forward with new interest. Danner looked up at the sky and noticed the stars had dotted the dark sky with endless sparking points just as the fireflies had done.

"I'm from Charleston," Danner began. "My father was a lawyer and businessman, my mother a teacher. My father kept a close watch on the political positioning of the states and decided that if war broke out, he would align himself and his family with the side he believed had the best chance of succeeding. So when Fort Sumpter was fired upon, we left our home and headed up north as fast as we could since my father felt the north was in a better position, what, with all the money, industry, and power," Danner explained. His tone verified his disagreement with his father. "It didn't matter that my mother, brother, and I wanted to remain in Charleston and defend our home. It's not that we were slave owners or even believed in that, but my mother believed in state's rights and honoring our homeland. My father cared about none of that. We ended up in Washington, where my father encouraged my brother to join the Union Army in order strengthen his position. So my older brother, angry with my father, joined the Confederate Army. I was only twelve, so I stayed in school and watched the war unfold. After all, it was only going to be a short fight anyway, right?" Sarcasm crept into Danner's voice. "Four years later, I learned that my brother had been killed at the Battle of Cold Harbor. I got angry and joined the Union the day after I turned sixteen. By the time I got involved, the war was almost over, and the soldiers I fought with and against were tired and just wanted it all to end. By then, most of the new recruits were young like me. When it did end, I went back to Washington to learn that my father had died of illness and my mother wanted to return to Charleston. When we got back to Charleston, we found the city we left was gone and the people were rioting among themselves. We turned around and went back up north to Pennsylvania, where I finished school and then spent two years at Franklin & Marshall College in Lancaster, Pennsylvania." Danner stopped abruptly. "That's my story," Danner added.

Danner looked up to see Elizabeth looking at him intently, and Chance staring into the fire as if in a trance. Elizabeth stood without saying a word, turned, and walked over to the buckboard where she had arranged her blankets for her night's sleep. Chance stayed silent for a long time before speaking.

"I was at Cold Harbor," Chance confessed apologetically. "They say we won that battle, but I thought different. We lost a lot of good men on both sides there, and for what?" Chance was agitated now and kept his sights on the flickering fire. "Tired and just wanted it to end," Chance repeated Danner's earlier statement. "You're right about that, partner," Chance added as he began to share a memory of his own.

"I remember a fight in March of '65," Chance began. "There were about twenty of us pinned down behind some rocks next to a creek. The Yanks were firin' from the other side of the creek hidden in heavy brush. We shot at each other all damn afternoon with neither of us knowing if we hit the other. I must've crouched behind that damn rock for hours, tellin' my men to do the same. We knew it was about over, and I didn't want any more of my men killed for nothing. Our colonel had split the troop in half a couple of days earlier and went in different directions. Damn fool, it didn't make sense to me, but I followed orders, moved on, not even sure where I was when the Yanks pinned us. After no shootin' for a while, this Yank starts yelling, 'Don't shoot! Don't shoot! We surrender!'

"So I yell out to the Yank that we won't shoot and to step out toward the creek. I tell my men to hold their fire and I stand up and step out from behind that damn rock! I drop-holstered my gun and saber and stepped out into the creek. This Yank, he looks like he's fourteen years old, face all dirty and bloody from moving through the thickets. He steps out with his hands up, and I yell at him to put his damn hands down," Chance recalled with a bright face and laugh. "This kid meets me at the creek, salutes, and starts to tell me his name and rank. I stop him before he can say much because I didn't want to know anything about him. I return the salute and tell him my name and rank. He repeats, 'We surrender, sir,' and says there's only three of them and they're out of ammunition. I lower my salute and asked him what the hell he was doing there in the middle of nowhere with only two other soldiers. He looks around and says we had just killed the third and they were lost in the woods. I can tell, the way this kid talks, he's no Yank from up North. So I ask him where he's from and he says somewhere down South. So I ask him what's he doin' in a Yankee uniform. He says, 'That's just the way it worked out, sir.'" Chance laughed. Chance paused and looked up at Danner, who had a faint smile on his lips.

Chance continued. "So I tell this kid to have his men drop their weapons at the creek and turn around and head east down the creek to the river until he found his Yankee army. The kid thanks me, salutes again, and orders his two troopers to bring their rifles out and leave them with me. Sure enough, two more young fellas come out, drop their rifles. I tell them that I wasn't accepting their surrender and that we would bury their dead soldier. They all thank me, turn, and start east down the creek. I have no idea if they ever made it to their outfit, but that was one of the saddest and funniest times I had in that damn war." Chance began to laugh.

Danner had joined Chance's laughter. Danner's laughter tailed off.

"He did make it back to his outfit," Danner stated bluntly. Chance stopped laughing, cocked his head to the left, and looked keenly at Danner.

"How would you know that?" Chance asked.

"Because I was that dirty-faced, thicket-bloodied Yank that surrendered to you," Danner announced. Chance fell back against his saddle, startled by Danner's proclamation.

"I'll be damned," was the only response Chance could muster. "What the hell are you doin' here, now!" Chance commanded.

"I never forgot your actions and promised myself that one day I would find you and express my gratitude," Danner stated with a wide smile.

"Oh, hell. It was the right thing to do, is all," Chance said.

"Well, there were plenty of men that didn't do the right thing in that war," Danner replied solemnly.

"Well, goin' after Ryker's gang with me is sure a foolish way to say thanks." Chance was shaking his head.

"That's not entirely why I'm going with you," Danner stated as he looked over at the buckboard where Elizabeth was sleeping.

"I see," Chance answered, glancing toward the buckboard. "Well, I reckon a woman has done worse to a man than this." He chuckled as he leaned back and slid his hat down over his eyes to sleep. "I'll be damned."

"First watch is yours, Yank," Chance muttered from under his hat. Danner smiled, picked up his Winchester, and disappeared into the dark.

CHAPTER 29

ANNER WALKED BY THE BUCKBOARD to check on Elizabeth, mindful of keeping as quiet as possible. He was still bothered by the rider or riders that he was certain were following them. It made no sense to follow as they had no money or anything of value outside of the horses and wagon. Still, he was certain they had a tail, so he decided to backtrack and have a look-see.

The arced moon wasn't providing much light, and the trail proved to be difficult to navigate in the black abyss. Danner brushed up against a tree branch that gave away his position. Immediately he stepped sideways across the trail and lay down, listening. Staring into the yawning black opening of where he believed the trail to be proved worthless. After several minutes, he began to move forward again. He tried to stay near what he thought was the middle of the trail. Not the safest position, but he was convinced the only eyes that could cut through this blackness were those of an owl. After moving what seemed like five or six hundred feet down the trail, he stopped again and listened. Nothing. Crickets and cicadas were the only sounds piercing the night's silence. Deciding his efforts were worthless, Danner retreated back to the campsite, where he found Chance away from the fire near the tree line.

"Where the hell did you go?" Chance asked in a muffled but harsh tone.

"Doubled back to see if I could find our tail back there," Danner explained.

"Don't worry about our tail. They'll make their appearance when they're ready. We need to make sure we're ready when it happens. Get some shut-eye. I'll watch for any visitors."

Danner said nothing. He laid his gun belt across his saddle next to his bedroll, and a few minutes later he allowed himself to drift off to sleep.

The rack of a Winchester broke Danner's slumber. He instinctively rolled to his side drawing one of his Russian .45s from its holster. A shot rang out, and dirt exploded near his left boot. The muzzle flash gave away the assailant's position. Danner pointed and pulled the trigger, but the Russian failed to fire. Danner quickly rocked the hammer back and squeezed off another round. The gun failed again. Danner yelled for Chance as the Winchester launched another round that struck square into Danner's saddle. Danner grabbed his other Russian and pulled the trigger with every bit of his strength. The Russian resisted. Danner banged the gun against his saddle, screaming for Chance. Danner again pointed and pulled back on the trigger that refused to move. Another crack from the Winchester rang in his ears. This time the bullet found its mark and exploded inside Danner's right shoulder, knocking him back onto the ground. His shoulder was rocking back and forth…

"Danner! Danner!"

Danner opened his eyes and swung at his attacker.

"Snap out of it, kid!" Chance was yelling, doing his best to avoid Danner's flailing fists.

"It's Chance! It's Chance!"

Suddenly, Danner recognized Chance and stopped his assault. He was sweating profusely and breathing hard. He peered at Chance, then to Elizabeth, who stood nearby wide-eyed and horrified at what she had just witnessed.

"Settle down, kid. You were dreamin'," Chance rhetorically stated.

Danner laid back, closed his eyes, and took several deep breaths. Chance stepped back and waited. Danner sat up and looked around in the dim fire light. Wiping the sweat off his face, he looked over at his gun belt still draped across his saddle.

"I'm sorry," Danner exhaled the words in a low voice.

"I'll get you some water," Elizabeth offered, turning to the keg on the buckboard.

"That was a bad one, partner," Chance said as he limped over to his saddle on the opposite side of the glowing embers of their fire.

Danner sat up against his saddle and accepted the tin cup of water offered by Elizabeth.

"Thank you. I'm sorry you had to see that," Danner again apologized to her.

"Don't worry about her! I'm the one you socked in the jaw!" Chance stated with a chuckle.

"Sorry for that, Chance. Things get a little crazy when I have one of those," Danner offered.

"Happen much?" Chance asked.

"Enough," Danner replied. "Now you know why I carry two guns."

"Oh?" Chance responded.

Danner drained the cup of water and handed it to Elizabeth.

"I have nightmares where my guns won't fire. I pull on the trigger but it won't move, or I squeeze the trigger and the hammer won't fall," Danner explained.

"How long ago that start?" Chance asked.

"About four, five years now," Danner answered. "Funny thing is, I've never had a gun fail on me. After a couple of these, I decided to wear two guns…just in case."

"You got any other ailments me and the young lady need to know about?" Chance asked with a grin.

"No, I reckon that's enough."

"Good. Well, it's a little earlier than I had planned, but since we're all up and awake, might as well get the day started. Let's bump up that fire a little and have breakfast," Chance suggested, looking toward Elizabeth for approval.

"That's a great idea," she stated, then headed for the wagon.

By the time breakfast was over, the sun had begun its ascent beyond the skyline. Its bright orange rim peeked over the eastern ridge like a child at a candy store counter. Elizabeth finished cleaning up while Danner hooked up the plow horse to the buckboard. Chance saddled the horses, then quickly replaced the bandage on his hip before Danner or Elizabeth could catch a glance of it. Chance knew the wound was bad, but there was no reason for his young accomplices to worry since there was nothing that could be done out here.

Danner helped Elizabeth up onto the buckboard's bench then retrieved his horse from Chance.

"Still figure on riding through the valley?" he asked.

"Yep. Don't see any need to beat around the bush. We should make it to the ranch with plenty of daylight left," Chance stated. "Now help me up on my horse, will ya."

Chance led the way with Elizabeth behind and Danner falling back several yards to the rear. With any luck, the valley floor would be desolate this day but for three travelers heading to Thornton, Texas.

CHAPTER 30

C HANCE SLIPPED BETWEEN TWO MESQUITE trees and stopped. The sun was up, brightly illuminating the valley floor. The entire vale was in clear view. The only movement Chance detected was a couple of mule deer grazing on bunchgrass inside a sliver of shade to the east. Chance started down the trail pulling slightly on the reins, reminding his horse to proceed slowly. Elizabeth, watching Chance closely, snapped her reins and began to follow. Danner had ridden back on the trail a short distance and then stopped and listened. Nothing. Worse yet, he had no feeling of a tail anymore. He turned and hustled back to Elizabeth and the buckboard.

Chance made his way down the path between tall scrub to his left and a rugged rock face to his right.

The wagon should make it, he thought. As he passed the jagged edge of the rock face, the path opened into a yawning area lined by purple sage and prickly pear cactus. In the center of the oasis, mounted tall in the saddle was a lone rider.

Chance stopped abruptly. He nodded but said nothing.

"Good morning, sir," the rider announced in a voice that Chance thought was friendly enough. "Sorry to announce myself this way, but I couldn't think of any other way to do it. Name's Payne, Wes Payne."

"Ben Chance. You the fella that's been tailin' us since Canyon Creek?"

"Yes, sir, sorry 'bout that too. Your partner there kept a good eye on me though. I wasn't going to be able to follow without being seen down here, so I figured I'd show myself."

"What do you want?" Chance asked, leaning back in his saddle, twisting uncomfortably.

"Wanted to offer my services if you'll have me—"

"Wes!" Elizabeth shouted as she maneuvered the wagon around the rock barrier.

Wes removed his hat, but didn't move forward, uncertain of Chance's disposition. Chance looked over his shoulder at Elizabeth, whose face was nothing more than a smile with two eyes perched above it. She stopped the buckboard, jumped to the ground, and rushed past Chance to Wes, who swung himself down off of Ringo. As soon as Wes's boots hit the valley floor, he was engulfed in Elizabeth's arms, the recipient of a hug that would make a bear proud.

"It's good to see you!" she shouted.

"Nice to see you too, ma'am," Wes answered.

Danner pulled up next to Chance and watched the show.

"What the hell is this?" Danner asked, sounding annoyed.

"Seems this fella knows your girl. Says his name is Wes Payne. You know him?"

"Never met him, but I know who he is. He's the gunslinger that fought off the Indian attacks on the stage that brought Elizabeth to Canyon Creek. I heard talk in town about him. They say he's pretty handy with a gun," Danner explained.

"Well, before this cheerful reunion began, he said he'd like to join us. Any objection?" Chance smiled, sensing a bit of jealousy in Danner's demeanor.

Elizabeth looped her arm around Payne's and escorted him to Chance and Danner, wearing the same broad smile.

"Wes, this is Ben Chance and Luxton Danner. This is Wes Payne. If it weren't for him, I'da never made it to Canyon Creek to find you," she gushed. "He's offered to help get Father's herd back—"

"Only if Mr. Chance and Mr. Danner agree," Wes quickly interjected. "I don't want to cause any trouble," he added, looking at Danner.

"Trouble? What trouble?" Elizabeth shouted, losing the smile and sounding out of breath.

"No trouble here," Danner assured, ignoring the burning sensation in his chest. "I'll take point for a while," he announced, looking at Chance. Chance nodded then leaned down, extending his right hand to Wes.

"Excuse me, partner, but my hip's telling me to stay right where I'm at for the moment. Welcome to our merry rescue party."

Wes shook Chance's hand.

"Thanks for bringing me along," he offered with a smile.

"Well, if you're as good as we've heard, we sure can use you. Let's get moving, I'd like to make the ranch before dark."

Wes helped Elizabeth up onto the buckboard then swung up onto Ringo.

"I'll ride behind if that's all right with you, Mr. Chance?" Wes asked.

"That'll be fine, and it's just Chance."

Wes nodded then took up a position behind the buckboard. Elizabeth turned toward Wes.

"I'm glad you're here," she said, then started the buckboard forward.

Danner's thoughts collided like two boss mares battling over the herd. He knew they needed Wes's gun. Hell, they needed as many guns as they could get, but why was he jealous? Elizabeth was beautiful, educated, independent, but he wasn't looking to settle down. On the contrary, he was on his own quest when this task impeded his purpose. He had been drifting for years now, doing what he wanted, going where he wanted. A woman would just cause complications. Hold him back. He wanted no part of that, or did he?

Nope, get her out of your mind, Lux, he thought. *This is just a job. A job that'll pay with the satisfaction of doing the right thing. Besides, Chance couldn't do much himself anymore, especially now with only one working hip. Keep your head clear and your guns ready, Danner.*

The heat was beginning to bear down as the foursome made their way across the valley. An occasional tree provided brief shade, but the valley was exposed to the sun's piercing heat rays made worse by the stagnant dry air. There hadn't been any rain in over two months as evidenced by the gaping cracks in the Texas crust. The dust from the trail bed plumed upward with each clap of the horses' hooves then dropped back to the surface waiting for the next hoof to repeat the cycle. Chance caught up to Danner.

"We'll use that opening up to the left." Chance assisted his verbal direction with the point of a finger. Danner followed Chance's direction and noted the trail split near the north edge of the valley floor. The trail to the left was not as worn as its counterpart to the right.

"Shortcut?" Danner surmised.

"A little. It's not clear enough for the stage, but the buckboard shouldn't have any trouble. So what exactly did you hear about your buddy Payne?" Chance chuckled, unable to keep a straight face.

"Well, you heard about the Indian attacks on the stage. There were two from what I gathered. Ole Payne there charged head on into the raiding parties and kept 'em off the stage. Some card player was killed in the first raid, but he got the driver and Elizabeth through all right. Damn stage didn't have anyone riding shotgun, so they were exposed."

"Funny I never heard of this fella before," Chance added.

"He rides further south from what I hear," Danner answered.

"Oh, down on the Rio Bravo?" Chance asked.

"I believe so," Danner said.

"Hmm," Chance grunted. "We better keep an eye out then."

"Yes, sir," Danner replied. "Didn't figure it any other way," Danner added with a smile.

Sweat was rolling down Danner's face faster than he could wipe it away. The oppressive heat burned through his Stetson and felt like it was pushing him down into the parched dirt below. The less-trekked way chosen by Chance was more of a path than a trail. It obviously was not used by regular travelers as evidenced by the overgrown sycamore, cypress, and mesquite closing in on the once-passable road. If that wasn't bad enough, the insects were taking liberties with his exposed flesh that had already been marred by the abundant thorns piercing his path. Danner stopped in a small opening and waited for Chance to catch up.

"You sure this is passable?" he asked his senior partner.

"I'm sure. This is the worst of it. We'll be out of this dense scrub in less than a mile or so. It'll open up then, and we'll make good time."

"That buckboard squeezing through okay?" Danner asked.

"Here it comes now. Ask for yourself," Chance answered.

Danner looked back to see Elizabeth guiding the buckboard through the tangled course. She stopped at the edge of the opening and wiped her face with the tattered sleeve of her blouse.

"How much farther, Mr. Chance, Ben?" she asked, reaching behind her to retrieve a canteen of water.

"Not far. We'll be through this pretty quick. How you doing, Wes?" Chance called back. Wes said nothing, just nodded and raised his hand, indicating he was fine.

Danner wiped his face then heard the sound of breaking ground cover and twigs snapping up ahead near the end of path opening. Chance touched Danner's arm.

"I hear it," Chance assured his young partner. Both Chance and Danner covered their gun grips with open hands and waited. Wes saw their actions and immediately slid off of Ringo and took a position behind the buckboard, rifle in hand.

Three riders emerged from the brush and stopped at the edge of the opening. Each wore their hats low and looked out beneath their brims. One moved his horse up closer.

"Howdy?" the rider greeted his audience.

"Good afternoon," Chance answered with a nod from Danner.

"I didn't think I'd find anyone else on this sorry excuse for a trail," the ragtag rider added.

"Nor us. Seems we're blocking your way. Give us a moment and we'll move this wagon over to the side and let you fellas get on about your way," Chance announced.

"No hurry, sir, no hurry at all. Not making good time today anyway. Where y'all headin'?" the rider asked in a loose attempt to be friendly.

"Oh, we're just escortin' this young lady back to her ranch up north a bit," Chance answered ambiguously. "You?"

"Us? I reckon we'll eventually make our way over to the railroad camps."

Chance moved his horse over and motioned for Wes to help Elizabeth move the buckboard out of the main path.

"Railroad? Good idea. They're always lookin' to hire," Chance offered.

The young man saw Elizabeth and removed his hat.

"Pardon me, ma'am. I didn't see you right off," he said.

Elizabeth smiled and made a faint attempt to straighten her sweat-soaked blouse and skirt with her hands.

"That's quite all right, sir, no need to be formal out here," she replied. "I'm Elizabeth Thornton of Thornton, Texas," she announced with a smile.

"I'm Dave Rudabaugh. Pleased to make your acquaintance. This here is Mike Roarke and Dan Dement," he added, waving his hand toward the two riders behind him. Neither said a word or looked up from beneath their hats.

Danner, Chance, and Payne stopped and looked intently at the young man. Sensing his audience had recognized his name, the young rider put his hat back on and smiled.

"Dave Rudabaugh? Friend of Doc Holiday?" Danner asked.

"That'd be the one, mister. Any trouble with that?" he asked Danner.

"Not with us," Chance interjected. "If you'll step your horses aside, we'll be on our way," Chance added.

"Very good, sir," Rudabaugh answered as the three outlaws moved their horses to the path's edge.

Chance motioned with a nod of his head toward Danner to move on, then waited for Elizabeth and Wes to follow. Once they were through the clearing and down the path, Chance turned to Rudabaugh.

"Good luck with that railroad career," Chance stated with a tip of his hat then turned and headed down the path, leaving the outlaws quickly behind.

Chance caught up to Wes, who was lagging behind Elizabeth and the wagon.

"Wes, keep an eye on that path for a bit."

"Think they'll turn around and hit us?" Wes asked.

"Nope, I don't think so. No real reason, just a hunch," Chance added with a smile. He then headed down the path.

"Never know who you're gonna meet on the shortcut trail!" Wes called out after Chance.

"Nope, never do," Chance called back without turning around.

Chapter 31

Martha Rawlings lifted the tea kettle up from the stove and felt ample water inside. She lit the stove and waited for it to heat the top. After looking about the house briefly, she entered Thornton's room being careful to be as quiet as possible. Thornton looked drawn, and his face lacked any color of life. She pressed her hand against his neck, hoping to feel the bump of a pulse. Her fear subsided as Thornton exhaled and turned his head toward her. A moment later he opened his eyes.

"Good afternoon, Joel," Martha said with a smile, drawing the hand back to her apron.

"Martha?" Thornton asked in a quip.

"Yes, it's Martha Rawlings."

"What are you doing here looking down on such a mess of a man?"

"I'm looking at a fine man and neighbor who sent his daughter off on a fool journey." Martha gasped, immediately sorry for saying such a thing to her wounded friend.

"I'm sorry, Joel, that wasn't right of me to say."

Thornton coughed and winced in pain.

"I understand, Martha. I didn't feel I had any other choice, and I guess I'm just not thinking straight."

"You have a wonderful daughter and a very stubborn one! She reminds me of her mother, God rest her soul."

Thornton forced a smile at the thought of his wife. "I sure need her now," he whispered.

"Well, old man, you'll just have to do with me!" Martha joked. "Now, what can I do for you? Doc Langdon should be along in a little while to fix up your wounds. How 'bout a cup of tea?"

Thornton forced out his chin and narrowed both eyes. "Only if you put a drop of whiskey in it!"

Martha placed both hands on her hips and looked down at her patient. Her attempt at not laughing failed miserably. Together they both laughed loudly, with Thornton paying the price with pain.

"I'll fix you right up, Mr. Thornton, but don't you speak of word of this to Doc Langdon or Elizabeth!"

"Not a peep from me, Mrs. Rawlings! The whiskey is in the cabinet next to the gun rack in the den."

Martha spun and headed for the den, rambling around the archway into the den when she stopped abruptly. A reminder of what had occurred swept over her. The boarded-up window and the crimson stain on the floor where Moses Barber had died lay before her. She closed her eyes and held back tears. An image of Moses danced through her mind. His funny grin beneath snow-white hair burned in her thought. She began to feel sick, her stomach aching and her legs growing weak.

That's enough, Martha Rawlings! Joel needs you right now! They'll be time for sorrow later, she thought. She opened her eyes and retrieved the whiskey bottle from its roost then quickly scurried to the kitchen, where the steam emitting from the tea kettle announced its readiness.

Strong tea with a splash of bourbon is good medicine for any ailment, she thought.

Martha returned to Thornton's room to find him attempting to sit up in bed.

"Save your strength!" she ordered, setting the tea on the bed table and quickly propping a couple of pillows behind Thornton's back and head. "There you go."

Thornton nodded and accepted the cup of tea with a shaking hand. Martha kept her grip on the cup while Thornton took a long sip.

"That's the finest tea I've ever had, Mrs. Rawlings!" he announced.

"There's some bread in the kitchen, do you think you could take some?" she asked.

"Yes, ma'am, I believe I could if there was a little honey on it," Thornton stated, feeling stronger than he had upon waking.

"Well, you must be feeling better, what with all these demands of me!" Martha laughed. "I'll be back presently."

Martha returned to the kitchen and unwrapped a small loaf of bread that had been placed in a deep wooden bowl. Looking out the window, she could see a single horse carriage coming down the road toward the house.

Must be Doc Langdon, she thought. She pulled a couple of pieces from the loaf, then found the honey jar in the cabinet. She returned to Thornton's room with the bread and news of Langdon's imminent arrival.

Martha stepped out onto the porch as Doc Langdon whirled his carriage around to the hitching post in front of the house. Langdon stepped down clutching his bag.

"How's our patient this evening?" Langdon asked.

"Well, I'd say he's doing quite well, considering. He's been making special requests all afternoon. He's finishing up some bread and honey at the moment."

Martha stepped aside, shaking Langdon's hand as he passed into the house.

"I have fresh tea available if you like?" she asked.

"That sounds wonderful," Langdon replied, entering Thornton's room.

Thornton was working on his second piece of bread, attempting to look as healthy as he could.

"It's good to see you propped up and eating, Joel," Langdon announced, maintaining an emotionless expression. "How you feeling, honestly?" he asked, conducting a visual examination of his patient that confirmed dark sunken eyes, drawn cheeks, and a pale complexion.

"I've been better, but hell you already know that," was his reply. "The pain is awful and I can barely feed myself, but Martha doesn't need to know that," Thornton added. "Look, Doc, all I need to do is hang on until Elizabeth and Chance get back. I'm dying and I know it. I figure they should be here tomorrow afternoon. Just keep me going until then, okay?" Thornton asked.

Langdon let out a sigh, but said nothing. He began to remove the old bandages to see what he was dealing with. He hadn't written off his patient yet, but he knew that Thornton's chances of living were minimal at best. The wounds had stopped bleeding, but infection that appeared out of his abilities to contend with had set in. There was some new medicine available in the big cities, but out here in cattle country, he was limited, and he was still grappling with that inability to properly treat his patients.

"I'll get these wounds cleaned up and dressed with clean bandages," Langdon announced. "Your job is to eat what you can and keep rested."

"Well, with Martha here, I'll eat some, and I can't do a damned thing other than rest, Doc!"

Doc Langdon managed a chuckle and commenced to tending his patient. When he finished with the bandages, Langdon sat back and looked at Thornton.

"Joel, I understand your desire to see Elizabeth, but what's the issue with Ben Chance?" he asked.

"Doc, something's wrong with this whole thing. Sure, there's cattle thieves everywhere these days with the drought and all, but this was different. Jack Ryker and Blackie Gillum show up here? And I'm not so sure it was Ryker."

"What? Not Ryker? I thought you said it was—"

"I did at first, but with all that hair, beard, and he was between me and the sun. I didn't get a good look. Just went with the voice, but after I thought about it, something just didn't seem right. I need to tell Ben. Somethin's just not right," Thornton alleged, becoming uneasy, twisting in his bed.

"Take it easy, Joel. Won't do you any good getting worked up. Save your strength. I feel good you'll see your daughter and ole partner soon enough. Get some sleep now. I'll be back tomorrow."

Thornton closed his eyes and relaxed. Langdon picked up his bag and closed the door behind him. Martha had steaming tea waiting for him on the table.

"How is he, Doc?" she asked, wearing a frown.

CHAPTER 32

S AM COLEMAN SAT BEHIND HIS massive oak desk chewing on an unlit cigar and flipped through the cattleman's latest report on stock prices. The news wasn't all good. As a matter of fact, it was downright bad. Oh, the price of beef was up, that was good, but the drought, heat, and lack of water had killed thousands of head of cattle all across the rain-starved plains. Top cattle were bringing twenty-five to thirty dollars a head up in the Kansas rail yards, but the big ranchers like Coleman had lost thousands of dollars in dead stock. Coleman was impatiently waiting for his foreman to bring him the head count that would begin this drive. He knew he had lost plenty but was hoping for the best. He snapped a match across his boot and lit his cigar. Thick blue smoke billowed from its tip as his foreman Tom Jenney walked into the room holding a stack of papers.

"Well, Tom, what's the number?" he asked abruptly.

"The boys are finishing up the count, but it looks like we'll be around twenty-six hundred or so, boss," was the guarded reply.

Coleman paused. "How many we lose?" he asked.

"About six hundred," Jenney advised.

Coleman scratched out the figures. "At twenty-five a head, that's fifteen thousand dollars gone." He sighed. Coleman thought for a moment.

I'll need to get every dollar I can for this herd. If I can get top dollar for most of 'em, that'll offset the loss.

"Okay, Tom, get the boys ready to leave in the morning. I'll be joining you on this one," Coleman advised his trail boss.

Jenney's face went pale.

"That's not necessary, Mr. Coleman. You don't need to bother with this drive. We'll get all the beeves to market. No worries," Tom pleaded.

Coleman stood and walked to the window that framed his cattle operation.

"No, it's not you getting the herd to the railhead that's an issue here. I'll need every dollar I can get on each one. I'll need to be there for those negotiations," Coleman explained.

"I'm sure I can get you top dollar with your written direction. Give me a signed letter with your demands and we'll get the payout you're looking for," Jenney added.

"No, no, I'll join you on this one. I figured I'd be going along anyway. Shouldn't take but a couple of weeks to get to the railhead. I'll be ready early in the morning. We'll leave just before sunup," Coleman stated.

"Yes, sir. See you in the morning then," Jenney said, nervously fumbling with the papers he held. He turned and left the room.

"Connors!" Coleman bellowed, calling for his valet.

Wayman Connors had been Sam Coleman's assistant for better than ten years and knew by the big man's voice he needed to double-time his way to the office. A short slight figure of a man with a bushy mustache, he maintained a sharp appearance in his suit and tie and spoke in a low yet clear voice.

"Yes, sir, Mr. Coleman," he answered while snapping to attention at the entrance to the cavernous office.

"Relax, Connors. I'll be joining the drive tomorrow and will need provisions for a three-week journey. We'll be leaving just before sunup in the morning."

"Very good, sir," Connors answered before turning on his heel and scurrying off to his duties.

Coleman stood working his cigar hard, filling the area with a dense fog of burnt-tobacco smoke. Staring out the window, he let his mind drift back to the days when he and his men had to fight their way through Indian attacks just to get a thousand head to market. Now he was lamenting about an easy drive with nearly three thousand head to sell. Coleman shook his head.

Things aren't so bad, he thought. Getting top dollar was still a priority though, so joining the drive would be wise. Besides, he'd not been on a drive in a couple of years. *It'll be good to get back out on the trail,* he thought.

Coleman returned to his desk and eyed a letter he had received a day earlier. It had been delivered by a man who said he was sent by a John Adair and Charles Goodnight who were establishing a cattle ranch in the Palo Duro Canyon, southeast of Oneida. Coleman knew of Goodnight, who had brought cattle into Llano Estacado last year after the Kiowas and Comanches had been forced onto the reservations, but he was not aware of this John Adair fellow. Coleman took another drag from his big cigar and read through the dispatch. After finishing, he tossed the document onto his desk and leaned back in his chair. Adair and Goodnight had partnered to buy up thousands of acres of land rendered cheap due to the drought and failing ranches nearby. Wanting to expand their JA Ranch, they were interested in purchasing the KC and wanted to meet with Coleman and make an offer. Coleman shifted in his chair and thought for a moment. He wasn't getting any younger, and fighting the elements was beginning to feel like a lost cause. Selling and moving east would allow him to see his daughter and grandchildren.

Might not be a bad idea, he thought.

"Pete!" Tom Jenney hollered for his trail boss.

Pete Calhoun jumped down from the herding chute rail where he was watching the final head count of the cattle.

"Yes, sir," Calhoun shouted, looking at Jenney and knowing something was wrong.

"Plans have changed," Jenney announced.

"The old man is coming on the drive," he added.

"Damn, why?" Calhoun asked.

"Says he needs top dollar per head. I couldn't talk him out of it. We'll have to skip Six Shot," Jenney said in a low voice.

Calhoun looked at the ground and thought.

"What if we run the herd near Six Shot and pick up Ryker's cows and put 'em in the rear. No way is the old man going to ride back there," Calhoun offered.

Jenney worked the idea over in his head.

Could work, he thought. No chance Coleman would be anywhere near the back of the herd eating that dust.

"Okay, we'll pass near as we can without causing suspicion, then send a rider to Six Shot and tell Ryker what's going on. We'll use a few of his boys to run with those in the back, then have them sell those Tilted Ts up in Kansas," Jenney finished. He thought further.

"Hell, we'll keep that money for ourselves. Coleman's only expecting twenty-six hundred or so at the end of the line. Okay, when we get close, send a rider to Six Shot," Jenney ordered his nodding trail boss. The two connivers then went about their business getting ready for the morning.

CHAPTER 33

J OHN THOMAS STEPPED OUT OF the small shack he used as the marshal's office and stood on the top step glancing up and down Thornton's Main Street.

Usual afternoon business, he thought. Mrs. Owens was sweeping the front porch of the boarding house, and Mrs. McNally was doing the same at the general store. The Tumbleweed Saloon was open for business with the usual patrons milling around out front. Thomas looked down at the telegram in his hand. He was puzzled. Byron Parker, Club Smith, and Doc Langdon all had reported that Jack Ryker had led the raid on the Thornton ranch, and yet the word he had received was that Jack Ryker died in prison six months ago.

Thornton had put Ryker in prison, so he must had known him when he rode up to the ranch, and yet he was reported dead. Only one thing to do was ride out to the ranch and see how certain Joel was about the outlaw calling himself Ryker.

Thomas mounted his horse and headed for Doc Langdon's place. He'd let him know where he was going and why. With the exception of an occasional drunken drifter passing though, Thornton was as quiet a town as anyone could find on the range. He was certain he wouldn't be missed for the couple of hours he would be gone. Thomas brought his horse up to the front window of Doc Langdon's office.

"Doc! Doc Langdon!" Thomas shouted.

Fred Langdon quickly finished washing his hands, then peeked out the window, seeing his marshal before stepping outside.

"Hello, John, what can I do for you?" Langdon asked.

"Nothing, Doc, just wanted to let you know I'm headin' out to see Joel. I want to talk with him about who shot him."

"I thought he said Jack Ryker was leading the bunch."

"Yeah, I know, but according to this telegram I picked up from Sheriff Barkley, Jack Ryker died in prison six months ago."

Langdon shook his head in agreement.

"That makes sense now," Langdon exclaimed.

"What makes sense?" Thomas asked.

"Joel told me that something about that fella wasn't right. The whole thing didn't make sense to Joel. He didn't say anything about Ryker being dead, but he knew there was something wrong with the fella who said he was Ryker. I thought it might have been a result of his injuries and him not thinking straight, but it appears he's right."

"Okay, I'll go out and tell him about the real Ryker and see if we can figure out who this outlaw really is," Thomas offered.

"Mrs. Rawlings is out at the ranch taking care of him. Tell her I'll be out later this evening to check in."

"Will do, Doc."

Thomas turned, spurred his horse, and headed down the street. As he passed the Tumbleweed, he saw Jess McCoy, the owner, step out the swinging doors.

"Jess, I'll be gone a couple of hours. Headin' out to the ranch to see Joel on some business. Don't let things get out of hand in there." He laughed as he rode on.

"No problem, Marshal!" Miller joined in the laughter as he waved Thomas on.

Miller swept the endless dust from the porch and picked up a chair that had been knocked over during the night before he returned to his usual spot behind the bar. After sliding a few beers down the slick surface, Club Smith pushed through the doors.

"Hey, Jess, riders stopped at the end of town. Don't look good," he reported. Miller quickly stepped out and looked down the street. Sure enough, four riders were stopped at the edge of town. He shaded his eyes from the bright sun with a huge calloused hand. They were too far to recognize, but with Coleman's bunch heading out on a drive, he figured they were strangers. Miller wasn't usually bothered by strangers since it always meant new business. These days though he'd rather not see a face he didn't know.

CHAPTER 34

C HANCE PAUSED AT THE DRY creek bed that bordered Thornton's property to the south. The ranch looked different from when he last saw it. There was a new corral behind the house, and the north pasture looked like it had been cleared some. There were twenty or so cows in the east pasture.

Nice of Ryker not to bother with those, he thought.

Danner and Payne rode up and joined him. The three men scanned the vast property looking for anything out of the ordinary. Nothing they could see. A lone horse bobbed its head at the hitching post in front of the house. A further look into the horizon also confirmed no one on horseback. The land looked empty with the exception of the few cattle lazily grazing in the far pasture. A twitch of anger crept into Chance once again. Bad hip or not, he would live to see his friend's assailant pay for his decision. Danner and Payne sat quiet and waited for Chance to finish his thoughts.

"Anything wrong?" Elizabeth asked from her perch on the buckboard.

"Everything," was Chance's flat response before he spurred his horse and started forward.

Danner and Payne quickly glanced at each other, then followed Chance's lead. Elizabeth snapped the reins and brought up the rear with the buckboard. She was both worried and excited to see her father. She mustered up as much courage as she could just in case her father had passed. She did not want to break down in front of the men who had already sacrificed so much to help her.

The top half of the split sun sent deep orange beams across the land, delivering just enough light for Chance and company to keep a keen eye out for trouble. No one had mentioned trouble, but no one had to. Each man knew that an attack was possible. It would even make sense. By now, Ryker would know they were coming after him. Why not split the gang and eliminate them here once and for all. Chance paused again near a group of sage on the west side of the house.

"Elizabeth, you recognize that horse tied up out front?" he asked.

"No, sir, but I really haven't been here long enough to recognize anyone's horses," she replied.

Martha Rawlings stood still at the kitchen window. She had been watching the riders since they stopped at the creek bed. Her eyes weren't as good as they used to be, but she thought, more like hoped, it was Elizabeth and Ben Chance. As they approached closer, she recognized Elizabeth driving the buckboard and exhaled through a thin smile. She removed her apron and called to Marshal Thomas, who was speaking to Thornton in his room.

"Riders coming! Looks like Elizabeth and three men!" she exclaimed.

"Very well!" Thomas answered. "I'll be right there!" he added.

Martha hurried to the front door, then stepped out onto the porch to greet Elizabeth and her suitors.

The men paused near the house to allow Elizabeth to pass and be the first to arrive in front of the house. Elizabeth brought the buckboard to a stop, then leapt down and met Martha at the bottom porch step where they embraced tightly.

"It's good to have you back safely, my dear," Martha whispered.

"It's good to be back. How's Dad?" Elizabeth asked, pulling back from Martha's grasp.

"He's awake talking to Marshal Thomas at the moment. He's been anxious to see you and Mr. Chance."

Chance, Danner, and Payne had ridden up to the buckboard, remained on their horses, and sat three abreast facing the two women. Marshal Thomas stepped through the doorway and stood behind Martha, not saying a word.

Elizabeth turned and made her introductions.

"This is Mr. Ben Chance, Luxton Danner, and Wes Payne. This is Martha Rawlings and Mr. Thomas," she finished. As she stated each name, Chance, Danner, and Payne removed their hats and nodded.

"It's been a long time, Ben," Thomas stated as he stepped down from the porch and approached Chance.

"That it has, John," Chance answered, reaching down from his horse to shake Thomas's hand. Chance nodded toward Danner, who remained mounted next to him. "This here is Luxton Danner from South Carolina. He was good enough to save my hide back in Canyon Creek, then found it necessary to join me on this fool mission to help Joel and Elizabeth."

Thomas stepped around Chance's horse and shook Danner's hand. "Any friend of Ben Chance is welcome around here, Mr. Danner," Thomas announced.

"And the other fella is Wes Payne. We just met on the trail, but I understand he helped out Elizabeth a couple of times during her stage ride," Chance offered.

Thomas moved to shake Payne's hand, then paused briefly looking hard at his face.

"Have we met before, Mr. Payne?" Thomas asked.

"Not to my knowledge, Marshal," was Payne's quick answer.

Thomas turned to speak with Elizabeth, but found the two women had gone into the house, no doubt to see Thornton.

"Gentlemen, please get down off your horses and come inside. I believe Martha has some food prepared in anticipation of your arrival," Thomas advised.

With that, each man dismounted and loosed the saddle on their horses.

"I'll take care of the horses, you two go on inside. I'll be along later," Wes stated.

Chance and Danner tied their horses to the hitching post and headed into the house following Thomas. Chance stopped on the porch looking down at the bloodstains on the boards. He then looked over to the boarded-up window. Danner watched Chance and waited.

"Huh," Chance grunted then pushed the door open and went inside. Danner followed close at Chance's heels.

The three men stood stoic in the front room, Chance's eyes darting from wall to wall, corner to corner. He stopped when his eyes caught the bloodstains on the den floor. Danner followed Chance's gaze and saw the evidence of the gun battle that had already changed the course of many lives. The silence was broken by a weak man's call.

"Chance. You there, Chance?" Thornton called out in a voice that cracked and wheezed.

"You two wait here," Chance ordered, then took a deep breath, pushed his wide shoulders back, and headed for his former partner's bedroom door.

CHAPTER 35

C HANCE PUSHED THE DOOR OPEN and was struck with the pungent odor of death. The air in the room felt thick. His once soaring and strong star-packing partner was now an ashen, withered rumor of the man he once was. Elizabeth was seated next to the bed dabbing a tear from her eye while Martha Rawlings stood slumped at the foot of the bed staring into the bedding that covered the big man's wrecked body. Thornton looked up and greeted Chance with a wide smile.

"Good of you to come, Ben," he offered.

Chance returned the smile.

"Did I have a choice, JT?" Chance answered.

Thornton started a laugh that quickly turned to a cough, bringing a grimace, wince, and blood to the corner of his cracked lip. Thornton was taking rapid short breaths as he tried to speak.

"Take it easy, Dad," Elizabeth whispered.

"The girl's right, no energy to waste, JT. Can you tell me what the hell happened here?"

Thornton recovered and stared at Chance with a newfound purpose.

"It's not Ryker!" Thornton exclaimed. "It's some jackass said he was Ryker, but I've heard his voice banging around in my head since that day. Long hair, long beard, and hat pulled down low. Sun was to his back. I couldn't see very well. He had Blackie Gillum with him. He I recognized. There was someone else, but I can't remember now. I told 'em all to get off my property, the next thing I knew I took a hard hit in the side. Spun me off my feet. The shootin' started then. Ole Moses started firing from the window, but we were outnumbered, something awful. There must have been fifteen or more of 'em, Ben. I got hit again and was out. Next thing I know, Elizabeth is over me on the porch. I let 'em get me, Ben. They just rode up and took me." Thornton sighed, shaking his head.

"They ambushed ya, JT," Chance offered in an attempt to console his pal.

"No! No! Moses saw 'em comin', we knew it was bad. I figured they were rustlers. Damn drought has every big outfit in the country hirin' thugs to take what they can from small outfits like mine," Thornton explained. "John was just tellin' me about it before you showed up. Nope, I let this happen. I guess it's not like it used to be, huh, Ben?" Thornton rhetorically asked.

Chance let his mind drift to the pain in his hip.

"No, JT, I guess it's not like it used to be," he agreed. "I reckon they'll take the herd up over the border into No Man's Land and then on to the railhead in Kansas," Chance suggested.

"That's what I figured on. If you let out right away, you might be able to catch 'em before they got through the territory," Thornton stated.

"We need to rest the horses. I figure we'll head out at dawn," Chance answered.

Thornton looked as his brother in arms. "How many you got with ya?" he asked.

Chance hesitated, considered lying and inflating the number, but decided the truth was best.

"Two," Chance admitted.

Thornton coughed again and frowned.

"I fear you'll need more than that," Thornton sighed, whisking more blood from his lip with his gray tongue. "I wish I was goin' with ya, Ben, but I've seen my last chase."

"Nonsense, Dad, you'll be back on your feet soon," Elizabeth stated, knowing her words were in vain.

Thornton turned to his daughter and reached for her hand.

"This isn't how it was supposed to be, is it?" he said.

Elizabeth took a deep breath and shook her head. Chance turned and called for Danner, who had remained near the bedroom door catching as much of the conversation as he could.

"Danner, come in here," Chance ordered.

Danner tossed his hat onto a chair and stepped inside the room, sensing the same death scene Chance had recognized when he first entered.

"Yes, sir."

"JT, this here's Luxton Danner. He's one of the fella's I told you about."

Danner looked down at Thornton and nodded.

"Nice to meet you, sir."

Thornton looked Danner over from head to toe.

"You good with those guns, Mr. Danner?" he asked.

Before Danner could answer, Chance broke in.

"The kid's good, JT. I'm standing here right now because he's good. He saved my skin back in Canyon Creek."

"Thank you for that and riding with Ben on this one, Mr. Danner," Thornton answered.

"Yes, sir, we'll get the heard back for you," Danner assured.

"Not for me, son. Get it back for Elizabeth. I'll do well to make it through the night," Thornton admitted.

Martha Rawlings wiped a tear and quietly left the room. Elizabeth bit her lip, but no more tears were falling for her. Sorrow was turning to anger and revenge now. She knew he father was right. She knew he was dying and there was nothing anyone could do about that. But they could make sure his death would be avenged. Her thoughts raced through her mind like a runaway pony. She thought back to Ryker and his rancid breath holding the knife to her neck demanding the safe combination then laughing as he rode away. She had already killed two men since coming home. What would a few more do? Ruin her life? It was already ruined as far as she was concerned. Elizabeth's thoughts were interrupted by the sound of Chance's voice.

"Elizabeth, will you excuse us? I'd like to speak to your father alone for a moment," Chance was asking.

Elizabeth nodded then closed the door as she left the room.

"JT, you have any idea who's behind this raid?" Chance asked.

"Before you arrived, John was telling me he met up with a couple of Texas rangers and a US marshal in Oneida. They told him because of the drought, many of the big cattle outfits didn't have enough water and suffered big losses. The word was they were hirin' guns to rustle cattle from smaller ranchers. The rangers and marshals had their hands full right now. I figure these sons o' bitches were part of that," Thornton explained, gasping for breath.

"What big outfits are around here?" Danner asked out loud.

"There's a few, Broken Bar and Twisted River aren't far, but the KC is the closest, I reckon," Thornton answered.

Danner looked at Chance, who was staring off in the distance. Danner knew what he was thinking.

Could King Coleman be behind this? The cattle baron that Chance insisted was okay. Could Coleman have sent those two idiots to Canyon Creek to get rid of Chance? Danner thought. If that's the case, this was going to be far more than just getting Elizabeth's cattle back. This was going to become a no-prisoners saddle war.

CHAPTER 36

THE SUN WAS DIPPING BEHIND the horizon, sending a slow cool darkness across the land. Like the seed of a plague, Ryker rode just inside the edge of the dark rim, his black hat pulled down low over his eyes. He could see two riders waiting for him at the base of a mammoth pecan tree just up ahead. As the riders came clear into view, anger crept up inside Ryker like a geyser ready to explode. Ryker didn't recognize either of the minion messengers, which was not the agreement he had reached with his crime boss.

"Where's the boss?" Ryker scowled as he stopped his horse at the edge of the pecan's reaching branches.

"Not comin'," replied the big man mounted to Ryker's right.

"That wasn't the deal!" Ryker spewed, spitting a stream of tobacco juice onto a clod of bunchgrass.

"Boss said it's too soon to be headin' out. Look too suspicious," the big man added.

"Well, you go back and tell your boss that I can't wait forever. The longer I hang on to that herd, the better the chance for trouble," Ryker replied.

"You already have trouble," the man to Ryker's left announced calmly.

Ryker turned his attention to the second rider. "What kind?" he asked.

"Ben Chance left Canyon Creek with some gunslinger and Thornton's daughter," offered the tall skinny man on the left.

"When?" Ryker asked.

"Yesterday, I reckon. We let out before them, but the boss was certain they were on their way to Thornton's ranch, then out to look for you," the skinny cowboy said, cracking a slight smile.

Ryker looked down at his saddle horn and thought. He didn't know Ben Chance personally, but he knew of his reputation. It wouldn't take him long to get to Thornton's ranch, find Thornton dead, then figure out where he had taken the herd.

"Chance has only one man with him?" Ryker asked.

"Far as we know. He wasn't looking for posse volunteers last we knew." The big man was now doing the talking.

"Boss says for you to take the herd across the border into No Man's Land just south of the Black Mesa. There's a town there called Six Shot. It has some holding pens. Wait there until we come through with the big herd. Boss says he'll pay you for the trouble," the big man said just before dousing his own clump of bunchgrass with a gulp of tobacco juice.

Ryker didn't answer, just stared down at the stained bunchgrass. Would Chance be stupid enough to come after him and his boys with just one other gun? He had heard Chance was one of the best, but two against a dozen or more? That made no sense. No, Chance must have something else up his sleeve. He must plan on picking up some help in Thornton, then coming after him. That must be it.

Ryker tipped his hat back slightly and looked at his go-betweens.

"Fine, but first me and the boys will make a trip to Thornton and let those people know what it'll mean to join up with Chance," Ryker stated.

"Boss ain't gonna like that, Ryker. He said to head up to Six Shot right away and wait," the big man declared in a lurid voice.

Before the big man finished, Ryker cleared leather and fired a single shot at the big man. The bullet hit its target, ripping through the vest, shirt, and right shoulder of the big man. The big man yelped in pain and rocked sideways on his horse. His skinny partner reached for his gun, but Ryker was too quick, drawing a bead on his second target.

"Don't bother!" Ryker shouted.

The skinny cowboy stopped and froze, his right hand inches from the butt of his Colt.

"Now, both of you turn tail and git!" Ryker ordered. "Tell your boss his herd will be ready in Six Shot day after tomorrow. I'll give him two days, and if he's not there, I'll take the herd to the railhead myself. Go on!"

Both riders turned on their horses and spurred them on without question. Ryker watched as they disappeared into landscape, then turned and headed back to the box canyon where Blackie Gillum and the boys were waiting. He knew he had little time to waste. The visit to Thornton would be necessary. He'd have to send a message to the townspeople discouraging them in helping Chance. Stopping by the Thornton ranch wouldn't be necessary with Thornton and his man already dead.

So Thornton's daughter had gone and got Ben Chance to hunt me down? I should have killed her when I had the chance, Ryker thought. He wouldn't make that mistake the next time they met.

Ryker rode into the night, not wasting any time. He'd meet up with Blackie, take a couple of men with him to Thornton, and send the rest with the herd to Six Shot. Six Shot, that was another problem. It was a town only in name. It was nothing more than a few line shacks, tents, and a ramshackle barn that doubled as a saloon filled with whores and gunfighters. Sure, there were holding pens there, but also plenty of bandits, horse thieves, killers, and renegades running from the marshals out of Fort Smith. Trying to hold on to the herd there would be fight in itself.

This deal is getting worse all the time, Ryker thought. He would have gone on alone had big money not sprung him from Yuma. Taking Thornton and delivering his herd was his debt to pay, and he was anxious to cash out.

It was half past midnight when Ryker approached Blackie Gillum's campfire at the edge of the box canyon where his plunder quietly grazed on bunchgrass and clover. Blackie quickly stood and cocked his Winchester, unable to see into the fire's dark perimeter.

"It's me," Ryker called out, sending Gillum's rifle down to his side.

"Well? What's the word?" Gillum asked.

"Not good," was Ryker's cold answer as he reached for the coffeepot resting on top of a rock in the middle of the fire. Ryker filled a tin cup with the black liquid. After a long gulp, he looked over to

Gillum. "The boss wants us to take the herd to Six Shot and wait for a couple of days until his boys come through with the main herd."

Gillum said nothing, just stared into the fire. Ryker knew what he was thinking. *Bad idea.*

"It gets worse," Ryker added, sending Gillum's eyes back to Ryker's stone face. "Thornton's daughter went to Canyon Creek and found Ben Chance. Seems Chance and some gunslinger are wearin' out their horses headin' to Thornton's ranch, then on to hunt us down."

"Ben Chance!" Gillum shouted simultaneously, breaking out in a wide grin.

"Know him, huh?" Ryker asked.

"Oh, me and Marshal Chance go way back!" Gillum exclaimed. "He and ole Thornton tracked me down a long time ago. Dragged me all the way back to Fort Smith only to have Judge Parker cut me loose!" Gillum broke out in laughter. "Bastard Parker didn't have any witnesses! That son-of-a-bitch Chance was madder than rabid coyote!"

Ryker managed a thin toothless smile. He tipped his cup up and finished the last of his brew.

"Well, looks like he'll have another shot at ya."

Gillum stopped laughing. His face turned to a long frown.

"I look forward to another meeting with the high and mighty Marshal Chance."

"I need a couple hours' sleep, then you, me, and a couple of the boys are going to visit the town," Ryker announced.

"Why we wasting time going there?" Gillum asked.

"Need to deliver a message to anyone thinkin' of joining up with Chance and comin' after us," Ryker explained.

"Why, you think he'll go there lookin' for guns?" Gillum asked.

"Just makes sense. He knows how many guns we have. Them idiots the boss man sent said Chance left with only one other gun. He ain't comin' after us with just that. Figures he'll stop off there and look for help."

"Ben Chance ain't lookin' for no help." Blackie Gillum exhaled abruptly. "By now he knows we killed Thornton and his boy and took his stock. It'll be personal with him now," Gillum informed his credulous leader. "On top of that, he thinks you're Ryker. He'd be satisfied with just killin' you, I reckon," Gillum added.

"You think he'll know I'm not Ryker?"

"Hard to say… You fooled ole Thornton," Gillum said, then lay back onto his saddle and closed his eyes.

Ryker stared back into the fire's flames and counted off his men. *Two killed at the ranch, that leaves…fourteen. Fourteen to two.* The man who called himself Ryker liked those odds. That thought made it easier to have some shut-eye.

CHAPTER 37

RYKER JERKED AWAKE, HIS EYES darting in all directions. Nothing. Gillum was snoring a few feet away. Another man sat quiet on top of a berm next to the camp, keeping watch. Ryker sat up and tossed his empty tin cup at Gillum, hitting him square in the face. Gillum jumped, cussing beneath his breath.

"What's the idea!" Gillum growled.

"Time to get a move on," Ryker advised. "Grab a couple of the best gunmen and tell the rest to keep the herd here until we return. Time to send a message to the town of Thornton." Ryker's smile was met with Gillum's. Ryker gathered his rifle and horse then thought about his plan.

Ride in, do a little shootin', then talk to the town's leaders. He couldn't remember if Thornton had a marshal, but it wouldn't matter.

We'll ride in and hit the saloon first. If there's a marshal, I'll call for him, get him on my terms, Ryker thought. Gillum returned with two men. Ryker looked them over. He knew Carlton Baines, but the other was a stranger.

"Who are you?" Ryker asked his unknown gunman.

"Name's Shaw," was the quick reply.

"Okay, we'll ride into town and head for the saloon. Anyone know if Thornton has a marshal?" Ryker asked his trio.

"Yep," Gillum replied. "Fella named John Thomas. Friend of Thornton. Old man. Shouldn't be a problem," Gillum offered.

"We're not lookin' to shoot the place up, and I don't want any killin' unless it's necessary. We go in there and kill the town marshal, we'll have the rangers on us before we know it. We got enough problems without the rangers huntin' us," Ryker explained. "Understood?"

All three men nodded, then fell in behind Ryker as he turned his horse and headed for Thornton.

Ryker stopped at the far end of town. He scanned the main street. Like most small prairie towns, this one had the usual trades. Boarding house, church, stable, corral, store, feed shop, blacksmith, and the obligatory saloon. There were few people on the street and no sign of the law. Ryker spurred his horse onward, his men following in silence. A bald-headed thin man sat on a bench in front of the stage office glancing up as they passed. A fat woman wearing an apron over a green dress was sweeping dust from the front steps of the store. The boarding house displayed a large wood sign with white letters saying "Vacancy," and the bartender at the Tumbleweed Saloon was standing on the steps wearing a similar apron as the fat woman in front of the store. The four riders were joined by a hefty cloud of dust as they brought their horses to a stop in front of the saloon.

"I'm beginning to think it'll never rain again," Jess McCoy stated, waving dust away from his face.

"I know what you mean, friend," Ryker answered as he and his men dismounted and tied their horse's reins to the hitching post. "We could stand to wash this dust out of our throats," Ryker added.

"I can help with that. Come on in," McCoy offered, then stepped through the swinging doors.

Blackie Gillum and Carlton Baines paused and looked up and down the street, sizing up any possible resistance. None seen, they joined Ryker and Shaw inside the Tumbleweed.

Never one to miss anything or anyone in town, Kate McNally hurried into the store to fetch her husband.

"Harold!" Kate hollered toward the back room where her husband was working on his ledger. "Harold McNally!" she called again slightly louder.

"Yes, dear," Harold answered, emerging from the office door.

"Four men just rode into town and stopped at the saloon. All wearing guns and looking suspicious."

"All men wear guns, Kate. What made them look suspicious?" Harold asked.

"I don't know, but with Joel Thornton being shot and robbed and this whole business of young Elizabeth fetching that gunfighter Ben Chance, I don't like strangers showing up just now," Kate explained.

Harold removed his round glasses and began cleaning the lenses with his kerchief. His nosey wife had a point this time. Might be trouble.

"Maybe I should go tell Mr. Thomas," Harold offered.

"Marshal Thomas just rode out a little while ago. I heard him tell Doc Langdon he was going out to see Mr. Thornton on business. Figures he'd be gone when we need him."

"We don't know if we need him, Kate. It's just riders passing through. Not like we don't have that regularly," Harold stated, moving over to the front window to have a look across the street at the Tumbleweed. "Just stay inside for now," Harold suggested, knowing his wife would do what she wanted anyway. Harold looked out and saw Club Smith and Byron Parker hurry down toward the boarding house. "Looks like Club and Byron don't like the looks of the riders either. They're running down to Mrs. Owens's boarding house, probably to tell Billy Morgan."

"Good, he'll not take any gruff from them strangers," Kate stated.

"I don't know, there's four of them and only one Billy Morgan. I know his reputation from the late war and his prowess with a gun, but he's also smart enough not to take on four gunmen, if that's what they are." Harold tried to calm his animated spouse.

"What'll you fellas have?" McCoy asked his four customers, taking a position near the double-barreled shotgun he kept handy under the bar.

"Beer," Ryker answered, waving at his three comrades.

McCoy expeditiously filled four mugs with beer and placed them on the bar.

"That'll be four bits," McCoy announced to the men. None of the men reached for money.

"Marshal Thomas in town?" Ryker asked.

"The marshal's around, I reckon. You friends of his?" McCoy asked, knowing better.

"Nope, just need to deliver a message," Ryker clarified before draining half of his beer mug.

"If you'll trust me with the message, I'll be glad to pass it along to the marshal when I see him," McCoy offered.

"Right friendly of you, mister. Now step back from that gun you have under the bar," Ryker ordered then drew his gun. Ryker looked to his men and nodded, then began firing his pistol, sending lead into the mirror and whiskey bottles shelved behind the bar. Gillum, Shaw, and Baines joined in firing bullets all over the saloon and sending McCoy to the floor for cover.

Billy Morgan heard the gunshots as he was approaching the Tumbleweed's doors. Drawing his gun, he slowly crouched down and looked into the saloon under the doors. There were no others in the saloon, only the four strangers firing randomly around, sending broken glass and wood splinters into the air. Morgan picked out the shooter on the end to his left and fired one shot, hitting Shaw in the rib cage, spinning him wildly to the floor. Ryker, Gillum, and Baines stopped shooting as Shaw fell dead. Ryker leapt over the bar followed by Baines. Gillum turned and fired blindly toward the saloon doors then dove behind a table. Morgan fired two more rounds into the table shielding Gillum. Ryker pointed his gun at McCoy behind the bar.

"Unless you want one between the eyes, you tell whoever the hell that is out there to back off!" Ryker roared at his hostage.

McCoy held up his hands and nodded.

"Hey outside! Whoever you are! Back away from the doors and don't shoot! Don't shoot anymore!" McCoy called out. Billy Morgan kept quiet. People were starting to run out into the street behind him. He looked around. Nobody but well-meaning farmers and merchants. No help here.

"All right! I'll back away. Your horses are here out front. I'll clear the street so you can ride out of town!" Morgan answered.

"We'll shoot the first face we see! Got that!" Ryker howled.

"Yeah, I got it!" Morgan replied. He then turned and yelled for everyone to get off the street and stay away from the saloon. "Okay, I'll clear the street, no shooting!" Morgan yelled, gritting his teeth, not wanting to bow to outlaws. Morgan then ran across the street into the general store, where Harold and Kate McNally were hiding behind a barrel. Kate began to speak, but stopped when Morgan held up his hand.

Ryker and Baines stood and saw Gillum do the same.

"Get to your feet," Ryker ordered McCoy. McCoy stood, then walked around the bar to the front, where Shaw lay dead in a pool of blood. "You're going out first. Any wrong move and I'll kill you, understand?" Ryker barked. McCoy nodded and began to walk slowly toward the doors.

"Get his guns," Ryker told Baines, nodding toward Shaw. "Stop right there!" Ryker told McCoy as he reached the swinging doors. "This is the message for your marshal and anyone else who thinks joining up with Ben Chance is a good idea. We'll kill everyone who comes for us, and after, we'll come back here and burn the town down! Got it!" Ryker was screaming loud enough for anyone nearby to hear.

"I got it," McCoy assured the outlaw. "Who should I say delivered the message?" McCoy asked.

"Tell everyone Ryker was here. Jack Ryker. Now move out the doors," Ryker demanded.

McCoy led the way with Ryker, Gillum, and Baines following in single file. Each of the outlaws untied their horses, mounted, and then kicked their horses into a full gallop, firing their guns wildly toward passing buildings.

Morgan ran out of the store to McCoy.

"You okay, Jess?" Morgan asked.

"Yep, they got the drop on me, Billy. I didn't have much of a chance," he explained.

"Good thing, Jess. They'da killed ya fer sure. I got one of um anyway," Morgan stated.

"Leader says he's Ryker, bastard that shot Thornton," McCoy added.

"Yeah, we all heard his message. I don't know if Ben Chance is coming here or not, but if he does, I figure I'll be the only volunteer to go with him," Morgan said as people crowded around McCoy asking endless questions.

"I'll take care of the dead one," Morgan told McCoy, who nodded in appreciation.

Doc Langdon pushed through the crowd. "Anyone hurt?" he asked no one in particular.

"Just a dead outlaw in the Tumbleweed!" Byron Parker yelled, followed up with a laugh.

"Was it Ryker?" Langdon asked McCoy.

"Yep, that's the name he gave," replied McCoy, turning to begin cleaning up his saloon.

"Interesting, more trepidation from a dead man," Langdon said under his breath.

"What's that about a dead man, Doc?" Harold McNally asked, the crowd quieting to hear the answer.

"I don't know for sure, but Marshal Thomas told me that Jack Ryker died in prison six months ago. That's what he was riding out to see Joel Thornton about. I just wonder who this fella calling himself Ryker really is," Langdon rhetorically stated before heading back to his office. On the way, Langdon stopped at the stage office, where Bill Wright had just returned to after joining the crowd outside the Tumbleweed.

"Bill, I'm riding out to see how Joel Thornton's doing. I won't be back until later tonight if anyone comes looking for me," he informed the little stage office manager.

"Sure thing, Doc. Tell Joel I said hello."

Fred Langdon nodded and headed down the street.

CHAPTER 38

RYKER, BAINES, AND GILLUM KEPT their horses at full speed until the town was a dot on the horizon. Ryker slowed up his horse with the others following.

"That didn't go the way I thought it would," Gillum broke the silence with the obvious.

"Damn fools!" Ryker growled. "You get a look at who shot Shaw?" Ryker asked.

"Nope," Gillum answered.

"Me neither," Baines offered. "We should've made that town pay," Baines added.

"You just do as you're told, Baines! I'll do the thinkin'! This whole thing is turnin' bad!" Ryker shouted, pounding his fist on his saddle horn. "We'll run the stock up to Six Shot and wait a couple of days. If that idiot don't show with the main herd and our money, we'll take what we have up to the railhead and sell 'em ourselves."

"Now yer talkin'," Gillum stated. "I've had enough of this waitin' around already!" Gillum added. "Tanglin' with Ben Chance wasn't part of the deal."

"Ben Chance don't mean nothing right now," Ryker added. "He ain't getting no help now!" Ryker laughed.

Blackie Gillum said nothing. He knew better. He knew Chance. Chance didn't need help to cause them trouble, especially if he had a gunslinger riding with him. Anyone riding with Chance had to be damn good. Other than him, Ryker, and Baines, none of the others in their bunch seemed much good with a gun. Sure, they all talked big, but none of them seemed tough enough to go up against Chance. It could get mighty interesting if Chance caught up with them in Six Shot. And Gillum knew he would.

The trio rode in silence for another hour until they came up on the box canyon holding Thornton's herd. Ryker told Gillum to call the men in to the camp. He had a few words to pass along. Fifteen minutes later, Ryker's gang of misfits crowded around. Ryker took a head count of his men. Including himself, there were eleven. With Shaw killed in town, he thought he had a total of thirteen.

"Everybody here?" Ryker asked Gillum.

"Nope, seems Nabil Wexley let out earlier," Gillum explained.

"Let out? Where'd he go?"

"Nobody knows, Lucas here saw him leave his post and ride out a couple hours ago," Gillum offered.

Ryker glared at Lucas Hudson, a kid who looked no older than seventeen.

"He say anything to you 'bout leavin'?" Ryker asked the kid.

"No, sir, didn't say nothing to no one," Hudson answered.

"All right, we lost Shaw in town. Some bastard shot 'em in the back. We're gonna stay here tonight, then head out to the border early in the morning. Run the herd up to Six Shot in No Man's Land. We'll wait there for a couple days, and if we don't get paid, we'll run the herd up to the railhead and sell 'em ourselves. Keep a close watch out tonight. We got a couple of gunslingers headin' our way thinkin' they're gonna take back the herd."

"A couple of guns?" one of the men asked.

Ryker frowned. "That's right, two as far as we know. I figure ain't nobody in town gonna join 'em after our visit today. I reckon they'll go to Thornton's ranch tonight then head out after us in the morning."

"Hell, why don't me and a couple o' boys go back to the ranch and take care 'em tonight?" the tall leather-faced man asked.

Ryker gnashed his teeth. "Because I can't afford to lose any more men. I'll decide when and where we take 'em," Ryker snarled. "Get out to your posts and keep your eyes open!"

Carlton Baines approached Ryker while the rest of the men scattered.

"Hank there has a good idea. Why don't I take a couple men with me to the ranch tonight and take care of Chance? They won't expect us to hit 'em there tonight. Don't figure on that marshal formin' a posse to come after us. This Chance is all we got to worry about," Baines offered.

"We all stay here tonight. Got that, Baines!"

Ryker stood silent for a long pause, looking down at Baines.

I barely have enough men to run the herd up to Six Shot now. We lose any more and we'll start losing cattle along the way, he thought.

"No, if we had more men, but we need all hands right now to keep the herd together. We lose cows, we lose money. Everybody stays here tonight," Ryker ordered.

"What about the horses? We ain't sold one. They're just slowin' us down right now," Baines advised.

"Hmm, true. We'll take as many as we can to Six Shot, see if we can sell a few there. Ain't got time to mess with 'em anymore."

Baines said nothing. He turned and headed for his horse. Ryker kept an eye on him as he rode away.

CHAPTER 39

C HANCE PULLED HIMSELF AWAY FROM his thoughts about Coleman and the KC. He was both angry and disappointed in himself for missing the mark on the cattle baron. Although it was possible another outfit had sent the rustlers to the Tilted T, Coleman made the most sense. Coleman's herd would be heading north in another day or two. They could easily stop off at Six Shot, pick up Thornton's herd, then move on to the railhead in Kansas. The horses and money were bonuses for whoever was masquerading as Ryker.

"JT, there's another thing. You're right, it wasn't Ryker that came here. Ryker died in prison about six months ago. I just got the word myself about a month back. Whoever came here must've known Ryker in some way. Probably met him in prison. Learned about me and you putting him there and such," Chance stated.

"That makes more sense," Thornton exhaled.

A sharp knock preceded the bedroom door flying open.

"There's a rider coming fast down the road," Elizabeth announced.

Chance and Danner hurried out of the bedroom, Chance heading to the kitchen window for a look and Danner taking a position near the front door. Martha and Thomas stood behind Chance, attempting to see who the rider might be.

"That's my boy!" Martha exclaimed.

Danner walked out onto the porch and was joined by the others. Jake swung his horse around the corner of the house jumping from the saddle before his horse stopped. After stumbling against the porch rail, he looked up at his audience.

"Riders came into town and shot up the Tumbleweed telling everyone not to join Mr. Chance and come after them," Jake gushed in a quick breath.

"You know who it was, boy?" Chance asked.

"Said he was Ryker. He came with three other guys, but Mr. Walker shot one in the Tumbleweed. That's when they took Mr. White as a hostage and rode out of town."

"How long ago?" Chance asked.

"A couple hours, I reckon. I wasn't there to see it, but Ethan told me about it after. I figured I better come let you know, Ma. I didn't know Elizabeth had come back!"

Elizabeth stepped down from the porch and hugged Jake, who returned the gesture.

"It's good to see you, Jake," she said.

"I'm glad you're back."

"This is Ben Chance and Luxton Danner. They're going after Ryker's gang and get Dad's herd back," she explained.

Danner stepped down and shook Jake's hand.

"I'm Danner, the old fella there is Chance," Danner stated through a grin.

"It's getting late, I'll get supper started," Martha announced.

"Right behind you," Elizabeth said, jumping up the steps into the house.

"Anyone get hurt?" John Thomas asked Jake.

"No, sir, I don't think so. They let Mr. McCoy go then rode out of town shootin' out some windows is all."

"And Walker killed one of 'em, you said?" Thomas asked.

"Yes, sir."

"Well, I better get back to town and see what's happening," Thomas informed Chance, then headed for his horse without waiting for approval.

Chance, Danner, and Jake entered the house, which Martha had already filled with the smells of a hot meal. Chance went in to tell Thornton what had happened while Danner and Jake took seats at the table where they could watch Elizabeth work. It didn't take long for Danner to see the glint in Jake's eye when he looked at

Elizabeth. Danner began to wonder what relationship Elizabeth had with this fresh-faced kid when Chance entered the room.

"Danner," Chance called, nodding his head in the direction of the front door.

Danner followed Chance outside.

"If they went through the trouble of going into town to scare off anybody that might hook up with us, they might just decide to pay us a visit here tonight. Stands to reckon they'll know we'd stop here first then head up north after 'em. If I'm one of this fella Ryker's gang, I'm thinkin' I'd make the boss happy by getting rid of us before we start huntin' 'em," Chance rationalized.

Danner nodded, looking off into the distance.

It made sense, but for one thing, the house. They knew they'd have to attack the house. That didn't make sense. Better to take us out in the open, Danner thought.

"Why attack us here at the house? We could barricade ourselves in and fight them off for a week," Danner stated. "Besides, they don't know how many of us there are," he added.

"If Coleman is behind this, he knows it's just the two of us. He doesn't even know about Payne," Chance answered. "By the way, where the hell is Payne?" Chance asked, looking out into the dusk-drenched surroundings.

"That's a good question. I forgot all about him. He never came into the house after we got here. I don't see his horse either," Danner noted.

"Well, I guess it's just the two of us after all," Chance mused. "Maybe I'm giving this bunch too much credit. I don't know who this Ryker really is, although I know Blackie Gillum pretty good. He'd probably wait for us to get out in the open, especially if he thinks he has us outnumbered."

"Which he does," Danner finished Chance's sentence.

"Mr. Chance, Ma says supper's ready if you like," Jake called from the doorway.

"Be right there, son," Chance answered.

"You go ahead, I'll stand watch for a bit," Danner said, heading for the barn.

Chance joined his hostess and her party at the dinner table, not remembering the last time he ate.

"Looks mighty tasty, Mrs. Rawlings," he declared as he scanned the table's offerings. Beef stew, potatoes, and biscuits.

"We haven't seen a spread like this since we left the Sundown," Chance declared.

"Where's Mr. Danner?" Martha asked, looking toward the door.

"He'll be along shortly. He's keeping an eye on the place for now," Chance answered.

Chance looked at Elizabeth. "You see Payne after we arrived?" he asked.

Elizabeth's face dropped to a frown.

"No, I haven't. He's not outside?"

"Nope, his horse is gone too. I guess he let out without saying goodbye," Chance stated.

"No, he wouldn't do that," Elizabeth stated with a tone of voice that left no need for explanation. "He'll be back. Maybe he went to town or something," she added.

"Oh! I forgot! Doc Langdon said to tell you that he would be out sometime tonight or first thing in the morning. He wanted to come this evening, but Mrs. Sutton was having her baby, I guess," Jake explained.

"Oh my! Mary's finally having that child! She's been ready for days! Jacob, you'll stay here tonight. Make you a pallet in the barn after supper," Martha ordered as she dished out her stew. "With Elizabeth back, I can rest easy and look forward to a quiet night," Martha added.

Chance looked down at his plate and pushed beef around with his fork.

A quiet night? I'd pay good money for that, he thought.

CHAPTER 40

D ANNER SWUNG THE BARN DOOR open and lit a lantern that
was hanging from a nearby rusty nail. A careful look around
the barn confirmed Payne's actions before he disappeared.
The horses were all in stalls, saddles removed, with hay and water
full up. Danner's saddle was resting on top of the rail next to his
horse stall. Chance's in the same position at his stall. The plow horse
Elizabeth had leading the buckboard was also put up for the night.
Danner retrieved his Winchester from its scabbard and checked its
load. Full up. He retraced his steps back through the big barn door
and swung it shut, taking a seated position in some tall grass next to
the shed. The moon was up now, sending a wide beam of light down
upon the north pasture. Danner could see the tree line off in the distance. A light breeze drifted past, causing the tall grass tops to dance.

*I wonder where Payne went. Why leave without saying something
to someone? No chance he'd abandon Elizabeth. Didn't seem like the
kind to run. Would Ryker or his men be fool enough to attack us tonight?
Suicide. It'd be suicide,* Danner thought.

Wes leaned back against the big mesquite and listened carefully.
He and Ringo were tucked away inside a thicket of sage and cedar
that formed a ring of camouflage he couldn't have made better. He
was thirty, maybe forty feet off a split in the brush that would make
for a good path to sneak up on the Thornton ranch. Halfway down
the west side of the pasture, it would make good cover instead of
riding right through the open fallow itself. On a moonlit night like
tonight, that wouldn't be an option. If what he'd heard from Chance
was right, the herd and its suitors were about three miles or so north
of the ranch. They'd have to come this way and he'd be ready.

The hinges on the front door sent out a scream for oil as Chance swung it open and emerged from the house.

"Danner," he whispered, choosing not to light the lantern hanging to the left of the doorway.

"Over here," Danner replied, keeping his voice just loud enough for Chance to hear. "Next to the shed," he added.

Chance crept up to Danner and knelt in the grass, wincing at the pain shooting through his hip.

"Anything?" he asked.

"Crickets," Danner replied.

"Good. With a moon like that, it's damn near daylight out here. You could see riders coming across the pasture as soon as they cleared the tree line," Chance added.

"Payne took care of the horses before he disappeared. They're all tucked away in the barn," Danner informed his partner.

"That fella's a mystery," Chance stated.

"Yeah, I figure there's no way he lets out without talking to Elizabeth first," Danner replied.

"Never know with these gunslingers. By the way, it looks like you have more competition with that Rawlings kid in there." Chance laughed.

"He's just a kid," Danner chimed.

"So is she, pal. So is she. Go on in and get something to eat. I'll take over here."

Chance moved around to the front of the barn and cracked the door open just enough to slip through. Danner had left the lantern burning low, and Chance could see his saddle on the rail. Grasping his Winchester, he returned to Danner's spot next to the shed and listened. He could feel his heart pounding inside the gaping wound in his hip. He had grown numb to the ever-present pain, but tonight it was excruciating. He took the opportunity to replace the bandage with a relatively clean one that he kept in his vest pocket. His mind wandered back to Canyon Creek and Rachel. He didn't want to admit it, but he missed her. He missed her presence, her touch, her constant nagging about drinking less and sleeping more. He was no settler, no farmer, and no man to grow roots in one place. But if he got out of this alive…

A limb cracked in the distance. It was faint, but a limb for sure. Wes's senses shot to attention. He listened hard and stared into the brush even harder. One, two, three minutes, nothing. Could it have been his imagination? Hardly. The only question now was what pierced the hum of the crickets. *Snap!* Another sound of brush breaking under the force of movement. Ringo got restless. Starting to shift his weight, Wes stood quietly and stroked his companion's mane. He whispered into the big stallion's ear. Couldn't give away their position. They both stood motionless now. Something or someone was moving through the gap in the brush. Wes reached for his Colt, slowly drew, and paused. He'd wait for them to pass, counting how many, then he'd open fire from behind. They'd never know what hit them. The rustling of the brush was coming closer now, just about into view. Wes wiped beads of sweat from his forehead. He leaned forward as the big sage in front of him parted. He was right, this was the path! Suddenly, two javelinas pushed their way past Wes's ambush point and continued down the path.

Wes let out a breath. He couldn't keep the muffled laugh inside. He holstered his gun, took off his hat, and wiped his brow with his shirt sleeve.

"Well, partner, that was a close one," he said, patting Ringo on the neck.

I'm getting jumpy, he thought.

He stretched out his arms, turned back and forth at the waist, then sat and leaned back against the mesquite, straightening his legs then crossing his boots at the ankles. His spurs dug into the dirt. He stared into the brush and listened hard. Crickets.

CHAPTER 41

D ANNER ENTERED THE KITCHEN AND took the seat Chance had just vacated. The food looked and smelled good. Danner couldn't remember the last time he ate a good meal. *Had to be Rachel's cooking at the Sundown*, he thought.

"This looks wonderful, Mrs. Rawlings. Thank you."

"You're very welcome, Mr. Danner." Martha smiled and set a bowl of stew in front of the hungry cowboy.

Danner dug in to the stew and grabbed a biscuit for dipping. He then took a long look at the Rawlings kid. He could see Elizabeth watching him size up Jake. Jake also noticed Danner's gaze and shifted uncomfortably in his chair.

"So, Jake," Danner broke the tension, "can you handle a gun? I notice you don't wear one," Danner stated.

Jake put his fork down and looked Danner direct in the eyes.

"Yes, sir, I handle a gun just fine. Mr. Thornton taught me well. I just don't wear one cause Ma don't like me to, but I reckon that's fixin' to change," Jake announced, turning his attention to his mother, who had stopped what she was doing near the stove and was listening.

Danner looked toward Martha in time to see her grin turn to a frown.

"With any luck, kid, we'll take care of this business, bring Elizabeth what's left of the herd, and you'll be able to continue to follow your ma's wishes," Danner offered.

"Nope," Jake answered. "I'm going with you," he added.

"No!" both Martha and Elizabeth shouted in unison.

Jake stood up with clenched teeth and eyes narrowed.

"I'm not gonna stand around and do nothing after what those bastards did to Mr. Thornton!"

Martha wiped her hands on her apron and turned to Danner.

"Mr. Danner, please don't let him go with you," Martha stated in a surprisingly calm voice.

"Well, ma'am, that won't be my decision. That'll be up to Chance and your son," Danner informed the frightened mother.

"Jake, please come with me out to the porch," Elizabeth asked as she stepped away from the table and hurriedly headed for the door, not waiting for an answer.

Chance turned his attention to the squeaky door and watched as Elizabeth walked onto the porch with her arms folded across her chest. She quickly began pacing back and forth from the door to the railing. Chance made no sound, just watched.

This should be interesting, he thought as Jake pushed through the door and stopped in front of Elizabeth.

Chance strained to listen.

"Jake Rawlings, you are not going with us!" Elizabeth exclaimed plenty loud enough for Chance to hear.

"What do you mean 'with us'?" Jake shouted. "You're certainly not going!" he shouted.

"I'll decide what I'm going to do. You have no say-so in my decisions. Those cows are mine and Dad's, and Mr. Chance needs all the help he can get," she added.

"Exactly! Which is why I'm going with them," Jake explained.

Chance chuckled under his breath. Little did they know, but neither one of them was going with him and Danner. Chance was too amused to interrupt their lovers' quarrel though. He turned his attention back to the north and leaned against the shed.

"I don't want to anger you, Elizabeth, but your father has been like a second father to me, and I'm no kid anymore. It's time for me to be a man, and that time is now."

Elizabeth dropped her arms to her side. A tear rolled down her cheek. She then stepped toward Jake, who received her with a tight hug. His long arms wrapped around her slight body.

"I know you're a man, Jake," she said, burying her face into his shirt. "I'm just scared something will happen to you," she added.

Jake rested his chin on Elizabeth's shoulder and smiled. His question of her feelings toward him had just been answered.

"Nothing bad will happen to me. I figure Mr. Chance and Mr. Danner will make certain of that," he assured her.

Their intimate moment was shattered with a shout from inside the house.

"Elizabeth, come quick! It's your father!" Martha was yelling.

Jake and Elizabeth hurried into the house and followed Martha and Danner into Thornton's room.

Thornton was coughing, blood streaming from his mouth, turning the white bedsheet a bright red.

"Elizabeth!" he called out again. "Elizabeth!"

Elizabeth knelt next to her father and grasped his hand.

"I'm here, Dad," she answered the ole rancher's call.

Danner looked over Thornton and knew it was the end. Quickly he turned and rushed out to the door and called for Chance, who was already making his way up the steps having heard Martha's call for Elizabeth. Danner opened the door and stepped back as Chance entered.

"Looks like this is it, Chance," Danner stated solemnly.

Chance limped into his friend's room and looked down upon the man that had saved his life at least twice over the years. If only he could repay the favor now. Thornton's eyes were wide open, and his gray face was twisted in evident agony. Elizabeth held Thornton's hand and wiped the blood from his mouth as best she could.

Thornton bit off a cough and looked at his daughter, then Chance.

"It's been an honor, my friend," he whispered.

He then looked at his daughter, his pale face lighting up just a touch as he forced a smile.

"I love you, little girl. I'm sorry."

"I love you too, Dad." Elizabeth managed a smile of her own as she squeezed his hand.

Thornton settled back into his bed and closed his eyes. His chest heaved once, then twice, and stopped. Elizabeth buried her face in his chest and wept quietly.

Martha looked at her son, who was standing over Elizabeth. There were no tears, just a hardened look she had never seen on her son before. She walked out of the bedroom and took a seat at the kitchen table and put her hands together to say a prayer. Danner followed Martha but did not join her at the table for prayer. Instead, he headed out to the shed to watch for an attack hoping it would come.

Chance bent down and patted Elizabeth on the back and directed his words toward Jake.

"Stay with her as long as she needs," he said.

Jake nodded, showing no sign of weakness to this legend of man he had just met.

Chance joined Martha at the table, taking up a chair across from her. Martha opened her eyes and shook her head.

"Why?" she asked.

Chance looked down at the table and noticed a carving at the edge in front of him.

J. Thornton, 1875. That's odd, didn't notice that before, he thought.

"No matter how many good men die out here and go to heaven, there always seems to be another evil one we need to send to hell," he said.

"Is that how it's supposed to be, Mr. Chance?" Martha asked.

"I don't know, but that's how it is," Chance replied. "Mrs. Rawlings, I know your son wants to go with us in the morning. At first, I was against that notion, but seeing how things are now, he'll be welcome under one condition. Only if you are in agreement. It won't be my decision."

Chance slowly stood up from his chair. "And I'm sure you know, I can't guarantee his return," he added.

Martha's eyes followed Chance's up as he stood. She nodded in agreement, knowing she had just made the most difficult decision of her life.

Chapter 42

C HANCE LIMPED OUT ONTO THE porch and waited. Danner crawled out from his bunchgrass fort and joined him at the bottom step.

"How's things going in there?" Danner asked.

"About what you'd expect," Chance answered. "Sun will be up in a few hours, best you get some sleep," Chance suggested.

"I'll catch some out here. What time you figure on heading out?"

"Just before sunrise. I need to talk to the kid. Looks like he's going with us."

"What?" Danner quipped.

"I wasn't going to take him, but he deserves to go, and besides, if JT taught him how to use a gun, he's gonna be good enough. On top of that, we don't know if we're gonna see Payne again, and we could use a little help," Chance added.

"Well, I don't like it," Danner announced, turning to head back to his bunchgrass bed.

"You just worry about yourself, I'll worry about the kid," Chance called to his disgruntled partner.

Danner raised and waved his hands wildly without turning or saying anything.

Chance smiled then found himself the biggest chair in the house and fell into it with the idea he'd sleep a bit before morning. A moment after he closed his eyes, he sensed Jake was standing in front of him. Chance looked up.

"What can I do for you?" Chance asked.

"I'd like to go with you this morning, Mr. Chance," Jake asked. "Mr. Thornton taught me to handle a gun, and I assure you I can take care of myself."

Chance looked around and saw Martha working over the stove. "This morning? What time is it?"

"About five thirty or so. Sun's about to come up," Jake answered.

"What!" Chance shouted and attempted to jump up from the chair only to be reminded of his crippled hip by the piercing pain firing in every direction. He attempted to stand, but his left leg was numb.

Elizabeth approached Chance and stopped next to Jake.

"Settle down, Mr. Chance. I told Mrs. Rawlings and Jake to let you sleep a little longer. Lux is getting the horses ready, and Mrs. Rawlings is going to pack some food for us promptly. Jake and I are ready to go."

"Stop right there, kid!" Chance announced with narrow eyes and a frown. "We're not heading for a damn picnic! Jake here is all set as far as I'm concerned, but this is where you'll stay until we get back!"

Chance was standing now and not mincing any words.

"The only reason your father called for me was because of you. Without you, there's no need to go get the herd, horses, nothing. All of this would be for naught if I go and get you killed in some shit-hole town outside the Black Mesa. You stay here, give JT the burial he deserves, get this house repaired, and wait."

Elizabeth stood silent and listened. She wanted to scream at Chance, but knew he was right. Her father would want her to listen to Chance and do exactly what he had just said. Elizabeth stared off into the distance, and nodded her head slightly. Jake reached down and took her hand.

"Mr. Chance is right. We'll be back soon enough," he whispered.

Elizabeth kept nodding. Her mind was racing with so many thoughts it was blank. She was tired. Very tired. She felt like she could sleep for a month. Her eyes burned like fire and she couldn't cry anymore. There were no more tears to shed. Jake led her to her room and suggested she lay down and rest. She had no strength to argue. She sat on her bed and stared into a corner where her carpet-bag was sitting.

We've traveled a long way in a short time, she thought, looking at the crimson-and-brown bag.

Jake closed the door behind him and saw his mother pouring a cup of coffee for both Chance and Danner, who had come in from getting the horses ready to go. Jake walked into the den where the gun cases were and removed a Winchester and three boxes of cartridges. He then opened the cabinet door and found Thornton's Colt Peacemaker and holster. A quick examination found the gun unloaded, clean, and oiled. He quickly filled each empty bullet loop and then all six cylinders.

"Better take as much ammunition as you can carry, kid."

Jake heard Chance say from the other side of the room.

"Yes, sir. Elizabeth told me to take her father's guns since mine are over at our farm," Jake explained.

Chance said nothing, then limped back to the kitchen holding out his cup toward Martha in a gesture requesting a fill-up. Martha obliged by filling the cup with steaming hot black coffee.

"Thank you, ma'am," Chance replied. "Could you see to Elizabeth and the funeral arrangements?" he asked his hostess.

"Certainly will, Mr. Chance. Dr. Langdon is supposed to come by this morning. I'll get him to take word back to town and all the arrangements will be made. I promise Joel will have the best service we can provide."

"I have no doubt." Chance's smile was met by Martha's.

"No time like the present," Danner spoke up, shaking his head toward an east window that filled with a bright orange glow. "Looks like another hot one," Danner added.

Chance finished his coffee and handed the cup to Martha. "Thank you again, ma'am," he said then joined Danner as they headed for the door. Jake returned from the den armed and ready. Chance and Danner stopped to look over their new partner.

"Looks like you're ready to go, kid," Chance declared in as optimistic a voice as he could muster.

Martha scurried across the room and hugged her son. Chance and Danner quickly left mother and son alone.

"You be careful and follow Mr. Chance and Mr. Danner's orders," Martha instructed her only child.

"I will, Ma. Please don't worry too much. We'll all be back before you know it," he said without getting emotional.

Elizabeth's door flew open, and she came running up to Jake as Martha was stepping back to look at her son. Elizabeth replaced Martha's hug with one of her own.

"You come back to me, Jake Rawlings!" she cried. "I don't care if you find Ryker, the cows, or anything else anymore. I don't want to lose anyone else!"

Jake moved Elizabeth away at arm's length.

"I've got to go before they leave me behind," Jake said with a big smile.

Elizabeth managed a smile then followed him out to where Chance and Danner were waiting, already mounted and ready to ride.

CHAPTER 43

JAKE SLID THE WINCHESTER INTO its scabbard and mounted his horse. He was both excited and nervous. He had never done anything like this, especially with two famous gunfighters. He looked forward to finding the men who killed Mr. Thornton and hoped he was good enough to help Chance and Danner. Either way, it was time to find out.

"No matter how things turn out, thank you for everything, Mr. Chance," Elizabeth called from the porch. "Take care of yourself, Lux," she added.

Both Chance and Danner tipped their hats, but said nothing as they spurred their horses onward into the north pasture. Jake turned and hurried to catch up bringing his horse astride with Chance.

"There's a path cut through the brush toward the west side of the tree line, Mr. Chance," Jake offered, pointing in the direction he described.

Chance followed his young guide's aim and located the spot Jake referred to.

"Very well, kid, lead the way!" Chance ordered Jake, waving his hat toward the junior gunslinger.

Jake sat up straight and pushed his chest out at the confidence Chance was bestowing upon him.

"Yes, sir!" Jake yelled and kicked his horse into a gallop.

Chance flipped his hat back onto his head and laughed along with Danner as they watched Jake riding like he was leading the cavalry through Indian territory.

"We can't lose with that confidence!" Danner managed to yelp, still laughing.

Jake kept his hurried pace through the open pasture, pulling farther ahead of his fellow riders when movement to his left caught his eye. Startled, Jake jerked back on the reins and drew his gun, bringing his horse to a halt. Seeing Jake's actions, Chance and Danner immediately split apart and brought their guns into firing position as they approached Jake. Jake slid off his horse and peered into the tree line scanning for any movement. Danner's boots hit the ground fifty feet or so to Jake's right. Chance, unable to maneuver his hip well, stayed in the saddle behind Jake.

"What is it, son?" Chance asked.

"Not sure. Caught movement out of the corner of my eye toward the west tree line. I can shoot better from the ground than on my horse, so I jumped down just in case. There he is! On the left," Jake hollered, bringing his gun on target.

Chance saw the man on foot leading a big white stallion behind.

"Stand down, son. He's one of us," Chance told his young gunfighter. Chance glanced over to Danner, who had also recognized Wes and was holstering his Russian.

Jake holstered his gun and jumped back up on his bay. Danner did the same and joined Chance and Jake.

"We wondered what happened to you, Wes. Thought you might have let out," Chance called out.

Wes jumped up on Ringo and rode up to his welcoming party.

"Thought we could use a forward observer in case those fools got brave. I figured if they were comin' from the north, they'd need to use that open path up yonder. Besides, I ain't much on hangin' around a house with folks I don't know," Wes explained.

"Hear anything last night?" Chance asked.

"Naw, a couple of hogs was all," Wes answered.

"Okay, Jake, let's get a move on!" Chance ordered.

Jake snapped his rein and headed for the path with the others following. The sun was pushing up into a wide open sky and sending down rays of intense heat beating down the countryside. The ground was rock hard, and the brush cracked and snapped under the heavy hooves of the quartet's horses. Jake forced his way through the narrow path, his vison hindered by the beads of sweat that found their way into his eyes. His hat was already soaked, and it wasn't noon yet. After about an hour, he broke through the north edge of the thicket into an open savanna. Jake moved his bay to the side and dismounted, waiting for his comrades to join him. A few minutes later Chance, Danner, and Payne had all dismounted and were resting the horses.

Chance was looking off into the distance, shading the bright sun from his eyes with his hat.

"Just the other side of this clearing is the Johnson Trail," he announced. "About an hour beyond that is the border. We should be gaining on Ryker and the herd. I don't see any dust out there yet," he added.

"Johnson Trail?" Danner asked.

"Yep, it's not really a crossing you'll find on many maps, but it's been there since the end of the war," Chance explained. "The story is that Colonel Henry Johnson led a large group of Confederate soldiers and their families west from Georgia after the war ended. Seems they weren't much on reconstruction. About half of 'em camped out on the banks of the Red River east of here. Built the town up some. They call it Range. The rest headed west to California cutting a trail along the way. It's been used regularly ever since. Seen a bit more travelers since the silver rush hit in the Nevada territory," Chance concluded. "All right, let's get goin'," he added. "Danner, take the lead. Wes, the rear. Kid, you stay with me for a while," Chance ordered. "Keep yer intervals, we don't want to bunch up just in case Ryker has a couple of rear guards lagging behind," Chance added.

Danner kicked up to a gallop and took point, curious about this Johnson Trail and the possibility of rear guards waiting on them. He hadn't thought of that. He was disappointed in himself. He should have considered the guards. The sun was beating down hard now, heat waves rising up from the rock-hard ground. Danner slowed his horse and checked off in the distance north, east, and west. He could see the trail, such as it was now, and a lone rider off to the east. Danner stopped at the trail and peered down its path. One rider moving slow with a pack mule in tow was approaching him. Danner waved his hat back toward Chance and Jake, then pointed to the east.

Chance, Jake, and Wes joined Danner at the trail's edge and waited for the rider.

"Looks like we've got us an old-timer headin' our way," Chance stated with a chuckle.

Their visitor was an old man, long shaggy gray beard to go with the same-type hair riding a mule with another one in tow.

"Afternoon, fellas!" the old man called out. "Nice to see someone fer a change. I haven't had no one to talk to 'cept ole Bessie and Bart here," the man said as he waved his hand over his two mules. "Augustus Leon Booker at your service, gentleman," he announced, removing his hat, displaying a large round bald spot on top of his head.

"Good afternoon, sir," Chance answered. "This here is Luxton Danner, Jake Rawlings, and Wes Payne, and I'm Ben Chance."

"Nice to meet you, fellers. Where you all headin'?" Booker asked.

"We're headin' north toward the border," Chance vaguely answered. "How 'bout you? Looks like you're headin' west to do some digging," Chance offered after seeing pickaxes and shovels protruding from the pack mule.

"Yes, sir, ain't much doin' back in Tennessee, so I thought I'd head west to Nevada and dig up a little silver," Booker declared. Booker's face darkened, his eyes narrowed, and his smile faded. "I met up with a couple of fellas' last night that weren't as friendly as y'all though. They took my poke and my horse after drinkin' my coffee. By the looks of y'all, I reckon you're lookin' to dig up somethin' else," he said quietly as if not to sound bellicose.

Chance smiled. "Well, Mr. Booker, you're right about that," Chance stated. "You see a dust cloud earlier this morning or yesterday?"

Booker slowly nodded his head. "Yepper, early this mornin' just after daybreak. Good-size ruckus to the west here. I reckon it was a cattle outfit, if that's what yer lookin' fer," Booker answered.

"Yes, sir, that'd be it," Chance stated. "A little late for a silver hunt, ain't it? I hear the prospectors have all been pushed out by the big outfits," Chance stated.

"Yep, heard that too. Just didn't know what else to do with myself, I guess."

"Well, a couple of hours south of here is a spread called the Tilted T. There's a young woman by the name Elizabeth Thornton there who could use a hand. She has a good-lookin' plow horse and buckboard that could be had for some help around the ranch. If you're interested, head down there and tell her I sent ya," Chance offered.

"That's a mighty fine offer, sir. Things bein' what they are, I think I'll take you up on that."

"Very good, Mr. Booker. We'll see you back there when we finish with our business," Chance added.

"Thanks, fellas, and the name is Gus."

Chance waved his left hand toward Danner, motioning him to head out. Danner turned and spurred his horse into a gallop heading north, keeping an eye out for signs of the herd. Twenty minutes later Danner found what he was looking for. A wide deep trail of heavy hooves making their way from the southwest of their position. Danner stopped and looked beyond the plateau's edge. He could see dust now, billowing up from the moving animals. Chance and Jake joined him. The three horsemen eyed the evidence of their prize.

"Well, boss, how do you want to handle this? We can overtake and hit them out in the open before sundown, or we can follow 'em all the way to Six Shot," Danner continued.

"Thanks for the promotion," Chance answered without taking his eyes off the distant dust cloud. "Wes!" Chance called back to his rear guard.

Wes rode up next to Chance and peered out toward the rising dust.

"Time to decide how we want to handle this. From what we know, we're outnumbered about four to one," Chance stated.

Wes nodded. "Won't be any cover if we hit 'em in the open," Wes offered.

"Any chance Ryker will get help from cowboys hanging around town?" Danner asked.

Chance shook his head no. "Nobody's joining a fight without getting paid, and I figure Ryker don't have the authority to spend his boss's money," Chance answered.

"If we hit 'em in the open, those cows are gonna scatter like flies at a picnic. We'll lose quite a few that way," Wes said.

Chance nodded in agreement. "Okay, the herd's about five hundred or so. That's small enough to use the pens on the west side of town. We'll wait for the herd to get penned up, then make our move. Agreed?" Chance asked.

"Fine by me," Wes replied.

"Sounds good," Danner answered.

Chance looked back at Jake.

"Yes, sir, okay," he chimed in.

"All right. Let's spread out. Watch those damn sage. Wouldn't put it past Ryker to have a couple guns waitin' to jump us," Chance warned.

"That'd suit me fine. Close the odds when the real shootin' starts," Wes added.

"Sure, long as they don't pick a couple of us off," Chance stated.

Wes nodded in agreement then moved Ringo out to cover the right flank.

"Nothing seems to rattle that fella," Danner said.

"If he's who I think he is, this is just gonna be a Sunday go to meetin'," Chance said, moving forward.

Danner drew a frown and pushed his square jaw forward. "Who the hell does he think he is?" he asked Jake.

Jake shrugged his shoulders and smiled.

Danner moved out to cover the left flank. "You go up the middle with Chance," he called over his shoulder to Jake.

"He's right, son, stay behind me."

Jeremiah Walker pushed himself into the Oklahoma dirt, keeping an eye on the four riders coming his way. He was well-hidden behind a large sagebush, but didn't like the fact he had no horse to escape on if the plan went wrong. He glanced over and saw his ambush partner, Ross Kline, in the same prone position behind another sage about one hundred feet to his left. Ryker's orders rang through Walker's head again. *Wait till they're close in and kill'em, then use their horses to hightail it back to the herd.*

Sure, that was fine when they thought there was only two, but the game changed with the sight of four riders.

We better not miss, Walker thought.

CHAPTER 44

RYKER AND BLACKIE GILLUM WERE leading the herd listening to the constant cattle calls of the men behind them. They were safely into No Man's Land, and the Black Mesa was just ahead beckoning their pilfered prize. Ryker felt some relief now, knowing he was out of Texas and inside a lawless land. Six Shot was only an hour away with yawning pens ready to house Thornton's herd. Coleman's big herd should only be a couple of days behind, and that meant payday and fulfillment of his debt. With any luck, the welcoming party he left back on the plateau would take care of Ben Chance and whoever was foolish enough to join him in his hopeless attempt to take back the herd. With Chance out of the way and money in his pocket, Ryker planned to get his fill of drink and whores in Six Shot, then head west into New Mexico, where hired guns were in high demand.

"I reckon we'll be in Six Shot in about an hour or so," Blackie Gillum interrupted Ryker's thoughts.

"Yep. The main herd should only be a day or two behind. Then we can get out of this territory," Ryker replied.

"Where you figure on headin'?" Gillum asked.

"New Mexico. I hear there's a saddle war in damn near every county. I reckon I'll join up in one of those. You?"

"I'm gonna go up to the Nevada territory. See if I can dig up a little silver."

"Or just take it from some poor bastard miner who had the good sense to dig it up for ya!" Ryker shouted, laughing and spiting tobacco juice in the process.

"No sense working for it!" Gillum replied, laughing along.

Jeremiah Walker wiped the sweat from his forehead then squeezed his Winchester tight and waited.

Sons o' bitches. They damn sure know what they're doin'. Spread out keepin' a close watch, he thought. The sweat was pouring down his face, aided by his anxiety more than the baking sun. *We better not miss.*

A hundred feet left, Ross Klein was repeating Walker's actions. His eyes were burning from sweat. The brim of his hat was soaked and dripping into the dust below his chin.

There weren't supposed to be four. We better not miss, he thought.

Chance's eyes darted across the terrain from one scrub bush to another. He had a bad feeling, and his hip was stiff and bursting with pain. His left leg had gone numb and wasn't recovering. He knew if gunfire started, he'd be unable to maneuver his horse or jump to the ground for cover.

I'll just fall. Falling off a horse is easy enough, he thought. He glanced over his shoulder and saw Jake closing his gap. Chance whistled, getting Jake's attention, then pushed his hand palm first toward Jake, motioning for him to move further back.

"Stay behind me, son!" he called.

Jake nodded and pulled his reins back, expanding the distance between him and Chance.

Jeremiah Walker had fought in the war and knew to take out the flanking threat first. He'd fix his sights on the rider to his right, then come back and take the one directly in front. Besides, the rider to the right was an obvious gunfighter and the one in front was distracted.

Wait, wait, just a little closer.

Ross Klein had no knowledge of military tactics. He figured he'd shoot the closest target first then worry about the other next. Plus, the rider in front of him was older and bigger.

Easy target. No time like now!

Klein rose to his knees. *Crack!* The bullet hit Chance in the ribs on his right side, sending him spinning off his horse into a dead sage. The sound of the rifle startled Jake, causing him to pull hard on his reins triggering his horse to rear up on its hind legs. Jake was thrown backward landing on his back, forcing all his breath out of his lungs.

His left arm hit a rock at the elbow and cracked loud. Sharp pain fired through his arm. Danner and Wes cleared leather and kicked their horses into full gallop going wide as they watched Chance and Jake hit the dirt. Walker, stunned by the early shot, wildly swung his rifle to the right and squeezed off a wild shot, missing Danner. Seeing his ambusher, Danner fired his Russian .45 twice, the second shot finding Walker's forehead, blowing the top of his head off. Wes had pulled both guns and was laying down fire in the direction of his assailant. Klein was frantically cocking and firing his rifle, sending bullets over Wes's head as he closed the killing gap. Wes let out a blood-curdling yell as he jumped off Ringo squeezing off a round from each of his pistols in midair. Both rounds found their mark, hitting Klein in the chest, blowing him backward before Wes's boots hit the ground. Wes approached his wounded attacker on foot. Klein was gasping for breath, blood oozing from his chest. He looked up at Wes, raising his hand as if to say, "No more."

"You son of a bitch!" Wes yelled then fired another round into Klein's head, ending the outlaw's fight.

Danner had circled around, confirmed his kill, and was looking for more. Nothing else stirred. Jake was lying on the ground trying desperately to suck air into his deflated lungs and fight the pain in his arm.

Broken, he thought.

Chance was on his back careful not to move. The pain in his hip was nothing compared to the fire he felt in his side. He tasted blood, which could only mean one thing—his lung was punctured. His ability to only take short breaths was further evidence of the damage the bullet had caused. He stared into the clear blue sky. Thoughts began to swirl around in his head. Leaving his father's farm as a teen. Cattle drives, Joel Thornton, the war, the marshal's office, and Rachel in Canyon Creek. He closed his eyes and pictured her in his mind.

Beautiful skin, flaming red hair, and matching lips that any man would fight for. She let him know many times he would never have to fight for her. She was his if he wanted her. Damn fool. She had made him a better man. He should have handled her differently, but he never was any good with women. Never knew how to handle them. He knew he'd never see her again. In all his life, that was only his second disappointment.

Danner rode up and jumped down next to Chance, checking the severity of his wound. Wes and Jake were right behind, kneeling at his side. Danner pulled Chance's bandana from his neck and began packing the wound.

"Get some water!" Danner called out.

Jake hopped up holding his left arm and retrieved his canteen, handing it to Danner.

Chance opened his eyes, reached for Danner's arm, and clutched it with his massive hand.

"Don't bother, Danner. It got me good," Chance said flatly.

"Take a drink," Danner ordered.

Chance pushed the canteen away from his lips.

"Keep it. You need it more than I now. Sorry I can't finish the trip with you boys," he said.

"Nope, we'll patch you up and have the kid here get you back to Thornton as quick as possible. The doc there will get you fixed up. You can make it," Danner said.

Danner's attempt at optimism was appreciated but swept aside by Chance.

"You get those bastards that killed JT. I don't care a lick about the herd anymore. Just get those miserable sons o' bitches," Chance said through bloody gasps of breath. He looked at Wes, then back at Danner. "You've got the infamous John Duncan ridin' with ya. No doubt you two can get the job done," Chance continued.

Wes smiled and cocked his head toward Chance. "How long you known?" he asked.

"I figured it out when I saw those scars on your hands," Chance replied, grimacing in pain. "One more thing, Danner. Go back to Canyon Creek and tell Rachel what happened. Tell her she was right, she was right all along." Chance squeezed Danner's arm, cutting off the circulation, his eyes wide and distant. One last spasmodic exhale and the legendary Benjamin Franklin Chance was gone.

Jake's shoulders dropped. His arms hung at his side. He no longer felt the pain of his broken arm. Tears began to flood his eyes and then rolled down his face. He quickly turned to his horse not wanting these men to see him weakened by emotion. Danner and Wes bowed their heads and said nothing for several minutes.

Wes broke the silence. "We've got nothing to bury him with."

Danner looked around as if a digging tool would magically appear.

"This ground is so damn hard, we'd need a pickax," Danner said. "We'll put him on his horse and look for a spot to leave him until we come back this way," Danner said, then stopped and looked at Jake. "No, Jake will take him back to Thornton's ranch. They can bury him there next to Thornton. That's the right thing to do," Danner announced.

Jake pulled himself together. "No way, Mr. Danner. I'm going on with you and Mr. Payne," Jake insisted, clutching his arm in a failed attempt to hide the injury.

"What's with the arm, kid?" Wes asked.

"Nothing, I'm all right," Jake answered with a wince.

Wes looked closely and felt the arm.

"It's broke," he announced to Danner.

"That settles it," Danner replied. "Look, Jake, we're not leaving Chance out here to be picked apart by the buzzards and coyotes. He deserves far more than that. He needs to be buried back in Texas next to his old partner. You're no good to us now with that arm. Get back to the ranch as quick as possible," Danner told his wannabe gunfighter. "Besides, I ain't getting you killed for a herd of cows. Miss Elizabeth Thornton wouldn't stand for that."

"Danner's right, kid. The best thing you can do now is get back home," Wes interjected.

Jake stood quietly, knowing his elder partners were right. He nodded his head then headed over to collect Chance's horse nearby.

"I'll get him on his horse. See if those two have any ammunition we could use," Danner told Wes.

Wes nodded and headed for the dead outlaws.

We'll need all the ammunition we can carry, he thought.

CHAPTER 45

D ANNER WRAPPED CHANCE'S BEDROLL TIGHTLY around his body, tying it with his rope. Danner felt empty inside. Despite barely knowing the man that spared his life years ago at the end of the war, he felt connected to Chance. Anger mixed with duty and sorrow. The once feared duo of Joel Thornton and Ben Chance was now dead. Gunned down by cowards for cattle money.

They'll pay, he thought.

Jake brought up Chance's horse and helped Danner place Chance's body over the saddle. Danner then tied the ropes around Chance's body to the stirrups. Danner nodded toward the makeshift splint Jake had tied to his arm.

"You going to be all right?"

"Yep, I'm fine," Jake replied without acknowledging his wrecked arm.

"Okay, you get back to the ranch as quick as you can," Danner ordered the young cowboy. "Remember, there has been Indian activity all around. They likely didn't bother us because we were four, but now they'll see you're alone and not hesitate. Got it?" Danner asked.

Jake nodded. "Got it," he firmly replied.

Wes rode up.

"Ready when you are, Danner," he stated.

Danner looked up and saw Wes covered in pistols and bands of ammunition.

"I reckon you know the way to Six Shot?" Danner asked.

"Yep," was the singular answer. "Good luck, kid," Wes offered to Jake before swinging Ringo around and heading up the trail the stolen herd had cut into the scorched terrain.

Danner shook Jake's hand, mounted, and followed after Wes. Jake watched for a moment, then set about his duty of delivering Ben Chance back to the Thornton ranch.

Danner caught up to Wes and brought his horse to an equal canter. Both men remained silent for several minutes before Danner asked the question.

"Who's John Duncan?" Danner asked.

Wes remained silent for several minutes. The question hung in the air like a storm cloud ready to break loose. Wes looked down and patted Ringo's mane.

"Before I was Wes Payne, I was John Duncan," came the cool reply.

"That's it?" Danner asked.

Wes took a deep breath, then exhaled slowly.

"That's okay, Wes, none of my business, I guess," Danner cut the tension.

"I reckon you have the right to know who you're riding into battle with," Wes stated. "When I was born, my mother wanted to name me Wesley Payton Duncan after her father. My father wouldn't hear of it. He insisted I be named after him and his father, John Duncan. They settled on John Wesley Payton Duncan. I was John Duncan until a few years ago when things changed."

Danner said nothing, just listened.

"I was playin' cards in a saloon down in San Antonio one night when this fella walked in. An obvious lawman, probably a ranger or marshal. Big, tall, straight, walked with a purpose, pounding his boot heels into the floor. It was obvious he was there to take care of business, so everything sort of stopped. This fella walks up to the table next to me eying a little skinny dude shuffling a deck and announces he's a Texas ranger. Pulls his vest back showing a ranger badge and tells the scrawny dealer he's under arrest. I see this clod standing at the bar watching the ranger close. Clod goes for his gun, and I stop him. The ranger looks at me so the scrawny dude draws, but the ranger beats um. Turns out, both the skinny card player and the one at the bar were both wanted. So I help the ranger get the two over to the sheriff's office, and the ranger thanks me by offering me the bounty money under one condition. I join the rangers."

"You're a Texas ranger?"

Wes didn't answer, just continued with his story.

"A couple years later I get sent to Presidio down on the border. There was a bandito gang crossing the border, stealing from the town folk, then hightailin' it back to Mexico. It wasn't a ranger issue until the town named a marshal and he was killed by the bandits."

"They just sent you?"

Wes cracked a grin and continued. "While I'm there, the bandits raid the town. I killed a few but got hit. Next thing I know I'm hangin' on the side of the stable wall with nails through each hand. They're taking potshots at me seeing who can get the closest without drawing blood. The leader, Juan Carlos Diego, figured killin' a ranger wouldn't be good for business, so I hung from my hands for a couple hours until they got bored and let out. After witnessing that, the town folk knew his message was clear. Once I could use my hands again, I resigned and tracked down Diego and his bunch myself. It took me a couple months, but I found 'em all. After that, I decided to go by my middle names, Wesley Payton. I became Wes Payne."

"Why did you…"

"Rangers couldn't cross into Mexico."

Danner said nothing. He now knew what kind of man he was riding with and felt better about their chances against Ryker and his boys. A short time later, Danner caught a glimpse of dust up ahead. Just a wisp, but he knew it was the herd.

"Looks like we found our herd," Wes stated.

Both riders stopped and stared at the ominous cloud of dust now within striking distance.

"How you want to handle this?" Danner asked.

Wes took a deep breath, removed his hat, and wiped his brow with a sweat-soaked sleeve before replacing it.

"With two of us and a bunch of them, I reckon we do it Indian style. I reckon Ryker will leave a couple of guards near the pens to watch over the herd. Probably the two youngest and least experienced. The rest are gonna want to hit the town for whiskey and women. We sneak in, kill the guards quiet like, then head into town just before dark, creating as much of a ruckus as we can. Ryker's men will be the only ones that have anything to lose, so they'll come runnin'. When they do, we get as many as we can before they know what hit um. That should even things out a bit. Then we just start huntin' 'em," Wes offered.

Danner listened, and slowly nodded in agreement.

"Sounds like as good a plan as any. If we can create enough chaos, we should do well," Danner added.

"It'll be best to hit um before Ryker can hire a few more guns," Wes said.

"Before we do this, there's something you oughta know," Danner said.

Wes turned and looked closely at Danner, his right eyebrow raised. "Oh?"

Danner reached inside his vest pocket and removed a United States deputy marshal badge and held it out for Wes to see.

"US deputy marshal! Why the hell didn't you say so days ago?" Wes asked, his voice cracking with annoyance.

"I'm here working the rustling, and I needed to be sure who I was dealing with," Danner explained. "My orders were to keep my position unknown until it was necessary," Danner clarified.

Wes turned his attention back to the horizon where the dust cloud had been. "Chance know?" he asked.

"No, I never had the opportunity to tell him," Danner replied in a low, shuddered voice of obvious regret.

"US marshals don't usually get involved in plain rustling. Why they send you?" Wes asked.

"I'm on the trail of a killer by the name of Bert Cullen. He's known to join up with rustlers. He killed a farmer and his wife near Texarkana while stealing a few cows. One of the men with him got arrested and turned on him. I was given the warrant and told to bring him in. I tracked him to Canyon Creek when I ran into Chance. You know the rest," Danner explained.

"Well, that's that," Wes said, biting off a chunk of chaw. He then offered the tobacco to Danner.

"No, thanks, never did pick up the habit," Danner announced.

"Gives me somethin' to think about while I'm getting shot at," Wes answered.

Both men spurred their horses on. It was time to get down to business.

CHAPTER 46

RYKER AND GILLUM COULD SEE Six Shot just ahead. The pens were empty, but the town sounded full. Music could be heard coming from the old saloon barn, and there were a mix of men walking and riding up and down the path that served as a haphazard main street. A couple of gunshots sounded, which meant nothing to Ryker or Gillum as that was routine for this clutter of ramshackle buildings and lost souls masquerading as a town. Gillum swung his horse around and headed for the men at the head of the herd. Ryker paused and looked back, getting a full view of his prize. It would be dark soon, and once the beeves were locked up, he could get about doing some damage in the saloon. He turned and headed for the pens.

"Push the herd over to the pens, we'll make sure they're open!" Gillum called to the lead riders.

Both answered with a wave of their hats. Gillum turned and spurred his horse up toward the pen openings. Ryker had already dismounted and was taking care of the first pen. The pens, four in all, were huge round structures lined with split rail timber. Each pen could hold up to two hundred fifty cows. They would use the two closest to the road leading into town. They'd be close to the saloon if trouble started. Gillum rode past Ryker, who was pointing to the other pen he wanted used. Gillum slid off his horse and opened the wide gate, which was secured by a looped piece of rusted barbed wire over the top of the gate pole. Gillum pulled a pocket watch from his vest. It was near seven o'clock.

Walker and Klein should have returned by now. If Chance was as close behind as we thought, they should have hightailed it back already, he thought.

Ryker stepped toward Gillum.

"Put four men on the pens. I don't like that Walker and Klein aren't back yet," he said.

"Ya, I was thinkin' the same thing," Gillum admitted.

"Put the young guys on guard duty, we'd have to fight the rest to keep um from getting to the saloon," Ryker snarled.

"Sure enough," Gillum answered, then headed over to the pens to oversee the operation.

Watching while the cows were being moved into the pens, Gillum called out to Roy Baker, who heard Gillum and saw him waving his hand up over his head. Baker joined Gillum directly.

"What is it, boss?" Baker asked.

"Post four of the younger guys at the pens to keep watch tonight. And tell them to stay alert. Klein and Walker never came back. Once they're in position, come join us over at the saloon," Gillum ordered one of his better men.

"Will do, boss," Baker answered, then returned to the pens keeping a watchful eye on the cows as they found their way into the pens.

Gillum continued to watch as Baker pointed toward four riders bringing up the rear of the herd and motioning each to their positions for the evening. After most of the herd had been contained, Gillum vacated his post and headed for the saloon a short distance away. Despite the short ride to the saloon, Gillum was propositioned by two whores looking for fresh cowboy money. Gillum ignored the women, who cursed him as he passed.

Now this is my kind of town, he thought.

Six Shot had begun as a town true enough. A few years earlier, a Baptist minister had traveled from the East and decided it was a good place to build a church and begin preaching the Good Book. In addition to the holding pens, the place already had a couple of barns and a few other buildings mainly used as boarding rooms for passing cowboys driving herds north to the Kansas railhead. A makeshift livery stable and corral followed, along with several tents housing whores for the weary cowboys starved for female attention. The minister thought spreading the word of the Lord would cure the town of its sordid habits. The church structure didn't make it past a floor and a couple of walls before it was requisitioned by outlaws running from US marshals out of Fort Smith. Eventually the minister realized his error in judgement and moved on. One of the barns became a saloon, the other a lively brothel. The town earned its name after rumors began that it took at least six shots to make it out of town alive.

Blackie Gillum had passed through Six Shot on a few prior occasions, sometimes driving legitimate cattle, other times not. As long as the saloon didn't run out of whiskey, a frequent problem since it wasn't on any supply line, the place suited him and others like him just fine.

Gillum tied his horse to a hitching post and took a moment to wash his hands and face, cupping handfuls of water from an adjacent trough. Music, laughter, and loud chatter emanated from inside the saloon. Gillum straightened his hat and pushed through the swinging doors looking to rinse the aridity from his throat.

Baker swung a pen gate closed and secured it with the rusted barbed wire, then gave final instructions to his guards. He didn't really know any of the four outside of them joining the outfit outside El Paso weeks ago. Ryker and Gillum took care of those things. Baker just wanted his pay and a fresh horse back to Texas. He didn't care much for the Indian territories and trusted no one, including Ryker or Gillum. The rest of the boys followed him into town, sans two who didn't make it past the two whores on the street hawking their wares. Both disappeared into tents whooping and hollering. Baker swung down off his horse and looked to the western sky that had suddenly become dark and menacing.

"Looks like a storm's comin'," he announced to his remaining companions. All followed Baker's gaze toward the west as a white bolt of lightning split the distant black sky in half. A loud clap of thunder followed, sending tremors through the hitching post.

"Just what we need. Rain and the mud that comes with it," Baker said aloud to no one in particular.

Several people, including Ryker, came out of the saloon at the sound of the thunder and looked toward the threatening sky.

"Yep, looks like a storm's comin'," Ryker proclaimed then hurried back into the bar.

CHAPTER 47

J AKE'S EYES DARTED BACK AND forth, then over his shoulder. Other than the black sky approaching from the west, he saw nothing threatening. He was moving as fast as he could considering his arm, Chance, and the growing wind. All things considered, they were moving fast enough. If he kept up this pace, he would be back to the ranch about midnight. He had already decided he wasn't stopping other than to briefly rest the horses. It wasn't long before he passed Johnson Trail, where they had met the old-timer and his mules. He was glad that Chance had offered the wannabe prospector a job back at the ranch. He knew Elizabeth would welcome the old man and his assistance. The thought of that visit seemed a long time ago now with Chance dead and Lux and Wes off to Six Shot.

Keep your head straight, Jake. Don't wander, he thought.

Jake hadn't considered the Indian issue while he was with Danner and Payne, but now he was obsessed, thanks to Danner's warning. Every bush, every tree or rock could be hiding an Indian. Jake's eyes kept searching the terrain, looking for any movement. The black sky was inching closer and lightning was flashing off in the distance.

No way will I beat the storm. I'll just keep riding. Maybe the storm will keep the Indians away, he thought.

The wind was picking up, sending dust about in snaking spindles down the trail. A gust blew past him, bringing cool relief to the overheated cowboy. Jake pressed on, attempting to relax as much as he could. His eyes darted back and forth, then over his shoulder. He couldn't get back to the ranch fast enough. His arm hurt with pain he had never experienced before in his young life. Once he fell off his horse and hurt his side, but that was nothing like this. He adjusted his makeshift splint. The pain brought tears to his eyes. His stomach was tense and his chest felt hollow. Despite the gust of cooler air, he continued to sweat heavily. He wished he hadn't insisted on going now.

Elizabeth was right. I should have stayed at the ranch and helped her bury her father.

He was angry with himself. In his attempt to prove he was a man to Elizabeth, he had made the wrong decision. Chance was so worried about him he failed to protect himself and died. Jake began to blame himself.

Chance would be alive if I'd only listened.

The thoughts rushed around in his head faster than he could control them. He began to get dizzy and felt sick.

I'm no gunfighter. I'm just a farmer making a fool of myself for a woman.

The thunder rumbled and rolled across the darkening sky with bolts of lightning breaking it like a pane of glass. Rain began to fall, at first intermittently, then picking up steam worthy of a rail engine. After a few minutes it was falling with force, stinging the back of Jake's neck. He pulled down on his hat, turned up his collar and leaned forward, exposing his back to the large drops that were now pelting him mercilessly.

I need some cover, he thought.

He began looking about for the inviting shelter of a tree canopy. A hundred yards up and to the left was a big mesquite that would provide ample refuge.

Jake brought his horse to a stop next to the twisted trunk and slid off his saddle, careful not to risk his fractured arm to further injury. He looked at Chance's body astride his horse. He knew he should pull Chance down in order to rest his horse, but with only one good arm, he knew he wouldn't have the strength to get his body back up onto the saddle.

"Damn it!" he yelled out loud for none to hear, attempting to release his built-up frustration. He felt the arm up and down slowly, gauging the pain. He closed his eyes, gritted his teeth, and squeezed.

Not too bad. I can do it.

He stepped back to Chance's horse and released the rope, catching Chance in one motion, then lowering him to the ground. His horse snorted, then stepped back and forth showing his gratitude. After feeding the horses some grain, Jake pulled his rifle and sat down against the tree. The storm was none he had ever seen in his nineteen years. The thunder was deafening and the lightning blinding. Despite the clustered leaves above him, raindrops forced their way through, smacking the ground around him. The air had cooled and the gusts of wind whipping though his shirt sent a chill over his body. He retrieved his blanket from his saddle and wrapped it tightly around himself. He hunkered down keeping an eye on his surroundings as best he could. He was tired, hungry, and wet. On top of that, having the responsibility of returning Ben Chance's body to the Tilted T made his mind numb. He had never been this close to a dead man, and it made him nauseous. He had always thought that when this time came, he would be tough and strong. Instead he just kept feeling sick.

The rain continued to blister Jake as he moved around the big tree looking for protection. No luck. Didn't matter, the downpour continued to be relentless. His hat was soaked through, allowing streams of water to glide down his face. He scanned the land as best he could. No movement as far as he could see. The pain in his arm was beginning to feel like the bolts of lightning looked. Razor sharp. He needed to get to the ranch and see Doc.

Nothing moving in this weather. I might as well head for the ranch, he thought.

He pushed himself up, then grabbed Chance as best he could. He grit his teeth then yelled out in pain as he lifted Chance's body onto his horse. After tying Chance to his saddle, he mounted his horse, tapped his spurs, and started off. The black sky had already made it difficult to see, but what little light there was would soon disappear with the onset of the night. Jake could barely make out the trail but kept his head down and horse moving. The thunder continued to pound the earth, and the lightning lit the land for sparks at a time.

I should still make it to the ranch well before daybreak, Jake thought. His thoughts drifted to Elizabeth. He pictured her on the front porch waving goodbye. The image brought a smile to his face and new sense of purpose. With all that had happened, it seemed like he had been gone for two weeks, not two days. He spurred his horse and picked up the pace. He looked forward to seeing her again.

Lightning lit up the sky and gave Jake a good glimpse of the trail. He kept his horse straight, its hooves slapping in the mud. He tucked his left hand into his gun belt in an effort to keep it from moving too much. The rain kept up its assault. It seemed like it was trying to make up for the two years of drought all in one storm. Jake wondered how Wes and Danner were doing.

Wonder if the storm changed their plan? Whatever the plan was, he thought.

Didn't matter now. His job was to get back to the ranch as fast as possible. He didn't look forward to telling Elizabeth about Chance. He had grown up a lot in the last few days. It's not what he expected two weeks ago when he found out Elizabeth was coming home from Philadelphia. He remembered the boyish crush he'd had on her when she left. He was excited and nervous to see her again. Then Ryker and his gang changed everything. He took a deep breath to let the anger out.

Pay attention, Jake. Still got a job to do!

Thunder exploded, bringing Jake back to reality. Lightning followed with a gust of wind nearly pushing Jake off his horse. Instinctively he grabbed the saddle horn with his left hand, sending pain shooting up into his shoulder. He clenched his jaw and felt his chest tighten.

I can't get frustrated!

He pushed down on his soaked hat then wiped the water from his eyes.

This is a day I won't soon forget, he thought, forcing a grin.

CHAPTER 48

S AM COLEMAN WAS CUSSING HIMSELF for insisting he go along on this drive. The rain was unrelenting, peppering him as he slowly rode between his foreman on his left and guard Clinton Wade on his right. Tom Jenney was calling out orders to his cowhands while Wade was silently watching the trail ahead. Quick and deadly with a gun, Clint Wade was well known in the territory as the best trail guard around. Coleman paid big money for Wade's services, of which he hoped he'd not have to use. Coleman's oilskin trail duster was doing its best to keep him dry, but the rain was so intense, the ole sou'wester was failing miserably.

"Son of a bitch! It hasn't rained in months, now it's damn near beaten us to death!" Coleman shouted to Jenney.

"Yes, sir! This may add a half day or more, maybe longer!" Jenney replied.

"At least we made good time before this blasted storm set in!" Coleman offered.

"Maybe we should head toward Six Shot if this keeps up!" Jenney suggested.

"No! No! We're staying as far away from that hell hole as we can, Tom," Coleman declared.

"Yes, sir! I'll be back, I need to check on the boys!" Jenney told his boss, then reined his horse to the left and disappeared into a wall of rain. Coleman returned to cussing himself.

Jenney rode astride of his trail boss Pete Calhoun, who was snapping a rope toward a couple of wandering cows on the edge of the herd.

"The old man wants nothin' to do with Six Shot!" Jenney informed Calhoun.

"No surprise! No boss wants his men around whiskey and whores!" Calhoun shouted through laughter.

"We're just going to have to leave Ryker on his own!" Calhoun continued.

Jenney nodded. "He's a big boy, he'll figure it out!"

"Sure, he'll figure it out, I just don't want to be the one who sees him first is all!" Calhoun answered with only a hint of laughter this time. Jenney rode on to the rear of the herd.

"Keep pushin' 'em, Dave!" he hollered to his rear teamster.

Dave Conlen was a veteran cattle driver of twenty years and had been with Sam Coleman for the last ten. He had little respect for his foreman Jenney and wondered why Coleman kept him around. He didn't trust him or his trail boss, Calhoun. Although he had never caught them stealing from the boss, he'd gone to guns on Jenney during a card game that went bad six months back. Calhoun quickly had Jenney's back, and the matter was settled with a new deal.

Any man who cheated his friends damn sure couldn't be trusted.

When Coleman heard about it, he dismissed it as drunk cowhands fighting over cards.

He waved toward Jenney, keeping his head lowered away from the stings of the rain. It was starting to get muddy now, and the cows were slowing down trudging through the muck.

Lightning flashed and thunder boomed overhead, causing a few stragglers to bob their heads and bolt. Conlen spurred his horse and quickly got around the startled bullocks and brought them back into the group. Communication with his rear cowhands was reduced to hand signals as the sounds of the storm made verbal communication impossible. Conlen looked up to see Jenney move on to bark orders at the other riders.

Luke Smith rode up next to Conlen and leaned over.

"Can't stand that son of a bitch!" he hollered to Conlen.

"Nor I! Got a bad feelin' about this drive, Smitty! Stay alert and let me know if you see anything you don't like!"

"Sure enough!"

Smith returned to his position, snapping his rope at a reluctant bovine.

Jenney rode back to report to Coleman.

"Starting to get bogged down, Mr. Coleman!" he reported.

"Can we keep moving?" Coleman asked.

"Yes, sir! We'll be okay! We'll be reachin' Johnson Trail in another hour or two! Wish this damn rain would stop so we could see what we're doin' though!"

"I'll tell ya what we're doing! We're losing cattle is what!" Coleman shouted. "Can't see a damn thing!"

Jenney said nothing, knowing his boss was right. There could be a dozen or more strays wandering off with little chance for his riders to see them. Lightning cracked the murky sky open, and thunder rolled right through it, echoing off its black walls.

Wade dropped back to Coleman.

"I'll ride up ahead a bit. Try and see what we're in for," he called to his boss.

"Okay, just don't go too far," Coleman ordered his gunslinger.

Wade nodded and disappeared into the darkness. He was certain something was wrong with this drive. Jenney and Calhoun had been having too many private conversations, and it was damn obvious Jenney wasn't happy with Coleman's presence. Wade wasn't sure if they were riding in to an ambush, or if there'd be trouble from within the group. Since he wasn't a regular at the KC, he didn't know any of the men very well other than Conlen and Smitty. With his position, he preferred that.

He wanted to get some distance between himself and the herd to get a feel of what was ahead. He couldn't see much due to the storm, but he trusted his instincts as much or better than his eyesight. Things weren't always as them seemed, and as far as he was concerned, this trip was shrouded in suspicion.

CHAPTER 49

Danner peered upward into the abyss. The sky was riven as if it had an identity crisis. The distant horizon shone bright and looked like the top of a cotton field while overhead the iron black clouds were being sliced into fragments by razor-sharp lighting. Thunder rolled in the distance, and large drops of rain were beginning to plummet downward, crashing into rock-hard ground that had once been a fertile field offering feed and shelter to its inhabitants. The temperature was dropping rapidly, bringing brisk wind that stung Danner's sweat-soaked skin. He tugged on his hat, tightening its grip, and turned up his collar. The rain was pelting his skin with the sting of a hornet. From a hundred yards away, he and Payne scanned the terrain and noted the placement of the pens, saloon, and various structures comprising Six Shot. The storm shielded them from the cattle guards.

Impeccable timing, Danner thought, thinking the storm would offer perfect cover for his and Payne's attack while hindering Ryker's defense.

Danner reconsidered the plan. Under the protection of the storm, he had a better idea.

Why not bring them to us? he thought. Create enough of a ruckus at the pens, then meet the rushing outlaws as they came to save their contraband.

Danner called over to Wes, who quickly joined him under the pounding rain.

"I'm thinking we would do better if we raise some hell at the pens and draw Ryker's riders to us. This storm is just what we needed!" Danner offered his gun-slinging partner. Wes nodded in agreement, then motioned with his hand which way he would approach the pens. Danner motioned the opposite way, and each understood the other's strategy. Both dismounted and started on foot toward their unassuming prey.

Lightning blew up the sky, and the thunder shook the ground. The rain was now coming down sideways in bullets, punching holes in the dirt. The daylight had been erased by the black sky. Danner and Payne ducked and darted their way to opposite sides of the pens. Both saw that each pen had two guards huddled near the gates.

No reason to stay quiet and use this, Wes thought, sliding his hefty knife back into his boot. Wes took position near a huge purple sage, then fired a shot over the pens. The shot did its job, causing all four guards to jump to their feet instead of hugging the ground like a seasoned gunfighter would have done.

Crack! Crack! Crack! sounded as Wes dropped his two guards in three shots. Wasting no time, Danner responded to Wes's shot over the pens and put down both his guards with a single shot from each of his Russians. Wes and Danner ran to their fallen enemies and checked their aim. Three dead, one was writhing in pain yelling into the muffling rain. Danner reloaded then slid the Russians into their holsters. He double-checked his third gun and tucked it behind his back. Wes was looking past Danner, checking the street for a stampede of gunfighters heading their way. Nothing. The storm had kept their attack from sounding an alarm.

Danner glanced over his shoulder and looked down the street. Nothing.

"Back to the original plan!" he shouted at Wes. Wes nodded as he reloaded and holstered his guns. Danner looked back at the wounded guard. He was dead. Danner held up four fingers to Wes, then pointed down. Wes shook his head.

"Watch those tents on the right side. I didn't see if any of 'em went in!" Wes ordered.

"I'll take the tents, you watch the saloon!" Danner answered.

Both men started to move when Danner stopped, suddenly grabbing Wes's arm.

"Wait! Let's run some cattle right down the middle of the street!" he suggested. "That'll bring 'em out!"

Without answering, Wes turned and whistled for Ringo, who appeared through the dense rain, hooves clapping in the mud. Wes swung into the saddle and lifted the barbed wire off the gate post of the pen nearest the edge of town. Danner jumped over the rails and landed inside the pen. Both men began herding the cows toward the gaping street. Wes pulled one of his outlaw guns and fired into the air, causing a stampede. The startled herd began chugging through the mud into the street toward the middle of town. The mass of angered animals pounded the wet ground, sending streams of mud in all directions.

The enemy fighters in the tents and the saloon heard the ruckus. None were prepared to defend themselves.

"Here we go!" Wes yelled, reaching for another pilfered gun, spurring Ringo toward the left side of the street while Danner sprinted toward the tents on the right, both guns cocked and locked. As if the heavens were on their side, a flash of lightning illuminated their targets.

CHAPTER 50

D ANNER CLOSED IN ON THE first tent, watching the door closely. As the cattle sped past, the tent's door opened, exposing a half-dressed cowboy, gun in hand, frantically watching the cattle rush by. Danner dropped to one knee and slid on his right hip through the muddy surface. As he passed the startled outlaw, he fired two shots, each hitting the target dead on. The outlaw flew backward, knocking his trailing female cohort to the ground. In one motion Danner sprang to his feet and rushed the next tent, meeting another outlaw at its opening. One shot through the neck took care of him as Danner kept moving with the heard.

The sound of gunshots and rushing cattle penetrated the storm's clatter inside the saloon and brought Ryker and his men to their feet. A cowboy rushed in.

"Stampede! Riders shootin'!" the cowboy cried.

"Chance!" Ryker boomed. "Get out there!" he yelled at his men, jumping to his feet and sending a chair flying.

Blackie Gillum ran to the swinging doors pushing the squawking cowboy aside.

"Get the hell out of the way!" Gillum yelled, drawing a gun as he crashed through the doors onto the street. Just as Gillum cleared the doors, Wes was charging forward. Wes fired. *Thud!* A bullet ripped through Gillum's left leg, spinning him to the ground. A second outlaw followed, only to take two bullets in the chest, ending his fight at the door. Ryker saw his two men go down and stopped inside the saloon.

"Hold on!" he yelled, firing a wild shot over the still-swinging doors.

As Wes rode by, he fired into the doorway.

"Ryker!" he yelled as he and Ringo flew by.

Danner was running down the opposite side of the street looking for cover and waiting for the herd to pass. He saw Wes ride by the saloon. He also saw Blackie Gillum stand and limp back into the saloon holding his leg.

Boom! Danner heard the sound as a stinging pain peppered the back of his legs. He turned to see one of the whores holding a shotgun on him. He dove under a wagon then crawled behind an empty barrel. He checked his legs.

Small bloody holes dotted his pants.

I didn't come here to kill a woman! he thought. "Damn it!" he hollered. *Boom!* A second blast from the shotgun sent buckshot into the wagon and barrel. Danner looked up to see his assailant loading two more shells into her double-barreled accomplice. He crawled out from under the wagon and sprinted toward the woman, firing at her feet. She flinched and dropped the gun into the thick mud.

Danner lowered his head, tucked his arms in, and hit her with full force, knocking her back into the muck. A shot rang out and smashed into the side of a water trough to Danner's left. He turned to see the shots coming from a saloon window.

Danner dove to the ground, grabbing the shotgun. He rolled over, sat up, and fired both barrels into the window, shattering what glass was left and sending the outlaw to the floor. Danner then rolled back behind the trough and reloaded his Russians.

Two outlaws ran out the door, and a third jumped through the broken window, all firing their pistols at Danner's position. Wes spun Ringo around and was charging back into the fight. The gunfighter at the window turned, saw Ringo, and fired at Wes, who was leaning low on Ringo's right side. Wes retuned fire, taking down the outlaw with a single shot to the chest. Danner reached over the trough and opened fire on the two gunfighters near the door. Bullets flew in both directions, smacking into bone, flesh, and wood. Two more Ryker men went down. Danner emptied his guns just before Wes sped past the saloon.

"Ryker!" Wes yelled, firing into the three outlaws down in front of the saloon, making sure none would rise again. The rain continued to pound the town with a fury matching that of Wes and Danner's attack. Thunder exploded overhead, and lightning fractured the sky.

Ryker paused and looked at Gillum, who was turning the saloon floor red with blood.

"How many?" Ryker asked Gillum.

"I couldn't tell, Jack. At least two or three, maybe more. I think that crazy whore got one of 'em," Gillum said. Ryker looked around the room filled with a few drunken excuses for men.

"I'll hire anyone who wants to join us and save the rest of that herd!" he announced. The ragtag group of nobodies looked around the room to see who was willing to join the fight.

"How much?" one drunk asked.

"Nothing for a worthless drunk!" Ryker yelled.

"You son of a bitch!" The drunk went for his gun, but Ryker was too fast and sober. *Boom!* Ryker's bullet knocked the drunk backward over a table onto the floor. He looked around the room and saw what was left of his men gathered at the bar. He had four left. Five including himself. The rest of the drunks staggered out the back door wanting no part of the battle. Ryker looked down at Gillum, who was tightening his belt around his wounded leg.

"You any good, Gillum?" Ryker asked.

"I'll be okay!" he barked back.

"Okay, two of you slip out the back and find positions up and down the street. Don't shoot unless they see you. I want to know how many there are. Maybe I can cut a deal with this Chance fella," Ryker finished.

"They'll be no deals if that's Ben Chance out there," Gillum declared.

Nobody moved, but the bartender grunted something under his breath. Ryker spun around and pointed his pistol at the bartender.

"You know this Chance fella?" Ryker asked.

"Know of 'em, a little. About two years back, he came in here lookin' for a guy. He was over in one of the tents, but a couple of his boys were here drinkin'. The two fellas tried to stop him from goin' to get 'em. He was fast, killed 'em both, warned everybody else the same would happen to them if they interfered," the brawny bartender recalled.

"What happened?" Ryker asked, figuring he already knew.

"Chance walks over to the tents, finds the guy, shoots him, then ties his naked dead ass over his horse and left. A fella who does that ain't makin' any deals, I reckon."

"The hell with this, Ryker! Let's just give them the herd and get out of here," chirped Donnie Mathews. Ryker looked at Matthews.

"They ain't here for the herd. They wouldn't've run 'em down the street if they were wantin' the cows. No, they're here for us. Might as well end this right now."

Ryker looked at Gillum. Gillum nodded.

"Ryker's right. We wouldn't get far in this rain anyway. They'd get us out in the open."

"Ryker!" Danner's voice cut chatter.

Ryker pulled Gillum to his feet and waved at Mathews and Jarred Cole to get behind the bar.

"You two move!" he yelled at his other unknown rustlers.

Both men turned and headed for the back door. Guns drawn, they kicked the door open and rushed out. *Crack! Crack! Crack!* Gunfire erupted. One of Ryker's men flew backward into the door-way, blood oozing from head and chest.

"Ryker!" Wes yelled into the open doorway.

Ryker, Gillum, Matthews, and Cole all opened fire, splintering the door frame and sending pointless bullets through the yawning doorway into the storm beyond.

"Who are you?" Ryker yelled in a wild rage.

"Who the hell are you!" he screamed again.

"Don't matter who we are, Ryker! Toss your guns out the front door and come out with hands up high! That's the only way you get out of here alive!" Danner shouted from across the street.

"Not gonna happen! Just ride on if you know what's good for you! They'll be fifty more guns here tomorrow. Ride on!" Ryker answered.

"You shouldn't have killed Thornton! We know you're not Ryker! You can die here in this hell hole or hang. Your choice. What'll it be!"

Ryker stared into space. His pulse quickened, and his chin quivered under his scraggly beard.

"There ain't enough of 'em to rush us in here," Gillum stated.

"Yeah, but there ain't no help comin' either," Ryker said.

"I didn't kill nobody, I ain't hangin'," Cole said.

"Me neither," Matthews chimed in.

"Shut up!" Ryker yelled. "Nobody's hangin'!"

"That's it! I'm getting outta here!" Matthews hollered. "Don't shoot, I'm comin' out!" Matthews started toward the front door with his hands up. Ryker drew and fired a bullet into Mathews's back, pushing him through the swinging doors onto the wet planks.

"Nobody surrenders!" Ryker yelled, then swung around pointing his gun at Cole, who had stepped back and raised his hands.

"Don't shoot, I'm with ya, boss," Cole assured his crazed leader.

"Well, what now?" Gillum asked in between short breaths through gritted teeth. "I lose any more blood and I'm done for," he added.

Lightning flashed, lighting up the street for a moment. Ryker could see their horses were still tied out front.

"Kill the lights in here. We'll make a break for the horses. Stay low in the saddle," Ryker ordered.

Ryker looked around the bar. Except for the bartender and a few vacant tables, the room was empty.

"Nobody moves until we're gone," he ordered.

Cole doused the oil lamps. He and Gillum crept toward the front door with Ryker. Ryker said nothing. He waited a moment and cocked his gun. Cole and Gillum did the same.

Wes peeked in the rear door, but it was too dark to see. Danner kept his position behind the trough and waited quietly.

Thunder boomed overhead, and Ryker burst through the doors, grabbing the reins of his horse. Cole followed with Gillum limping behind. Danner opened fire in the direction of the sounds. Ryker swung up onto his horse, lying flat on the saddle. Cole jumped up onto his mount but stayed too tall. *Crack! Crack!* Danner fired two shots at the reckless bandit. Both bullets hit their mark, sending Cole flying off the saddle onto the hitching post. Wes came sliding out from under the swinging doors and fired up at Ryker and Gillum, who were spurring their horses. Both bullets found their target, Gillum taking a round in the back and Ryker in the hip. Danner was rushing across the street and fired at Ryker as his horse began to run. The bullet shattered Ryker's shoulder, knocking him off his horse. Gillum had managed to spur his horse on out of the onslaught of bullets being fired by Danner and Wes. Wes whistled for Ringo.

"I'm on him!" Wes yelled.

"No, let him go. We got who we came for," Danner stated.

The two gunfighters stood over Ryker, who was still alive wallowing in the mud. The saloon doors swung open, and Danner spun around his gun barrel stopping an inch from the big bartender's nose.

"I sent everybody that was hidin' out the back door. You can come inside if you like," the bartender offered, turning without waiting for an answer.

Wes pulled Cole off the hitching post and let his body thump to the ground, making sure he was dead. He and Danner then each grabbed a boot and pulled Ryker past Matthews's body into the saloon, where the bartender had lit the oil lamps. Wes looked behind the bar. Nobody there. Just a double-barreled shotgun hanging on rusted nails. The saloon was empty like the bartender said.

"Just two of you?" the bartender asked.

"That's all we needed," Danner said.

The bartender whistled and shook his head.

"I seen a lot of gunslingers come through this town, but I never seen nothin' like that," he exclaimed. "Get you fellas a drink?"

"You reckon there's anybody else in this town that'll give us a problem?" Wes asked.

"Nope. Weren't nobody of any importance in town today. You just missed Marshal Reeves. He was here yesterday and plucked a couple of fellas. The rest let out after that." The big man examined Danner and Wes.

"I remember what Marshal Chance looked like. Neither of you are him."

"Who said anything about Chance?" Danner asked.

"Them hombres you just killed said it was Marshal Chance lookin' for 'em."

"Which one is this?" Danner asked, pointing to Ryker.

"They called him Ryker."

"Thought so," Danner added. "You mind if we stay here tonight?"

"Nope."

"Thanks, I'll take that drink now," Danner said.

"Make it two," Wes stated as he slung water off his hat.

The big bartender poured two double whiskeys, then set the bottle down next to the glasses and stepped back. Danner walked out and pulled some rope from a horse still tied to the post out front. He pulled Ryker over toward the front wall and tied his feet together, then his hands. Ryker called out in pain. Danner paid no attention, just turned and joined Wes at the bar.

"What's your name?" Danner asked the bartender.

"Everybody calls me Billy."

Wes finished his drink, but didn't move toward the bottle for another.

"Thanks, Billy. What we owe ya?"

"Oh, no, nothin', fellas. After that shootin', it's on me. I seen a lot of outlaws, losers, and gunslingers here, but nothin' like the two of you!"

CHAPTER 51

WES TOOK FIRST WATCH, TAKING up a position at the broken front window. Having retrieved his soggy bedroll, Danner propped himself up against the bar and tried to catch some sleep. The storm had moved on, leaving behind a light steady rain that peppered the roof with the sound of a horse's trot. Wes looked up and down the empty street, which was now more of a bog. Other than a dim light inside one of the tents, there was no movement. Ryker remained unconscious with an occasional groan. He was breathing hard with quick short breaths. Wes paid little attention, not caring if he lived or died. Billy the bartender had lowered the oil lamps and gone to bed, which was no more than a ragged cot in the back storage room. A light breeze whisked through the swinging doors, when the back door burst open and two cowboys came rushing through, guns firing in all directions.

Danner quickly rolled to his right, simultaneously drawing both Russians and pulling triggers. Wes opened fire from the front of the bar, scoring hits with both shots from his Colt. The first cowboy through fell dead from Wes's efforts, but the second zeroed in on Wes and fired. Danner was frantically pulling his triggers, slamming his guns against his hips trying to clear the jams. Wes yelled out as a bullet shattered his side, spinning him to the floor. Danner wildly threw one of his pistols at the gunman, then fanned the hammer on his other. The hammer refused to move, causing Danner to rip his hand open. The cowboy fired again, this time point-blank at Danner.

"Danner! Danner! Wake up!" Wes was yelling and shaking Danner by the shoulders. Billy came rumbling out of the storage room.

"What's happening?" Billy yelled, leveling his double-barreled shotgun as he entered the bar.

"Nothing! Put the gun down!" Wes ordered the big bartender.

"No! Stop! Wes!" Danner was disoriented, screaming and jerking his body in all directions trying to free himself from Wes's grip.

"Danner! It's okay! It's okay!" Wes yelled at his partner.

Danner woke and stared at Wes. His ashen face covered in sweat.

"I'm all right, Wes. I'm all right now, sorry." Danner grabbed Wes's arm, his eyes darting around the room. Danner was gasping for breath, his hands shaking.

"That was a bad one, partner," Wes said, standing.

Danner said nothing, just looked over at the back door, which was still nailed shut, compliments of Billy's earlier carpentry skills. Danner caught his breath. Wes waved at Billy, who returned to his storage room.

"I'll take over now," Danner advised Wes.

Wes nodded and moved over to a corner of the bar, where his bedroll had been drying. Wes laid down and watched Danner for several minutes before allowing himself to drift to sleep. Danner stepped outside and caught some rainwater in his hand and wiped it over his face. He scanned the street. Nothing.

Couple hours till daylight, he thought. He sat down at the front door and checked his guns. They seemed to be working fine.

Danner buried his face in his hands and rubbed hard. The nightmares were coming more often and getting worse. His heart continued to race while he made an unsuccessful attempt to calm down. He rubbed the back of his neck, then noticed he was tapping his boot against a spittoon near his feet. He took several deep breaths and rocked back and forth to shake the feeling. After several minutes he regained control of himself. There was never any fear of his guns malfunctioning while he was awake. No hesitation, no hindrance to his skills. But when he slept, everything changed. Confidence, skill, his weapons, nothing functioned. He stood and started to take a step when he was reminded of the buckshot in his legs. The wounds burned more than they hurt. He returned to the inside of the bar and propped himself up near the front window. He looked over at Ryker. He was still alive.

Good. He needs to hang, not die in a gunfight, Danner thought.

Danner turned his attention back to the muddy street. He kept an eye on the tents. He didn't know if the woman who shot him might have another gun, or if Billy was mistaken about troublemakers in town.

Time passed slow. Danner took a seat at a table and put his guns on the surface. Finally, there was a dim light on the horizon. Daybreak was arriving. Ryker began to move. He tried to speak but began coughing instead.

Wes woke to the sound of Ryker coughing, mixed with mumbling about where he was. Daybreak was coming with what looked like a clear day ahead. Danner was sitting at a table cleaning his guns.

"You fellas want some coffee?" Billy asked, emerging from his room.

"That'd be mighty nice," Danner answered.

"I'll need to start a fire out back. It'll be a few minutes," the big man stated as he pushed through the swinging doors. As usual, there was no movement this early in Six Shot. Anyone here was usually drunk late into the night, and waking early was not the norm. The only exceptions were the cowhands who occasionally stopped off to rest their herd. Billy looked down to the pens and saw one full up with cows. He paused and chuckled to himself.

Well, them rustlers all dead, he thought, ducking behind the saloon to the fire pit.

Danner walked over to where Ryker lay and looked down at the bloodied outlaw. Ryker looked up through shallow, bloodshot eyes.

"Who the hell are you?" Ryker growled.

"The real question is, who the hell are you?" Danner repeated. "We know you're not Ryker. He died months ago in prison."

Wes joined Danner in the interrogation.

"I'm guessin' you somehow knew Ryker either in prison or before," Wes added. "And since I doubt it was before, you must have been inside with him."

"Which one of you is Chance?" Ryker asked.

Danner and Wes took a quick glance at each other.

"Chance ain't here right now," Wes informed their prisoner.

Ryker's matted black beard split open with a smile, exposing his rotted teeth.

"He's dead, ain't he? My boys got him back in the flats." Ryker began to laugh, but was interrupted by coughing that sent a trickle of blood down the side of his mouth.

"We don't really care who you are. If you live long enough, you'll hang in Thornton," Danner advised.

Wes headed for the door when Billy returned with a steaming coffeepot. Wes paused and waited for Billy to pour him a cup. Armed with a hot cup of coffee, Wes headed out the front door to tend to the horses.

"That fella there is a mean one," Billy said to Danner.

Danner took a long sip of coffee.

"Thank you, Billy. That's good coffee. Don't get the wrong impression about Wes. He's a good hand. He just doesn't care for talk much," Danner explained.

Danner drained his cup and held it out for a refill, which Billy obliged.

"You two reckon on takin' that herd out this morning?" Billy asked through a wide smile.

"Not sure what we're going to do about what's left of the herd. I guess we'll do the best we can with just two of us. There doesn't seem to be anyone around here to hire."

"Naw, like I said last night, Marshal Reeves came through, took a couple of fellas, and the rest rode out after he left. Just whores and drunks today."

"One of those whores shot me with a shotgun last night. I picked up a couple of buckshot in my legs. No too bad though," Danner stated, looking at the back of his pants.

"Well, I'm no doctor, but I've taken a bullet or two out of a man these last couple of years. Want me to take a look?" Billy asked.

"Don't mind if you do, Billy. Just don't tear up my pants too bad, they're all I have until I get to a real town."

Billy slipped behind the bar and came out with a small bag of tools.

"Medical kit?" Danner asked with a chuckle.

"Hahaha! Not quite! But it'll do. Crawl up on the bar and let me take a look."

Danner eased himself up onto the bar facedown. The wood reeked of bad booze and stale beer.

"Hmm? One, two, three, four, looks like three in the right and one in the left. This shouldn't take but a few," Billy confidently announced as he poured whiskey into each puncture wound, sending fire up each leg. Danner gritted his teeth, pressing his forehead into the sticky wooden surface.

"This is gonna hurt." Billy dug into the wound on the left leg. After a minute or two, which felt like ten, Billy pulled the first piece of round lead out of Danner's leg and dropped it into Danner's empty coffee cup.

"One."

Billy then repeated the surgery three more times, pulling each lead pellet from Danner's right leg.

"Done. Don't move yet, I'll bandage these as best I can."

"Thanks," Danner managed between clenched teeth. He took a deep breath.

Billy made quick work of the bandages, then returned his tools to their place behind the bar. Danner swung his violated legs around and sat on the bar. He reached into his vest pocket and withdrew a damp ten-dollar bill.

"Don't argue." Danner laid the money on the bar.

Billy snatched it up.

"Thought never entered my mind."

CHAPTER 52

A BENEFIT OF THE PRIOR DAY'S torrential rains, the cool pre-dawn air was fresh and uncharacteristically clean. The once rock-hard ground had turned soft with patches of mud here and there along the path that Clint Wade was blazing. Daybreak had begun with the promise of a bright sun-drenched day. The land would soon see the return of the season's intense heat. Wade's eyes weren't what they used to be, and the dim early morning limited sight in all four directions. It was shadowed movement to the west that caught his attention. Stopping his horse, Chief, to steady him-self, he used a strong squint to penetrate the hazy view.

Looks like cattle mulling around, Chief, he thought. Just a few heads, no wranglers in sight. He reined his horse left and popped his spurs, sending his mount in the direction of the quizzical sight. Bringing his speed up to a full gallop, he closed in on the animals quickly.

Yep, they're cows all right. A dozen or so wandering unattended. Must have got separated from the herd during the storm. Wade slowed and swung off his horse. He decided to approach one of the cows on foot in order to check for a brand. Tying off his horse to a purple sage, he closed in on one of the grazing bovines. At about twenty feet, the animal ceased to graze and watched closely.

"Whoa, take it easy, girl, settle down," he spoke in a low voice, not wanting to spook the animal into a run and cause the group to flee. A whisk of its tail signaled Wade could come closer. An examination of the hindquarter revealed the Tilted T brand of Joel Thornton's ranch.

What the hell? Wade thought. *I thought that Ryker fella stole all of Thornton's stock days ago.* Wade took a head count of the cows he could readily see.

Looks like eighteen of 'em. Wade walked back to his palomino, Chief, and swung up into the saddle. He scanned the area all around.

Wait, looks like a lone rider further west. Tapping Chief's sides with his spurs, he headed west, bringing Chief to a trot. Wade was no beginner when it came to suspicious actions of cowboys out on the range. He kept an eye on his surroundings, staying focused as the image of the rider came into view.

Looks to be alone all right, he thought. Then he noticed the rider's position. He was slumped forward hanging partially off the saddle. His horse was keeping a slow pace. Wade positioned him and Chief in the path of the stranger and stopped, choosing to wait for the rider to come to him. As the horse and rider came closer, Wade could see the rider was in bad shape, clinging to his saddle horn. Wade met the duo and stopped the horse. Looking over the rider revealed blood-stains on both shirt and pants. The rider was unconscious with his head hanging down past the saddle, shielding his face. Wade took a strong grip of the cowboy's shoulder and lifted his upper body, exposing the weathered, unshaven face of outlaw Blackie Gillum.

Well, Gillum, you've seen better days, Wade thought. It looked like he was alive, barely.

"Gillum! Gillum!" Wade shouted, shaking Gillum's shoulder. Gillum slowly came to, mumbling and coughing. Wade offered his canteen, which Gillum could not handle on his own. Wade gave Gillum water, then waited to see if he was up to answering a few questions.

"What happened to you?" Wade finally asked.

Gillum looked at Wade, blinking several times in a failed attempt to focus.

"Who are you?" Gillum muttered.

"Clint Wade, riding with Coleman's outfit. You Blackie Gillum?"

"Yeah," was his reply.

"What happened?"

"Got ambushed last night by Ben Chance and his gunslingers in Six Shot."

"Ambushed, huh? Why would Ben Chance ambush you?" Wade asked.

"Old grudge, I reckon."

"Anything to do with Thornton's cattle running wild out here?"

"Don't know nothin' 'bout that," Gillum lied, then began to violently cough blood oozing from his mouth. "Coleman's outfit you said?" Gillum managed to ask.

"That's right."

"Tell Jenney…" Gillum paused, then fell from his horse, hitting the mud with a thud.

Wade looked down at Gillum, having no feeling of compassion for the outlaw who appeared to finally get what he had coming. Wade dismounted and squeezed his neck looking for a sign of life. Nothing. Blackie Gillum was dead.

"Well, Chief, what does Tom Jenney have to be told?" he asked his trusted companion.

Don't trust that son of a bitch anyway, and now Blackie Gillum is bringing up his name, he thought.

Wade left Gillum facedown in the mud, avoiding the urge to take the time to bury him. He grabbed the reins of Gillum's horse then swung up onto Chief.

No sense leavin' a good horse out here.

Wade brought Chief around and headed back to Coleman's drive.

The sun's bright orange rays pierced the skyline on the mesa. Life had returned with the sharp sounds of wildlife both near and far.

Sam Coleman pulled back the rain-soaked canvas flap of his tent and stepped out to the smell of fresh air and frying bacon. His cook, George Shaw, was a top hand with a chuck wagon and kept his men well fed.

"Good morning, Mr. Shaw," Coleman said in between taking deep breaths and stretching his arms out to each side. "Smells awfully good!" Coleman added.

"Good morning, sir. I have hot coffee, bacon, eggs, and biscuits if you like," Shaw announced with a wide gap-toothed grin.

"Fine! Fine! Don't mind if I do."

"The men have already eaten and are out with the herd. We should make some good time today, sir."

"Indeed, we should. I'll look forward to drying out!" Coleman accepted the hot coffee and plate of food. "Can you have my tent loaded onto the buckboard when you're finished?" Coleman asked his cook.

"Yesiree, Mr. Coleman. Already told Mr. Jenney I'd need a man for that."

"Thank you, Mr. Shaw, you're a good man."

"Hey, Pete, how does the herd look?" Tom Jenney asked his trail boss after joining him on a rise overlooking the water-logged cows.

"Not bad, considerin'," Calhoun answered without taking his eyes off the herd. "We'll get movin' in a few," he added flatly.

"Fine, looks like the old man is up. Can you tell if we lost any?"

"Nope," Calhoun answered. "I'm sure we did though. Couldn't see a damn thing yesterday or last night. If we're lucky, we'll come across a few on the way."

"All right, I'll let Coleman know," Jenney quipped as he rode off.

Jenney rode up and slid off his horse, tying it to the chuck wagon.

"Good morning, Tom," Coleman addressed his foreman.

"Morning, sir. Get any sleep last night?"

"Some once I got used to that blasted rain pounding on the tent. How's the herd look?"

"Looks okay. Can't tell if we lost any yet. If we did, it looks like only a few. Maybe we'll find a couple along the way."

"Very well. When do we get started?"

"The boys are getting in position. Should get rolling here quick. You want us to wait for you and George?"

"No, no, I'll be ready in a moment. George can fall in behind the herd. That okay, George?"

"Yes, sir. I'll be cleaned up here shortly. By the time the herd moves past, I'll join in."

"Tom, have you seen Wade?" Coleman asked.

"He rode up ahead early, before dawn. Didn't say why."

"I see. Anyone with him?"

"Not that I saw."

"Hummm. Okay," Coleman mumbled, rubbing his unshaven chin.

Hard to ride guard when you're not with the herd, Coleman thought.

"Wade's a good man. Never let me down before. I'm sure he had good reason. Okay, Tom, let's get going," Coleman ordered his foremen.

"Yes, sir," Jenney answered before mounting and riding off.

George Shaw stepped forward.

"Mr. Coleman, I saw Mr. Wade real early this morning. Gave him some coffee. He said he had an uneasy feeling. Was gonna ride ahead and make sure things looked okay. I didn't think I should say anything in front of Mr. Jenney."

"Thank you, George. Yes, it was good to keep this between us."

Sam Coleman sat tall in the saddle and looked over his heard as the men were shouting cattle calls all around. Considering what they had been through, both cattle and men looked good. Coleman spurred his horse and headed for the point where Jenney had assumed his position.

"The herd's exceptionally loud this morning, Tom," Coleman said.

"Probably that bath they took last night!" Jenney laughed.

"Where are we, Tom? I don't seem to recognize this area. This the same trail we've used in the past?" Coleman asked.

"Yes, sir, mostly. We're a little further east than usual, keeping our distance from Six Shot as ordered."

"Oh, that explains it, I guess."

Jenney looked further north and saw a lone rider with a horse in tow.

"Looks like we got company comin'," Jenney stated, pointing ahead.

Coleman followed Jenney's direction and strained to see the rider.

"Looks like Wade, boss," Jenney announced.

As the distance closed, both men confirmed it was Wade bringing in another saddled horse. Jenney and Coleman veered off to their right to allow the heard to pass while they talked to Wade.

"Hello, Clint. Run into some trouble up ahead?" Coleman asked his guard.

Wade paused without looking at Jenney.

"No trouble for me, Sam. This horse here used to belong to Blackie Gillum." Wade made sure to catch a quick glance at Jenney when he said Gillum's name. As expected, Jenney lowered his face beneath the brim of his hat, but not before Wade caught a glimpse of gritted teeth partially hidden behind a frown.

"Blackie Gillum? The outlaw that stole Thornton's herd?" Coleman asked.

"That's the one. I came up on him shot to hell. He lasted long enough to tell me he was ambushed by Ben Chance and a couple of gunslingers in Six Shot."

"Hmm? Sounds like Ben caught up with 'em then," Coleman stated. "I wonder if he and that Ryker fella still had the herd."

"Can't say for sure, but I also spotted about twenty heads with the Tilted T brand grazing unsupervised up a ways. Nobody else around."

"Boss, me and few of the boys could ride over to Six Shot and see what happened," Jenney blurted.

"I'll bet you'd like to do just that, Jenney," Wade stated.

"What's that supposed to mean?" Jenney snorted.

"Don't know yet, but I figure on finding out," Wade said coolly.

Coleman sat astride his horse saying nothing, just listening and watching his two cowhands' exchange.

"I believe that's a good idea. I suggest you both go and I'll go along. No need for anyone else. Tom, keep the herd moving. Have them pick up the Thornton strays along the way. Ain't there holding pens over there in Six Shot?"

"Yes, sir, couple of big ones," Jenney advised. "I'll ride back and let Pete know what we're up to." Without waiting for a response, Jenney turned and rode off.

Coleman looked back at Wade. "Clint, what was that all about between you and Tom?"

"Just before Gillum died, I told him I was ridin' for you. He mumbled Jenney's name. Before he could finish, he fell off his horse and was dead. I'm not surprised, I've never trusted him."

"George told me he spoke to you this morning. Said you had a bad feeling. Is that what you meant?"

"That's part of it. This whole business about Thornton, the rustlin' in the territory. I heard all about it when I was in Fort Worth a couple weeks back. Heard rangers and US marshals are around takin' a look-see."

Coleman listened intently, sporadically nodding his head, but said nothing. Coleman reached into his pocket and withdrew a big cigar, bit the end off, and burned the other end, sending a thick blue loop of smoke around his head.

"Let's see what the hell happened in Six Shot first. Then I'll think about Tom."

"Yes, sir. I'll run this horse back to Shaw, then I'll be ready to go."

CHAPTER 53

Wes called in through the door.

"Riders comin'. Looks like three stopped at the edge of town."

Danner hobbled out onto the porch and followed Wes's gaze to the east of town. Three mounted riders were framed against the backdrop of the morning sun. After a moment's scan of the town, the riders spread out and began slowly moving down the street.

"Well, looks like they know about this place," Wes stated.

"Yep, I wouldn't think that would be hard to figure out though," Danner added.

"Mounted or on foot?" Wes asked.

"Let's see what they're up to first. Maybe they're not interested in us at all."

"Why do I doubt that." Wes exhaled, then pulled his Winchester from its scabbard on Ringo.

Both men walked back into the saloon and leaned out the door watching the riders approach. One of the whores came out of her tent and started down the street, failing at an attempt to make herself presentable. She stopped in front of a collapsed building and watched as the three men rode past, not paying her any attention. Wes and Danner stepped back from the door and stood near the bar.

"I'll see what they want," Billy offered.

Billy stepped out onto the wooden planks passing as a porch. The area in front of the swinging doors was still stained in Matthews's blood. Billy had hauled the dead outlaw's body around to the back when he went to make coffee earlier. The three riders stopped next to Ringo and Danner's horse and turned to face Billy. The big older fella in the middle spoke.

"Good morning, sir," Sam Coleman started.

"Morning, fellas. What can I do for y'all?" Billy answered.

Danner and Wes peeked through the door opening, getting a good look at the riders. Danner recognized Coleman instantly while Wes did the same with Wade. Danner waved Wes toward the rear door of the saloon.

"The old man in the middle is Sam Coleman," Danner whispered.

"The gunfighter to his right is Clint Wade," Wes responded in the same low voice. "Don't known the other one."

"Me neither," Danner admitted.

Both men walked quietly back to the bar and listened.

"My man here came across an outlaw named Blackie Gillum about a mile or so east of here. He was shot up pretty bad and died. Before he died he said he was ambushed by Ben Chance. Would you know if Ben Chance is still here?"

"Or maybe the two fellas in the saloon would know?" added Wade, leaning down, looking through what was once a glass-filled window frame. Both Wade and Jenney reached for their guns.

"No, no, we'll have none of that!" Coleman shouted. "Gentlemen, please join us if you have any information. See, in addition to finding this Gillum fella, we found twenty or so cattle out there. They all had the Tilted T brand. I know that Ben Chance let out after the gang that stole 'em from Joel Thornton's place," Coleman explained. "I'm a friend of Chance, name's Sam Coleman," he continued.

When Danner and Wes stepped to the front door, Coleman recognized Danner.

"You're the fella that joined Chance, ain't you?" Coleman asked Danner.

"That's correct, Mr. Coleman. I'm Luxton Danner, and this is Wes Payne. I started out with Ben in Canyon Creek, and Wes joined us at the Thornton ranch."

"Where's Ben?" Coleman asked, his voice trailing off.

"Ben was killed in an ambush a few miles south of here by a couple of Ryker's gunmen," Danner stated.

Sam Coleman removed his hat and swallowed hard.

"Oh no, not Ben too." Coleman sighed. Coleman looked at both Wade and Jenney.

"Get down, both of you," he ordered.

All three men dismounted and tied their horses.

"I know it's early, young man, but you have any whisky in there?" he asked Billy.

"Yes, sir, come on in."

Wes, Danner, and Billy stepped into the saloon with Coleman and his men close behind.

"You look familiar, but I don't recall ever meeting a Wes Payne," Wade asked Wes once inside.

Wes put some distance between him and Wade, but paid closer attention to Jenney, who stopped abruptly and stared at Ryker lying in the corner. Sensing Jenney's actions, Coleman and Wade turned to see what had gripped Jenney's attention.

"What is this?" Coleman asked, keeping his distance while Jenney walked closer to the fallen outlaw.

"Is he dead?" Jenney asked in a cracked voice.

"Wasn't earlier. Don't know now," Wes answered.

"Who is that?" Coleman demanded in a sharp tone.

"That's the one who calls himself Ryker," Danner answered.

Danner checked on Ryker, who was still breathing, but unconscious again.

"He's alive. If he stays that way, he'll hang for Thornton's murder," Danner announced.

"You look a little nervous, Jenney," Wade stated, watching Jenney's hands shake a bit.

"Not me, never seen this one before, just heard of him is all," Jenney explained.

"Never seen him before, huh?" Wade pressed.

"That's what I said, Wade!"

"Tom, you sure you don't know this fella?" Coleman asked his foreman. Coleman turned to Wade. "Tell 'em what you told me, Clint."

Jenney's face turned pale, and he stepped toward the door. Wade drew his gun and aimed at Jenney.

"Nope. Stay right there," Wade ordered.

Danner and Wes each gripped their guns and waited, not sure what was happening.

"What's this all about?" Danner asked.

"Right before Gillum died, he took interest in me riding for Coleman and started to ask me to tell Jenney something. Died before he finished. Now why would Blackie Gillum want me to tell Jenney something?" Wade concluded.

"Well, Tom, I'd like the truth, if you don't mind," Coleman stated.

"Let's see what Ryker has to say about this," Wes said.

Jenney's eyes were wide as though they would fall out of their sockets. They dashed around the room. Wes stepped over and kicked Ryker in the boot.

"Ryker! Wake up, someone here to see you!" Wes shouted.

Ryker came to, muttering noises and straining to open his eyes.

"What'd you want, son of a bitch!"

"Seems as though you have a friend here, Ryker. Name's Tom Jenney. Mean anything to you?" Wade asked from across the room.

Ryker looked up and saw Jenney.

"Where the hell you been, Jenney!" he howled.

Jenney turned and started to run toward the door, drawing his gun, but Wade opened fire, killing him with two shots. Jenney sprawled onto the floor, his gun sliding over to Coleman's boots. Coleman picked up the gun and walked over to Ryker.

"Look, mister, I don't know who you are and I don't care, but Tom worked for me and I'd like to know what his business was with you," Coleman calmly asked.

Ryker looked up at the big rancher and smiled.

"Hahaha. Business? Okay, Mr. King Coleman, I'll tell you what business. Jenney arranged for me to get out of prison as long as I did a job for him. I was told you had lost a lot of cattle, and Jenney wanted to replace as many as possible any way he could. So he hired me and the boys to steal Thornton's herd, bring it here where he would pick it up and sell 'em at the rail station. You'd never know. Things went bad at Thornton's and I lost a couple of men. I tried to meet him a couple days ago and tell him what happened at Thornton's, but he didn't show. Sent two others in his place. Jenney knew Ben Chance would get involved, so he sent a couple of boys to take care of him, but they didn't kill him. Instead he came after us. That's what business we had," Ryker finished, coughing up more blood. "I need a doctor!" he yelled.

"Ain't no doctors in Six Shot. Are there, Billy?" Danner asked.

"Nope, not for miles," the big bartender answered with a smile. "I do have some frontier whiskey though, if anybody is still wantin' it?"

"I'll take a whiskey," Coleman said, stepping to the bar. "Who around here buries the dead?"

"Well, they just find their way into boot hill out back, sir."

Coleman put twenty dollars on the bar. "Give that to whoever buries my foreman."

Billy snatched up the money. "I'll see to it myself, sir."

"Thank you. Clint, gather his belongings and put them on his saddle. I'll deal with it when I get back to the KC."

"Yes, sir," Wade answered then got about his task.

"Gentlemen, I have a proposition for you," Coleman said to Wes and Danner. "Please join me at a table."

CHAPTER 54

S AM COLEMAN GRABBED THE BOTTLE from the bar and set it down on a table before taking a seat. Wes and Danner joined him. Two men walked into the saloon and headed for the bar paying no attention to Ryker or the three men seated at a table. Recognizing each, Billy poured two glasses of beer from a barrel he had tapped the day before. One of the whores came in and joined the men at the bar. She had a bruise on the side of her face and favored her right arm. Danner wasn't sure, but he guessed she was the one who shot him last night before he hit her like a charging bull.

"Gentlemen, I know it's early, but it doesn't seem to matter much right now," Coleman stated as he poured himself a drink. Wes and Danner passed, each holding up a right hand.

"What's on your mind, Mr. Coleman?" Danner asked.

"Please, call me Sam. I'm both shocked and angry that a man in my employ would be responsible for the deaths of two men I had a great deal of respect for."

"Hahaha! Who said it was just one man?" Ryker blurted.

Coleman looked at the outlaw with narrow eyes and a stone-cold frown.

"You have more to say?" Coleman asked.

"You'll want to talk to a fella named Calhoun. I only saw him once when I met Jenney, but he was in it with Jenney all right."

"Pete Calhoun?" Coleman asked.

"Don't know the first name, just Calhoun."

Coleman looked at Wes and Danner.

"I don't know what the truth is these days, but my trail boss is Pete Calhoun. Tom brought him on last year. Seemed to know his business, so I allowed it. I never had any trouble out of either one."

"Sure you did," Wade announced, walking back into the conversation before taking a seat at the table.

"Well, there was the one time they got cross with some of the hands during a poker game in the bunkhouse. I took care of that. There's a big difference between cards and murder, Clint," Coleman added.

"Lyin' is lyin', Mr. Coleman. Don't matter what you're doin' when you get caught," Wade stated.

"Okay, okay. I see your point."

"Hahaha," Ryker laughed.

Wade drew his Colt and pointed it at Ryker's head.

"I don't give a damn who or what you are, you laugh again I'll kill ya. Understand?"

Wade holstered and looked up to see the three locals staring at him from the bar.

"That goes for the three of you too," he added.

Coleman spoke up.

"I feel a sense of responsibility for the events at the Thornton ranch. Therefore, I'd like to buy the remaining head from Joel's herd at the current price. No discount. I'll add them to my herd and sell them up north. All money will be paid to Joel's daughter as soon as my drive team return to Canyon Creek. I understand there were horses taken also. I will cover the cost of the lost horses once I receive a count from the Tilted T. I know you two don't know me, but everyone in Canyon Creek and Thornton knows I'm a man of my word. Would you agree to that?"

Wes and Danner exchanged glances and thought for a moment.

"Chance chose you to get the herd back, Danner. I just came along for the ride. It's your decision," Wes stated.

Danner shook his head.

"No, we both agree or no deal. It's a fair offer, and Wes and I can't run the herd up to the railhead by ourselves." Danner nodded.

Wes nodded in agreement.

"That settles it then. If you two will help us move the remaining head east to our group, I'll send them on from there," Coleman announced.

"We can do that," Danner stated.

"What about him?" Coleman asked, pointing to Ryker.

"We'll tie him to a horse and bring him with us. I want him to hang," Danner added.

"Could just as easily hang him here," Wade stated.

"Yep, but I can't do that," Danner said without further explanation.

"Let's get movin' then." Wade scowled before walking out of the saloon.

Coleman watched his gunman leave.

"He's good at what he does, gentlemen," Coleman explained.

"That's what I hear," Wes offered. "I'll get the horses."

"Use Jenney's horse for this outlaw here," Coleman ordered.

Danner untied Ryker's feet.

"Don't do anything that you're not willing to pay for with your life," Danner told Ryker. Danner lifted Ryker to his feet and helped him to the saloon door.

"Thanks, Billy."

The bartender waved while pouring another beer. Wade brought Jenney's horse up to the saloon. Coleman and Wes stayed mounted.

"I'll move your hands to the front. No stupid moves, Ryker," Danner stated.

Danner loosened the rope, and Ryker slowly brought his hands around in front of him rubbing his wrists. Danner began to push Ryker up onto the horse when Ryker spun and reached for the Russian on Danner's left hip. Danner grabbed the top of Ryker's hands. *Crack!* Ryker's head exploded, sending blood all over Danner and the limp body to the mud. Danner looked up to see a wisp of smoke rising from Sam Coleman's drawn Colt .45.

"That simplifies things. Now let's get moving," Coleman stated then headed for the pens.

Billy came out and was met by another twenty-dollar bill from Danner.

"Can you take care of this, Billy?" he asked.

"Sure enough, Mr. Danner," Billy answered.

"That's Marshal Danner, Billy," Danner corrected his quasi-undertaker, removing his badge from his pocket. "Do you know how to sign your name?"

"Yes, sir."

Danner removed a folded paper and pencil from his pocket. He opened the paper revealing an image of the man caller Ryker.

"Sign this for me," Danner asked.

Billy signed his name. Wade took the paper from Billy and looked at it.

"So that's Clete Walker? Fella that broke out of Yuma?" Wade asked.

"Was. He walked out the door with a dozen prisoners that were being released. One of those being released was Jenney's brother. That's how Jenney hired him," Danner explained.

"And you're a US deputy marshal. Huh, never know who you're going to run into out here. Now I know why you couldn't hang him," Wade said.

"Judge Parker frowns on things like that," Danner offered.

"I heard that about ole Parker. Heard he likes you boys to bring 'em back alive," Wade stated.

"When we can."

Danner ended the conversation abruptly when he realized Ryker's horse was standing at the trough getting a drink.

Ryker took money from the safe. I wonder…

He stepped over to Ryker's horse and unbuckled the left saddlebag. Nothing. Stepping around to the other side, he opened the right saddlebag and reached in. He felt stacks of paper. Pulling one bundle out, it confirmed his suspicion. A stack of greenbacks. He put the money back into the bag and unlatched it from the saddle. He tied the additional bag to his horse.

"Let's get these beeves over to Coleman's drive," Danner told an astonished Clint Wade.

"Yes, sir!"

CHAPTER 55

SAM COLEMAN WAS HAVING FUN. It had been years since he actually herded cattle, but it was like old times as he moved back and forth keeping his edge of the herd contained. Wade was leading the way while Payne and Danner were taking care of the opposite edge and rear respectively. The sound of Coleman's cattle calls brought back fond memories of a younger man in simpler times. He was beginning to question his thoughts on selling to the JA Ranch. Their offer was fair, but maybe he still had a few years left in him before packing up and heading east to join his daughter and her family.

Wade looked ahead and saw the loose Thornton cattle still grazing on an elevated mesa. He waved his hat back to his companions and pointed forward toward the strays. Coleman, Danner, and Payne responded with hat waves and kept the cows moving. Coleman hoped the strays wouldn't spook and scatter. With only four of them, he knew they couldn't chase after them.

Danner kept moving, bringing up the rear of the group, which wasn't easy. Normally there'd be three or four cowboys with a herd this size. Fortunately this group was containing itself, with a short distance to Coleman's main herd. His thoughts drifted back to Elizabeth and the ranch.

Carrying back the news of Coleman's offer should bring relief to her, but then what? Will she sell the ranch and return East? Keep the ranch and run it herself? He knew that wasn't possible. He also knew he was in no position to help. Not unless he wanted to turn in his badge and become a rancher.

Would she even want that? He answered his own question. No, if she stayed, it would be because of young Jake, not him or Wes. *That's the way it should be. Snap out of it, Lux!*

Danner cleared his mind and returned to the task at hand. They were approaching the strays. Time to go to work.

Wade sped up and circled around four cows, pushing them toward a few others and back at the herd. A handful of strays further up kicked up dirt and moved away from the herd. Wes let them go, knowing they'd lose a few anyway. Wes angled himself and pushed ahead of a few more of Thornton's cows, pressing them back toward the main group. He returned to his edge, and they kept moving east.

Coleman watched Wade and Payne bring the strays into the group, impressed they had only lost a few. He figured they should see his herd in a few minutes. He had given Calhoun instructions to stop the herd on the high ground of the Black Mesa and watch for his return, then send out as many men as he could to assist if needed. He assumed Calhoun would follow his orders, but now he wasn't so sure. His trust had been destroyed by the two men he relied upon the most.

How could I've not seen that? I used to be a better judge of men. Maybe I should just sell and get out of the business, he mused. His thoughts were interrupted with the shriek whistle from Wade. Coleman looked out and saw several riders coming their way from the east. His boys.

Am I glad to see that, Coleman thought.

Coleman's men met the group and assumed positions around the herd. Jessie Thomas, Marshal John Thomas's son, rode straight to Coleman.

"Glad to see you, Jessie!" Coleman greeted one of his longtime hands. "Did Pete stay back with the herd?"

"No, sir, right after you left, Pete put me in charge and rode out. Never said where or why, just let out," Thomas reported.

"It's true then. Son of a bitch!" Coleman yelled out in frustration.

"What is it, sir?" Thomas asked.

"Never mind, Jessie. I'll tell you about it when we get back to the herd. You've just been promoted to foreman. Jenney's not coming back. Pick a good man to be trail boss when we reach the drive. Let's go!"

"Yes, sir, Mr. Coleman!" the new KC Ranch foreman answered.

With ample help, Danner moved out from the rear of the herd and rode over to Coleman.

"Looks like you have enough hands to take it from here, Mr. Coleman. Wes and I are going to head back to the Thornton ranch. I'd like to get there tonight."

Coleman shook his head emphatically.

"No, please accompany us back to my herd. I have a little more business to take care of with you and Payne. It shouldn't delay you much."

"Very well, I'll see you later then," Danner agreed then returned to his rear-guard position.

Now that's a good man, Coleman thought.

Thirty minutes later, Coleman's men were pushing the Thornton cows into the main herd, which was lazily grazing atop a fertile area of the Black Mesa.

Danner and Wes joined Coleman and Thomas at the chuck wagon, where Coleman insisted they eat and help him drain a coffeepot.

"Jessie, this is Wes Payne and Luxton Danner. Mr. Danner here is a US deputy marshal. These fellows took care of the gang that killed Joel Thornton and stole his herd," Coleman advised.

"Mr. Payne, Marshal Danner," Thomas acknowledged, shaking each hand.

"Have you an idea for a trail boss?" Coleman asked his foreman.

"Yes, sir, I asked Smitty," was the answer.

"Fine choice, Jessie. Long overdue for Smitty. I have reached an agreement with these gentlemen to buy the Thornton cattle and run them up north with our herd. I want you to cut them out at the railhead and keep count so I'll know what to pay Miss Thornton. Understand?"

"Yes, sir, no problem," Thomas replied.

Coleman turned to Wes and Danner.

"I'll be returning to Thornton with these men, if it's all right with the two of you, that is," Coleman asked.

Wes and Danner nodded in approval.

"Good. I would like to meet Miss Thornton as soon as possible and offer my condolences. Gentlemen, please finish your meal and coffee while I attend to business with Jessie."

"If we can start out here soon, we should make it to the ranch before midnight," Danner stated.

"I'm not going to the ranch with you, Danner," Wes declared. "I'll ride with you as far as Johnson Trail, then I'm heading to Fort Griffin. There's a ranger company assigned there."

"I see. Figurin' on joining back up?"

"Don't know yet. I'll decide by the time I get there."

"Elizabeth will be disappointed," Danner said.

"Naw, she's got plenty to think about other than me…or you." Wes smiled.

"You're right about that, pal."

"You boys ready?" Coleman asked.

"Yes, sir, let's get going," Danner answered.

CHAPTER 56

J AKE STOPPED AT THE EDGE of the north pasture and looked down at the Thornton ranch. He felt like he'd been gone for weeks instead of days. With all that had happened, he was no longer the wide-eyed boy who left on a manhunt to avenge Mr. Thornton's death. He felt like he was returning as a man with the scar of death attached forever. Wet, tired, and in pain, he dreaded delivering the news he was bringing. He spurred his horse slowly onward, giving himself more time to prepare for his meeting with Elizabeth and his mother.

Halfway through the pasture, the front door opened, and his mother emerged with what appeared to be a large pot of liquid. Walking to the end of the porch, she poured the contents over the rail and turned to see him slouched in the saddle with Ben Chance tied over his horse close behind. Jake watched as his mother screamed something, dropped the pot, and ran back into the house. A moment later she and Elizabeth appeared at the door. A faint smile managed to invade Jake's face as he fixed his sights on Elizabeth. Her long blond hair was tied back, and she looked wonderful in her print blouse and brown prairie skirt. Quickly Jake's thoughts focused on his disheveled appearance and foul smell that he was certain to have acquired on his brief but prodigious journey.

As Jake approached the house, he noticed two mules in the corral. A glance beyond, he saw the old-timer they had met on the trail was tending to the few cows in the east pasture.

He decided to stay. What was his name?

His mother, clearly crying, rushed to meet him, holding her hand over her mouth. Elizabeth remained a pillar of strength, standing on the porch her father was killed on. Her face expressionless, hands to her sides.

"Jacob Rawlings!" Martha screamed as she reached her son.

He pulled the reins, stopping his horse, but said nothing.

"Oh my God! You're hurt!" his mother continued, recognizing the gruesome disfigurement of his left arm. The arm was bent midway between the elbow and wrist.

"It's okay, Mother," Jake managed in a low voice, remaining mounted on his horse. "I'll be fine. Hello, Elizabeth."

"Hello, Jake," she answered in a shaking voice, holding in her emotion as best she could.

"Who's with you?" Martha asked her son, nodding toward Chance's body.

"It's Mr. Chance," was the flat response.

The announcement hit both women like bullet.

"Oh my," Martha softly stated.

Elizabeth, hearing the name, sat down on the top step and buried her face in her hands.

"Come down off that horse this minute so we can get you fixed up in the house," Martha ordered her son.

"No, not yet, Mother. I need to take care of Mr. Chance first."

"Nonsense! You come into the house this instant, young man!"

Elizabeth looked up and quietly watched. Jake said nothing. Just turned his horse and headed for the rear of the barn near the growing Thornton family cemetery.

"Jacob Rawlings!" Martha called one more time.

"Mrs. Rawlings," Elizabeth called out.

Turning her attention back to the house, she saw Elizabeth standing with her arms reaching forward. Martha understood and hurried back to the house, where she embraced Elizabeth, now uncontrollably shedding more tears of sorrow. The two women stood for a moment then walked into the house.

Having seen Jake's arrival, Gus made his way to the barn where Jake stopped. Jake slid off his horse with his soaked boots, splashing mud in all directions. Gus quietly stepped up and helped remove Chance from his horse. They placed his body under the big mesquite that stood guard over the graves, its outstretched branches embracing its residents underneath.

"Who is it, young man?" Gus asked.

"It's Mr. Chance."

Gus removed his hat and paused a moment to wipe his nose.

"Let's get these horses in the barn," Gus stated, taking the reins of Chance's horse. After putting the horses in the barn, the two returned to Chance's body and covered it with burlap until a proper burial could be arranged. Jake sat for a moment to gather his thoughts.

"What happened?" Gus asked hesitantly, not knowing if the young cowboy could repeat the story.

Jake stared into the distance. After several deep breaths, he described the events as best he could remember.

"It's my fault he's dead," Jake added to the story.

Gus shook his head vigorously. "No, no, no! Don't think that way. Miss Elizabeth told me all about Mr. Chance. Who he was. Fact he'd been shot and was probably dying. You can't blame yerself, young fella. Won't do ya no good," Gus pleaded. "Let's get ya together and have the lady folk fix up that arm," he added, picking Jake up.

"I don't remember your name, sir," Jake stated.

"The name's Gus, my friend!"

Jake shook Gus's hand then headed for the house and the barrage of questions he had no answers for.

Chapter 57

J AKE STEPPED INTO THE HOUSE and found his mother and Elizabeth hurrying about gathering their things. Elizabeth emerged from her room wearing a hat and carrying her carpetbag. His mother put a few items inside her large carrying bag and headed toward him.

"Don't bother coming in, Jacob. We're taking you to town to have Doc Langdon look at that arm," his mother advised. She hurried past him and opened the door. "Come on now!" she ordered, holding the door open for Jake and Elizabeth.

"I'll get—" Jake began.

"You'll get into my carriage. Gus will take care of Betsy," his mother interrupted.

Gus had already opened the barn and was bringing Betsy, Mrs. Rawlings's horse of ten years, out to her carriage. Jake followed orders and got into the carriage. He was doing his best to hold his arm, which now felt like it was the hot iron target of a blacksmith's hammer. He also realized he was burning with fever. Elizabeth joined him while Gus quickly hitched Betsy up then handed the reins to Martha.

"We'll be back as soon as we can, Gus," Elizabeth advised her new ranch hand.

Gus waved and headed back to close the barn doors. Martha snapped the leather straps, and they were off.

Martha settled Betsy into a double-timed trot then spoke.

"What happened Jake?" she asked.

"Are you well enough to answer?" Elizabeth asked, wiping the sweat from his face.

"We were out in the open. Mr. Chance told me to ride behind him because it was a good ambush spot. Wes and Danner each spread out to the sides. We all kept a close watch, but there were two of

Ryker's men hiding in the sage. One of 'em shot Mr. Chance. His horse jumped, and I was too close behind. My horse reared up and I fell. I hit my arm on a rock and knocked the wind out of me. Mr. Chance yelled for me to stay down while Wes and Danner charged 'em. Wes and Danner killed them, but Mr. Chance was already hurtin' bad. They shot him in the chest. There was nothing we could do. I wanted to go on with them, but they told me I needed to bring Mr. Chance back since we couldn't bury him out there. Plus my arm was broke, so I headed home. The storm came, so it took me longer to get back. I'm sorry, Elizabeth. It was my fault. Mr. Chance was protecting me and he got shot."

"Nonsense! Ben Chance knew exactly what he was doing. He knew he was already dying. There's no use gettin' you killed too! Those outlaws killed him, not you!"

"Your mother's right, Jake. It's not your fault. I should have just let them have everything. It's not worth it, and we don't even know about Lux or Wes. They could be dead for all I know."

"Don't worry, Elizabeth, not those two. They know what they're doing and they're really good. They'll be back. You'll see," Jake stated confidently.

Jake closed his eyes and leaned into Elizabeth's shoulder. She wrapped her arm around him and leaned back, allowing him to sleep. Martha caught the scene from the corner of her eye and smiled.

Doc Langdon's office was open, but he wasn't there when Martha and company arrived. Elizabeth helped Jake into a chair in the office, then joined Martha in the hunt for Langdon. Elizabeth checked in the store where Mrs. McNally quickly took charge and began calling for the doctor in front of the store. Elizabeth and Mrs. McNally then saw Martha come out of the hotel with Langdon close behind, black bag in hand.

"Thank you, Mrs. McNally," Elizabeth said to her self-proclaimed surrogate mother.

Mrs. McNally waved, then headed down the street to announce the news to anyone who would listen.

"Hello, Jake. How do you feel?" Langdon asked, reaching to feel the boy's forehead. A brief touch provided the answer he sought.

"Elizabeth, bring him into the examination room. I'll get him out of those clothes and under blankets, then I'll take a look at that arm. Looks like a bad break."

Elizabeth got Jake to the bed, then returned to the waiting room and took a seat next to Martha, who was content watching Elizabeth care for her son.

"I'm sure Dr. Langdon will have Jake's arm fixed up soon," Elizabeth said with a touch of optimism in her voice.

Martha nodded, but her smile had been replaced by a weak frown producing lines of worry across her face.

"If you'll stay, dear, I'd like to find someone to ride out to the farm and let Mr. Rawlings know Jake's back and what happened."

"Certainly. I'm not leaving without him."

"Thank you."

Doc Langdon peeled the damp clothes off Jake, cutting his shirt away from his broken arm. The area near the break had turned black with a bright red ring around the bruise. Langdon held the arm gently and pressed on the flushed area of the skin.

"Aaah!" Jake called out.

"Sorry, son. Checking on how far the infection has travelled."

"How bad is it?"

"Not too bad considering the bone damage. I'll be able to set it, but I'm not going to lie. It's going to be a very painful process. The good news is I have chloroform I can give you. That will put you to sleep."

Langdon left his patient and entered the waiting room, seeing Martha was no longer there.

"Is Martha returning?"

"Yes, she went to find someone to go tell Mr. Rawlings Jake had returned. Can I help you with something?"

"Yes. I'll need help setting his arm. Can you do that?"

"I believe I can."

"Very well, I'll take a moment to prepare, then call for you."

Minutes later Elizabeth joined Langdon in the examination room. Jake appeared unconscious, and his broken arm was lying on a table next to the bed. The sight of his discolored skin brought a low moan of sadness. Langdon explained that Elizabeth would need to hold Jake's shoulder down hard while he manipulated the fractured bones back into place. Langdon took hold of Jake's arm above and below the break.

"Ready?" he asked his assistant.

"Ready," she answered, then using her weight, she pushed firmly down on the shoulder and nodded.

Langdon carefully separated the two sections by pulling hard on Jake's wrist. He could feel the jagged edges of the bones grating against each other. He pulled as hard as he could. The bone edges cleared each other and pressed together as he slowly released his grip.

"Okay, Elizabeth, you can let go now."

Elizabeth stood and exhaled. She hadn't realized it, but she had held her breath while Langdon worked the arm. Langdon removed a handkerchief from his pocket and wiped beads of sweat from his brow.

"Whew. That was easier than I expected."

"Hello! Dr. Langdon!" Martha called out from the waiting room.

"I'll be right out, Martha! Elizabeth, would you tell Martha everything looks fine. He'll be all right."

Elizabeth delivered the news and received a warm embrace from a relieved mother and an enthusiastic storekeeper's wife as Mrs. McNally had returned with Martha. Doc Langdon entered the room behind a wide smile.

"Well, Jake's lucky to have three pretty admirers. He'll be all right, Martha. You can go in and see him. He's just waking up from the chloroform."

"Thank you, Doctor!" Martha said as she hurried past him.

Langdon turned to Elizabeth. "Martha said Ben Chance was killed?"

"Yes."

"Any word on the other fellas that went with him?"

"No, not yet," Elizabeth said, looking to the floor with slumped shoulders.

"You don't worry, young lady. Those boys will come back," Mrs. McNally declared. "Come with me over to the store. You'll stay with us for a bit."

Kate McNally escorted Elizabeth out the door. Doc Langdon followed onto the porch and saw Marshal Thomas waiting in front of the store to greet the ladies.

Thomas removed his hat. "Hello, Elizabeth. I was wondering if you had a few minutes, I'd like to speak with you."

"Of course, Mr. Thomas. Can we talk inside the store?"

"Of course, you can talk in the store, come in, Mr. Thomas!" Mrs. McNally snapped, slamming her hands on her hips, obviously displeased with Thomas's intrusion.

CHAPTER 58

T HE GROUNDSWELL OF LIFE WAS evident all around. The water-starved land had been replenished. Rain-nourished tentacles of vegetation reached toward the sun, looking like it had returned from the dead. Leaves were full and vibrant. The sage burst with purple floras sending a blanket of color over the land-scaped floor.

Coleman, Danner, and Payne rode in silence, making good time. They would certainly reach the ranch well before midnight as hoped. Danner's thoughts rested squarely on the question of whether the mission had been successful. Losing Chance screamed loudly of failure, but Coleman's offer to buy Elizabeth's cattle and recovering some of the money from Ryker said otherwise. On the other hand, Wes was simply satisfied that Ryker and his bunch were dead. Getting the cattle and money back was fine, but his mission had been completed. Coleman remained disappointed with himself and carried a sense of guilt. He genuinely liked Joel Thornton and respected Ben Chance. Two good men were dead because he hadn't seen the evil in his men. He had fought and killed for his cattle in the past, but that was in defense of his property. He rolled the sequence of events in his mind.

Jenney's brother was in Yuma and knew Walker. That's how he sprung Walker and knew when to bust him out. Why did Walker call himself Ryker? That made no sense. He'd probably never find out.

"Coleman! Hold up!" Wes called to the preoccupied rancher. Coleman looked around and saw Payne and Danner looking ahead. Coleman moved around Payne and saw the reason for the abrupt order. Up in the distance stood a dozen or so mounted Indians lined side by side. Coleman had heard of the mini raids and skirmishes, but he had not witnessed any himself.

"What'd you boys think?" Coleman asked.

"We're outnumbered, and that formation isn't a welcoming party," Danner offered.

"Nope," Payne agreed, looking around for cover. "There's a group of trees to the right. Might give us an advantage," Payne added.

Danner looked over. *Better than nothing*, he thought. "We won't outrun 'em," Danner added.

"Let's go then," Payne ordered.

"Sure enough," Coleman agreed and kicked his horse in motion.

The three cowboys headed for the trees, sparking the Indian charge. The warriors recognized the tactic and charged, spreading out in order to circle their enemy position.

Winchesters cleared their scabbards as Danner, Payne, and Coleman each took a tree.

"Hold your fire until we open up, Mr. Coleman," Danner called out. Coleman gulped hard. Sweat began to run down his face, which felt like it was on fire.

Two warriors swung out far to each side and opened fire with rifles. Bullets hit the trees sending bark and branches into the air. Wes opened fire trying to hit the warrior flanking him. Danner did the same, but the braves were moving too fast. The remaining warriors charged straight on, sending a barrage of bullets and arrows into the trio of gunfighters. Wes and Danner continued to fire at the flanking braves who were now circling behind them. Sam Coleman lowered his Winchester and fired, knocking the flanking brave on the right from his mount. The brave on the opposite side made it behind and fired. Both Danner and Wes redirected their fire to the attacking group in front. *Crack! Crack! Crack!* Two charging warriors went down. Incoming bullets ravaged the tree trunks into splinters.

"Damn it!" Coleman hollered.

Danner turned to see Coleman on his knees grasping his left shoulder. "You okay?" Danner called.

Bullets hit all around Coleman's feet. He dropped the Winchester and pulled his pistol. "I'm still in it!" Coleman assured his fellow combatant.

The brave that circled behind jumped from his horse, knife in hand, and charged Coleman on foot. Coleman raised his Colt.

Crack! The brave fell backward, the result of a bullet from Wes's Winchester.

"Thanks!" Coleman yelled, then turned and fired at the charging warriors.

Wes spun around and was met with piercing pain in his collarbone. He fell forward into the tree, his vision temporarily blurred. He reached up and felt the end of an arrow sticking out.

Crack! Crack! Crack! Danner fired as rapidly as he could work the Winchester. Two more warriors went down. Wes fell backward and fired point-blank into an Indian hulking over him. A warrior jumped from his horse onto Danner, knocking him on his back. *Crack!* A single shot from Coleman's Colt ended that fight. Danner pushed the dead brave off only to have another jump on him feet-first, knocking the air from his lungs. *Crack!* Coleman dropped Danner's second attacker. Danner rolled onto his side and gasped for breath. Coleman moved over to Danner and continued to fire at the warriors who were turning to retreat. Four Indians ceased the attack and rode off to the west. Coleman and Wes reloaded in case a second charge was coming. It wasn't. The warriors continued on, not looking back.

"I'm okay, check on Wes," Danner told Coleman.

Wes was looking at the arrow that had hit him just to the right of the neck, hit the collarbone and continued through his flesh. The bloody arrowhead was fully visible behind his shoulder.

"Son of a bitch," muttered Coleman. "That just missed, my friend."

"Missed? You see something I don't, Coleman?" Wes replied, wincing in pain.

"It's above your collarbone and back shoulder bone. I can take care of this," Coleman assured Wes.

Coleman slid his knife from its sheath. "Hold on to the front. I'll cut off the head and we'll pull it out from the front," Coleman advised.

Wes nodded in agreement and took a firm hold of the arrow. He leaned his head back and grit his teeth. Coleman cut the arrowhead off and put it in his pocket. He moved in front of Wes and grasped the arrow with both hands, wincing in pain as his shoulder sent a reminder that he had also taken a bullet.

"Ready?"

Wes nodded.

Coleman took firm hold of Wes's shoulder and nodded.

Coleman swiftly pulled the arrow out.

"Aaah!" Wes yelled. He took multiple deep breaths, fighting the pain. "Okay. Thanks."

Danner quickly retrieved a bandana from his saddlebag and tore it in half. He then bandaged Wes's wounds by pushing a portion of the bandana into each puncture. He turned to Coleman.

"Let me see what you have here, Mr. Coleman."

"Please! Call me Sam for God's sake!" he exclaimed.

Danner smiled and tore Coleman's sleeve open, exposing a clean-through wound. "Well, pretty lucky. Bullet went clean through."

Danner pulled Coleman's bandana off his neck and tore it in two. He repeated the same bandage procedure as he performed on Wes.

"You two able to ride?" Danner asked.

Wes whistled for Ringo. Coleman picked up his Winchester and headed for his horse. The trio mounted and headed south, knowing another Indian encounter would be fatal.

CHAPTER 59

I N ADDITION TO REFRESHED FOLIAGE, the wildlife had been invigorated and were seemingly everywhere. Jackrabbits and javelinas scurried about. Two hours passed without conversation. Danner, Payne, and Coleman were consumed by their thoughts, each facing critical decisions. Danner needed to return his focus on his pursuit of Bert Cullen. Payne considered returning to the rangers, and Coleman was conflicted on whether to sell his ranch and move on. The sun was slowly sinking behind the western ridge, mixing a thick orange hue with vibrant ground colors of purple, green, and yellow. Danner could see the break of the Johnson Trail up ahead and slowed his horse.

"I'd like to see you join us in Thornton so you can get that shoulder looked at by the doctor," Danner told Wes.

"Been thinkin' about that. Probably a good idea. Wouldn't be any good to the rangers with one arm anyway. Captain Tobias would just send me to the infirmary when I showed up. Might as well heal up in Thornton," Wes reasoned.

"Captain Tobias?" Coleman asked. "Would that be Jed Tobias of J Company?"

"That's the one," Wes acknowledged. "You know him?"

"Yes, sir, back about ten years ago he and a few of his boys helped me with a few raiders that attacked my ranch. I lost my wife and several good men in that fight," Coleman explained.

"I didn't know your wife was killed, Sam. I'm sorry," Danner added.

"Hold your sorrow, Lux. She wasn't killed. She decided after that mess, she and my daughter were heading East. She'd had enough. Indians, the war, and then banished ex-soldiers running roughshod. I couldn't blame her. She'd put up with an awful lot. Fact is, I'm thinking about selling the KC and headin' East myself. I have a grandson I've never met."

"Wouldn't blame ya if you did, but Thornton and Canyon Creek wouldn't be the same without the KC," Danner stated.

"There's a couple of new fellas moving in starting the JA Ranch. They've been buying up a lot of land and made me an offer. Pretty good one also. Seeing Thornton and Chance killed over beef has me thinkin'."

Wes and Danner remained silent and kept moving up and over the trail and beyond. The sun had disappeared, bringing a clear star-filled sky into view. The crescent moon sliced through a starlit ceiling, keeping the trio shrouded in semi-darkness. The Thornton ranch was about two hours away, where a washroom and good food waited. At least the three cowboys hoped that's what awaited them. All three were grateful for the protection the darkness provided. The threat of an Indian attack remained very real despite night setting in. No one was in the mood for a fight.

Ten horse lengths ahead of Wes and Coleman, Danner stopped at a rain-made pool, allowing his horse to drink. Coleman and Wes followed. A branch snapped nearby. All three men dismounted and worked to keep their mounts quiet. Several minutes passed with nothing but the night's usual sounds.

"You two get going. I'll stay back and make sure we're not being followed. I'll catch up. I'll whistle when I'm getting close," Danner whispered.

Wes and Coleman mounted and continued south down the trail. Danner found some scrub and waited, rifle in hand. Another fifteen minutes passed. Nothing. Satisfied, Danner swung onto his saddle and proceeded south as fast as the dark trail would allow. Coleman, unsure of his surroundings, followed Wes in single file, keeping an ear for Danner. Soon, Coleman heard the low sound of a whistle.

"Wes, Danner coming up."

Wes stopped and waited for Coleman to ride up next to him.

"Spread apart," Wes whispered to Coleman. "Just in case it's not Danner."

Wes moved Ringo left, and Coleman went right a few feet. Another whistle, this one a louder shot-out.

"Danner?" Wes called, pistol in hand.

"Don't shoot, it's me," came the reply.

Danner came into a shadowy view.

"Seems okay," Danner reported to his partners.

"Good, let's get to the damn ranch then, I'm gettin' jumpy," Coleman blurted out.

Coleman's admission brought quiet laughter to all three as they headed for the ranch.

A short time later, Danner led the trio through some tall brush and into a clearing on the far side of the Thornton ranch's north pasture. The three men looked down on the main house. Other than a light burning on the porch, there was no sign of activity. There didn't seem to be any lights on inside. Danner surmised it was around ten or eleven o'clock. Certainly, late enough for Elizabeth to have turned in for the night.

I wonder if Mrs. Rawlings had stayed once Jake had returned. That's if Jake made it back, Danner thought.

"Well, let's see if anyone's home," Wes stated and started off toward the house.

As they moved closer to the house, a dim light in the kitchen shone through the front window. Danner checked the barn door. Closed. The shed was also closed. No horses were tied to the front rail. There were two horses in the corral though. The three men approached the corral. Danner recognized the animals in the corral were mules, not horses. They dismounted near the corral.

"Looks like that old-timer's mules," Wes stated.

"Sure does. I'll take care of the horses. See if anyone's home," Danner said in a low voice.

Wes paused at the steps, waving Coleman toward the door. Coleman stepped up onto the porch and looked through the window. He could see a young woman reading by candlelight in the front room. Moving to the door, Coleman knocked lightly and stepped back, not wanting to alarm the girl. Elizabeth looked out the window and saw Wes standing on the step. She flung the door open and rushed out past a startled Coleman and hugged Wes, who returned the hug, biting off the pain in his shoulder.

Elizabeth's head whirled with excitement. She couldn't focus or speak. Tears ran down her cheeks as she squeezed as hard as she could.

"Aaah!" Wes couldn't help himself.

Before Elizabeth could comprehend Wes was hurt, Danner approached from the corral. Elizabeth hurried to Danner and nearly jumped into his arms.

"I'm so happy you're back!" she finally yelled. She kissed Danner and threw herself into another hug.

"Good to be back," Danner said. "We brought a guest if that's okay," he added.

Elizabeth turned and saw Coleman standing on the porch wearing a huge grin.

"Oh my gosh! I didn't see you! I'm so sorry!" Elizabeth gushed.

"That's just fine, young lady. I don't blame you for hugging the young fellas. I'm Sam Coleman. You must be Elizabeth Thornton."

Elizabeth accepted Coleman's outstretched hand.

"Mr. Coleman! Yes, I'm Elizabeth. I barely remember you! My father spoke highly of you and your ranch. Please, come inside!" Elizabeth said, still short of breath.

"Yes, that would be a good idea, I believe!" Martha announced from the doorway in her nightgown.

"Sorry, Mrs. Rawlings, we didn't see you," Danner stated on behalf of everyone.

Martha entered the kitchen and lit a lamp.

"Is Jake here?" Danner asked.

"No, Doc Langdon told him he had to stay in town tonight so he could look after his arm," Elizabeth answered.

"Did he make it back with Ben?" Danner asked.

The room went quiet. The mood dropped like it fell off a canyon cliff. Everyone felt twenty pounds heavier and out of breath.

"Yes, he's out by the cemetery. We're going to bury him tomorrow," Elizabeth spoke through quivering lips.

"There'll be time for all that in the morning. Right now, you three need to wash up and I'll get some food on the table," Martha ordered.

"Yes, you'll all have something to eat and get some sleep. We'll catch up in the morning," Elizabeth added.

CHAPTER 60

S AM COLEMAN WOKE TO THE snap and sizzle of bacon frying in the kitchen. It sounded like a warm, friendly campfire. The sweet smell of fresh biscuits also permeated his room. Danner had used the sofa in the front room and was roused early by Mrs. Rawlings working in the kitchen. After his offer to assist was quickly dismissed by Martha, he choose to stay put and watch the activity. He couldn't recall the last time he felt this worn-out. He looked forward to Elizabeth's meeting with Sam this morning. He hoped his buying the herd would please her and soften the heartache she must be experiencing. A sharp knock on the door drew a loud response from Martha.

"Come in!" she hollered over her shoulder as she battled the crackle of the bacon grease.

Wes stepped inside holding his right arm close to his body and his chin tucked down toward his chest. After a heightened discussion with Elizabeth last night failed to change his mind, he slept in the barn claiming he'd be more comfortable.

"How was that hay bed last night?" Danner asked.

"I'm positively certain it was horrible!" Elizabeth exclaimed as she exited her room.

Wes chuckled. "Well, my shoulder didn't take very too kindly to it."

"I tried to warn you, but no! You'd be more comfortable!" Elizabeth continued through a smile.

"I could smell the cooking from out there and had to come see Mrs. Rawlings in action," Wes offered.

"How'd you know it wasn't me?" Elizabeth asked with a full laugh.

Wes said nothing, just found his way to the table.

"May I?" he asked.

"Of course. Coffee's ready," Martha announced.

Danner headed to the washroom and met Coleman walking out.

"Good morning, sir!" Danner said as he moved past the big rancher.

"Good morning, ladies. That breakfast smells mighty good, Mrs. Rawlings," he added.

"Thank you. Please take a seat and we'll get started," Martha stated while setting a large basket of biscuits on the table. Elizabeth stood back and looked at the scene, which eerily reminded her of the morning her father and Moses were shot. She bit back a rush of emotion and poured coffee for everyone. Danner joined the group, who all attempted to wait for Martha to join them.

"Nonsense! I'll have mine soon enough, then I'll be on my way, dear," she said to Elizabeth.

"What will I do without you?" Elizabeth exclaimed emphatically, putting her hands on her hips.

"The same thing you did before I arrived, my dear," Martha answered. "I'm sure Mr. Rawlings will be quite happy about my return. He's probably been starving this past few days!" she laughed.

"Where's Gus?" Elizabeth asked Martha.

"Said he needed to go into town. He left early," Martha advised.

"*Early* isn't the word. More like last night," Wes offered.

Coleman cleared his throat. "May I discuss a little business with you over breakfast, Elizabeth?" he asked.

"Yes, of course."

"Well, in your absence at Six Shot, I made an offer to Lux and Wes regarding your remaining cattle. I offered to buy the herd at the railhead market price, then pay you in full when my men return with the count and price. Lux and Wes agreed on your behalf, so we put your cows with mine. I hope that is all right with you. If not, we can try to reach a different agreement."

Elizabeth looked at Danner. "Only part of the herd was saved?"

"About half. We used the other half to stampede the street."

"Did it help?"

"Yes, it gave us the advantage we needed since there were only two of us."

"Good. Mr. Coleman, thank you for the kind offer. Had I been there, I would have agreed. May I ask why you made the offer?"

Coleman squirmed in his seat, then looked at Danner and Wes before turning to Elizabeth.

"The truth is I felt responsible for the death of your father and theft of the herd. I discovered that my foreman, Tom Jenney, and trail boss, Pete Calhoun, were behind the hiring of that Ryker fella and his gang. They thought they could add your herd to mine and bring in more money without me knowing. Thanks to these young men, that didn't happen, and at least you'll recover some of the money you lost."

Elizabeth said nothing. She stared into her plate without blinking.

"Did Ryker get away?" she asked openly.

"No, Mr. Coleman made sure of that," Danner answered.

"Mr. Coleman?"

"The man made the decision to try and escape and grabbed for Luxton's gun. I was fortunate not to miss," Coleman responded. "My guard found Blackie Gillum out on the range early that morning with a few of your cattle. He died from wounds he got during the gunfight in Six Shot."

"What happened to Ben?" Elizabeth asked.

"Ben had a feeling that Ryker, whose real name was Walker by the way, had an ambush set up for us. Jake was riding next to Chance and was exposed, so Ben directed him to get behind him. He was turned making sure Jake was behind him when he was shot," Danner explained.

Martha, who had been cleaning up the kitchen, stopped at Danner's recount of the shooting.

"You mean he was paying attention to Jake and got shot keeping my son safe?" Martha asked without turning to face the table.

"Yes, ma'am," Danner answered, with Wes nodding in agreement.

Martha said nothing, wiped her eyes with her apron, and went about her business.

After several minutes of silence, Coleman asked the question that was on everyone's mind.

"Elizabeth, do you know what you're going to do now? No one would blame you if you left the ranch and went back East."

"I have given it some thought, but I've not made a decision yet. Obviously, I would need to hire help if I decided to stay, and I don't know if there will be enough money. Gus has said he will stay and help me in exchange for the buckboard and plow horse we brought from Canyon Creek, but I don't know how long he'll be here."

"Well, if you decide to sell, I know of a couple of new ranchers that are looking to buy up property. They seem to have enough money to buy the whole territory. They've made me an offer and I'm considering it myself."

"Who are they?" Elizabeth asked.

"The fella with all the money is John Adair. He's from Europe or somewhere. His partner is Chuck Goodnight. Their main ranch is a little southeast of Oneida, but they have big plans, I hear. They might be interested."

"I'll keep that in mind, thank you for the information."

"You're very welcome."

The troop finished their breakfast in silence. After helping clear the table, Danner spoke up.

"I'll see if there's wood for a casket and bury Ben," Danner said.

"I'll help you with that," Coleman advised.

"No, that's okay, you take care of that arm," Danner stated.

"Lux, please let me know when you're ready so we can join you," Elizabeth asked.

Danner found ample wood in the barn and, with Coleman's stubborn assistance, went to task, finishing before noon. Though hindered by his bad shoulder, Wes had the grave nearly completed when Coleman and Danner brought the casket. After lowering Chance into the grave, Danner summoned the ladies from the house. Once gathered at the graveside, Coleman spoke up.

"If you all will permit me, I'd like to say a few words since I knew Ben the longest."

After everyone nodded in agreement, Coleman spoke a few words and recited Isaiah 57:1–2, the only Bible passage he had committed to memory.

"The righteous perish, and no one takes it to heart; the devout are taken away, and no one understands that the righteous are taken away to be spared from evil. Those who walk uprightly enter into peace; they find rest as they lie in death."

Alone, Danner completed the burial by mounting a wooden cross bearing,

Benjamin Franklin Chance
Born Unknown
Died August 25, 1877

"I'll excuse myself and get ready to head back to my ranch," Coleman stated upon returning to the house. "Thank you for your hospitality, Elizabeth and Mrs. Rawlings," he added.

"You're welcome anytime, Mr. Coleman," Elizabeth offered.

"Please, call me Sam."

"I'll head out with you. I need to go into Thornton and see if the doctor is around," Wes added.

"Mr. Payne, I'm going to Doc Langdon's and pick up Jake. Would you mind waiting for me?" Martha asked.

Wes nodded and headed out to the barn. Danner entered the house and approached Elizabeth.

"Elizabeth, I need to ride over to Canyon Creek and see Rachel at the Sundown. I need to tell her about Ben and deliver a message from him," he advised.

"Will you stay in Canyon Creek?"

"No, I've got an assignment I need to continue with."

"Assignment?"

"Yes, I haven't told you, but I'm a United States deputy marshal."

Elizabeth was speechless. Her face showed no expression. She turned and went to her room, closing the door.

"Now I don't like to get into people's business, but is something wrong, Mr. Danner?" Martha asked.

"No, ma'am. Nothing wrong. I just surprised Elizabeth with the news that I'm a US deputy marshal. I have been on assignment looking into the rustling in the territory and trailing a fugitive at the same time. I had to keep my identity unknown for a while. I trailed the fugitive to Canyon Creek. That's when I met Chance, and you know the rest."

"I see. She knows you're not coming back." Martha patted Danner on his chest. "I understand her disappointment," she added with a grin. "It's been very good to meet you, Marshal Danner. Make sure you stop and say hello when you're back in these parts."

Martha went to Elizabeth's door, tapped once, and went in, closing the door behind her. Danner headed out to the barn where Wes and Coleman were saddling their horses. Danner took care of his, then hitched Betsy to Mrs. Rawlings's carriage and brought it to the porch.

"Gentlemen, it's been an honor riding with both of you. Stop by the KC anytime you can. You're always welcome. Here, take this and show it to Doc Langdon. May be useful," Coleman advised Danner, handing him the arrowhead from Wes's wound. Two quick handshakes later, Coleman was on his way to the KC.

"Is Mrs. Rawlings coming with us?" Wes asked, fidgeting with his guns, anxious to get going.

"Yes, she's talking to Elizabeth right now. I just told her I was a marshal, and that seemed to upset her, I guess."

"Well, pal, if you weren't out before, you are now." Wes laughed.

"It was never like that anyway. I need to give her the money we took from Walker's bag though. It'll be enough to hire a hand if she chooses to stay on out here."

"She oughta just go back East. Ain't nothing to keep her here now," Wes said.

The conversation ended with the appearance of Elizabeth and Martha on the porch. After exchanging a hug, Martha stepped down and put her bag in the carriage.

"Thank you to whoever hitched Betsy up for me," she said.

Danner pulled the bag from his saddle and met Elizabeth, who had stepped over to him and Wes.

"We were able to salvage some of the money Walker stole. I didn't count it, but it looks like enough to keep you going until Coleman's men return with the cattle money," Danner stated.

Elizabeth accepted the saddlebag and set it down.

"I don't know how to thank you both. I have no words. Just know I'll never forget either of you."

She hugged Danner, then took Wes's scarred hand and rubbed it gently. She then turned, retrieved the bag, and went into the house, saying something to Martha on the way.

Martha cracked her buggy whip and headed for the road. Danner and Wes followed behind. Neither man looked back. Men in their business couldn't afford to look back.

Less than an hour later, Martha led her gunfighter escort into Thornton and up to Doc Langdon's office, where Jake was rocking in a chair on the front boardwalk. When Jake realized Wes and Danner were riding up, he jumped to his feet and ran onto the street to greet them.

"Wes! Danner!" he called across a wide smile. "You two all right? What happened? Did you get Ryker? What about the herd?"

"Take it easy, kid. You're going to blow up," Danner said, swinging off his horse and shaking Jake's hand.

"Wes took an arrow, but I'm sure Doc will fix him up in no time."

"Arrow? You run into an Indian raid?"

"Yep, on the way back. Sam Coleman was also wounded with a bullet in the arm. Not bad though," Danner explained.

"Doc's inside, Wes. I'll take Ringo," Jake said, reaching for the reins.

Wes and Danner went into Langdon's office and found him reading up on combating infections.

"Doc, this here's Wes Payne, he has an arrow wound," Jake announced like a little kid.

"Glad to meet you, sir. Looks like it entered in the front near the collarbone, I see," Langdon stated.

"Yep, caught me here on top of the shoulder and went through the back."

"What type of head did it have?"

Danner stepped forward and removed the arrowhead from his pocket.

"Sam Coleman thought you might ask for that, Doc. Here it is. Sam wasn't sure if we needed it, but I figured you'd want to take a look."

"Well, that's something most cowboys wouldn't think of," Langdon said, examining the edges of the arrowhead.

"I actually had a medical class in college. I knew it would make a difference on the type of treatment needed," Danner boasted.

Langdon paused a moment and looked at Danner closely.

"Can't say I've ever seen a gunfighter that went to college," he offered. "Come on back to the examination room. I'll get you fixed up."

"You went to college, Mr. Danner?" Martha chimed in. "Jake here says that reading and writing is all he needs and that college is a waste of time."

"Mother," Jake moaned.

"Well, college isn't for everyone. Out here there are more important skills to have. I went for a while, then decided it was time to move on. Sometimes I wish I'd stayed, but a man has to decide what's best for himself, Mrs. Rawlings."

"Huh!" Martha grunted, then left the office.

"Thanks, Lux. She keeps telling me about schooling and all. I read and write really good. I reckon I don't need any more school."

"First, you read and write really well, and like I said, every man needs to decide for himself."

CHAPTER 61

A FEELING OF DREAD CAME OVER Danner as he made his way into Canyon Creek. The conflict between honor, duty, and trepidation had engulfed him the closer he got to town. Now he felt the weight of an anvil on his shoulders as he passed the marshal's office and headed for the Sundown. He had delivered death notices before, but this one was going to hurt. Danner tied his horse to the post in front of the hotel and gathered his thoughts.

No sense waiting any longer.

Danner walked into the hotel and was met by Adeline.

"Hello, Mr. Danner. Mommy's in the kitchen."

"Hello. Could you tell her I'm here?"

Adeline ran toward the big archway leading to the kitchen.

"Mommy! Mommy! Mr. Danner is here!"

Danner stepped into the empty dining room. Rachel appeared in the doorway in a beautiful ruffled blouse and dark blue prairie skirt partially hidden behind a fresh white apron. Her red hair was pulled up away from her face, allowing her green eyes and red lips to shine. Her smile quickly disappeared when she realized Danner was alone. Danner said nothing. He didn't have to. His slumped shoulders and lowered eyes shouted the news loud and clear to Rachel. She stood still for a moment, then took a seat at the long dining table, which was covered in a bright white cloth. She began to fold the towel she had in her hands. Danner took a seat at the table. To his surprise, there were no tears in those striking green eyes.

"I'm sorry, Rachel." Danner didn't know what else to say.

"Was it the wound in his hip?" she asked, keeping close watch over the folded towel in front of her.

"No." Danner didn't offer any more in case she didn't want to know.

Rachel softly bit her bottom lip and moved her gaze to Danner. "Tell me please," she asked.

"We were in the open. Ben was concerned about a young man we had with us. He was making sure the kid was behind him when we were ambushed by two of Ryker's gang. They were lying in the brush. We didn't see them until they fired. Ben was hit immediately."

Rachel slowly nodded her head and smoothed out the table-cloth in front of her.

"He knew he wasn't coming back," she said.

"He was struggling with the hip," Danner explained. "He also told me to tell you that you were right. You were right the whole time."

Rachel managed a smile, then took a deep breath followed by a sigh.

"I have something to show you," she advised, then went into the lobby. Danner heard her open and close a drawer in the front desk. Returning, she handed Danner a thick sealed envelope. On the front it simply read "Judge Parker."

"Ben gave this to me the night before you all left. He said if he didn't return, I was to have this letter delivered to Judge Parker in Fort Smith. He said that the judge would know what to do."

"If you'd like, I can deliver this to Judge Parker. I'm leaving for Fort Smith in the morning."

"Why are you going to Fort Smith? I thought the only men who go to Fort Smith were marshals and their prisoners? Which one would you be?" she asked with narrowing eyes.

"I'd be a deputy marshal," Danner answered with a weak chuckle.

"Ben and I knew you didn't just show up here by accident. Did you know Ben when he was with the marshal's office?"

"No, I joined about a year after he left. That's how I knew where to look for him. Before you ask why, I'll tell you. Ben and I met in Alabama at the end of the war. As you probably know, he was a Confederate captain. I was a sixteen-year-old Union private who surrendered to Ben during a fight. He refused to accept my surrender and directed me and my troopers to our basecamp. I never forgot that gesture. He didn't remember me, but I always said if my path ever passed near his, I'd find him and thank him again. He was as honorable as a man could be."

"Yes, he was. More honorable than I wanted him to be at times," Rachel added, staring into the distance. "I'd like to hear that story someday. I'll get you a room for tonight," she said, hurrying off to the front desk.

Danner smiled at Rachel's comment, then headed out to get his saddlebags.

There's a woman who could change a man's plans, he thought.

Other than boarding his horse with Davy Garcia at the stables, Danner avoided contact with other town folk. He sought and found a quiet night in Canyon Creek. Early the next morning, he said goodbye to Rachel over a cup of coffee then started back to Fort Smith. His curiosity about the contents of Chance's envelope gnawed at him like an South Carolina tick.

Maybe Judge Parker will share some information with me. Chance had no family, so whatever the instructions were, they were directed at Parker. What could Judge Parker do for a retired marshal?

Barring trouble, it'd take about two weeks to get back to Fort Smith. He'd find out then. Besides, he had his own business with Judge Parker, who wouldn't be happy that he was returning without Cullen. Once the judge heard of justice being served for the deaths of two of his marshals, all would be forgiven though.

What began as a simple hunt for another Fort Smith fugitive became the heroic actions of what legends were made of. Outnumbered and outgunned, three strangers set out to right a wrong and bring justice its due. Western justice maybe, but along the way several people's lives were touched and changed forever because of a gunfight fought by unknown men in a town that nobody cared about. Here's to the next wrong that honorable men yearn to make right and the people they touch and change forever.

About the Author

John is a longtime veteran of law enforcement, beginning his police career with the Houston Texas Police Department in 1981. He has held numerous positions over the years, including the last twenty-four years as a detective. He is currently a senior detective for a statewide law enforcement agency in North Texas.

His writing career began in the sports industry where he wrote articles for national magazines and online publications. He held the position of sports editor for two years where he wrote on professional, collegiate, and amateur athletics.

He grew up watching Western movies and reading stories of the Old West. His theatrical influences included actors John Wayne, James Stewart, and Clint Eastwood, as well as directors John Ford and Howard Hawks. He drew literary inspiration from Louis L'Amour, Zane Grey, and C. J. Box. His passion for history and the classic Western genre moved him to write short stories of the Old West and his first novel, a classic Western set in 1877 Texas.

John is an avid sports fan and horse enthusiast and loves all things Texas.